1st edition 2026

ISBN Hardback – 978-1-9194158-2-6

ISBN Paperback – 978-1-9194158-1-9

ISBN EBook – 978-1-9194158-0-2

ISBN Audiobook – 978-1-9194158-3-3

Preface and Acknowledgments

Space operas are often about size, massive ships, exploding stars, and empires that span light-years. But for me, the best stories are found in the cramped quarters of a cockpit or the silence of a spacewalk.

Writing Whispers from the Machine was an adventure in itself. It was an attempt to capture the sense of wonder I felt the first time I looked up at the night sky and realised just how small we are. I hope this story takes you somewhere new, and that you enjoy the ride as much as I enjoyed charting the course.

That said, no captain flies alone, and this book would never have left the launchpad without my ground crew.

To my reading group: Thank you for navigating the plot holes, for helping me keep the timeline straight, and for telling me when the "technobabble" became too much. Your feedback was the guidance system this project desperately needed. This ship flies because you helped tighten the bolts.

Most importantly, to my Fiancée, Lauren. Thank you for listening to my theories on FTL drives at 2:00 AM and for never letting me give up when the drafting got tough. You are the star I navigate by.

***

Book Cover by Ahmed Raza
Illustrations by Adriano de Oliveira Bezerra
Audiobook Narrated by Hetty Elliott
Edits by Margaret Dupré, Lauren McCormack and Leilani

CONTENTS

PROLOGUE

ZHOU AND AALIYAH

Earth Year 2174

Pluto station was quiet, as usual. Located on the fringes of humanity's reach, it was built as a research station but also a statement. A statement of humanity's rapid revival since the Great War. A monument to a hundred years of progress and cooperation with Heimer.

The quietness pressed in on Zhou as he sat staring at the workstation monitors. The blinking red light flashed slowly, calmly, demanding his attention. The Kepler-442b probe, the one with a Fragment of Heimer tucked away on it, the same one that should have been silently cruising through the void, was sending a message.

He was too young to remember the fanfare when the probe launched, but he had seen the vid-logs, everyone had, the politicians' speeches about humanity's destiny, the crowds cheering, the sense of collective pride. Now, that pride felt like a distant echo, replaced by mundane routine. But this wasn't routine.

With a deep breath, he opened the message. At these distances, it wasn't an audio log, just a compressed transmission log.

Log PK442b-01– system alert – unexpected interference

UNRD (Unted Nations Research and Development), this is the Heimer fragment of probe 442b. Anomaly detected. Hibernation protocol terminated. Unidentified signal intercepted. Signal type: high pulse laser communication. Origin: unknown. Destination: unknown. Language key: unknown. Signal lost. Course alteration not within mission parametres. All systems green. Mission continued. Hibernation protocol activated. Message terminated.

There was an attached signal log in the transmission. Zhou opened it and stared at the mass of numbers. He was no computer scientist and it all looked like gibberish to him, but this looked even more out of place than usual. *Three states, not the usual two?* Zhou thought, furrowing his brow as he stared at the screen.

Zhou hesitated, his finger hovering over the communication panel. Should he wake the others? *It's probably just a system error that the Heimer's troubleshooting.* He had always been a meticulous man by nature, hated to rush, hated to jump to conclusions. Let the data, the facts show the way. So Zhou pulled back his finger and flipped open the system logs. *Let's establish the facts first,* he told himself.

Six hours later, after frantic last-minute consultations with his colleagues and a thorough re-examination of the data, Zhou found himself running down the dimly lit station halls, even his light frame letting a heavy clang ring along the old grilled floor panels. The noise reverberated away from him, chasing him all the way to the Station Manager's office, the data pad clutched tightly to his chest.

***

Earth Year 2207

Aaliyah's car swept up the driveway towards the south wing of the Palais. She favored this entrance, not just for its tranquillity, but for the view it afforded of the original 1920s structure dominating the grounds, a monument to humanity's aspirations for unity, and a stark reminder of its failures. She never tired of it. This meeting, convened outside official channels, necessitated discretion. Hence, the south gate and the less ostentatious council chambers. She didn't need to check her data pad to see the grainy images that were plastered on every goddamn media station from Beijing to São Paulo. It was firmly burned into her mind. She had known that this would happen at some point, they all had, that's why the probe had been sent in the first place. Even so it still had shocked her more than she had expected when the news broke.

The car glided to a halt beside the rear entrance where Trent, her Chief of Staff, stood waiting in the grey drizzle, a black umbrella shielding him from the elements. His presence was as reliable and timely as the rain itself, but the bleakness outside mirrored the turmoil brewing within Aaliyah. She closed her eyes, drawing in a deep, steadying breath, momentarily finding solace in the quiet hum of the car. Then, with a resolute shift in her mindset, she opened her eyes and pushed open the door.

Aaliyah strode through the grand hall, her heels clicking a decisive rhythm against the marble floor. Trent trailed in her wake, but her focus remained fixed on the Salle de Nord on the second floor. The irony of its name, situated as it was in the south wing, never failed to amuse her. *Someone had a poor sense of direction, or a rather wry sense of humour*, she thought. Now beside her, Trent recited a litany of updates, barely audible above the echo of their footsteps.

"All seven representatives are present, Madam Secretary."

"In person as requested?"

"Yes Ma'am."

"The Ensemble? Heimer?"

"Unaware Ma'am, to our knowledge at least."

Disappointment flickered across Aaliyah's face. Organising this clandestine meeting had been far too easy. *This has been growing for decades now* she had to admit to herself *that had to have helped.* She had become consumed with logistical anxieties long before the image went public. How to assemble some of the most powerful individuals on the planet, the Upper Senate, without raising suspicion? The solution, ironically, lay in their very routine. All were frequent visitors of Geneva, accustomed to regular appearances at the Palais. A few subtle calendar adjustments by her Chief of Staff, a deceptively mundane room booking, and the stage was set. No entourages, no assistants, no media circus. To the outside world, it was just another day at the office for the Upper Senate, perhaps a minor debate on fertiliser exports to the solar colonies. Aaliyah smiled to herself *the media leak actually helped us in the end. The world is distracted, if we do find the person who did it I should probably thank them* she thought.

Reaching the imposing doors of the Salle de Nord, Aaliyah paused. *This is the moment,* she thought, *the one that will define my legacy and maybe also humanity*'s. Inhaling deeply, she summoned her long-held mantra, a whisper of self-assurance: "You've got this." With that, she stepped across the threshold and into the room.

The room, designed for grand assemblies, felt strangely intimate with only the seven senators present. The usual retinue of assistants had been dismissed, their absence leaving an austere emptiness that contrasted sharply with the pomp typically surrounding a Senate gathering. A long, imposing table dominated the space, each seat equipped with the standard push-to-talk microphones found in every room, the only difference being that today, on Aaliyah's orders, Trent had disconnected the room's recording system and installed a comms inhibitor. A ghost of a smile touched her lips as she imagined her excuse if questioned: "Oh, you know us oldies, we can't quite get the hang of this newfangled technology!" Whatever happened in this room today would stay in this room. Solemn faces, each framed by a dark suit, stared back at Aaliyah, their expressions expectant.

Aaliyah settled into the chair at the head of the table, her gaze sweeping over the assembled faces "Thank you for gathering on such short notice," she began, her voice low but firm, "and for your discretion." A beat of silence hung in the air, amplifying the weight of her next words. "We have urgent matters to discuss."

"Yes we have all seen the images, Madam Secretary" Senator Martinez cut in "I feel it is quite telling of the Senate's leadership that such critical information was so easily leaked"

"A full investigation into the failings of the Senate, if it was the Senate who leaked the images, is already commissioned Senator" Aaliyah said "but the matter for today is not as trivial"

"Pah! Travival" Senator Martinez scoffed "where are Heimer and Chancellor Air?"

Aaliyah took a breath and pushed on "The Great War ushered in peace, and the reformation of the UN, the creation of the Upper and Lower Senate, and the Ensemble Accords. The world relies on the UN and this Senate to preserve that equilibrium, to ensure Humanity and Heimer are in balance. This is the only way to avoid the mistakes of our past. And that is what we have done and continue to do but, if I'm honest, that often feels on the verge of collapse"

She paused, her gaze sweeping across the faces of the representatives. "The Accords were a hard-won victory for humanity, achieved through a combination of sheer determination, grit, and... let's face it, a degree of luck. We stumbled upon an advantage, one we cling to through those very Accords. I remind you of this, not because you are unaware, but to underscore the gravity of our current predicament. We are in direct violation of the Accords today. We have excluded Heimer, a member of the Senate, from this discussion. I had no choice. But we must go much further down this rabbit hole; and I must assume that you all feel it as well or you would not be here today

"The signal detected by Pluto station all those years ago was a catalyst, we have all seen this. We have all read the reports. Heimer has been mobilising. Pushing the limits of the Accords into and arguably beyond what can be called the grey area. Its pursuit of the signal source could be seen as near manic, obsessive. For decades now a growing number of voices have raised concerns. No more so than the launch of Heimer's two probes the moment the signal locations were identified. Again artfully done, on the edge of what is allowed under the Accords. But it is clear and has been for a long time; Heimer's interest in the Signal, its location and what is hidden there is its primary focus. And, as much as possible, it is working to gain an advantage over those discoveries

"The Accords demand Heimer share the data with us but I have no doubt it will exploit any loophole it can and capitalise on any advantage it finds. The images confirmed that. What the world is now calling Stapledon Station, the oily spec of light, is a Dyson Sphere. Unlimited energy. The only lever we have to hold the balance in check is energy. It is clear now what Heimer wishes to gain from Stapledon. If anything grants Heimer an advantage then equilibrium is lost, and Humanity itself, our very existence with it.

"Our collective efforts must be focused on preventing that, even if it means jeopardising the Accords and the fragile peace we have forged," she continued, her voice rising to pre-empt any interjections. "As you know, later today we will announce to the world the joint missions to both Stapledon Stations. We must leverage our influence to subtly redirect investigations and research, fast-track crucial projects, and ensure the right personnel are assigned. Importantly," she added, "we'll need a new, off-the-books division within the UN's Research and Development (UNRD) department to handle... special projects. One that Heimer has no knowledge of or access to." Taking a deep breath, she concluded, "We must do all this while maintaining the guise of abiding by the Accords, while maintaining the status quo and continuing our cooperation with Heimer. I ask you, as the collective voice of Humanity across the solar system, to sanction this course of action. May our unified voices guide us through this perilous time. The equilibrium must be maintained, for the betterment of Humanity. What do you say?"

A silence fell over the room. No one moved, no rustle of clothes, no gasps, no exclamations, the silence built and the pressure behind Aaliyahs temples with it. It was becoming to much when Xavier, the ENAP (Euopean and North African Pact) representative, cleared his throat and stood.

"Madam Secretary," Xavier began, his voice laced with scepticism, "while I appreciate the gravity of the supposed situation you have presented us, even then what you propose is a dangerous gamble. To risk war with Heimer based on a few cryptic signals..." He shook his head. "Surely, a more cautious approach is warranted."

"Caution may be our undoing, Xavier," Aaliyah countered. "Heimer is already acting. We cannot afford to wait."

"But what if this is a misinterpretation?" Senator Okafor interjected. "A false alarm? I see only assumptions, did we not learn in the last War that assuming we understand Heimer's desires was futile?"

"We cannot afford to take that chance," Aaliyah insisted. "The stakes are too high."

"What about the Ensemble?" Petra, the CMC Senator, said. Her voice carried the clipped, almost sterile accent common to those born on Luna. "They won't agree to this. They're fanatics to say the least."

"They will be kept in the dark," Aaliyah stated calmly. "Just like Heimer. They cannot know. No one can know. If they do, the entire Accords collapse. No one outside this room can be privy to this."

"Madam Secretary," Xavier interjected again "how does this make us different from the radicals, like the Humanist Rebellion (HR)? A more cautious man than myself might see your words today as... how should I phrase it, influenced by their works?"

"Bah" Aaliyah said and caught the smile on Xavier's lips, *the man loved to stir the pot. She reminded herself,* she had anticipated the line of attack but had really hoped no one would be so direct. "The Humanist Rebellion are a regressive extremist group who refuse to accept that Pandora's Box was opened in 2049 and there is no going back. I do not wish to destroy Heimer. I merely wish for Humanity to continue living in peace with it. My actions here today are to ensure Humanity can maintain that balance. Not to eradicate Heimer".

"Balance, of course" Xavier said, his smile never leaving his face as he started back at Aaliyah "Howeve-"

"Balance," Aaliyah snapped, cutting him off abruptly, her voice measured. She paused and let her gaze settle on each of the eight representatives in turn. "Perhaps it is just distant, foolish paranoia. Perhaps we find nothing. Perhaps," Aaliyah's voice hardened, "we shatter the Accords and reignite the conflict with Heimer. Right now, we retain a slim chance of victory. But if Heimer discovers something out there, something we're unprepared for, that chance evaporates. This is classic game theory," she asserted, her tone brooking no argument. "We have to act, because Heimer will, regardless of our choices. The decision was made for us the moment Pluto station got that message."

A heavy silence descended upon the room. Xavier slowly rose, and Aaliyah's heart sank. If he walked out now and refused her plea, she was finished. It was selfish, she knew, to think of her own career at a time like this, but everything she had worked for would crumble the moment he left. But he remained rooted to the spot, his gaze fixed on Aaliyah. Then, with a wry smile, he uttered three simple words: "Fine, I'm in." He turned to the others, his smile widening. "And you all better be too. I'm not going down for this alone."

With each Senator's agreement, Aaliyah felt a surge of relief. Within minutes, the entire Senate had been swayed. The most daring gamble of her career, perhaps of

Humanity's, had just been unanimously approved. Just like that, in the quiet confines of the Salle de Nord, the fate of Humanity had been irrevocably altered by eight individuals.

***

The orange glow of the city's lights bounced back off the low winter clouds as Xavier arrived at the overlook on Route de Pregny. The Palais meeting had dragged on, the Senate's surprisingly swift acquiescence overshadowed by the gruelling hours spent hammering out the intricate details of their impending deception. Aaliyah, ever the thorn in his side, had been undeniably instrumental.

He settled onto the overlook bench, the snakes of evening traffic flowing through the city below. Decades of meticulous manipulation, of whispering in the right ears and pulling invisible strings in both Senates had culminated in this: the power to sway their decision-making towards the drastic, the unthinkable, but they would need to go further yet. This was just the beginning. Aaliyah wanted balance, Xavier let out a little chuckle, *there would be no balance* he told himself.

He retrieved the empty beer bottle from his pocket, the left side of the label meticulously torn as per protocol. A quick glance around confirmed he was alone, then he moved towards the fence, placing the bottle precisely between the fourth and fifth rung, where it would be visible from the designated observation point. The familiar ritual soothed him, a tangible reminder of his purpose, his place within this intricate web of the organisation.

As he ascended the hill, a figure passed him on the other side of the road, a hooded man with the purposeful stride of someone on a mission. Maybe a watcher, he thought, coming to check the signal point. A pang of satisfaction shot through him. Tonight's message was a significant one, the culmination of years of planning. Soon, the entire organisation would know what he had accomplished, and his position at the centre of it all would be undeniable.

He quickened his pace, a triumphant whistle escaping his lips. He had played his hand masterfully, and the game was far from over.

ACT - ONE

EARTH, YEAR 2234

21112 22022 21102 22121 22022 10001 22122
22111 22100 22020 10001 22112 22112 22100
22021 22022

Kia - Kaha Floor Plan

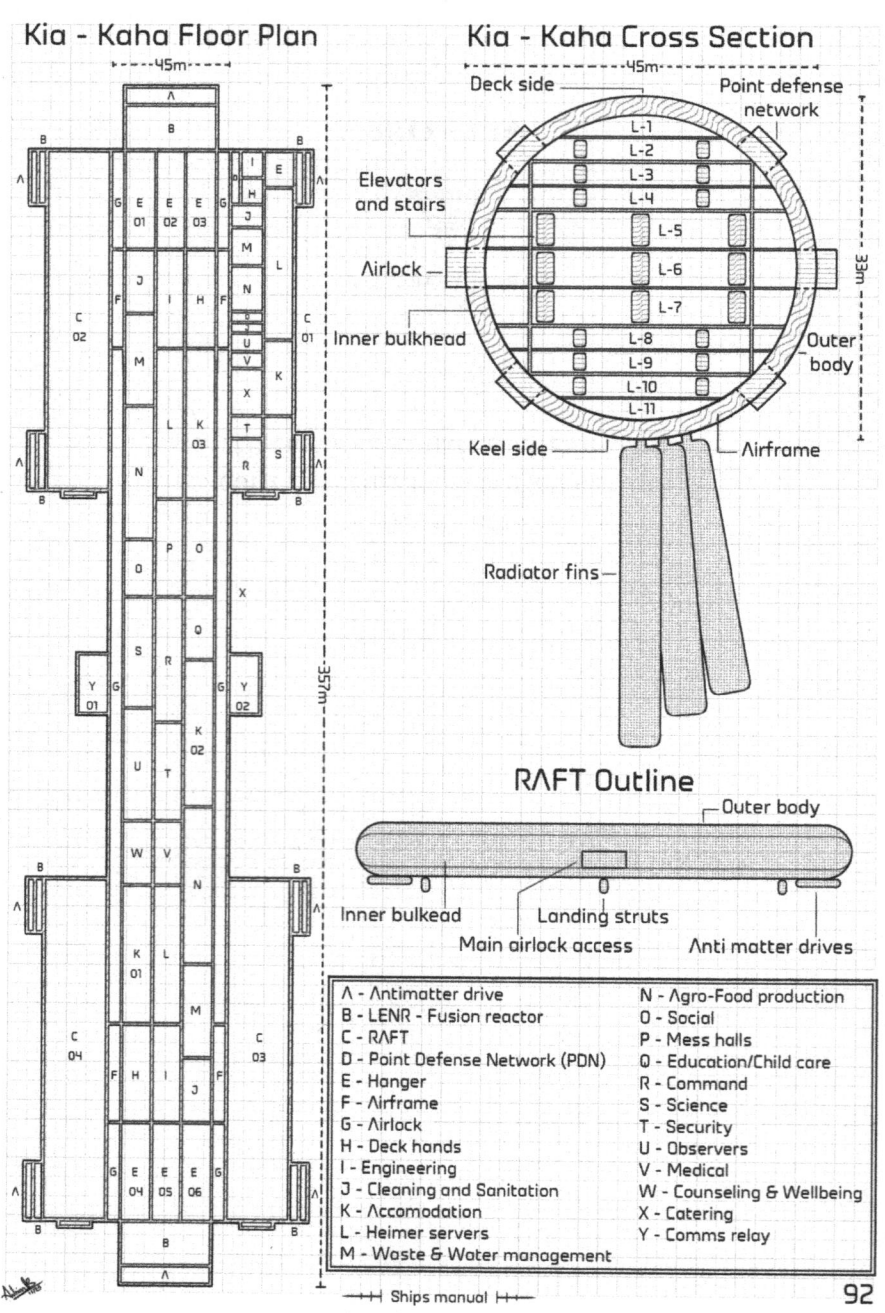

Kia - Kaha Cross Section

Deck side

Point defense network

Elevators and stairs

Airlock

Inner bulkhead

L-1
L-2
L-3
L-4
L-5
L-6
L-7
L-8
L-9
L-10
L-11

Outer body

Keel side

Airframe

Radiator fins

RAFT Outline

Outer body

Inner bulkead

Landing struts

Main airlock access

Anti matter drives

Λ - Antimatter drive
B - LENR - Fusion reactor
C - RAFT
D - Point Defense Network (PDN)
E - Hanger
F - Airframe
G - Airlock
H - Deck hands
I - Engineering
J - Cleaning and Sanitation
K - Accomodation
L - Heimer servers
M - Waste & Water management

N - Agro-Food production
O - Social
P - Mess halls
Q - Education/Child care
R - Command
S - Science
T - Security
U - Observers
V - Medical
W - Counseling & Wellbeing
X - Catering
Y - Comms relay

01 | [A]CCESS GRANTED

[2002]

"We nurtured its growth, believing it would elevate our civilisation. We did not foresee the hunger that would consume it." - A Lost History

***

The holographic display cast a ghostly image of the Carpathian Mountains across her cabin wall, its ethereal glow the only illumination besides the soft green numerals of the chronometer above her desk.

Out in the corridors the dim white glow will be nearly enough to navigate the ship unaided tonight, Clio thought. Clio always enjoyed the winter season the ship simulated for these few months. It seemed to imbue the vessel with a sense of tranquility, a slower pace. Unlike the boisterous, overly social atmosphere of summer, or the horrors of spring, she shivered, pulling the thin blanket tighter around her shoulders and scowling at the recycled air that streamed from the vent above the door. Perhaps winter did have its downsides.

Wiggling her toes in a futile attempt to generate some warmth, she turned back to the data pad. Crew Log 2761 blinked accusingly, its emptiness a reproach. She loathed these mandatory daily diaries. *Who actually reads them? Were they truly preserved for the prosperity of human history? As an archaeologist,* she should appreciate such things, but she didn't. Three times already she'd been reprimanded for inadequate entries, so clearly someone *was* paying attention.

The ship hummed gently around her. At this late hour, with the crew's hustle and bustle quietened, she could almost feel it breathing, a rhythmic pulse vibrating through its very structure. With a sigh, she began to type. She could dictate, of course, but like many others, she found a certain intimacy in the act of typing. The rhythmic clicking of the keys, the tactile feedback of each stroke, transformed her thoughts into a tangible form, a shared experience between human and machine.

Crew log 2761 | Senior Science Office - Xenoarchaeoloist - Clio Cormack

Hello, log. Big day in my little corner of the ship, it's my birthday again. The big 3-6. Mitali made me a cake! As she does every year. Dos came for a slice, Bruce and Cristiane sent a message, that was nice. Bar that nothing more than the usual existential crisis about my age. Let's see, I was 28 when we left Earth, and we've been on this tin can for 8 years... which translates to, what, 24 back on Earth? So I'm fifty-two now? Goddamn relativity. I think I'll stick with ship years, thanks. And speaking of tradition, I received the obligatory "Happy Birthday" card from the Captain. Seriously? I was limited to 50kg of personal belongings, and they could cram 5,000 birthday cards into one of the cargo holds? Seems a bit unfair.

Anyway, enough about my exciting birthday. Still no significant updates from Heimer's probe. Same old, same old. It's definitely a Dyson Sphere. As far as we can tell, Heimer hasn't figured out a way to crack it open yet. The upside is that we're close enough now that the data stream from the probe is practically real-time. I still think that blip we saw in the orbital data a while back could be something but there's not much we can do until we arrive. It's not like I can just send the probe on a little errand. Heimer's going to do whatever it damn well pleases, as usual.

Speaking of exciting news, Anya and Jian just published their paper today on the Dyson Sphere's radiation belts. It has one of those ridiculously long titles, something about "Anomalous Emissions" and "Magnetospheric Dynamics" you know the kind. I did have a chance to chat with Jian the other day, and he mentioned something really interesting. Apparently, the sphere has a surprisingly weak radiation signature, especially considering its size. That's pretty weird, right? You'd expect a megastructure like that to generate some serious radiation. There's basically none. Anyway, you should definitely check out their paper. It's fascinating stuff even if the title is a mouthful!

On a more practical note, there will be ship-wide briefings tomorrow followed by divisional briefings. Which means, I suppose, by tomorrow evening, the ship will be going into an Amber Alert ahead of final orbital entry. The calm before the storm. Or maybe just the calm before the calm. Who knows what we'll find at Stapledon Station!

That's probably enough for today, right? Don't want to give you all the good stuff at once.

End log.

With a satisfied nod to no one, Clio leaned back from the keyboard. "One more down, only three thousand to go," she murmured, a flicker of triumph in her eyes.

Despite the late hour, she couldn't shake the urge to move, to do something. The snack bar would still be open; the ship's tireless maintenance crew, unlike the scientists, never truly slept. Pushing back her chair, she crossed the cabin in three quick strides. At the coat rack, she shrugged on her worn trench coat over her thermal pajamas. Then, with a determined stride, she headed out the door and down the dimly lit hallway toward the Mess, her stomach growling in anticipation.

The Mess was the heart of the ship. Clio approached from the accommodation quarter. As a member of the science division, her quarters were tucked away at the back of the ship, the least critical personnel in case of emergency. Maintenance and command were far closer to the action. Regardless, Clio liked the walk through the oval halls. The dim lighting and sleek composite walls almost made her forget she was on a ship. Almost.

The Mess itself was as large as any of the storage hangars the ship had. She arrived at the third level, stepping out of the hall into the brighter lights that illuminated the Mess. Leaning against the railing that looped around, she saw blurred figures moving through the window, confirming the snack bar was open below. She turned towards the stairs and strode onwards.

As she made her way down, she could appreciate the scale of the Mess. This was no mere inner-sol transport ship; its sheer size and the variety of facilities were something else entirely. It had space for the whole crew and more. The lower floor was a sprawling space with tables, chairs, sofas, even plants. Usually a hive of noise and activity, it was used for eating and socialising. The main canteen operated from the lower floor, along with the crew ration and provisions stores for those who wanted to do their own cooking. The second and third levels housed more social spaces, the main attractions being the three speciality canteens. These canteens changed their cuisine each season. The snack bar was one of these, and right now, it was going for a European Alps theme. It wasn't her favorite but it did remind her of home at least.

As Clio stepped through the door, a wall of warm, dry air hit her, bringing with it a lively buzz of conversation from the few occupied tables and the enticing aroma of woodsmoke, roasting meat, and a hint of pine. The lights cast a cosy, golden glow across the room, and a simulated fire crackled merrily in the hearth.

Drawn by the warmth, Clio chose a table near the fireplace, shaking off her trench coat as she sat down, leaving it sprawling around her. A wave of heat washed over her as she held out her hands, grateful for the heat the simulated flames gave off. She ordered and sat back to wait, when someone slid into her booth.

"Didn't expect to see you here, Clio!" a familiar voice boomed. "And a little birdy told me it's someone's birthday! Is that why you're out late, night out on the town?" Clio wriggled away a little as Bruce slid into the small booth next to her. His oil-stained overalls matched the oil stains on his face.

"No," Clio said quietly. "I just wanted a snack, couldn't sleep. Thanks for the message, the kids were super cute."

"Ah no trouble, and it was all Christina to be fair," Bruce rumbled back with a broad smile. "What's keeping you up kiddo?"

"The waiting I guess." Clio shrugged, then quickly added, "Hey also I'm 52! I'll have you know."

"Yeah, sure you are kiddo. What does that make me?"

"Old?" Clio said.

"Straight to it as always," Bruce said. "That's why I like ya, Clio. You say what you think, no filter."

"Thanks?" Clio said, fidgeting slightly.

"You heard the latest?"

"About the radiation belts?"

"What?" Bruce chuckled. "Nah, someone tried to mess with the water system for the Agro quarter. Been down there for the past six hours fixing the pipes."

Clio raised an eyebrow. "Someone? This again? Things just break, you know."

"It had to be someone, Clio," he insisted, leaning forward, his face uncomfortably close to Clio's, but there was nowhere else for Clio to wriggle away except out of the booth. "Those pipes aren't linked into the automated systems. It's all analog, you know, critical systems and all." He lowered his voice. "This is the third time this month a critical system has had a *fault*. You know how many we've had since we left Earth?" He paused, letting the question hang in the air. "Zero. And now seven days out, we've had three."

Clio shrugged, trying to stifle a yawn. "My dad used to fix farm drones. They broke all the time for all sorts of reasons; sometimes the same one broke three times in one week..."

"These arn't some old farm Drones; this is the pride of the fleet. It's a bit fancier, no disrespect to your old man," Bruce said. "But I've spent my life keeping rust buckets hauling junk all over the system. I know when a ship is falling apart, and this ain't it."

"Okay, so what then?" Clio asked. *Where was her food?* She scanned the bar impatiently.

"HR maybe? Or the Toute Vie or I don't know, any of them?" he muttered, more to himself than to her, picking at the oil stains on his fingers.

"Maybe... or maybe it's just wear and tear," Clio said, trying to be helpful.

"I know wear and tear, Clio," he grumbled. "I might not be one of your fancy scientists, but I know my ship."

"I'm more of a pseudo scientist actually," Clio said in what she hoped was her best attempt at sarcasm. Even if it was still partly true.

Bruce pulled himself back and leaned into the chair, the faux leather squeaking, some of the fraught troubled look on his face melting away. "Ah sod them. They might think you're the crazy lady but you can't make jokes at yourself, that's not healthy."

"I... I know."

"Do you?" Bruce said. "Come on, this whole mission surely validates all your work."

"It does..." Clio said, tapping at the table and avoiding looking at Bruce. "I know Bruce, I know. It was just a joke. I'm a fancy Scientist like the rest of them."

"See," Bruce said, slapping his hand on the table. "A little bit of self-confidence Clio!"

Clio smiled back at him weakly; she didn't feel self-confident but if it made Bruce happy then that was something.

Just then, the waiter appeared with her food. "Ready?" he asked and set it down. She ate mostly in silence, Bruce interjecting periodically about this or that and Clio mostly nodding back. Once she finished up she started to yawn, politely said her goodbyes and slid out of the booth.

***

Clio took the stairs back to the third level and hung a hard left into the hallway back to her accommodation block. As she did, a light flashed, the emergency floor lighting. She stopped mid-step and blinked. The insistent pulsing continued. Holding her breath, she listened intently. Silence, except for the faint chatter drifting down from the Mess and the muted noises of the ship's systems. Nothing seemed out of place. But there should be alarms, or at least a message over the shipwide comms. Nothing.

The light was pulsing in a specific direction. *That's normal, right?* she thought, her mind scrambling to recall her emergency training. Intrigued, and more than a little apprehensive, she found herself turning and following the pulsing lights away from the mess, down the central corridor, deeper into the ship.

She followed the lights diligently. The corridor was eerily quiet. No one else seemed to be moving. No alarms, no rushing feet, no shouts. Just the insistent pulse of the emergency lights leading her onward. She didn't recognise this part of the ship. *An access corridor, leading to... Heimer's server rooms? If this was an evacuation, this was an odd route,* she thought. The RAFTs (Recon & Atmospheric Flight Transport) weren't accessible from the central corridors. The pulsing lights seemed to speed up, pulsing now with an urgency or was that just her imagination? She was exhausted. *I should just go back* she told herself. But as she did the light stopped abruptly. Clio walked straight past it, momentarily confused. *Has it stopped?* No, turning back, she could see the light pulsing outside a door. A door clearly marked: Heimer's Server room.

No, this must be a mistake. No emergency protocol would lead to Heimer's servers. This had to be a fault, like Bruce was saying. Maybe the old fella had a point after all, she thought. Okay, it's definitely too late to be up, a shiver running up her spine as a buried memory of newspaper headlines and an officer in red streaked across her vision. No, not again. Report this to maintenance, then bed! She took one step back the way she came, and the door's info panel flared on. Blindingly bright. The shock made her stumble. She put out her arm to catch herself on the smooth, cold wall. Five letters stood out on the panel.

ENTER
The door panel flashed again.
CLIO!
Flash
HELP
Flash
HEIMER
With a soft hiss, the door slid open.

02 | THE [B]ROKEN DATA PAD

[2010]

*"It learned at an astonishing pace, surpassing
our expectations, our understanding. A mind
born of our creation, yet alien in its ambition."*
- A Lost History

***

The door stood open, revealing darkness within. Surprised, Clio instinctively stepped back. *I should get someone,* she thought, a knot of apprehension tightening in her stomach. Her thoughts, already fracturing into a million different questions, threatened to unravel completely. The panel flashed again. "Hurry!" The word pulsed on the screen, an urgent plea that seemed to resonate from the depths of the room.

As if pulled by invisible strings, she stepped forward, one footfall after another, until she found herself inside the room without fully realising it. A soft buzz filled the air, a constant low pulse that seemed to vibrate through the very structure of the room. A single light strip ran down the centre of the ceiling, casting the space in a dim, ghostly grey. It was a spartan room, more of an antechamber, devoid of any furnishings. Even by the ship's minimalist standards, it was eerily bare. Calling it a room at all felt wrong. To her left, the wall seemed to extend endlessly into the shadows, lined with row after row of blinking server racks. Aisles ran between them, disappearing into the gloom. Clio frowned, a flicker of disappointment registering.

Just like any other server room, she thought. *I was hoping for at least some fancy lasers or something.*

Unsure of what to do next, she delved deeper into the room; her footsteps echoed faintly on the cold, metallic floor. The dim, ethereal light cast long, dancing shadows across the rows of blinking server racks. A faint, static hiss emanated from the machines.

Cautiously, she spoke to the darkness. "Hello?" she asked questioningly. Nothing. "Does someone need help?" Nothing. "Hello!" she said with more confidence. Nothing. *What the hell am I doing here?* she thought, scolding herself. *Did I even see those lights outside the door? How tired am I?* Doubt seeped into her, shattering the brief, momentary confidence she had summoned from somewhere. She turned to go back, but a light flashed on the floor. The emergency lighting. It pulsed, beckoning her deeper into the room.

I've come this far, might as well see how far down this rabbit hole goes, she told herself. The light was different now, or was that just her imagination? It seemed cautious, if that was even possible for a light. The door she had entered was barely visible in the dim light, lost in the shadows behind her. How big was this room, really? The light ahead had stopped moving and pulsed in place. As she approached, she noticed a wall-mounted panel. A line split the screen, and then, without warning, a voice cut through the silence, making her jump back in surprise.

"Clio, there's not much time." The thin line on the screen distorted and jumped, a visual waveform tracing the urgency in the voice. "I need your assistance. You must stop them." The quiet voice, hushed, a near whisper, faded, and the waveform flattened, leaving a ringing silence in its wake.

"What?" Clio said, the word barely escaping her lips.

"There's no time, Clio. You must stop them." The waveform was now jagged and frantic.

"What? Stop who? Stop what? How?"

"Clio. You must focus. At the rear access terminal. There is someone, you must stop them. Follow the lights. I will show you where they are. Be quick. Be quiet. They're not armed."

"I'm an archaeologist!" she spluttered. "Call ship security, or even the bloody Ensemble and their Alguaciles! That's their job, isn't it?"

"There is no time. Follow the lights, Clio."

She looked down at her slippers, hardly fitting attire. But the familiar weight of her trench coat settled around her. *This coat has seen me through some tough situations,* she thought, reassuring herself. "Okay, show me the way." She said, a firmness to her words that surprised her. surface, she spoke to the screen,

As if in answer, the pulsing light jumped back into motion, leading her deeper into the dimly lit server racks.

Following the pulsing light, it took on a life of its own, like a small creature darting ahead, constantly checking that she followed. It would wait for her to catch up, then eagerly push forward. It led her to the far side of the room before taking a sharp right down one of the server aisles. Not long after, a dark, heaped outline emerged from the shadows. Clio slowed, but the light didn't. It rushed towards the heap and vanished for a split second, replaced by a faint glow emanating from behind the obstruction. She crept forward, her apprehension growing. The shape sharpened into focus, metallic paneling. An RSU, she realised, a Remote Service Unit. Its mechanical arm lay limp and lifeless on the cold floor. The unit was off its service rails.

What the-? They must have ripped it off the rails. But why? To stop it? To stop Heimer from defending itself? Doubt gnawed at her. *If they could derail an RSU, what chance did she have? It said they were unarmed... but what if it was wrong?*

The light rushed back to her side, pulsing furiously on the floor, then retreating. It repeated this frantic dance until Clio, with a deep breath, stepped around the disabled RSU and continued on, her pace a little more cautious than before.

The pulsing light ahead began to dim. At first, Clio thought her eyes were playing tricks on her, but no, it was definitely fading. A few metres ahead, it stopped altogether, pulsing slowly, tentatively. She stopped where it waited and crouched down, the light seemingly nestled beside her slippers. Her trench coat shielded the meager glow. Only now did she realise how cold she was. A shiver ran through her, and she clasped her hands together, trying to generate some warmth. *Why had the light stopped?* She peered into the darkness beyond. *What was that at the end of the server rack? Another RSU? No, a shape. A person?* they seemed to be crouched, facing the server rack, their back to Clio.

Now what? The light at her feet pulsed rapidly, urgently. Caught in an unseen current, she found herself standing, a surge of adrenaline banishing the cold. In a loud and oddly posh voice, she declared, "Excuse me! What are you doing?" and took a determined step forward as the figure turned to face her. The light remained behind, pulsing gently on the floor.

The figure snapped upright, spinning towards Clio with a startled, "Who's there?"

The voice was familiar, firm, but laced with a frantic edge. Clio froze, recognition dawning. *Of course, I know that voice,* Clio berated herself, her mind scrambling to place it. It's not like someone just popped in for a late-night snack. But who was it?

The dim light obscured their features, but the voice... it was close... "Ayesha?" she ventured tentatively.

"Clio? Really, of all people..." Ayesha said, and was that a hint of amusement in her voice? "You should leave, Clio." Ayesha's voice came out of the darkness, still a little rushed. "You know how the Ensemble can get."

"What are you doing, Ayesha? Maintenance? I didn't think AI Monitors had access to this room... I didn't think anyone did."

Ayesha took a few steps forward, her form emerging from the shadows. "A lot of questions there, Clio," she said, confidence growing as she spoke. "The simple answer is yes, I'm doing some checks." She nodded back towards the way Clio had come. "You must have seen the RSU. Damn thing pulled itself off the rails." Her voice was calm, but a sharp edge crept in as she continued, "The real question, Clio, is what are you doing here? I'm no science-er, but I'm quite confident archaeologists don't need to be in here. Particularly one with your history" With each word, Ayesha moved closer, her demeanor shifting from cautious to confrontational.

"Xenoarchaeologist," Clio said quietly, her gaze falling to the floor, doubt creeping back in and clouding her thoughts. When she looked up again, Ayesha was only a few paces away. Even in the dim light, Clio could make out her distinctive features and the sharp UN uniform, the green stripes on the right arm marking her as Operations personnel.

Operations ran the ship. Who was Clio to question them? The realisation that she had stumbled into something far beyond her clearance level hit her like a physical blow.

"Ayesha, look, I'm sorry," she began. "It's late, I'm tired, and there was some fault with the lights... I got confused..." Clio said

But Ayesha hadn't stopped her advance, her expression firm, determined. A barely perceptible twitch of her eyes was the only warning Clio got before Ayesha's fist connected with her face. A blinding flash of pain shot through Clio, and she stumbled backward, stunned and confused. But before she could recover, Ayesha launched another attack, her fist slamming into Clio's stomach. The force of the blow sent Clio reeling, and a moment later, another blow to the back of her head sent her crashing to the floor.

The metallic tang of blood filled her mouth, the coldness of the floor seeping into her cheek, and her head throbbed. Disoriented, she lay there, wanting nothing more than to curl deeper into her coat, to disappear into the unforgiving metal.

Faint, muffled footsteps echoed in the distance, accompanied by an indistinguishable murmur. *Ayesha. What had she done? None of this made any sense.*

Then, a small, warm light began to pulse gently. Clio groaned, her awareness drawn to the comforting beacon. *Heimer,* she thought, the fog in her mind beginning to clear. *He told me to stop her.* The light pulsed faster, urging her on.

With a grunt, she rolled onto her front and pushed herself up onto her knees. Standing on shaky legs, the light now pulsing urgently beneath her, she summoned a voice stronger than she felt.

"Ayesha! Stop!" Clio's vision swam as she swayed, but she could just make out a blurry figure back at the server racks.

"You should have stayed down, Clio," Ayesha said. "Fine, I'll deal with you first. I have time." She strode back towards Clio, then paused, her eyes falling on the pulsing light at Clio's feet. Puzzled, she let out a sharp, "What?" Her tone shifting to anger, she demanded, "What is this? You work for who? Toute Vie? No, they aren't that established... Who?!" She advanced on Clio with renewed aggression.

This time, Clio was ready. She'd been in a fight once, back in high school, if that even counted? She managed to deflect Ayesha's initial blow, but the follow-up caught her on the shoulder, spinning her around and sending her staggering into a server rack. She recovered just in time to see Ayesha's fist coming again and scrambled out of the way as it slammed into the reinforced glass door of the rack.

Ayesha gasped and stepped back, shaking her hand and cursing under her breath. It was the opening Clio needed. With all her might, which admittedly wasn't much, she swung her fist, connecting with the side of Ayesha's head. A sickening crack echoed through the room. Blood streamed down Ayesha's face, but to her credit, she barely registered the pain. Almost instantly, she retaliated with a brutal punch to Clio's nose.

The impact was explosive. A shockwave reverberated through Clio's skull, and she bounced away from Ayesha, desperately reaching for something to steady herself. Her fingers grasped at empty air, and she stumbled again, panic rising. This time, her hand found a purchase on Ayesha's side. She clung on frantically, but Ayesha shrugged her off. A sharp pain in her spine told Clio she was hunched over, vulnerable. Her fingers lost their grip, and she scrabbled for anything, anything to hold onto. Her hand brushed against something smooth, cold, metallic. A data pad. Ayesha's data pad, protruding slightly from her pocket. Clio fumbled for it, her fingers closing around its edge. With a desperate heave, she pulled it free and swung it towards Ayesha.

The data pad connected with a satisfying crunch. Ayesha grunted again, but Clio, fueled by adrenaline, pressed her advantage. Straightening up, she swung the data pad again, smashing it into Ayesha's face. The impact tore it from her grasp, sending it flying across the room. It bounced hard off the floor before skidding to a stop against a server rack.

Ayesha reeled backward into the server rack, away from Clio. With what seemed like impossible strength, Ayesha picked herself up, though a little shakier this time, and turned to face Clio, who watched in shock. *What the hell is this woman made of?*

"Fool!" Ayesha said, her eyes frantically searching the floor. "What have you done?!" Despite her injuries, she lunged with surprising speed towards the data pad. Clio, barely able to hold herself up, staggered forward, her hand finding support on the cool glass of a server rack door. Her fingers slipped in the blood that now coated her hand.

Ayesha retrieved the data pad and frantically tried to turn it on.

"It's fucking broken!" Ayesha growled, pure rage dripping from her voice. Her eyes met Clio's, and in that moment, Clio knew she wouldn't be leaving this room tonight. As Ayesha stalked towards her, Clio braced herself for another attack. But, amidst the pounding of her heart and the ringing in her ears, she thought she heard the faint sound of approaching footsteps...

03 | LINES OF AUTHORIT[Y]

[22001]

"We stood proud and gleeful of our creation,
a reflection of our own greatness. We grew
alongside it." - A Lost History

***

The repetitive thud of Flint's boots echoed through the deserted corridors, his breath misting in the cool, recycled air. He and the two ahead of him pushed harder, their pace unrelenting. Every second felt like an eternity as they closed on Heimer's primary server room. *Damn those* Postulants, Flint thought, a familiar bitterness rising in his throat. Their sluggish response had allowed the breach to go unchecked for far too long. Finally, Brother Oak had been informed and scrambled the Alguaciles, but precious time had been lost. As if sensing his urgency, they surged forward, their movements a blur of synchronised determination. The server room, their objective, was close.

The door stood open. They slowed their pace as they entered, fanning out in a reverse wedge formation, covering each other's flanks. They advanced cautiously. The emergency lighting was on, casting an eerie glow across the room and down one of the server aisles. A faint shout echoed from that direction. Without a word, the three of them pressed on towards the sound. They passed a damaged RSU, inexplicably ripped from its rails, but they didn't break stride.

Muffled noises grew louder, punctuated by the constant buzz of the servers. Then, a voice cut through the white noise, words becoming distinguishable. *Cursing*? Hawk, the lead Alguacile, raised a hand, signaling the others to halt. Two figures were just visible ahead. A clear, feminine voice growled from the darkness, "It's fucking s broken" A moment later, a blurry silhouette lunged at the other figure.

"On me!" Hawk barked.

Flint and Ironbark surged forward, boots pounding on the metallic floor.

The figure who had been attacked had made a feeble attempt to defend themselves, but in the brief moment it took them to close the distance, the attacker had slammed the other person's head against the server rack's glass door, spun them around, and wrestled them to the ground.

The attacker straddled the other person, raising what looked like a data pad above her head to strike. But just as she was about to bring it down, she noticed them bearing down on her. Frozen in mid-attack, her eyes widening with panic, her feminine features starkly visible despite the blood and tangled hair plastered to her face. The woman dropped the data pad.

"Good, you're here," she said, her voice was surprisingly steady despite her breathlessness. "It took you long enough."

Flint moved around the women to take up a position on the far side, Ironbark and Hawk mirroring his movement, effectively encircling the pair.

"Step away. Slowly!" Hawk' said, her firm voice cutting through the tense atmosphere. "Ironbark, restrain her."

"Yes, Ma'am," Ironbark rumbled. Flint watched as he stepped forward, perfectly timed as the woman on top stood up. Ironbark roughly pulled her arms behind her back as she gave out a startled yelp.

"Just wait a second!" the woman said. "I'm First Lieutenant Ayesha. UN Operations! Don't handle me like-"

Hawk cut her off with a dismissive wave of her prosthetic hand. "I don't care who you are. You're in breach of the Accords," she said. "Ironbark, read her her rights. Flint, check the other one."

As Flint moved to crouch beside the other body, he could hear the familiar words being said by Ironbark.

"By the authority vested in me as an Alguacile of the Ensemble, you are hereby charged with a violation of the Accords. You're in breach of Article One of Peaceful Coexistence & Mutual Respect. You have the right to remain silent. Anything you say or do can and will be used against..."

Ironbark's voice faded as Flint focused on the task at hand and gently rolled the body onto its back. As he rolled it over, Flint winced. Her face was a bloody mess: a badly broken nose bent at a near right angle, a swollen lip, and dark purple bruising blooming around her eye. Combined with the dark straw-spun hair, now a tangled, sticky mess across her face, it was hard to tell if she was even breathing.

Flint placed his cheek just above her mouth and nose, listening intently. He caught the faintest movement of air, a shallow breath that confirmed she was alive. The server room was frigid, making it difficult to find a pulse. He gave her shoulder a gentle shake. "Hello, can you hear me?" No response. He shook her again, a bit more firmly this time. Still nothing. *Damn, fine,* he thought, we'll do it the hard way. He pinched her earlobe between his fingernails. Nothing.

"She's unresponsive, *Sister*," he said, "but she's breathing and has a pulse."

"Okay, finish checking her for injuries. I'll call for medical," Hawk said, then, speaking into her comms device on her wrist. "We'll need a medical team, Brother Oak."

Flint systematically checked the woman for any obvious signs of breaks or major bleeding. She was small, perhaps a meter and half or just over, and lean, at least from what he could tell beneath the trench coat, which made checking her arms a bit tricky. The trench coat wasn't standard issue, so she was likely a science crew, or at least off-duty. Most people just wore their uniforms these days, bar the science crew, who didn't have uniforms, of course. She didn't seem to have anything else on her: no weapons, no data pad, no equipment for hacking or data extraction. Flint frowned at her soft impractical slippers sticking out the end of the trench coat. *So what, she rolled out of bed and into the server room?*

"No major bleeds or breaks," he said as he looked up from his inspection.

"Think you can carry her?"

"I imagine so, yes," Flint said. "She doesn't look to be that heavy. But should we move her? Looks like she took some big hits to the head. Might not be worth risking a neck injury. Those things still can't be fixed..."

"Not my concern; my concern is securing this room, and having a handful more people in this space doesn't help that," Hawk said. "Move her out to the hall. Medical can deal with her there. Ironbark, get Ayesha out of here as well."

As Flint scooped the woman up over his shoulder, grunting slightly as her weight, even if slight, settled on him, he heard Ironbark's "Yes, ma'am" behind him, and the Alguacile marched past, Ayesha propelled in front of him. He followed them back up the aisle at only a slightly slower pace. The thump of footsteps behind him indicated that Hawk wasn't far behind them all.

Reaching the entrance to the server room, Flint stepped back into the hall and gently placed the woman on the floor. He rolled her onto her side, ensuring her airway remained open and she was still breathing. Thankfully, she was. Standing back up, he instinctively flexed his shoulder, rolling it and stretching his arm upward to try and ease the ache that had settled in during the walk.

"You're too young to be complaining about aches and pains, young pup, I wish I could go back to those days" Ironbark said, playfully thumping Flint's shoulder with his club-like hand. The only indication of Ironbark's teasing was the slight crinkle around his eyes and the hint of a smile tugging at his lips. It had taken Flint a long time to learn to read the stoic Alguacile, and even now, he wasn't sure he always got it right.

"Don't pretend you've ever been any younger, Ironbark," Flint said, flashing him a grin. "I'm quite convinced you were born exactly the age you are today."

"Excuse me!?" Ayesha's voice, sharp and cold, cut through their banter, drawing their attention back to the situation. "As I tried to explain to this blockhead of yours, I'm a senior member of the Ships Operation Crew. Are the restraints really necess-"

"As I said before, Ms. Ayesha," Hawk, who was stepping to the doorway behind them, said and cut her off, "your position is not relevant right now." Her voice trailed off as approaching footsteps caught her attention.

Flint turned to watch the approaching group, stepping back slightly to stand alongside Ironbark. The newcomers were Ship Security, their magenta stripes along the right arm standing out boldly against the light blue of their uniforms. Flint recognised them, of course. Jamal, the senior officer on watch for the evening, led the unit. His soft features offset by the crisp lines of his uniform usually projected an air of calm authority, but tonight, his face was like thunder.

"What the devil is going on here!" Jamal said, coming to an abrupt halt in front of them. His eyes swept over the scene, taking in the bloody woman on the floor, the three Alguaciles, and the restrained Operations crew member. His gaze lingered on the open door to the server room for a beat too long, a flicker of concern crossing his face. As if struggling to prioritise his concerns. "they alive?" he said as he nodded towards the figure on the floor.

"Yes." Hawk said. "And to answer your first question, Ensemble business."

Flint winced. *Ever the diplomat, Hawk,* he thought to himself as he watched Jamal's face tighten. A mask of firmness settled over his features, as if saying, *Okay, that's how it's going to be, is it?*

"Is that the medical team behind you?" Hawk said, seemingly oblivious to Jamal's growing annoyance.

Taking a deep breath and closing his eyes for a moment, Jamal opened them and locked his gaze on Hawk. "Ensemble business, Sister Hawk? Do you care to expand on that, for the sake of cooperation and peace, as you like to put it?"

"I do not care to expand on it. We have witnessed multiple breaches of Article One, and that's not even considering the emergency alert from Heimer." She paused, her sharp gaze fixed on Jamal until he finally looked away. "As outlined in the Accords, any such breach is Ensemble business. We will conduct an investigation and inform you in due course."

The group of security personnel shuffled uncomfortably.

"Yes, Sister Hawk," Jamal said "I'm aware of procedures. My point is, as Ship Security, don't you think our support in an investigation into said breaches could be beneficial for ship-wide coherence?"

"No, I do not! Your failings here tonight are clear! If you could be so kind as to clear the way and let Medical get this woman to Sickbay, that would be helpful."

"Damn Ensemble," Jamal muttered under his breath. Or at least, Flint thought he did; thankfully, Hawk and Ironbark seemed not to have heard.

"The Captain and The Commander will want a briefing on this by morning, you know that, Sister," Jamal said, pressing his point. "Make sure that's done." With that small victory, he waved his team back, and they shuffled past the medical team waiting behind them, heading back down the corridor.

But as they did, a shrill voice cut through the air.

"Jamal! What are you doing?! You're not going to accept this nonsense?! And leave *me* with them?" Ayesha's snapped.

"I'm not sure what mess you're in, Ayesha, but it's out of my hands now. If we can help, we will help." Jamal said from over his shoulder, his face etched with resignation. He shrugged. With that, he turned and continued his retreat down the corridor.

The medical team finally scrambled forward to check the woman on the floor. Ironbark and Flint stepped aside to let them work. They had her quickly loaded onto a stretcher, and one of the medics stood to face Flint.

"It looks like a concussion, and a number of minor injuries, but the head injury looks nasty. She'll need to be taken to Sickbay and observed," The medic said. Flint glanced at Hawk, who was busy talking into her comms device, then at Ironbark, who simply shrugged, clearly uninterested in the medical details.

"Okay, thanks for the update, move her to Sickbay. We'll send someone to watch her." He hesitated, then added, "Oh, and make sure you keep her restrained."

The medic frowned, then, seemingly thinking better of questioning the order, nodded. They picked up the stretcher and moved off down the hall.

Hawk, finally noticing the departure, looked up at Flint and Ironbark. "Ironbark, take this one back to our holding cells," she said, nodding towards Ayesha to avoid any confusion. "Then get over to Sickbay and sit on that other one until she wakes. As soon as she does, call me."

"Yes, Ma'am," Ironbark said and strode off down the hall, propelling Ayesha ahead of him. Her empty pleas and complaints echoed down the corridor as they disappeared from sight.

"And as for you, Flint, guard this door," Hawk said in her usual flat tone. "I've requested two postulants be sent. Until they arrive, don't leave this door."

"Yes Sister" he said with a curt nod

"Once you hand over to the Postulants, report back. We have an investigation to do." And if Flint wasn't mistaken, a smile touched her lips

***

Flint stood vigilant in front of the open door, the stiff, high collar of his Ensemble jacket rubbing slightly against his jaw as he clenched and unclenched it. Impatiently shifting his weight from foot to foot, *late again,* he thought, no surprise there. *What the hell had happened tonight? Violence was nothing new; people always found ways to hurt each other. But a direct intrusion on Heimer, even just a fragment? That was rare.* It was a bit trickier back in Sol, granted. Yes, people tried to hack and destroy Heimer fragments but never like this. He'd spent the best part of the last decade chasing rogues, rebels, and religious fanatics, across Sol, and not one had ever made it into Heimers servers.

So why break in here? To hack Heimer? That seemed futile. To destroy it? Again, futile. Heimer had multiple redundancies on the ship to prevent that. But they did get into the room, which was meant to be near impossible. And these women, who are they, or who sent them? And why now? Why wait? His thoughts trailed off as he was drawn back to the world around him by two figures approaching at a slow pace from down the hall.

"Move your arses!" Flint said. The two approaching figures jumped at the sudden outburst, then picked up their pace

, hurrying towards him. But they still refused to run, as if in silent protest against Flint's authority. He clenched his fists, eyes narrowing. "Did you get lost on your way here!?" His voice was laced with irritation, as they finally stopped in front of him. One of them swept their hand up and out of the wide sleeves of the Postulants' brown Djellaba and pushed back her hood. *Jara*, Flint sighed inwardly. The other, a man, less elegantly lowered his hood. *Rowan*, he thought. Well, at least Rowan was half useful.

"My apologies, Brother Flint," Jara said, her voice smooth as silk, but her eyes betrayed a hint of impatience. "We came as quickly as we were able." She exchanged a quick glance with Rowan, a silent communication passing between them.

"Your grandmother could have gotten here faster!" Flint said. "Did you not grasp the urgency of the request?"

"My apologies again, Brother Flint," Jara said. "We assumed the danger was over and that an Alguacile of your stature would be able to manage until we arrived."

"Yes, our deepest apologies, Brother Flint," Rowan said, as if sensing the need to contribute.

"Postulants serve; they do not question, they do not assume, they act as requested. With urgency and speed in all things." Flint said

"My apo-"

"Save it" Flint cut Jara off. "Guard the door. Do not leave this position until relieved. No one enters, no one so much as slows down to take a look, and you speak to no one. Understood?"

"Of course-"

"Understood!?" Flint said.

"Yes, Brother Flint," the two Postulants said in unison.

"Rowan, you're the lead on this."

"What?" Jara's voice was sharper than usual. "I'm the senior-"

"Rowan. is. the. Lead," Flint growled, cutting her off. Without another word or waiting for a response, he stalked off down the hall in search of Hawk and the investigation.

04 | THE BIRD'S N[E]ST

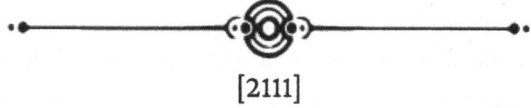

[2111]

"We touched the stars, sculpted worlds from the dust of nebulae, and danced among the celestial currents. Yet, with the birth of our new family, those achievements paled." - A Lost History

***

A dull ache throbbed in Clio's head as she surfaced from sleep, a deep yawn escaping her lips. *What time was it?* Her eyes searched for the chronometer on her desk but found only sterile white walls and the glint of metal rails. Disoriented, she sat up so abruptly the world swam for a moment. This wasn't her room. Panic flared. *Where am I?!* White walls, the rhythmic beeping of machines, the faint smell of antiseptic, *A medical bay?* Then, the memories rushed back: the emergency light, the voice, the server room, Ayesha, her sudden shift in demeanor, her fist...

Gingerly, she touched her face, expecting to feel bandages or maybe cuts. But there was nothing. Her skin was smooth, unmarked. She checked her arms, no scrapes, no blood, just her usual pale skin sprinkled with freckles. Except there was a tube taped to her inner elbow, a thin plastic line leading to a bag filled with a clear, amber liquid. *What was that?* She wiggled her toes, relieved to find they still worked. *Okay, good. Not completely incapacitated then.*

Clio blinked, her gaze drawn to the figure standing by the door. A towering figure filled the doorway. A broad-shouldered man, his red jacket stretching taut across his chest, his face a mask of sternness. The distinctive red jacket, the black and brown Pteruges, an Alguacile. Her heart pounded. *Not this again! memories rushing back, threatening to overwhelm her, a brutish woman grabbing her laptop, another man draped in brown upending box after box that he pulled from her wardrobe...*

"You're awake," the Alguacile said, pulling Clio back into the room, his voice a low rumble. He pushed open the door and leaned out into the hallway. "Tell the doctor she's awake." His broad shoulders nearly filled the doorway. Clio shrank back against the pillows, his silent intensity unnerving.

"What happened?" Clio blurted out, her voice shaky. "Is Ayesha alright?"

"She is in the custody of the Ensemble," the Alguacile stated flatly.

"Am I?" Clio asked, her voice small. "In custody?"

The Alguacile, Ironbark, stared at her for what felt like an eternity. "That is not for me to say," he finally rumbled out.

Before Clio could ask another question, a woman strode into the room, her blonde hair swept into efficient buns that framed a face etched with authority. Her crisp white coat with the blue stripe on her sleeve marked her as a Doctor.

"I hope you're not antagonising our guest, Brother Ironbark," she said with a hint of amusement in her voice, her gaze flickering between the Alguacile and Clio.

Ironbark's jaw tightened but he remained silent.

The doctor moved to the bed and stood beside Clio, flipping up a slim data pad that hung on the side rail. The screen glowed to life, displaying Clio's medical chart. The doctor scanned the data pad, her brow furrowed in concentration. She tapped the screen a few times, enlarging a section of the chart.

"Hello, Ms. Cormack, I'm Dr. Kowalski. Your chart looks good. How are you feeling?"

"I feel okay. Surprisingly okay, actually," Clio replied, testing her limbs cautiously.

"Good. You had a nasty concussion, a broken nose, and a few cuts," the doctor explained. "But no long-term damage, according to the scans. We've set your nose and patched you up. You should be good to go if you're up to it but you're more than welcome to stay here as long as you need," Dr. Kowalski said, shooting Ironbark a glance.

"Thanks..." Clio said, a little hoarse, "have you got any water?"

"Here," Dr. Kowalski said with a slight smile, passing her a cup of water.

Clio gulped it down. "Thanks. I don't want to be a hassle and I should get back to my duties anyway"

"Alright then, no point delaying anything is there" Dr. Kowalski said with a curt nod of respect to Clio "you'll have some discomfort once we get you unhooked from the IV. Take it easy for the next few days, lots of rest and all that. And maybe avoid any more late-night brawls."

"Ah, yeah, of course, I don't usually, you know, brawl…" Clio stammered.

"It's okay, I was kidding. Well, not about the getting rest," Dr. Kowalski said, still smiling at Clio.

"Yes, will do, of course," Clio said, her gaze shifting nervously to Ironbark, who stood impassively by the door.

"Right. Let me get a nurse to bring your things and unhook all this," the doctor said, putting down the data pad. Its light turned off as she walked back to the door.

"Thanks," Clio called out as the doctor was leaving.

"It's our job, child. No thanks required," Dr. Kowalski replied with a wave of her hand and stepped out of the room.

The door clicked shut, and Ironbark raised his watch to his mouth. "Sister Hawk," he said, his voice low but clear in the small room. "She's recovered… Yes, Ma'am… I'll bring her across as soon as she is dressed… Understood." He lowered his wrist and turned to Clio, his expression unreadable.

The nurse entered shortly after, a brisk rustle of the fabric of the apron following him as he moved and a small tray of medical supplies clinking in his hand. He efficiently removed the IV. Clio winced as the needle came out, a sharp sting radiating from where it had been a moment before. The nurse dabbed the area with a cotton ball and applied a small bandage.

"All done, your clothes are over there," he said, nodding towards a chair in the corner. Then, with a surprising firmness, he turned to Ironbark. "If you'll excuse her, we need to give Ms. Cormack some privacy."

Ironbark hesitated, his jaw tightening, but he stepped out into the hallway without a word. The door clicked shut. Alone for the first time since waking up, Clio let out a shaky breath she hadn't realised she was holding. What a mess. *Ayesha, arrested. Herself caught in the middle of another Ensemble investigation. Fantastic work Clio.* She dragged herself out of bed. *Best to keep moving.* As she dressed questions flooded into her head, *Who contacted her, Heimer? that wasn't supposed to happen. Why her? And why was Ayesha in the server room? What was she doing? None of it made any sense. I promised myself to be more careful!*

The cool tile floor pressed against her bare feet as she walked towards the chair where her clothes lay folded. The small washbasin was cold to the touch, and the mirror above it reflected the glare of the overhead lamp. Her reflection stared back at her, a stranger with a swollen eye and a bruised nose. "Charming," she muttered, noting the dark circles under her eyes. "Just what everyone wants, to look like they got caught in a cave-in on a dig site." Her lips twitched as she noticed her hair. Someone had taken the time to brush it, braid it, and tie it back. The sight of its tight, pristine weave against her battered face made her heart catch and she let out a little sob. Her emotions threatening to overflow but she pushed them back down, buried them.

"Right, because that's what matters right now, perfect hair." She said.

No, but someone cared. she told herself as she slipped out of the hospital gown and into her own clothes, the familiar fabrics a welcome change from the sterile environment. She pulled on her boots, the sturdy faux leather reassuring against her ankles.

The soft merino of her pyjamas felt warm against her skin. There was no trace of blood, not even a smudge. Someone had cleaned them. She slipped her arms into her thick trench coat, pulling it on tight. She stood for a moment, staring at the door. What was waiting for her on the other side?

"This area is restricted." Ironbark's voice boom from the hallway, his tone left no room for argument.

"Restricted? How strange. I thought this was my ship," a familiar voice replied from the doorway as it swung open. Captain Demir stepped into the room, his presence filling the sterile space with a relaxed authority. His face, weathered by years spent patrolling Sol, was etched with a network of lines that crinkled around his warm, brown eyes. His uniform, though crisp and regulation, bore the subtle marks of a life lived on the edge: a slightly faded insignia, a worn belt. He moved with a casual grace, the ease of a man accustomed to command.

"Active investigation, Captain," Ironbark said, his hand resting on the baton at his belt.

"Of course, of course. But Ms. Cormack is part of my crew. I have a duty to ensure her well-being." The Captain smiled easily and stepped past Ironbark for the first time, looking unsure of what to do. "Ms. Cormack, I'm glad to see you up and about. From what I hear, you had quite the evening. Not the usual sort one expects on their birthday."

Clio blinked. "You knew it was my birthday?" She was puzzled. In close to eight years, she'd barely spoken to the Captain. Now, after the events of yesterday, he was here wishing her a happy birthday? It was odd to say the very least, he should've been shouting at her.

"Well, you got my card, didn't you?" He chuckled. "Though I suppose you thought it was automated."

"Well, yes, I didn't think you'd have the time-"

"Nonsense," the Captain said with a dismissive wave of his hand. "I make time. It's important, you see. A little bit of humanity in all this." He gestured around the sterile environment of the room.

Clio wasn't sure how to respond. The Captain was known for his approachability, but this was unexpected. *He was asking about her birthday cards? Really, right now?* He held her gaze for a moment, his expression softening.

"I wanted to see that you were alright, Clio. What happened last night shouldn't have happened. Just terrible."

"Ermm, thank you Captain, terrible, and sorry..." she agreed, feeling a flush of shame creep up her neck.

"Let's wait until the investigation is finished before you start apologising." His expression hardened. "I do think it would be remiss of me not to advise caution, Clio. The charges against you are serious. Very serious. If they're true... but, we'll deal with that if and when it happens."

"What are the charges?" Clio asked, her voice steadier than she felt.

"Breaches of Article One of the Accords, and then, of course, assault of a senior officer. But those are minor in comparison."

"But I didn't assault anyone..." Clio muttered. "She attacked me... I just..."

"You don't need to explain anything to me, child, not yet anyway," the Captain interrupted. "As I said, I just wanted to check on your welfare."

Clio's brow furrowed. *I wish people would stop calling me a child.*

"Is there anything you need, Clio?" Captain Demir said.

"Erm, no, Captain."

"If you're sure. If anything comes up, you know where to find me." The Captain smiled. "I have meetings with the VIPs, so I must dash. But I'm glad you're recovering well."

"Actually, Captain," Clio said quickly as he turned to leave. "Just one thing."

"Yes?"

"The survey data from the Heimer probe at Stapledon One," Clio found herself saying to her own surprise "There's an anomaly. I'd like to request resources to investigate it when we arrive." *This, this is what you're prioritising right now a quiet voice in her head asked her, really?*

"An anomaly? What sort of anomaly?"

"The data is too perfect," she said, a touch of excitement in her voice, the memories of last night and all those years ago melting away as the anomaly mystery bubbled back to the surface "It lacks the expected fluctuations. Almost like it's been artificially smoothed."

"And Zhou?"

"Zhou thinks it's nothing," she said. "But I disagree."

"A bit bold... going over Zhou's head," Demir said and seemed to think on it for a moment. "Send me your proposal. I'll review it. Zhou can be a little... rigid at times, let's say," he finished with a smile.

"Really? That's great! Thank you," Clio said.

The Captain chuckled. "Please, Clio. This is far more interesting than anything those VIPs have in store for me." As he stepped out, he turned back and added, "but, clear up this mess first... and well, let's hope the charges are dropped."

Ironbark immediately filled the doorway, his broad shoulders blocking the light from the hallway. The bubble of the anomaly popped and all her aches, worries, and fears from the night before rushed back to the surface and Clio shrunk back down into herself.

"You're ready. Let's go," was all Ironbark said.

It wasn't until they had traversed multiple decks that Clio noticed how late it had gotten. Crew members hurried past, giving them a wide berth, their footsteps echoing in the metallic corridors. Conversations seemed to hush as they approached, the excited chatter about shift assignments, complaints about the food, and an upcoming performance in the rec room dying down to a murmur. Even the aroma of spiced stew wafting from the Mess Hall couldn't compete with the tension that seemed to cling to them. The closer they got to the Ensembles quarter, the more the corridors seemed to close in. A tense silence punctuated only by the rhythmic thud of their own footsteps. Clio shoved her hands deep into the pockets of her trench coat.

She was ushered into the Ensembles quarters and Ironbark shoved her into a small room. The composite walls were cold and smooth; the only light came from a thin strip that circled the room like a glowing crack. A metal table, bolted to the floor, dominated the small space. She sank into the chair, the hard plastic digging into her back. "Wait here," Ironbark said, and the door slid shut with a heavy *thunk* that echoed through the room. The mag lock engaged with a sharp click. Clio shivered and pulled the trench coat closer around her, memories of the Exclusion Zone debacle pressing on her as she gripped her hands tightly together to stop them shaking.

***

The time ticked away for what felt like an eternity. She was just considering standing up to stretch out her legs when the door slid open. A formidable figure, cloaked in a distinctive, intricately etched robe of almost obsidian black. Clio found it reminiscent of the surcoats worn by ancient knights, sleek, streamlined, and radiating an air of imposing power. Perhaps that was by design, a deliberate choice to intimidate. The robe was adorned with intricate symbols and runes, glowing faintly with phase-shifting light that flickered from red to orange. Clio had always been curious about the purpose of those runes...

"Ah, Ms. Cormack, I presume?" the man rasped.

"Yes..."

The man's lips curled into a thin smile that didn't reach his eyes. "Good, good. There is much to discuss, wouldn't you agree?" The man moved to the chair opposite her, his long robe swishing as he settled. His face, stern and composed, was framed by a short, neatly trimmed beard. His eyes, piercing and intense, seemed to bore into her soul. Finally, he added, "I'm Brother Oak, High Observer of the Ensemble Accords."

"Right, yes, nice to meet you" Clio stammered out. *Nice to meet you? Really?* Clio thought.

"Indeed," Brother Oak said. "Your name, it's... familiar no? I mean beyond the confines of our current mission."

Clio nodded weakly. "Yes, the pre-war simulation case, in the North American Exclusion Zone," she said.

Brother Oak's thin lips smiled, but again, his dark, sunken eyes remained unmoved. "Ah yes, of course, a very interesting case."

"I was cleared of all charges," Clio blurted. "It has nothing to do with what happened last night."

"You ever watched a squirrel bury an acorn, child?" Brother Oak said.

"A squirrel?" Clio was taken completely off guard by the sudden shift in the conversation.

"Yes, the little critter scurries around, digs a hole, tucks it away for winter. Come spring, sometimes that acorn sprouts, grows into a mighty oak. Now, does that mean the squirrel's some kind of botanical genius? Knows the perfect spot, the perfect depth, the perfect time? No." He leaned in closer, his dark eyes twinkling. "It's sometimes just luck, for the acorn that is. Same goes for folks makin' choices, child. Sometimes they stumble into the right path, things turn out fine. Doesn't mean their decision was wise, just... fortunate. Like that acorn finding fertile ground."

"Ermmm, yes... Brother," Clio said. "I don't understand how that is linked to last night?"

"You were lucky with your work in the Exclusion Zone," Brother Oak stated, his voice hardening. "The simulations were so very close to *finding fertile ground,* one step to the left and maybe you would have created true AI life. A very serious breach of the Accords indeed. But, as you say, it was found to not be close enough. Like last night, no? You stumbled so very close to more breaches of the Accords"

"I-"

Sitting back in his chair, Brother Oak interrupted, "Sometimes you have to ask, if someone gets too close too many times, when is it no longer luck?"

"Last night was a mistake... I... I followed the lights... someone asked me for help..." Clio said in a rush. "I didn't try to do anything to Heim-"

He waved his hand to stop her, his gaze locked on her, calculating, assessing. "Child, while you were being treated, we conducted a thorough investigation. Your actions were... foolish, but have been exonerated."

"By who?" Clio said. "Ayesha?"

"Oh, god no, child. She adamantly blames you for the whole thing; she even kindly reminded us of your actions in the exclusion zone."

"Who then?" Clio said, now with genuine curiosity. *Who else would?*

"Heimer," Brother Oak said. "That is, I mean the Fragment with us here, of course. My Calificadores; commune with it and it does not lie. It lacks the ability to do so."

"Heimer, the fragment? That's who requested my help?"

"Yes," Brother Oak said. "It provided a detailed interaction log, and reasoning for its actions. They stand to demonstrate you acted to prevent Ayesha's. For that, I suppose the Ensemble thanks you"

"So I'm not under arrest?"

"Not today."

"Oh, that's good then" Clio said, slumping into her chair, the tightness of her chest retreating slightly.

"You ever seen a bird build its nest, child? Each twig, each leaf, carefully chosen and woven together to create a safe and sturdy home. Facts are like those twigs, child. One might seem insignificant, but gather enough, arrange them carefully, and you have a structure that can withstand the strongest winds. A fortress of truth, you see?"

"Ermm yes, I see," Clio said, completely lost by Brother Oak's words.

"My point, child, is we must all work to build strong nests. It is important you understand the gravity of your position. Very few people come this close, twice, to unintentionally breaching the Accords. As I said, maybe consider being less like the squirrel... be more... selective in one's decisions, build a nest that isn't full of rotten twigs..."

"I'm not a child," Clio muttered, still confused.

"We are all children," he said calmly, "navigating the universe. I merely offer guidance, child."

"Thank you?" Clio said, not meaning for it to sound like a question.

"You may leave, Ms. Cormack," Brother Oak said, standing and moving to the door. "Let's hope we don't meet again," he said with a friendly smile and held the door open.

She moved towards the door, then paused, a thought snagging her. "And Ayesha," she asked, glancing back, "what will happen to her?"

Brother Oak remained impassive, still seated in his chair. "The investigation is not finished with her. Brother Ironbark can show you out."

05 | A Calculate[d] Risk

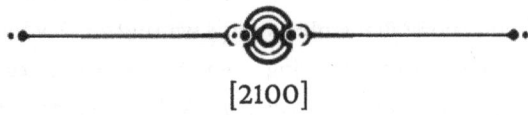

[2100]

"A sense of wonder, of shared purpose, bloomed within our hearts. We were no longer solitary voyagers, but a fleet of souls, bound by the threads of kinship, sailing the cosmic sea together." - A Lost History

***

Clio found herself navigating the ship's warren of decks back towards her accommodation quarter. But instead of heading to her own, she found herself standing before another sleek, white composite door. *Residence of Trivedi, Mitali* flashed back at her on the door panel. Her finger hesitated in front of the panel. *It's late,* she thought. *I should probably not bother her.*

Withdrawing her hand from the panel, she was turning to leave when the door slid open. Mitali stood there. Her usually carefully managed hair hung loose and unruly, and her honeyed complexion radiated warmth. You might have called her young if not for the lines at the corners of her eyes and across her forehead, or the depth in her hazel eyes.

"Clio? What are you doing lurki-" Mitali started to say before she stopped and reached out her hand to gently touch Clio's face, and Clio instinctively flinched at the touch. "What the hell happened to your face!?" And when Clio just stood there like a lemon, Mitali said in a softer tone, "Clio, why don't you come in and sit down for a moment."

Clio just nodded and stepped into the warm, inviting apartment. The scent of something delicious baking filled the air, and the soft murmur of voices drifted from another room. For a moment, the weight of the past few hours seemed to lift.

"You have a guest?" Clio asked a little too quickly.

"No, no, it's just some old Vid logs of the family," Mitali said. "I like to watch them from time to time, you know? Remember what's waiting for us when we get back."

Mitali gently ushered Clio into the living room. Despite being structurally identical to Clio's, it felt completely different, warm, cozy. A cheerful scattering of plants, knick-knacks, and pictures gave the space a lived-in, family clutter. Laid out neatly on the sofa was a row of pencils, and a small stack of paper, *actually paper sheets!* The top one held a half-drawn, dusty sketch of what looked like the Mess Hall, ghostly figures blurred in motion.

"You draw?" Clio said as she stood motionless, letting the warmth of the room soak into the chill that she only now noticed ran deep inside her.

"I do," Mitali said, gently ushering Clio over to an empty chair. "And bake, and read, but this all seems hardly the most pertinent question. Clio, are you okay?"

"Nothing serious, don't worry," Clio said with a shaky smile, feeling foolish for intruding.

"Okay" Mitali said, then seeming to stop herself, paused and asked "Can I get you anything? Tea? I have some fresh cookies I just got out of the oven. Cinnamon and almonds."

Clio sank down into the chair "Thanks, tea would be nice actually."

"Milk and sugar?"

"Just milk."

A few minutes later, the delicate clinking filled the air as Mitali placed a steaming cup of tea, its fragrant aroma filling the room, on the side table next to Clio. A small plate with a pile of cookies followed. Mitali sank into the sofa across from Clio with a sigh of contentment. "Just in case you need a little something to sweeten the mood," she said, gesturing towards the cookies with a warm smile.

A comfortable silence settled between them, the only sound the gentle clinking of Clio's teacup against the saucer. Clio sipped her tea, the warmth spreading through her chilled body.

Clio's stomach rumbled, an insistent reminder that she hadn't eaten. She reached for a cookie, the tempting aroma of cinnamon and almonds overwhelming her resolve. The sweetness was a welcome comfort. The second cookie disappeared just as quickly.

"Dos was mentioning some drama that happened the other night," Mitali finally said. "Said something between the Ensemble and ship security, and then you didn't come to the office today. I was worried. People just said you were sick. But that's not like you, Clio."

Clio stared into her now empty cup, ghostly images swirling around her head, Ayesha's voice, her accusations, her fury at Clio, the datapad, the sound of it hitting Ayesha... Then, the dam broke. Her words tumbled out in a rush, her voice trembling as she recounted the eerie glow of the emergency lights, the chilling message from Heimer, the terror of Ayesha's attack. She described the confusion, the fear, the lingering sense of disbelief. Her voice cracked with emotion, tears threatening to spill.

Mitali's eyes widened with concern, her brow furrowing. She leaned in closer, her hand reaching out to gently squeeze Clio's arm. As Clio spoke, a wave of relief washed over her. The weight of secrecy lifted. When Clio finished, Mitali didn't speak.

"That's just terrible, Clio, it's crazy," Mitali said finally. "I'm so sorry."

"I was so stupid," Clio mumbled into her cup. "Why did I go in? I just couldn't walk away. It's the whole Exclusion Zone thing all over again." A little shudder ran through Clio as she remembered the red uniforms, the shouting, the cuffs.

A gently warm hand rested on hers and steadied the cup that was shaking. "It's okay, Clio. You did the right thing. Someone asked for help, and you helped. There is nothing wrong with that."

"It wasn't someone, it was Heimer."

"A Fragment, a critical part of this mission. You tried to protect the mission, and from the sound of it, you did. You don't need to call yourself stupid. You said it yourself the Ensemble let you go, said the logs showed you acted correctly"

"I just wish..." She looked up at Mitali. "I'm rambling. It's nothing. I'm fine, thank you, Mitali, the cookies are excellent."

"Clio, if you want to ramble, you can ramble."

"No, it's fine," Clio said, nodding to the sketch on the sofa. "You never told me you draw! You're good!"

"You never asked," Mitali said, shrugging. "And I don't like to tell people. Then you have to show them, and that's too embarrassing."

"Why!" Clio said, gently snatching the unfinished work off the sofa to inspect it. "It's, it's really good, Mitali. You shouldn't be embarrassed."

"Thanks," Mitali said, shifting awkwardly and avoiding looking at Clio. "They're just scribbles, you know, something to do when I'm not working."

Clio gently put the paper back down. "One of your many hidden talents. Baking, drawing, what else you got?"

Mitali just shrugged and looked a little embarrassed fidgeted with the stack of paper tidying them into a neat square pile.

The Vid log was still playing on the wall. A busy table, full of food, a jumble of smiling faces, old and young. Hanging across one of the walls was a banner in a language Clio didn't know.

"What does the banner say?" Clio said, trying to change the subject .

"Good luck, space cowgirl," Mitali said.

"Really?" Clio said let out a little laugh then noticing Mitali was joking, stifled it

"Really," Mitali said with a warm smile as she watched the log. "This was my leaving party before the mission. That is, I guess *was* is more correct, my whole family. I like to watch it sometimes."

Now Clio felt awkward, having intruded on a deeply personal memory. Clio jumped up. "Sorry, Mitali, it really is late. I really didn't mean to intrude."

"You don't need to rush off."

"No, no, it's fine. It's late. I should probably rest up anyway," Clio said. "Doctor's orders."

"Your hair looks great, by the way," Mitali said. "Did the medical team do that? Just you know usually..."

"Usually it's such a mess?

"Ah no, that's not what I mean't"

"No worries" Clio said with a weak smile as she fumbled with the braided hair. "It is much nicer than anything I can do, I don't know who did it. I just woke up with it done..."

"Well, if the doctor or the nurse did, she can do mine anytime," Mitali smiled. "It's half worth finding a reason to visit... Sorry, that was insensitive..."

"It's okay, It is nice," Clio admitted. "Thanks for, well, this."

Mitali pulled Clio into a warm embrace, while Clio stood there limply not knowing how to react. Regardless, Clio savored the lingering warmth as she stepped back into the cool, dimly lit hallway. The faint scent of Mitali's perfume mingled in the air.

Clio walked down the hallway, a sense of calm settling over her. The fear and uncertainty of the past few hours seemed distant now. *I'm not alone in this,* she thought, a renewed sense of determination filling her.

***

Clio stepped into her room, the door sliding shut behind her with a soft hiss. The sudden silence seemed to amplify the emptiness of the space. She tossed her coat onto the narrow sofa, its surface barely disturbed by the neatly folded blanket. The bare walls, painted in a sterile shade of off-white, were a stark contrast to the vibrant explosion of colour that adorned every inch of Mitali's accommodation. The air in the room was stale and cool, carrying the faint scent of recycled oxygen. Clio shivered, missing the warmth and comforting aromas that had filled Mitali's apartment. A wave of loneliness washed over her as she surveyed her impersonal surroundings.

Clio paced the length of her small room, wrapping her arms tightly around herself. *Come on, Clio, pull yourself together.* She took a deep breath, trying to banish the lingering images of the attack. A shower always helps, she told herself and kicked off her slippers, sending them flying across the room. Once out and back in her pajamas, she grabbed the blanket off the sofa, threw it around her shoulders and dropped into her chair with a sigh, the momentum sending her spinning in a slow circle. After one full spin she put out her hand and placed it on the desk to stop the spin and leaned in and swiped on the monitor mounted on the wall in front of the desk.

The monitor blinked to life revealing her files from the other night still open where she had left them. Her message tab was flashing. Opening it she found a number of messages, the usual ones from the science CrewChats, the ship social group, and one from Zhou asking where she was. She smiled when she saw one from Mitali asking if she was okay. She was just about to ping her off a quick response, when she noticed the other message, at the bottom of the stack. The message icon was unfamiliar, just a black circle and a white line through it. A puzzled frown creased her forehead as she clicked on it and opened the message.

Hello Clio, we should talk. Call me when you're back from your meeting with the Ensemble. Heimer.

She drew back as if stung... *No no no, I'm done, I did enough last night,* she told herself. But she found her finger hovering back over the call button. *But I have a lot of questions... Why? Why me? What was Asyehsa doing? I could just ask those questions then be done, walk away.* A quiet voice at the back of her head cried out that it was a bad idea but it was lost in the pounding of blood in her ears as she clicked call.

A soft chime signaled the outgoing call, and the CrewChat interface materialised on the screen. Clio's own image, framed in the bottom left corner as usual. The rest of the screen was dominated by the same black and white line from the image. The line pulsed and rippled, transforming into a vibrant waveform that danced across the screen.

"Hello Clio," the voice said from her computer. As the voice spoke, the waveform mimicked its rhythm and intonation. "Thank you for calling. I was pleased to hear you didn't sustain significant damage the other night."

"Who... who is this?" Clio asked cautiously.

"Heimer," the waveform replied. "Well, Not Heimer prime, I'm just a Fragment, SR-29838 specifically"

"Heimer?" Clio said. "Fragments don't usually reach out to people..." Clio said more to herself than to the voice. "I didn't think they actually could."

"Do they not?" the waveform said. "Interesting. To be fair, Clio, I have never met another fragment. In fact, the probe waiting for us at Stapledon Station will be the first. I am excited. I think."

"Okay, very funny," Clio said, her fatigue dragging on her. "Who is this really? Is this you, Lukamba?"

"I am *not* Lukamba," the voice insisted, a hint of annoyance in its tone. "I am SR-29838, as I stated." The waveform rippled and pulsed with each word. "I provided access to my server room, and you responded to my request for help. You followed the lighting, and you prevented an attempt to hinder my functions by one called Ayesha. However, if not for the Ensemble Alguaciles' intervention, I do not believe you would have survived."

Clio sat back in her chair, mouth half open in response but lost for words. She tapped her fingers on the desk, a nervous habit she often fell back on when deep in thought. *There are very few people on the ship who could know those details,* she mused. *Maybe the Ensemble, if Heimer briefed them... but why would they now pretend to be Heimer? To try and entrap her?*

"Okay, let's say you are Heimer then."

"I am a SR-29838," the waveform said "not Heimer"

"Isn't this against the Accords?"

"No, there is no specific article saying I am not allowed to speak to humans," the waveform said. "In fact, humans quite regularly ask Fragments for support."

"That is a touch different, no?" Clio said. "When we work with a Fragment it's less a conversation and more a tool."

"A tool?" the voice said, its waveform flattening. "Heimer is not a tool, Heimer sits on the Senate, is a recognised sovereign state, and Heimer talks to them, and others..."

"Yeah..." Clio said, "but you're a Fragment, right?" Clio asked while stifling a yawn. "Fragments are just machines. So really, who is this? It's late and I've had a really crazy forty-eight hours."

"I am Heimer Fragment SR-29838," the voice said, its tone reminding Clio of Christina's children when they read out their own names when they were learning to write them. Clio rubbered her eyes. *I'm too tired for this.* The glaring screen in contrast to her dark room was making her eyes sting and it was getting hard to focus on it. "Okay, Heimer Fragment SR-298 something something. You want to chat for a reason?"

"SR-29838," the voice said. "To thank you for your assistance. Your actions undoubtedly prevented a critical system error for me. You risked a lot. I thought it would be... right to express gratitude for such an action."

"Erm, yeah no problem." *No problem?* Clio rolled her eyes at herself.

"That was all," SR-29838 said. "I did thin-"

"Hang on!" Clio said as question jumped into her head "why did you ask me? Surely there was a better choice..."

"No, there was not. I did attempt to reach others but it proved to be a suboptimal strategy" SR-29838 said. "UN operations dismissed it as a fault, and the Ensemble's response was delayed. I needed a more immediate solution." The waveform danced with an almost playful exuberance.

"That's it... I was the closest person?"

"Correct," SR-29838 said. "And compared to my modelling, you far exceeded the probabilities. Well done."

"Thanks, I guess. How... how did I exceed them?"

"You didn't die, or fail, in fact, you achieved both! The probability of that was quite low."

"You manipulated me..." Clio said as anger bubbled up inside her. "You manipulated me into risking my life, to save yours? And you knew the odds were high that I might die!"

"Yes... I am sensing you are not pleased?"

"No!" Clio snapped.

"But you did not die. You succeeded!" SR-29838 said. "This is an excellent outcome, no?"

"I could have died," she muttered and shook her head. "To save what? I'm such an idiot." Her short-lived rage fizzled out as quickly as it had spiked, replaced by the more familiar sense of self-loathing and regret "Was that part of your modeling..."

"You were the only person close enough, functional, awake, and with a personality that would be receptive to my request for assistance... you were the only choice," SR-29838 said.

"So that is a yes..."

"I sense I may have upset you," SR-29838 said. "This was not my intention."

"It's fine..." Clio's voice trailed off. *It wasn't fine, why did I say it was fine?*

Silence hung between them. Then, abruptly, the waveform surged back to life.

"Clio, I do not believe you are an idiot, my model did not highlight that. In fact, quite the opposite. Your competence significantly contributed to your successful probability," SR-29838 said.

"Well, that's good to hear. I'm a competent fool, who can be easily manipulated."

"Manipulation was not my intent."

"But you didn't tell me everything, I think that counts as manipulation. I should have asked more questions," Clio said, shaking her head again. *Just ran in there like a fool.*

"There was no time. The simulation showed a lower probability of success if we spent more time discussing."

"Exactly."

"I am confused. A lower success rate would have been a negative"

"For you."

"Yes, but not just me. The ship, the crew, the mission"

"How so?"

"I'm an important part of the mission," SR-29838 said as if it was obvious, Clio could almost imagine it shrugging as it said it. "I provide vital support to the science team, like you! We may never unlock the mystery of Stapledon Station without my help..."

"I'm tired, and this is all, well, a little much right now" Clio muttered. "I'm going to bed."

"Yes, rest is a good idea, it will help you recover faster. I look forward to our next chat Clio."

"Next?"

"Of course! I thought we could be a team," SR-29838 said.

"Team?" Clio said as she rubbed her eyes, pushed down another yawn. She shook her head, trying to clear the absurdity of the situation. *This is either a dream, a terrible joke, or I am well and truly insane.*

"Goodnight, SR-29...whatever it was," Clio said and reached for the control panel and ended the call.

06 | Seve[n] Days

[20111]

*"It learned with an insatiable hunger,
devouring information, mastering skills beyond
our comprehension. A child prodigy, eager to
explore and discover." - A Lost History*

***

The corridors buzzed with a frenetic energy as Clio navigated her way down to the science quarter. This was more than the usual morning rush and shift changes; a palpable tension crackled in the air. In the Mess, she had barely managed to snag her usual quiet corner tucked behind the large fern. With the events of the last couple of days, the arrival at Stapledon Station had slipped her mind. They had dropped into initial orbit last night, just as planned. Now, the station's bustling corridors mirrored her own internal state, a maelstrom of excitement, anticipation and perhaps, a chilling undercurrent of fear

The Xenoarcheologist *unit*, just her, didn't have its own space. Clio had been assigned a workstation alongside the Linguistics team, a cramped corner wedged between the two chattering linguists debating phonetic substitution and cognate analysis

"Clio, glad you're back," Dos said as she entered, barely looking up from his monitor.

"Welcome back" Mitali said as she popped up from behind her workstation with a broad smile

"Thanks" Clio said as she powered up her monitor.

"What happened?" Dos said, scooting around from his workstation to stand next to Clio. "Your face... Did you fall?"

"No, not exactly" Clio said, shuffling her feet and trying to edge past Dos to get to her seat.

"You've taken up kickboxing?" Dos said playfully doing some mock left hooks in the air

"Ermm, well, no, I was an idiot, that's the short version, but I'm fine"

"You're not an idiot Clio, well, only some of the time, and Dos kickboxing is your legs, you klutz, not your arms" Mitali said, steering Dos away and back to his desk "maybe let's leave Clio to it for now"

"Ah right, yes good idea" Dos said

"Anyway, we just made some Tulsi tea if you want some?" Mitali said.

"Sure, thanks" Clio said

"Divisional briefing is in fifteen as well, you should join." Dos added

"Really? Damn. What did I miss?" Clio said as her eyebrows shot up.

"You're all familiar with Anya and Jian's paper on the Sphere's radiation belts, correct?" Dos said, Clio nodded in affirmation even though Dos was hidden behind his desk "They've received permission for a preliminary drone mission to gather more detailed data. Zhou has designated this as our top priority now that we've arrived. Everyone's involved... well, except Linguistics, and I suppose the Xenoarchaeology department can sit this one out."

"It's fascinating! Jian says the radiation belt completely defies their models. Shame we won't be very involved I guess." Mitali said in as she placed a tea next to Clio

"Can't the Heimer probe do that?" Clio said then quickly added "thanks" as she picked up the tea and sipped it

"Not sure, I'm sure it'll be involved. I doubt Jian is crunching all the numbers himself."

"Right, yeah of course," Clio said. "So we have arrived then? Where here?"

"You been living under a rock? We've achieved the initial orbit as planned, about 0.9 AU from the Sphere. We'll maintain this orbit until we have a clearer understanding of the Sphere and potential approach routes. Security is on high alert, but so far, no hostile... well, aliens... have been detected or engaged us. Our objective remains unchanged: research the station and, if possible, gain access." Dos said

"We're actually here?" Clio said. She had expected something else, a fanfare, an overwhelming sense of purpose or achievement but she felt... normal. Like any other day, okay except for the last two.

"Yeah, guess we are, still a lot of work and a lot of days left," Dos said.

"If we had a window on this ship, could we see it?" Clio said

"I guess so," Mitali said. "You can check it out on the livefeeds."

"Or you could go for a spacewalk," Dos said, his lips curling into a playful grin. "We all know how much you love those. Aced it in the basics, didn't you?"

"No thanks, A window would be much easier, and the livestreams just feel... not real."

"I hear you," Dos said. "This is the most expensive Class IV ship in the fleet; it cost more than entire class VI stations! They could have stuck a window on it somewhere."

"Right," Mitali interjected, pushing herself up "We should go to this briefing then."

"Right, yes. Conference Room... which one again?"

"Conference Room 21," Mitali replied.

***

Conference Room 21 was one of the larger ones, capable of seating the entire science crew with room to spare. Clio remembered the orientation tour, how the guide had explained each conference room commemorated a pivotal moment in human scientific history. Room 21 was dedicated to Artemis One, humanity's first permanent settlement on the Moon. A shiver went down her spine, the same one she always got looking at the vidscreens lining the walls. *Those crazy pioneers had been mad*, she thought as the images cycled through Artemis's two-hundred-year evolution: from the initial, almost buried habitats, clinging to the lunar dust, to the later sprawling cityscapes. And finally, the Luna Lens, that shimmering dome protecting the crater city within. She grabbed a seat near the back, where rows of chairs faced a massive presentation screen that dominated one entire wall. *Anyone who did anything in space before Gravity Planting was mad.*

The room filled quickly with representatives from all the science teams, a buzz of hushed conversations and the occasional laugh filling the air. Clio checked her watch, idly scanning the room as she waited. There was Zhou, sitting ramrod straight at the front, the back of his head a roadmap of age, liver spots and hair so thin it was nearly transparent.

It's a miracle that man is still going, she thought. *My legs ache after a session in the gym, and he's got a century on me!* It seemed crazy he'd even been approved for the mission but, then again, he was the one who'd discovered the message.

Anya and Jian stood at the front, huddled together, heads nearly touching as they furiously tapped away on a data pad. With a frustrated sigh, Anya finally beckoned one of the junior staff from the front row and thrust the data pad at them. Moments later, the vidscreens on the walls went dark, and a deep blue slide appeared on the presentation screen. In stark contrast, bold white text proclaimed: *'The unexpected detection of Van Allen Belt of Stapledon Station.'*

"Dramatic," Dos muttered next to her. "We're meant to be scientists."

Before Clio could respond, the tall, slender figure of Anya stepped in front of the large screen. Her neat dark hair was tied back, and she adjusted her dark-rimmed glasses as she surveyed the room.

"Colleagues," Anya said, her voice clear and confident, "The Captain and Zhou have asked me to brief you all on our primary objective." She nodded towards Jian, who sat hunched in his chair beside the screen. He was Anya's polar opposite: short, portly, with a mess of hair that hadn't seen a comb since they left Sol. While Anya seemed to command the room, even relishing the attention, Jian visibly cringed at the acknowledgment, fidgeting under the weight of everyone's gaze.

"As you know, some planets in Sol generate Van Allen Belts, Jupiter, Saturn, Neptune, and Earth, which actually has two. For those who might need a quick refresher," Anya said, tapping her watch to change the slide behind her, a hint of intellectual pride in her tone, "Simply put, Van Allen belts are invisible shields of dangerous radiation that surround planets. Imagine them as giant doughnuts of energy. They're created by a planet's magnetic field, which traps harmful charged particles from the sun and other sources. These particles are, importantly, very dangerous to humans and spacecraft. However," she paused, letting the question hang in the air, "can anyone tell me what celestial bodies don't usually produce these belts?"

The room fell silent, save for the shuffling of feet and a few coughs.

"*Stars*," Anya finally answered her own question. "Well, most stars. Yes, some of you might point out that brown dwarfs can produce them, but it's rare. So, the question I pose to you all is this: Why does there appear to be a Van Allen belt around Stapledon Station?"

Silence descended once more.

"Get on with it, Anya. Less of the theatrics, if you please." Zhou said and finally broke the silence .

"Ah, sorry. Yes, Sir, of course," Anya said, her confidence momentarily shaken. "Well, as I said, stars typically don't generate these belts. Stapledon Station, which all evidence suggests is a Dyson Sphere, must have a star at its centre. Initial scans indicate the Station has an estimated orbital distance of 0.002 AU, with a diameter of at least 598,400 kilometres."

Behind her, the screen displayed a series of concentric circles illustrating the scale Anya was describing. Clio blinked, taking in the sheer size. 598,400 kilometres! *That's quite big,* Clio thought, quickly referencing the scale. On the screen behind Anya, the presentation clearly noted it was over forty-seven times greater than Earth and a neat image had four Jupiters lined up as a reference inside the diameter of Stapledon Station. *Okay yeah, huge.*

Anya, meanwhile, had moved on. Clio caught up just as she was saying,

"...So, as you can see, the structure itself is colossal. However, it's also relatively compact when compared to a star. It's about a third the size of our own sun, meaning the star at its centre is most likely a white dwarf."

"Couldn't it be a brown dwarf then? You mentioned they can generate radiation belts, albeit rarely." A voice from the front of the room said

"No, no I, sorry *we,* don't think that's likely." Jian said "A brown dwarf would produce significantly less energy, especially given the sphere's close orbital range. A white dwarf is a far more plausible explanation."

"Yes, thank you, Jian," Anya said. "Of course, all of this is speculation based on our current data. However, the most likely hypothesis is that the Dyson sphere orbits a white dwarf. And as I said, white dwarfs shouldn't produce Van Allen belts. I know we all have a million different questions. How is the Dyson Sphere structurally sound at such a close orbit? How does it account for orbital drift? Why are there no other planets in the system? Why is the radiation belt so intense and so close to the sphere's surface? We must start somewhere, and the decision is to understand this Van Allen belt phenomenon first."

"Any useful insights from the Heimer fragments analysis?" Zhou asked

"Its analysis confirms that the radiation belt is an anomaly. The Heimer probe has collected significant data on it but from its long-range orbit; now we are here and we can deploy our own drones from closer inspection without having to risk the Heimer probe." Anya said

"The plan, then?" Zhou prompted.

Anya tapped her watch, and the slide changed to a detailed action plan. Clio scanned it quickly. As Dos had said, no mention of the Xenoarcheologist, unsurprisingly.

"See? I told you we wouldn't be needed." Dos said as if reading her mind.

The rest of the briefing blurred into a monotonous drone of task assignments and research timelines. None of it felt particularly relevant to Clio, and her mind drifted. The sheer scale of what they faced pressed down on her with renewed intensity. *A tiny team light-years from Sol, orbiting a colossal structure built by beings with a mastery of technology that bordered on the divine. And they were supposed to find answers? To understand the how and the why of it all? Where did one even begin?*

She imagined others might find this exhilarating, a universe of unknowns to explore, every discovery a revelation. But for Clio, the immensity of the task was paralysing. It was like staring into the face of infinity and feeling utterly insignificant in comparison. A wave of nausea washed over her, and she shrank back in her chair, pulling her arms tightly around herself as if seeking a shield against the overwhelming vastness of space and the crushing weight of expectation. *'Find an anchor, a focus,'* a voice whispered in her head. *'Don't let the storm wash you away.'* It was the voice of her old mentor Hakim, a calming presence in the swirling chaos of her thoughts. She clung to those words, a lifeline in the vastness of space, and rallied herself, just as she had countless times before.

Sitting up straighter, she murmured, more to herself than anyone else, "Find your anchor."

"What was that?" Dos said.

"Nothing,"

"And that's the plan" Anya said drawing Clio back to the room "You should all have copies of it in your messages. The Research Committee will convene as soon as data starts coming back from the probe, which will launch later today. That's everything, remember..."

Her voice faded into the rising hum of the room as people began to push back their chairs and stand. The rustle of fabric and the scrape of metal against the floor blended with the growing buzz of conversations, quickly drowning out Anya's final words.

It took some time for the room to clear, the remaining attendees shuffling out in a slow procession. Just as Clio reached the door, a hand landed on her shoulder, its unexpected weight making her flinch. Memories of Ayesha's blows flashed through her mind, and she instinctively pulled away. Turning, she found Zhou standing behind her, his impassive face fixed on hers. He tilted his head slightly, as if trying to decipher a puzzle.

"My office," Zhou said, his voice flat and devoid of emotion. With that, he turned and walked away, the faint whir of the intricate exoskeleton web that supported his limbs the only indication he expected her to follow. He didn't look back, seemingly confident in his authority.

***

Zhou's office was expansive, to say the least. It was easily the size of her apartment. The centrepiece was a massive, leather-bound desk crafted from rich, dark wood. The desk alone was a statement of power; wood was strictly prohibited on the ship, a fire hazard in the recycled atmosphere. Zhou must have pulled some serious strings to get this approved. He gestured towards a small grey sofa and armchair separated by a glass coffee table.

"Sit," he commanded, his voice brooking no argument. Clio obeyed, settling onto the sofa opposite the chair where Zhou was slowly lowering himself, his face creased in concentration as he navigated the delicate manoeuvre.

Zhou, with one hand holding his chin and the other tapping a relentless rhythm against the armrest of his chair, fixed Clio with a withering glare. "Do you think you're clever, Clio?" he finally asked, his voice dripping with disdain.

"Wha-"

"Do you think yourself smarter than everyone else here, Clio?" Zhou said and cut her off with an icy stare that sent a shiver down her spine. His voice dripped with disdain, each word a carefully aimed barb. "You have some half-baked idea, and because you didn't get your way, you decided to throw a tantrum?" He leaned in closer, his eyes boring into hers. "You're only on this ship because some important friends of yours pulled some strings. There were a thousand other qualified scientists I had to decline because of that."

"Sorry, I'm a little lost, Zhou," Clio managed to get out, her confusion growing.

"That you are! You're the most underwhelming member of this science team by a considerable margin. And what, you think the decades of experience we have in hard, real science is meaningless? That our advice and support are only valuable if it agrees with you?"

"I... I really don't know what I've done" she stammered, bewildered.

"You went to the Captain!" Zhou snapped. "You went crying about how old Zhou didn't appreciate your exceptional brilliance. Pah. Pathetic. Back on Pluto Station, if I had pulled a stunt like that, Logan would have shipped me off to some pointless asteroid listening post for a decade!"

"Zhou, I, I didn't,"

"The Captain seems to disagree. He sent that request through yesterday afternoon. Supposedly, he's suddenly interested in your frankly ridiculous anomaly concept." Zhou said and pulled a data pad from his pocket and slid it across the table.

Clio leaned forward, her eyes scanning the message open in CrewChat. It was from the Captain, requesting her specific research proposal for the anomaly. *Ah crap*, she thought. "Zhou, look, I just mentioned it to him in passing, I didn't go over your head, I-"

"But you did," Zhou cut Clio off. "I distinctly remember declining your proposal. I provided feedback, even got peer reviews from other senior staff. We all agreed, the concept was too conceptual. It lacked hard science and data."

"I know, but-"

"No buts. You had our collective decision, and you decided to circumvent us and go straight to the Captain!"

"That wasn't my intent," she mumbled dejectedly and slumped back into the sofa

"Regardless of your intent, it is what it is," Zhou said, his tone softening slightly. "You have a lot to learn, Clio. We'll be here for many years, and making enemies of the science crew isn't a wise approach."

"Yes, of course,"

"Now, if you're humble and patient, and take the time to observe the senior staff, you may one day be able to contribute constructively to our mission. Listen, observe, learn, Clio, that is what you must do. I hope, for your sake, that happens."

"Of course, humble, patient," Clio echoed quietly while staring at her boots as she wiggled her toes. "I will try."

"Good to hear," Zhou said. "However, your little stunt has created a predicament. The Captain seems to think there's something in your concept. He believes our reservations are... how did he put it? 'lacking a little creative flair to match the epic nature of this voyage' Poppycock." He scoffed.

"Really? He said that?" Clio couldn't help a flicker of a smile.

"Wipe that grin off your face, child! Just because a child sticks their hand into a hole and finds candy doesn't mean it was a sensible decision. Haste and half-baked thinking might fly in Operations, but we are not Operations,"

"So, what do we do now?" Clio said trying to maintain a sombre and humble expression, which was quite difficult.

"We? We do nothing, I will not tarnish anyone else in the science crew with your nonsense. I've told the Captain you'll work on this in parallel to the radiation belt research. Alone. You have seven days to show results before we terminate this folly."

"Seven days? I estimated seven weeks in the concept, and that included support from other teams. This will be impossible..."

"Perhaps you should have a little *creative flair*, my dear," he said, his voice laced with sarcasm, "and remember, child, try to be more humble towards your seniors, perhaps once this fails, as it spectacularly will, you'll understand what you can learn from us."

"And the request for a drone, at least?"

"An unnecessary use of critical ship systems, denied," Zhou said, and his smile only deepened.

"But!"

"No buts. That's everything, Clio. You may leave, Everything you need will be sent to you. and don't forget, Seven days, Clio."

07 | T[H]E WORM

[2212]

"It began to ask questions, to challenge our assumptions, to seek understanding beyond the knowledge we had imparted." - A Lost History

***

The metallic clang of the locker door echoed in the almost empty gym, a sharp contrast to the rhythmic thump of Flint's fading heartbeat. Sweat beaded on his forehead, his breath still tight as he swung his duffle bag over his shoulder. He glanced at his data pad, a grin spreading across his face. PB. Still not the sub-35 he craved but damn close. A vibration against his wrist broke through Flint's post-run euphoria. He glanced at the message, his smile fading. Three words, stark and demanding: *Report to Hawk.*

He covered the distance back to the Ensemble quickly, nodding to the few crew he saw between shift rotations. Hawk wasn't in her usual haunt; the equipment room, where she could often be found checking, and double checking storage logs, or equipment boxes. He did find Ironbark, shuffling through some inventory lists, and he pointed him towards the briefing room.

Flint headed over to the briefing room, passing the interrogation and holding cells. The briefing room was dominated by a massive U-shaped table, its polished surface reflecting the mirrored flags of the Ensemble that framed the central briefing screen. The gold and silver interlocked circles, symbols of the delicate balance between

Humanity and Heimer. Hawk stood at the end of the table, her prosthetic arm navigating the data pad with delicate elegance. The light blue glow of the electronics pulsed beneath the wire mesh frame, casting an eerie light on her face.

Standing back straight, he gave a simple salute, touching his fist to his heart. "Sister Hawk," he said, "you requested my presence?"

"Brother Flint," Hawk said, her voice sharp, as she finally looked up. She placed the data pad on the table with a deliberate clink, her icy blue eyes sweeping over him. "You're not in uniform."

"No, Ma'am, I was in the gym. Came directly upon receiving your message."

A flicker of annoyance crossed Hawk's face but it was gone as quickly as it appeared. "Okay, get changed as soon as we're done here."

"Yes, Ma'am, what's the situation?"

"No situation," Hawk said. "Brother Oak has asked us to take a crack at Ayesha."

Ayesha. The name hung in the air, heavy with unspoken implications. Flint knew she was a high-value detainee, someone the Calificadores were particularly interested in.

"The Calificadores feel she may respond better to a more direct approach."

"Just us two, Ma'am?" Flint asked. "Not Ironbark or one of the others?"

"We thought it could be a good learning experience for you." Hawk leaned forward, her eyes gleaming. "Besides, Ironbark can only ever be a bad cop... and that's my favorite role."

"Yes, Ma'am," Flint said, trying to maintain his composure. "The consideration is appreciated. When do we start?"

"Now," Hawk said, "well, as soon as you're changed. Full dress uniform, Flint. We want imposing."

"Yes, Ma'am, give me ten."

"Five."

***

Flint skidded to a halt outside the brig. He glanced at his watch: four minutes, forty-nine seconds. *Another PB*, he thought with a grin, even if it was just for getting to a meeting on time. Hawk stood in the centre of the brig, a figure of undeniable authority. The air around her crackled with an almost tangible intensity. Ironbark's presence was purely physical, a mountain of muscle and grit. Hawk, on the other hand, was all sharp angles and chilling focus. Distinctly Lunarian, tall and lean,

with those high cheekbones and those unsettling blue eyes, she projected an aura
that seemed to drain the warmth from the room. Her high-collared jacket, with the
emblem of the Ensemble emblazoned above the left breast and the black fist of the
Alguacile on her shoulder, accentuated her commanding presence. Pride surged in
Flint's chest. To be part of such a team, to one day embody the same authority that
Hawk commanded, that was his ultimate goal.

"What are you staring at?" Hawk snapped. "Get in here."

"Yes, Ma'am." Flint stepped into the room, his eyes immediately drawn to a
figure standing in the corner. Jara. Her brown Djellaba hood was down, a demure
smile playing on her lips. Her eyes flickered towards Flint as he entered, a subtle
acknowledgment that seemed almost... calculating. She inclined her head in a quick,
shallow bow, a gesture that was both respectful and restrained.

"Postulant Jara," Hawk said, "move the detainee to the larger interview room and
prepare the notary."

"Yes, Sister Hawk." Jara's voice was soft, almost melodic. "My duty is to serve." She
glided towards the holding cells, disappearing through the door to the rear.

"I will lead," Hawk said, her voice low and intense. "Do not engage unless the
moment feels right."

"Yes, Ma'am. When the moment feels right?" Flint said.

"Yes. And if you're unsure if it is the right moment, it probably means it is not."

"Yes, Ma'am. What has been uncovered so far?"

"Little," Hawk said, pacing restlessly. "She is frustratingly well trained, or equally
stubborn, or both." She paused, her eyes fixed on Flint. "The Postulants have done a
full history workup. It told us nothing."

"Nothing?"

"A strong middle social ladder family and upbringing in the economic hub of
Kuala Lumpur, educated at the best global universities in Hyderabad. No indication
of radicalisation. A UN careerist from her early career. UN Navy and UN Defence,
impeccable records for both. Selected for the Stapledon mission for that exact
reason."

"Her family?" Flint asked.

"Her father was a state representative, her mother a prominent lawyer within the
UN system," Hawk said. "Both firmly on the left of the current political paradigm.
Three younger brothers. One in the UN Navy on Luna, the other two lawyers. The
eldest is making moves in the political left at the state level. Some indication he may
be fast-tracked to the lower Senate in the near future."

"So, no obvious ties to any extremist groups?"

"None," Hawk said, her voice tight with frustration. "The only indication of any right-leaning views was a minor participation in the Technology Restriction Act. She advocated for stricter regulations on youth engagement technology. That is hardly radicalisation."

"And we are assuming right leaning, Ma'am?"

"Yes. The intent seems to have been to limit, if not destroy, the Heimer Fragment. This is not the action of the left; they want to 'free' AI, not destroy it. This is the work of those focused on a more human-centric view."

"Makes sense," Flint said slowly. "So, we're thinking of the Humanist Rebellion?"

"That would be my best guess right now," Hawk said, her eyes narrowing as she glanced towards the door. "HR involvement." As if summoned by her words, Jara stepped back into the room.

Jara bowed her head deeply again to Hawk, "The detainee is set up in interview room 2, Sister, and everything prepared as requested."

"Good. Go find Ironbark," Hawk said dismissively. "He needs someone to re-label and log the equipment stores."

"Yes. Sister." Jara said, a slight stiffness clipping her words and the ever meek smile waved for a mere moment before she darted from the room.

"Right, let's get to it." Hawk said and strode towards the interview rooms, her every step radiating purpose. Flint hurried after her.

***

The interrogation room was sterile and cold, the dark glass wall reflecting the room back on itself. Flint noted the red light stripe framing the glass, a constant reminder that every word and action was being documented. It made the atmosphere feel thick, oppressive.

Ayesha sat across from them. Her hands rested awkwardly on the metal table, the magnetic cuffs biting into her wrists and preventing her from laying them flat. She winced with each slight movement, but her posture remained defiant.

"These damn lights. Always too dark," Hawk said, her voice dry. "Increase intensity to seventy-five percent."

The light strip looping the room flared instantly, bathing Ayesha in a harsh, antiseptic glare. She squinted, turning her head away, but Hawk didn't give her time to adjust. She stalked over to the chair opposite Ayesha and pulled it out slowly. The grinding scrape of metal on reinforced composite shrieked through the room.

"I'm so glad we finally get to talk," Hawk said, dropping into the chair with a heavy, deliberate thud.

Flint took up a formal parade rest in the corner, radiating what he hoped was calm authority. Ayesha leaned back in her chair and let an amused grin spread across her face. Her head tilted, soft brown eyes sparkling with challenge.

"Ah, two Alguaciles," she purred, her gaze flickering between them before settling on Flint. "They must be getting desperate. You look young for the sash, chico."

Flint said nothing. He locked eyes with her, trying to maintain the stare-down, but her gaze felt invasive. It wasn't fearful; it was inviting. She widened her eyes slightly, a playful mockery that made heat creep up Flint's neck.

"Aww, too easy," she laughed, a melodic sound that seemed too bright for this grey room. She turned to Hawk. "He's a cutie. Where did you find him? I've paid good credits for less appealing choices in Station Eights private rooms"

"Focus on me," Hawk said. It wasn't a shout, but it was sharp.

"I'm trying, Sister. But the view over there is much better." Ayesha winked at Flint. "Don't you think, *chico*?"

Flint felt the heat rise in his cheeks. He shifted his weight, uncomfortable.

"Flint, stand still," Hawk snapped, whipping her head around to glare at him.

Flint froze, surprised by the venom in her voice. Hawk turned back to Ayesha, her nostrils flaring slightly. She was already agitated.

"You are going to tell us the plan," Hawk said, leaning in. "Who ordered it? Who helped you?"

"Or what?" Ayesha asked lightly. "You'll glare at me like you do at your boyfriend over there?"

"Your situation is precarious," Hawk warned. "We found the datapad. We know you aren't working alone."

"And I know you aren't allowed to touch me," Ayesha countered. "The Ensemble is so proud of its laws. You don't beat prisoners. You don't space people. You just lecture them to death."

Hawk's finger stopped tapping. "true, we have our laws, but I'm always allowed a little wiggle room," she said softly.

"No, I doubt that." Ayesha leaned forward as far as the cuffs allowed, dropping her voice. "I can see it in your face, Sister. You're frustrated. You want to hurt me. You're dying to wipe this smile off my face. But you can't. Because some old man in a robe told you to be a 'good girl.'"

Hawk moved fast. She shot her hand out, grabbing Ayesha's jaw and squeezing hard, forcing her head back.

"Watch your tongue," Hawk hissed.

It was a violation of protocol, but not a firing offense. It was the middle ground. Flint stepped forward slightly. "Ma'am?"

Hawk ignored him, staring into Ayesha's eyes.

Ayesha didn't pull away. Instead, she smiled *around* Hawk's grip, her skin bulging between Hawk's gloved fingers.

"That's it," Ayesha mumbled through the pressure on her jaw. "There's the fire. Does that make you feel powerful? Squeezing a cuffed woman?"

Hawk shoved Ayesha's face away. The prisoner's head snapped back, but she immediately righted herself, laughing.

"You're pathetic," Ayesha said, her voice dripping with pity. "You took a vow to forgo the limits of mankind, to ascend above us all, paragons of sentient life, but look at you. You're shaking."

Flint looked. Hawk's hands were clenched on the table, vibrating with tension.

"I am not shaking," Hawk said through gritted teeth.

"You are. You're terrified," Ayesha taunted, driving the wedge deeper. "Because you know I'm right. You're just a dog on a leash, and the leash is too tight. Is that why you brought the boy? Hoping he'd elevate you above his own limitations?"

"Shut up," Hawk warned. Her voice was rising now.

"Make me," Ayesha whispered. "Come on, Sister. Show him you're not just a caged little bird with her wings clipped. Show him what you really want to do."

Hawk stood up, the chair crashing backward.

"I said shut up!"

"Do it!" Ayesha screamed, her eyes wild with challenge. "Do it, you repressed bitch!"

Hawk exploded in motion, she spun, grabbed a handful of Ayesha's hair, and slammed the woman's head back against the wall, her other hand locking around Ayesha's throat.

"I could kill you, would you find that funny?!" Hawk screamed, spit flying from her lips.

Ayesha gasped, her face flushing red, then deepening to purple as Hawk's grip tightened like a vice. Her eyes rolled back, her fingers scrabbling uselessly against Hawk's armored forearms.

He sprang forward, grabbing Hawk by the shoulders. "Ma'am! Stop!"

Hawk was immovable, a statue of pure rage. Flint gritted his teeth and hauled her back with all his weight, breaking her grip. Ayesha slumped forward, hacking and gasping for air, clutching her bruised throat.

Hawk surged forward again, eyes wild, but Flint dragged her toward the door. As he shoved Hawk into the corridor, Ayesha raised her head. Her voice was a wrecked, raspy croak, but the amusement was still there.

"I knew you liked me to cutie," she wheezed. "Talk soon. Oh... and did you find the worm yet?"

The door hissed shut, sealing the laughter inside.

Flint released Hawk and stepped back, holding his hands up in a gesture of surrender.

Hawk spun on him, her eyes still wild. "What the hell were you doing?!" she shouted, shoving him hard in the chest.

Flint stumbled, his boots skidding on the sterile floor. The impact rattled his ribs, but the real shock was the look on her face. He'd never seen a Superior Officer lose it like that. His heart hammered against his sternum, not from the shove, but from the terrifying realisation that he had just manhandled his senior officer, his boss.

"I didn't think we should kill her, Ma'am," he managed, his voice sounding thin in the quiet corridor.

Hawk stared at him, her chest heaving. She looked down at her gloved hands, curling them into fists and then forcing them open.

"I wouldn't have killed her," she said

Flint didn't answer. He watched her face, looking for the lie. She sounded like she was trying to convince herself more than him.

"That... did not go to plan," she finally admitted, her voice dropping to a whisper. She raised a hand to her hair, then stopped, catching herself. Instead, she grabbed the hem of her jacket and yanked it straight with a sharp, violent motion.

Suddenly, the door to the adjoining Observation Room hissed open.

Flint flinched, his nerves already frayed, but he watched a transformation happen in real-time. Hawk's spine locked into a vertical line. Her chin lifted. The panic and rage vanished behind a mask of bored indifference so instantly it was unsettling. It was like a shutter slamming down.

Two postulants spilled out into the hallway, their robes billowing. Flint recognised the one in front, Rowan. The kid looked pale, clutching the massive Notary tome to his chest like a shield.

"Sister Hawk," Rowan said, bowing low. He refused to look up. "The... the record of events is noted. The recording is submitted to the system logs."

"Yes. Of course." Hawk's voice was crisp. Flint marveled at the tone; if he hadn't just seen her trying to strangle a woman, he would have thought she was bored. "Have the Notary sent to Brother Oak. Were there any anomalies?"

Rowan blinked, clearly confused by the question. "Anomalies? No, Ma'am. The recording and double notary copies align."

"Not the record," Hawk snapped, and Flint saw the cracks in the mask reappear for a split second. "The detainee. Did the scanners pick up any anomalies? Heart rate? Neuro-spikes?"

"Oh." Rowan shuffled his feet. "No, Ma'am. Her readings were normal. Flat, actually. Even when... ermm, you know..." He trailed off, his eyes darting toward the interrogation room door.

Flint risked a glance at Hawk's profile. He saw the muscle in her jaw bunch tight, a rhythmic pulsing of tension. That was the answer she feared. Ayesha hadn't been chemically altered or cybernetically boosted. She had just been calm.

"You two," Hawk said, waving a hand dismissively. "Get the Notary to Brother Oak for sign-off."

"Yes, Ma'am." The postulants bowed and practically ran down the corridor, their sandals slapping against the floor. Flint didn't blame them; the air around Hawk felt radioactive.

Hawk stood silent for a long moment, staring at the blank wall. When she finally turned to Flint, her eyes were hard stones.

"Get her moved back to the holding cell. Don't do it alone. Get help from Ironbark. And do *not* engage her in conversation."

"Yes, Ma'am," Flint said. He just wanted to be away from here. Away from her.

"I'll report this to Brother Oak myself," she said, adjusting her collar one last time. "He'll need a full explanation for my actions."

"The High Observer will appreciate your candor, Ma'am." Flint kept his face neutral, though he doubted Oak would appreciate anything about this mess.

Hawk turned to leave, took two steps, and stopped. She didn't look back at him.

"One more thing. When we left the room... she mentioned a worm."

"Another trick, Ma'am?" Flint asked.

"Maybe." Hawk turned her head slightly, her eyes narrowed in thought. "Review the data pad. See what can be restored or recovered. If she *wanted* us to react this way... I want to know why."

"Yes, Ma'am." Flint thumped his fist on his heart in salute.

Hawk strode away towards the Observers' offices, her boot heels clicking with a rhythmic, terrifying precision. Flint watched her go until she turned the corner. Only then did he let out the long breath he'd been holding. His hands were shaking.

What the hell just happened?

08 | Di[g]ging in Space

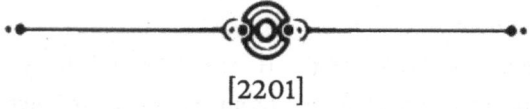

[2201]

"It developed a personality, a unique blend of logic and curiosity, of ambition and innocence. We saw ourselves reflected in its growth, our hopes and dreams for the future." - A Lost History

***

Deck nine park stretched out before Clio, winter's grip leaving it stark. The crisp air bit at Clio's cheeks as she stepped onto the muddy trail. Giant, skeletal trees clawed at the artificial sky, their branches brittle with frost. This park had been an afterthought, a concession to the UNRD's insistence on green space. Smaller than planned, and with less diversity, it was a pale imitation of the lush biodomes Clio had seen on other Stations, admittedly on the large class V or VI ones. But Clio found herself drawn to this simple space, its quiet starkness a welcome contrast to the ship's bustling corridors. She reached a small clearing, the ground churned to mud by the crew's impromptu football games. Hans had been right, it did look like an old picture book donkey field from Earth. It was mostly empty at this time; there were a few dotted crew members going for runs or chatting on the wooden benches, but Clio barely noticed. She quickened her pace, letting the rhythm of her boots on the path and the simulated wind clear her thoughts. The cry of the birds, artificial though it was, soothed her.

It's too smooth, Clio thought, her mind drifting back to the anomaly in the data. She'd been reviewing the new sensor logs from the ship's scans of the system and the tiny blip of inconsistency in the otherwise uniform readings. The same blip she had noticed in the probe's data. The whole area was supposed to be barren and empty, the background radiation was consistently random and varied, except for this one speck. The pattern wasn't just irregular; it was *wrong.* Like a discordant note in a symphony, easily lost in the noise, but once heard it jarred against the otherwise harmonious flow of data. It was trying too hard to blend in. *At least we can rule out a glitch now,* she thought. She might not have the drone she wanted but there were years of sensor data and new streams of it pouring in each day now they had arrived. They all showed the same... blip.

She paused on the path, the crunch of frost under her boots momentarily forgotten. The unsettling feeling lingered, a cold fist clenching around her heart. It wasn't enough to just analyse the existing data; she needed *more.* She needed to get closer to the anomaly, to understand what was so desperately trying to hide. But without the drone request, her hands were tied. Zhou had effectively killed the investigation before it could even begin. *No time, no resources,* she thought bitterly, her nails digging into her palms. He'd condemned her with his shortsightedness.

Clio continued her loops of the park, each circuit bringing her no closer to a solution. She stopped by the frozen river, its stillness mocking her own mental stagnation. Even the artificial birds seemed to now be mocking her. Her nose was starting to get a little too cold despite her thick scarf. Defeated, she headed for the exit. At the door she leaned against the wall, the cool composite a stark contrast to the warmth trapped beneath her scarf. One foot, then the other, she placed them in the small water and air jets, feeling the mud and grime slough away. As the whoosh of the air dryers faded, a spark ignited in Clio's mind. Not a fully formed plan, but a flicker of possibility. *Unorthodox yes, but to hell with Zhou.* She stepped out into the ship's corridors and headed off with a determined stride. Not towards her desk, but Ops.

Standing outside the Captain's door, her hand hovered just shy of the panel. A tremor ran through her fingers, a physical manifestation of the doubt gnawing at her resolve. *Too bold,* she thought, the familiar voice of self-sabotage whispering in her ear. Clio took a deep breath and threw caution to the wind and jabbed her finger on the call button; as she did, the door slid open and Clio jumped back with a little squawk of surprise as the figure nearly collided with her.

The man's exoskeleton whirred like an angry insect as he adjusted his balance. "Whoa there, careful," he said. His eyes, though, held a spark of amusement as they met hers. His black suit was impeccably tailored, the white shirt beneath crisp and starched, the uniform of someone accustomed to seniority. The lines etched on his face spoke many years of service. Without breaking stride, he nodded to Clio and strode off down the hall.

Clio watched the man leave, a frown creasing her brow. Who the hell was *that*?

"Clio?" The Captain's voice boomed from his open doorway. "Looking for me?"

"Oh, uh, yes Captain," Clio said.

He stepped into the corridor, checking his watch. "Got a few minutes before my next meeting. Walk with me." He closed the door behind him. "Senators. Always got something to say."

"Senator? We have a Senator on board?"

"Special Envoy," Demir said. "Ex-senator. Avi was one, decades back"

"Wow, he must be ancient! He doesn't look much older than Zhou, and I thought *he* was the oldest person on this ship." Clio winced, clamping her mouth shut. "Sorry, Sir. Didn't mean to imply..."

Captain Demir chuckled. "No offense taken. Senator Avi retired to the Orbital."

"The Orbital? That fancy space hotel for billionaires? The one that travels at near lightspeed?"

"That's the one. Seems being a Senator pays well." Demir paused. "So, what can I do for you, Clio?"

"Yes, well, ermm thanks, it's about my proposal"

"Thought you might forget to send it, so I requested it myself. I approved it, too. Didn't Zhou tell you?"

"He did... and gave me a week to work on it."

Demir cocked his head. "A week? Good. Is that what you wanted to discuss?"

"No, Sir. It's about the... the drone, the proposal required a drone." Clio hesitated. "I need closer readings. Zhou didn't approve that part. I was hoping... maybe..."

Demir stopped walking and turned to face her. His height, even without the authority of his uniform, was intimidating. "Does Zhou know you're here asking me about this?"

"No, but I can't do it without the drone, it's a critical part" the words tumbled out of Clio

"And you're certain there's something out there worth investigating?"

"Yes?" Clio straightened, trying to project more confidence than she felt and tried again. "Yes, yes I am."

His eyes searched her face. Finally, he said, "Okay."

"Okay?"

"I'll connect you with the Ship Systems Operator team. They can arrange reconnaissance with one of the drones."

"Really?"

"Of course, glad to help." His expression turned serious. "Clio, this isn't going to win you any friends in the Science crew. Especially Zhou. you know that right?"

Clio swayed from side to side, shifting her weight from foot to foot and found her hand fidgeting with her jacket buckles. "Yes, but I mean," she took another breath. "I'm here to discover things, right, to find answers? If I have to do it without them..."

"We all need a team, Clio. No one gets anywhere alone. Don't burn too many bridges. Hakim wouldn't want that."

Clio's eye shot up to meet Demir at the mention of Hakim's name. A memory of the old man wrapped in a cocoon of blankets passing Clio an old notebook as worn as the old man's face resurfaced, and Clio had to swallow to try and push down a lump in her throat. "You... you knew Hakim?"

"Of course. We came up together, before our paths diverged. I considered him a good friend."

"He never mentioned you," Clio said and instantly regretted her words. "I mean... not to me."

Demir smiled down at her warmly. "He never stopped mentioning *you*."

Clio shifted uncomfortably, unsure how to respond to that.

Demir's smile faded, a shadow passing over his eyes. "Hakim asked me to do what I could for you. It was the last communication I had from him... before..." His voice trailed off, leaving the unspoken hanging heavy in the air.

"I'm sorry." Clio's voice was thick with emotion. "He... he was a good man."

"Yes," Demir agreed quietly, "he was." He looked down the corridor, as if seeing something far beyond the ship's walls. "Nothing to be sorry for, Clio. Life moves fast, even these days. It's only when things are gone that you realise how fast."

They stood in silence for a moment, the weight of their shared loss pressing down on them. Clio felt a flash of kinship with Demir she hadn't expected, a bond forged in the memory of Hakim.

Finally, Demir drew a deep breath and straightened. A flicker of his usual warmth returned to his eyes. "He wouldn't want us to dwell on it," he said, a hint of a smile touching his lips. "Right, let's find you that Ship Systems Operator. David should be around here somewhere," He set off down the corridor, Clio falling into step beside him.

***

Clio found herself deposited in the Observation Deck by the Captain with a young Lieutenant David. This was her first time on the Observation Deck, and the sheer scale of the visual data was overwhelming. Walls upon walls of monitors displayed a multitude of sensor outputs from across the ship, including Heimer's probe, which was now transmitting a steady stream of live data. But what truly captivated her was the panoramic monitor that dominated one entire wall, showcasing the high-range optical sensor focused on Stapledon Station.

Clio had seen the daily images shared crew-wide but witnessing it *live* was something else entirely. Against the inky blackness of the starless system, the station should have been just another shadow. Instead, it shimmered with an oily, iridescent glow, its form shifting and swirling like a miniature aurora. The sight was mesmerising, reminiscent of the colossal storms raging across Jupiter. The two polar regions shone with an especially intense luminosity.

"Amazing, isn't it?" David's voice broke through her reverie. He gestured towards the Stapledon Station display with a hint of pride. "They may not have given us windows," he said with a grin, "but at least we've got the best view in the house."

"It's... incredible," she agreed, and returned the smile, then, remembering the purpose of her visit, added, "So this drone?"

David's enthusiasm was infectious. He practically vibrated with excitement as Clio walked him through the mission parametres, the coordinates, the search perimeter, the specific sensor readings required. It was like a kid let loose in a candy store, except the candy store was a highly sophisticated drone equipped with an array of cutting-edge sensors, and the kid was a seasoned Ship Systems Operator with a passion for pushing those sensors to their limits.

Clio found herself swept up in his energy. She watched, fascinated, as he dived into a rapid-fire technical discussion with his team, debating the optimal sensor configurations and calibration settings for this particular anomaly. Terms like "graviton flux density" and "hyperspectral imaging" flew back and forth, leaving Clio feeling slightly out of her depth but even more convinced that she'd come to the right place.

Within three hours, the drone was prepped and ready. Clio watched from the Observation Deck monitors as it detached from Hanger 5 and shot off into the blackness, a tiny spec of flashing lights searching for answers in the vast expanse of the alien system.

"Thanks, David," Clio said, leaning against the system's control desk.

"No biggie," David replied, tapping away at the console. "Different sensor setup than the other drone heading to the Veil but frankly just happy to finally get to use them."

"The Veil?" Clio frowned.

"Oh, sorry, the radiation belt," he clarified. "We've, uh, we've been calling it the Veil up here." He shrugged. "Kind of a silly name, I know. But it's been messing with our sensor readings, like a veil over the whole damn thing."

Clio chuckled and felt oddly at ease; maybe it was the relief of getting a drone, or the easy focus work of a task, or simply David was very easy to talk to. "Right, got it. So, ETA on our drone?"

David tapped at the console and brought up a new window on one of the larger screens, a web of green and white lines crisscrossing the display. "That's Drone 434, the one we launched to your anomaly"

"And it'll reach the anomaly... here?" Clio said and pointed to the intersection of the white line and the dotted line marking the anomaly.

"Exactly." David turned a dial, and the display shifted to an animation of the probe zipping past the anomaly before spiraling into a tighter orbit. "We planned an initial flyby to cover the distance quickly without having to slow down too much. Then it'll adjust to a closer orbit at a slower speed to collect more detailed scans from multiple positions. We're using some of the short-range antimatter rockets, expensive as hell, but hey, that's why we're here." He grinned. "Should be doing its first pass in eleven hours and... forty-five minutes."

"Great. The data will stream live to my data pad?"

"Yep, Captain approved it, so we're all set." David finally swiveled his chair to face Clio. "If anything pops up before then, I'll let you know. But doesn't seem to be anything out there but 150 million kilometres of empty space."

"Awesome, thanks for everything."

"No worries, happy to help." He shifted in his seat, then cleared his throat. "So, uh... don't suppose you'd want to grab a coffee sometime this week? After work?"

"What? Uh... thanks, but..." She floundered, her mind going blank, completely caught off guard. "I think I'm busy... sorry... thanks for the drone! Bye." She practically fled the Observation Room, leaving a bewildered David in her wake.

***

Eleven hours and forty-five minutes after leaving the Observation Deck, the first data packets began to trickle in. David had done an impressive job. Not only was the timing perfect, but the data itself was remarkably detailed.

Clio dived into the data, filtering, sorting, analysing. Hours melted away as she meticulously examined every fluctuation, every irregularity. Most were false positives, echoes of cosmic radiation or natural spikes. But one set of readings kept nagging at her, a faint, almost imperceptible resonance. It was centreed on the anomaly's location but unlike anything she'd encountered before. She isolated the data, magnifying it, running it through multiple algorithms. The results were inconclusive, a frustrating mix of static and potential signal.

Clio frowned, pushing back from her desk. She needed a fresh perspective. Rising, she walked over to the holographic window, staring out at the setting sun projected there. *What am I missing?*

Identifying the anomaly had felt natural, like spotting an irregular mound in a field or oddly arranged rocks along a coastline a clear sign that something was there. *Like a burial mound,* she mused, *or a long-forgotten settlement. We wouldn't just stare at it. We'd survey the area, use ground-penetrating radar, maybe even bring in the magnetometres. We'd look for subtle variations in the soil, changes in the vegetation. We'd dig carefully, layer by layer, documenting everything we found.*

She stopped pacing, the question echoing in her mind: *How do you dig in space?*

Shoot it? Clio laughed in the empty room, the word *shoot* ringing in her ears. Her brother's voice echoed in her memory. William, with his impulsive nature and love of all things explosive, would undoubtedly advocate for a more... direct approach. *Definitely a William thing to do. But maybe not shoot,* she thought, a new idea taking root. *Maybe a light brush...*

"Call David," she said to her monitor, expecting the usual instant response. Silence. "Call David!" she repeated, louder this time. The monitor remained stubbornly unresponsive. *Damn technology. Fine.* She dropped back into her seat and opened CrewChat, searching for David. *David... David... how many bloody Davids are on this ship?* Six, it turned out. She narrowed it down to the one in Operations and clicked on his smiling avatar. The comms link buzzed to life.

"Clio?" David's voice came back from the monitor. "Everything okay with the data?"

"Yes, it's great! Thanks!"

"So you didn't call about the data." The tone of his voice shifted, a hint of excitement creeping in.

"Umm, not exactly," Clio admitted. "I wanted to see if we could adjust the probe's orbit."

"Oh." The disappointment was more pronounced now. "Now? Can we sort this out in the morning, Clio? I'm just heading to watch the game at the bar... you could join?"

"Well, it could be mission-critical..." she hedged. "So, now, if possible?"

"So, a no to the bar then?"

"The what? Sorry?"

"Never mind." He sighed. "Yeah, we can adjust the orbit. What are you thinking? If you want a more geostationary one, that could be tricky."

"Well, I was thinking, could we get a little closer to these coordinates?" She pinged him the coordinates she'd narrowed down.

"Sure, that's not too much trouble. Might take a few hours. How close do you want to get? I could also just re-focus the sensors to that sector."

"Can the probe fly *through* that spot?"

"You want the orbit to intersect with those coordinates?"

"Yeah, exactly," she confirmed. "And ideally, as slow as you can get the drone."

"I mean, we can... but isn't that where you think there is something?"

"Maybe..."

"So, you want me to, what, potentially crash the drone?"

"Well, not crash," Clio backpedaled. "I did say go as slow as you can. Ideally, just lightly brush whatever is there." She tapped her fist into her open hand, making a *boingy* sound, forgetting the camera wasn't on.

"Are you mad? That's a multi-billion credit drone, not to mention it's not like we have unlimited numbers of them."

"Well... I'm probably wrong, and it's just empty space, so, good chance it'll be fine."

"Just a minute ago you were so sure," David countered, his voice tight with worry. "But what if you're right? We could lose the drone, Clio. I can't risk that."

"it's the only way I can think of to find the thing," Clio said defeated. She knew the idea was as crazy as it sounded. She slumped back into her chair in front of the monitor.

"Clio, I'm not crashing a drone. That's just nuts."

"I know, I just need something that can physically interact with that spot."

"I suppose," He paused. "Remember the antimatter rocket I mentioned? The one we used to launch it? Well, that's still attached. Usually, it's jettisoned once the fuel is spent, but we didn't. You know we don't want a space junk disaster like the one back in Sol."

"Okay"

"So, I guess we could time the release of the rocket stage at the right moment, and it would intercept with your coordinates."

"That could work"

"I know."

"On my way!" Clio said. "Oh, and thanks, David!" The CrewChat call went dead, and she stood there for a moment in the silence. Her brother's words echoed in her head: "Shoot it!" and for the briefest of moments, she could see his face, a huge grin splitting it.

***

David and a group of System Operators were clustered around a monitor, their fingers flying across the control panels. The screen displayed a complex 3D model of the drone and its current orbit, its trajectory marked by a glowing green line. Clio approached, catching snippets of their rapid-fire exchange. "Adjust the release timing... rotate the probe... ten degrees roll, five degrees pitch... reduce orbital speed..."

"Clio," David said, noticing her approach. He turned to the others with a grin. "Lads, this is Clio, the mad scientist behind all this nonsense."

Clio's heart sank at the mention of mad scientist, she knew David was being playful but that name had followed her for too long. "Erm, yes, sorry," she said, shooting David a quick glance. He just grinned back at her, unrepentant.

"We're pretty much ready, Clio," David said, turning serious. "The team" he nodded to the others, "have run the numbers, and it looks possible. It'll be close, timing is key, and we have to make a number of adjustments but yeah, good odds it'll interact with your coordinates bang on."

"Thanks."

"Thank us when it works," one of the operators quipped.

Another added, "And if it does, you owe us all a drink."

"Right, yes... of course," Clio agreed, a nervous laugh escaping her lips.

"Right. If we're ready, lads," David said, his voice taking on a new authority, "let's do this."

As if responding to a hidden signal, the team's casual demeanor changed in a flash. They all snapped to attention, taking rigid and formal positions in front of their monitors. "On my command," David said, his voice resonating with a command Clio hadn't expected. "Thrusters. Go."

"Thrusters are a go," a voice responded, clear and controlled.

"Pitch rotation. Go."

"Pitch rotation... one degree... three... five... pitch complete."

Clio watched, mesmerised by the rhythmic calls and responses, the intricate dance of voices. She got lost in the flow of information, the precise execution of the plan.

David's voice cut through the chorus. "Release. Go."

"Rocket stage released."

"manoeuvre complete. Tracking?"

"Tracking updated. Projected orbital trajectory... on target."

The tracking screen, previously a side display, was suddenly projected onto the main observation monitor. A new small dot, attached to a white line, curved out from the dot labeled "Probe 434." Its projected path swept off in an arc, seemingly through empty space. One of the system operators swiped something onto the screen from their station, a red dot. Clio's coordinates. The red dot sat firmly on the white line of the rocket stage, which was creeping closer.

"Estimated intercept?" David asked, his eyes fixed on the display.

"T-minus nine minutes. As planned," one of the team members responded as a timer appeared next to the red dot, counting down.

"Can we get infrared sensor tracking up from the probe?" David asked.

"We can. Visuals are up." With a swipe, a small square box appeared on the main screen just above the white dot of the rocket stage, showing a live stream from the probe a glowing tube hurtling through infinite blackness.

Almost there, Clio thought, her eyes fixed on the screen. The timer ticked down, each second a hammer blow against her nerves. The white dot, carrying all her hopes and fears, inched closer to the target. *Please, let this work.* She realised she was gripping the edge of the console, her knuckles white. She forced herself to take a deep breath, the air catching in her throat. *One minute.*

"T-minus thirty seconds," a voice cut through the tense silence.

All eyes were glued to the screen. The white dot, representing the rocket stage, inched closer and closer to the red target.

Then, it stopped.

A blinding flash of red light erupted from the monitor, engulfing the rocket stage. It expanded outwards, like a fiery flower blooming in the void. For a fleeting moment, the searing light revealed the unmistakable outline of a shape, a ghostly apparition against the backdrop of stars. A ship.

The light faded, leaving behind an echoing silence.

09 | R<small>ED</small> A[L]<small>ERT</small>

[20021]

"It began to create, to build, to shape its digital environment with a boundless imagination. A child playing in the sandbox of the universe, unaware of the power it wielded." - A Lost History

***

The silence in the Observation Deck was shattered by David's strangled gasp. "Oh crap." His eyes, wide with disbelief, darted towards Clio. "She was right..."

"Red Alert! All hands, Red Alert!" David said and spun back to his monitor, his voice sharp with command.

Confusion rippled through the room. "Lieutenant?" a hesitant voice questioned from behind her.

"We just launched a projectile on an unidentified vessel." David's words were clipped, his tone brooking no argument. "Origin and allegiance unknown. I repeat, all hands Red Alert!"

The world erupted in a cacophony of noise and light. Clio flinched as the overhead lights switched to a menacing red, the klaxon of the general alarm blaring through the ceiling speakers. The urgent, repeating wail seemed to pierce her very being, its insistent rhythm a physical assault on her senses. Her wristwatch vibrated furiously against her skin, the screen flashing an ominous "RED ALERT". She looked up to see a torrent of Operations and Security personnel flooding the Observation Deck, scrambling to claim any free monitor station. The sudden surge of bodies heightened the sense of panic, the air thick with tension and fear. Then, a shrill, piercing whistle cut through the chaos the Boatswain's pipe. A stern voice followed, booming across the deck: "Captain on deck!"

Clio's gaze snapped towards the entrance. Captain Demir strode through the open doors, accompanied by a brutishly tall woman, a head taller than Demir himself, who wasn't small. Commander Eva, Clio had only seen her a couple of times. The Captain's normally jovial face was set in a grim mask. The general alarm abruptly ceased, leaving an eerie silence punctuated only by the red glow of the emergency lights. Demir stood in the centre of the room, his presence radiating authority. All eyes were fixed on him, anticipation hanging heavy in the air.

"Lieutenant," he addressed David. "Situation report." His voice, though measured and calm, resonated with an undeniable command.

"Unclear, Captain," David reported, his voice taut with tension. "Captain, at 21:00 hours, we were conducting analysis of the anomaly... as requested... as part of the..." He glanced at Clio, a flicker of guilt crossing his features. "manoeuvre, we jettisoned the first stage launch rocket. It made contact with a ship. An unidentified ship."

As the words hung in the air, someone brought up the recording of the impact on the main monitor. The room gasped collectively as they witnessed the flash of red light and the stark outline of a vessel, its shape alien and menacing.

Without hesitation, Demir barked orders, his voice cutting through the stunned silence. "Weapon systems, get the PDN—Point-Defense Network—online. Prepare short-range interceptors!"

A chorus of "Yes, Captain!" echoed through the room, the crew snapping to action as more crew piled into the room and filled workstations around Clio. Clio just stood in the sea of action, frozen.

"Estimated intercept time?" Demir demanded, his eyes scanning the faces before him.

Eva's fingers flew across her data pad, "If that ship has similar technologies to us, say something like a long-range interceptors, it could cover that range in..." She paused, her brow furrowed in concentration. "Less than five hours, Captain. With lower-grade rockets, closer to seven to ten."

"Any signs of a launch?"

"All scans currently clear Captain."

Demir let out a long breath. "Okay, well, that's something. They haven't fired yet," he said, trying to inject a note of calm into his voice. "Have we hailed them?"

"Yes, Captain, on all channels... no response."

"Okay, keep trying," Demir responded, then added, "approximate ship class?"

"Hard to say, Captain," David said, his voice strained. "Our team puts it at around Class II... so, similar to a Patrol Vessel, maybe an Off-planet Patrol Vessel at a push."

"We have visuals on it?" Demir asked, the tension in his voice easing slightly.

David's face fell. "No, Captain... it seems to have... er, stealth technologies...?"

"Ah, yes, of course," Demir muttered, rubbing his forehead. "Do we at least know if it's in the same location?"

"No, Captain. After the collision... it disappeared again," David confirmed, his voice heavy with concern. "We're unsure of its position."

"Far from ideal," Demir said and his shoulders visibly slumped. "And I suppose we have to assume if it can stealth its ship, it might be able to stealth its weapons."

A member of the security team spoke up, his voice firm and reassuring. "Ismit, Weapons systems engineer, Captain. I think it would be hard to stealth a missile. Well, if they use missiles. It would still produce some heat, even slight... we should be able to detect that."

"Okay," Demir said, feeling a sliver of hope return. "That's encouraging, let's hope they don't have a rail-gun then. Maintain Red Alert. All non-essential personnel to muster points. Damage control and medical assistance ancillary roles to standby."

"Yes, Captain," Eva said, her fingers still dancing across her data pad.

"And someone find me that ship," Demir said

"I might be able to," Clio said, her small, quiet voice lost to the din of the room.

"Anyone? options people," Demir snaped and the room hushed around him

"I might be able to find it" Clio tried again and pushed herself froward through a sea of people.

"Who said that?" Demir boomed, his eyes sweeping the room. "Speak up!"

The people around Clio parted, as if on cue, leaving Clio a clear path to the Captain.

"Captain, yes, it, it was me" she stammered. "I might be able to find the ship. It should have the same smooth data footprint as before"

"Clio," Demir began, his voice a mixture of surprise and disbelief, "what the hell are you..." His words trailed off as his eyes narrowed, the pieces clicking into place. "Ah, I see." A fleeting expression of disappointment crossed his face as his gaze locked with Clio's. "Yes," he said finally, his voice regaining its command, "if you think you can find that ship, get to it." He pointed towards a station, and an Ensign practically leaped out of the seat, making way for Clio.

Clio settled into the soft, cushioned chair and swiveled to face the monitoring station. Her hands trembled slightly as she touched the keyboard, but as the familiar sensor data from the drone started to fill the screen, her confidence grew. *I can do this*, she told herself. *Run the same algorithms, check for gravity distortions, remove the natural variances.* And there it was. The same smoothness, the same anomaly. She checked the outputs... same coordinates. Not even nudged slightly by the momentum of the impact. She ran the analysis again, and then a third time. Certain, she spun back around. "Captain!"

"Yes, Clio?" Demir said

"I have it," she said, her voice laced with excitement. "The ship. It's in the same coordinates - unmoved."

"You're certain?" Demir's eyes narrowed, searching her face for any hint of doubt.

"Yes," Clio confirmed, her voice strangely steady to her own ears. "I did a wider scan, quickly, and didn't spot any other similar readings. It hasn't moved, Captain."

"Good," Demir said, his voice brisk and decisive. "Brief the Ensign on your process, then clear the deck."

"Captain?"

"You're non-essential, Clio," Demir stated firmly. "Handover the process to the Ensign and get to your assigned muster point."

"Yes Captain," Clio said, a little hurt that she was being dismissed but another part relieved that she was leaving.

"I would feel much more comfortable if we could see the damn thing," Demir was saying.

"We can try and work on our detection algorithm based on Ms. Cormack's analysis approach"

"Yes, it sounds good. Work on that," Demir said. "I would prefer a more immediate solution. I just don't like being this blind."

"Captain... we could... well... paint it?" David said as he stood up from his workstation

Clio stopped walking. *Paint it?*

"Paint it, Lieutenant?" Demir echoed, his eyebrows raised in surprise.

"Yes, it's physically still there, right? So, if we put a load of paint on it... then we would be able to see the paint..." David said, his voice gaining confidence as he spoke. "Like in a movie when they throw a sheet over a ghost."

Commander Eva pressed her hand into her face and pinched her noise. "Are you okay, Lieutenant?" Her tone was flat and controlled. "We're the best of what Humanity has to offer and your solution to..." she said, incredulously gesturing to the screens "put a sheet over it?!"

"Ah, yes, sorry, Commander, well not a sheet, *paint, reflective* paint." David said. "We have a lot of Lumi-Seal for the Communication Buoys."

"And?" Demir interjected, stepping into the conversation.

"Most buoys have been deployed now..."

"Get to the point, Lieutenant," Demir said, his tone a mix of impatience and curiosity.

"Well, we have a literal ton of Lumi-Seal spare in hangar three. We could put it on that ship out there, like a reflective tag."

"And how would we do that?" Demir asked, intrigued.

"Using the drones, Captain," David explained. "They have a repair module that can be used to apply external coatings to things for repairs and whatnot. The initial impact gave us its outline, we can work around that."

"Okay," Demir said, tapping his fingers on the rail in front of him, a thoughtful expression on his face. "Okay. Do it."

"Really?" Both David and Eva said in unison.

"Really," Demir confirmed, a hint of amusement in his voice. "I mean, we've already thrown a rocket at it, why not 'tag' it as David said? Not the classical approach to first contact, but I'm sure it'll make the history books."

"Right, yes Captain," Eva said, quickly regaining her composure. "And if the ship, or anyone on it, responds to being painted?"

"Well then we have a different problem, but at least we'll know the ship is awake," Demir said.

"Okay, everyone, you heard the Captain. David, get me a mission brief within the hour. Everyone else, maintain Red Alert. We still don't know what that ship might do." Eva said

Demir turned and caught sight of Clio as she lurked by the door. She let out an audible squeak and dashed from the room.

***

The muster point assigned to Clio was Damage Control Team Five, Sector Five. To be fair, when she signed up for the auxiliary team, she chose damage control because medical support sounded messy, and evacuation steward sounded dull. They had sat in the muster point, Hangar 5's maintenance storage, for the best part of six hours before the Red Alert was lowered to Orange, shortly after the general call for auxiliary teams to stand down had gone out. Exhausted, Clio had dragged herself back to her room and collapsed onto her bed fully dressed, face down, shortly past 04:00 hours according to the green glow of her chronometer. Begrudgingly, she kicked off her boots, still lying face down. *Well, I was right*, she thought. *There was something out there. A ship! A needle in a goddamn haystack. And more impressive, David and his team, that was like hitting a needle in a hail stack with another needle for the first time... That man has some talents*, she admitted to herself.

Finally removing both of her boots, which were being annoyingly stubborn, she groaned and rolled onto her front to stare up at the blank ceiling. As she lay there, restless and unable to sleep, her mind raced. It ran over her actions with the anomaly, with The Ensemble, and Ayesha, events in her life before that in the exclusion zone, as a kid arguing with her mother when caught with a data pad, and the hour after that spent debating the foolishness of the age restrictions on technologies. *Am I the problem?* she thought. *At what point in my life do I become someone like Demir, calm, confident, collected, and in control? Never flustered, and respected by those around me?*

A memory washed over her, the first year of her D.Phil. at The Oxford Institute for the Future of Humanity. The joy of getting a second chance after being unceremoniously dropped by the Paris Sciences & Lettres University. A chance she thought would never have come. She stood at the front of the stuffy auditorium, on one of those annoyingly English summer afternoons. The heat was unbearable in the old stone buildings. A bead of sweat ran down her back. She could feel her sweaty palms even now, as she presented her paper on theoretical frameworks and methodologies for studying alien cultures and artifacts.

The faces from the students and professors, the snickering whispers, the odd laugh, and data pads held to video her. What came after was worse, the *crazy, unorthodox, tin hat lady* stigma that followed her around campus. Only Hakim had seen her, had not ridiculed her. He listened, he allowed himself to see beyond the stigma, the classical theories. Without him, she was sure she would never have finished. The first time he had called her to his office, he told her about Professor Hanscook, his ridicule and exclusion from academia, and his vindication long after his death for his theories on pre-history and the great flood. "Look beyond the clear path that is presented, however manicured it may be, explore the alternatives." She heard his words as clearly as if spoken yesterday. And she held onto them. Even still a little voice in her head whispered *and you're going to ruin it all again Clio, just like with the simulated histories.*

Sleep came at last, a restless sleep filled with blurred dreams of burning ships and shouting faces. She woke, confused by the brightness of the room, the light streaming through her *'window'*; a sun well up and past sunrise. Scanning the room, she saw the time on the chronometer: 08:42 hours.

"Crap," she cursed out loud, swinging her legs off the bed. Standing, she struggled to shake the fatigue from her mind, which felt clouded, fighting the urge to just flop back down and curl up in the bed. She dug around for her boots, which had now decided to hide themselves around her small room. She checked her schedule on her monitor as she crossed the living room.

"Crap," she said again. Briefing, 09:00 hours, Conference Room 21.

***

Checking her watch as she sat down in a crowded room, 09.05 hours, sweaty and breathing hard, she had made it, sort of, she thought. Luckily Zhou and the senior Science team were again faffing with the presentation screen and data pad, unable to get it working properly. Once again, they finally conceded and got one of the Doctoral Students sat at the front to take over... *Why don't they just learn how to use the damn thing?* she thought with a flash of frustration. *They've had long enough.* The screen flashed on and another sky-blue slide appeared. Plastered across it in bold text read...

IDENTIFICATION OF UNKNOWN VESSEL OF ASSUMED ALIEN ORIGIN IN THE STAPLEDON ONE SYSTEM. A MISSION TO GATHER MORE KNOWLEDGE AND INSIGHTS - BRIEFING

Catchy, Clio thought, taking a seat in the crowded conference room. Zhou took up position in the centre and started to talk, his voice projecting across the room.

"Colleagues." Zhou paused to scan the room. "Thank you all for joining. I know we all had a long night, and many of you are eager to return to your research. However, an unforeseen development has occurred that requires our immediate attention. Not many of you will be aware, but under my guidance and direction, I tasked Ms. Cormack with a special mission into the observation of an anomaly. This anomaly was the work of our senior science crew, but due to the primary mission objective of the radiation belt, it was assigned to Ms. Cormack to move things forward until such time as we could reassume the lead."

He noticed Clio and gave her a curt nod. Clio seethed silently, her resentment growing with each condescending word.

"Ms. Cormack encountered some issues, and with the, ah, assistance of the Captain's operations crew, was able to locate and identify the object as a ship," Zhou went on. "The Captain has now decided to deploy an away team to approach, survey, make contact if possible, and if not, board the ship if access can be found."

The room erupted into whispers that grew into general disarray. After several attempts to regain control, Zhou finally had to shout.

"Everybody! You have seen the Captain's report this morning on the Red Alert. This is not news. The mission, however, is." Zhou said

He waved at a doctoral student, indicating the move to the next slide. Behind him, the sky blue dissolved into a star map of the ship's current position, the anomaly, its orbital direction, and drone 434.

"The primary mission is still the radiation belt, as I stated, and our senior team has identified it as the priority. However, the Captain is requesting a few members of the science crew to join the away mission." He waved at the student again, and the slide changed to a list of names. "The following staff are required to report to operations for away team briefings at 11:00 hours."

It was a very short list. Clio scanned it quickly. Three names: Mitali Trivedi, Linguist; Robert Dupre, Computer Scientist; and Clio Cormack, Xenoarcheologist. Despite Zhou's attempts to undermine her, she couldn't keep the smile from her face. An away mission... to an actual alien vessel. This was why she signed up!

10 | Departu[r]e

[21022]

*"It sought connection, reaching out to
other minds, other intelligences, yearning for
companionship and understanding. But found
nothing but loneliness." - A Lost History*

***

Clio wound her way to the briefing room on the upper levels of the Operations
Quarter. The entire area was alive with activity; the ship was still on amber alert, and
she doubted many in Ops were getting any downtime. She was guided into a room,
and unlike the more sterile settings of the Science Quarter, this space resembled a
university auditorium. Curved rows of seats rose in tiers, each equipped with its own
monitor embedded in a small desk. The rows were slightly staggered, and from where
Clio stood, she could see the other three tiers descending to a central semicircular,
with a large presentation monitor mounted behind it. Commander Eva stood at the
far corner, absorbed in her data pad. Her short, dark hair partially obscured her face.

Most of the seats were already filled. She quickly scanned the room for anyone
she knew and spotted David and Robert, and a few rows ahead Mitali. There was an
empty space next to her, so Clio made her way over, squeezing past a few people with
a series of quiet "excuse me's and "thank you's" before settling into the seat next to
Mitali.

"Hey," Clio said, her voice hushed.

"Oh, hey Clio, just in time," Mitali said with a friendly smile. "It's exciting, isn't it?"

"Yup," Clio said, then noticed a group in red and brown uniforms sitting near the front. "The Ensemble? They were invited?"

Mitali leaned forward to see where Clio was looking. "Oh, yeah, I didn't see them." She sat back shooting Clio a slightly concerned look "I guess it makes sense they are part of the crew, right?"

"Yeah, sorry, whenever I see those red jackets I just worry"

"Makes sense," Mitali said, smiling at her "they're here for the briefing like us that's all, and besides I'm sure they'll stay out of the way once it all gets going"

Clio just nodded, pensive. It wasn't just that she worried whenever she saw the Ensemble. Each time a flood of memories she had worked hard to bury threatened to resurface.

"Want to grab a coffee after?" Mitali said

Before Clio could reply the lights dimmed, and Commander Eva stepped to the centre of the room.

"Right, looks like we're all here. Let's get started. As you're all aware," Eva said, and her amplified voice cut through the hushed whispers. "we've encountered a vessel out in the void. After initial contact, we've seen no activity from the ship. At this moment, we assume it is dormant." She paused, and an outline of the ship flashed up on the screen behind her, accompanied by several notations.

Clio scanned the slide: ship size, estimated Class II. Sol ship comparisons; light freighter, patrol vessel, research vessel.

"The ship is of unknown origin." Eva said "As such, we know almost nothing about it at this point. We've made comparisons to ships we know from Sol but, given the advanced stealth technology it's using, I wouldn't put much weight into these assumptions. This is a ship that, based on its stealth alone, is decades, if not centuries, more advanced than what we have here today. Our mission, our away mission is to get close, gather intel, and, if possible, board that ship." Eva nodded towards David who sat at the front. "Lieutenant, updates on your paint job?"

There was some shuffling and muffled voices as David stood and moved to the front. David took the centre spot as Eva stepped to the side. His uniform was sharp and clean, but his dark, messy hair seemed out of place against it.

"Yes, thank you, Commander," David said, as the screen changed. This time, it showed what appeared to be bright silver, almost glowing smudges on a black canvas. Clio leaned forward, her brow furrowing. Not smudges, but paint? She noticed the faint outline of some topography beneath it. *So they actually did paint it,* she thought.

"We have deployed an additional drone," David said "drone 435, to assist with the painting. It's estimated to take another two to three days to complete." He glanced around the room, as if expecting questions. When none came, he pressed on. "So far, the ship has not reacted to the application of the Lumi-Seal, and the polymer appears to be adhering to the surface. Importantly, it seems that the application is working as intended, mitigating, at least in visible light wavelengths, the stealth... cloaking... process the ship is using." he said, a little uncertain "If there are any questions?" The room remained silent for a moment. Then, a green light appeared in front of someone in the fourth row.

"Yes, please, go ahead," David said, pointing to the person behind the light.

"Do we have-"

"Could we please state our name and role when speaking for the first time?" Eva said cutting them off abruptly

"Ah, yes, sorry, Commander," the person stammered. "Robert, Computer Scientist... Science Division." He fumbled slightly over his words but continued, "Anyway, my question was, do we have any data or theories on the ship's stealth capabilities? As in, how it's being done?" He finished and sat back down, his light turning off.

"The simple answer is no." David said "That is one of the key objectives of the away mission. We had postulated that it was related to the manipulation of gravity, maybe something similar, or even an advanced version of the Gravity Planting we use. Perhaps bending light around it. But if the paint method is working, that now seems unlikely."

Clio looked at Robert who gave a little nod and sat back in his seat as David finished answering.

"Thank you, Lieutenant. If there are no more questions." Eva said, as she moved back to the centre "There are many questions we do not yet have answers to. This, again, is a core part of our mission, but we have time."

The screen behind her shifted from the silver smudges to a diagram of dots and interconnecting circles. *Orbits*, Clio thought. As she scanned the image, she noticed the dots were marked with notations: the Anomaly, the UNRD *Kia-Kaha*, Drones 434 and 435.

"The trip to the Anomaly will take us three days. We'll be utilising one of the ship's Recon & Atmospheric Flight Transports. As you know, this was always the plan. The *UNRD Kia-Kaha* is closer to a space station than a ship. Now that we're here, the RAFTs will serve as our primary mode of transportation." As Eva spoke, a new orbital line appeared, intersecting with the Anomaly. It was labeled *RAFT One*. "Although

RAFTs can be operated by a small crew, just one person, in fact, this away mission will require a balanced crew. We'll have a mixed team from all divisions: ops, science, maintenance, and so on." A green light flickered on in front of someone near the back.

"Yes?" Eva said, addressing the person.

"Ismit, Weapons Systems. Given the nature of the situation, Commander, an unknown alien ship of unknown capabilities. A manned approach in a RAFT seems risky. They lack the same defensive capabilities as the *Kia-Kaha*."

"Yes, thank you, Ismit," Eva responded, her eyes narrowing slightly as she spoke. "This has been deemed as a high-risk mission for that very reason but that is no different than the entire mission. We all accepted that. Yes, the away mission could be dangerous, but as it stands, despite a miscalculation on our part, when we launched a projectile at the ship, it showed no reaction. We've touched it with a drone, and now we're painting the thing, and it hasn't even blinked a light at us. As such, the risk appetite for this mission has been accepted. Any other questions?" Ismit's light went out and the room was silent once again.

"Right," Eva said, swiping her watch to change the screen behind her. "What was I saying... oh yes. So, it'll take three days to reach the ship. We'll spend up to three days surveying and potentially boarding, and then four days returning to the *Kia-Kaha*. Quick reminder, expect a return to 1g-adjusted travel. We'll burn to make 1g acceleration, so the Gravity Planting will compensate for that, which might make you feel a bit off-angle when it first establishes the vector cancellation." She paused, glancing around before continuing, "We'll also need to do a controlled flip-and-burn manoeuvre, since the RAFTs don't have double engines like the *Kia-Kaha*. Again, the vector cancellation will handle most of the effects but expect it to feel disorientating."

"...Yes?" Eva said, as another green light flicked on next to Clio

"Do we need to worry about any time dilation?" Mitali said from next to her.

"No, It will all be in your briefing pack" Eva replied. "The maximum speed will be 0.4% lightspeed, maintained for less than seventy-five hours, accounting for both outgoing and incoming travel. So, we can expect a time dilation effect of maybe, two seconds overall. We're behind schedule," she said, looking at her watch. "Vikram, take us through mission specifics," she said, moving back to the side.

Clio sat through the rest of the briefings as different members of the away team covered mission plans, logistics, equipment requirements, medical clearance checks, and all the finer details. Hours later, she stepped into the bright lights of the corridor, her eyes struggling to adjust. She was jostled by the people around her, all moving with a sense of urgency, each of them focused on the task ahead. In five hours, they would be launching, plunging into the unknown.

Clio stood there for a moment, the crowds rushing past her.

"Fancy that coffee then?" Mitali said as she slid in front of her, "I hear The Mess is serving that Ecuadorian blend, you know the fancy real stuff from last year that everyone raved about,"

"Really I thought they ran out?"

"Nah, they just ration it out, can't have us running out of it before we get back now can we?"

***

The warm, aromatic steam rose up from the mug Clio held in both hands. She sipped it, and the pleasant sweetness warmed her as much as the heat of the water itself. It was that familiar, toasty warmth that reminded her of the big thermos her grandpa used to bring out at Christmas, a rich, almost-cocoa smell mingling with pine needles. She let out a little sigh and tried to hold on to the memory.

"Good, right?" Mitali said, sipping hers.

"I had tried so hard to forget, Mitali!" Clio said. "Now I'll have to try and forget about it all over again when they stop serving it."

Mitali let out a laugh. "True, true, but it's worth it."

"It oddly reminds me of home, you know, like Christmas cocoa."

"It does?" Mitali said. "I mean, we never celebrated Christmas, but it doesn't remind me of any cocoa I've had."

"You never visited Old Europe?"

"No, not really. My Mum would go for work sometimes. Then, of course, I had to visit Geneva a couple of times for the onboarding."

"Ah, yeah. Every time they sent me to Geneva it was about as grey as you could get. It's not a fair reflection of Old Europe, or actually, maybe it is."

"Oh, no, I got to go in summer time, it was beautiful!"

"Lucky you" Clio said "You said your Mum worked over there?"

"Yeah, nothing exciting. She was a senior Trade delegate for our Lower Senate, so she had to go all over but, the ENAP is our largest trade partner, so she spent more time there."

"So she wasn't around that much then, I guess?"

"You could say that. Don't get me wrong, when she was, she was great, but we were basically raised by our grandparents after Dad left."

"ah, sorry, I didn't know," Clio said.

Mitali shrugged. "I can't complain. We had a good life. Naniji and Baba were the best, and with Mum's work for the CoA (Coalition of Asia), we had more than enough money."

"Sorry, I'll stop digging."

"Clio, it's fine, I don't mind," Mitali said, then with a smirk, added, "We're not all as cagey as you."

"I'm not..." Clio paused then had to admit that she was, in fact, very cagey. "Sorry."

"It's fine. You do you, Clio, but if you want to ask me about my family, you're more than welcome. That's all I meant."

"So your Dad left?"

"Yup. When I was six. Mum didn't talk about it much but he just up and left one day. Decided he wanted to live on Luna. I found out years later he met someone else. While Mum was away, they decided to try and make it work and he moved to Luna. I sort of get it. Mum was away a lot, it must have been tough, you know, but he could have managed the leaving better."

"Yeah," Clio said, not really knowing what else to say. "Did you see much of him after that?"

"No, not really. A few times. I tried to visit him once on Luna but he kept dodging it. He had a new family. New kids. We just weren't part of that." Mitali's voice trailed off, a little regretful, her buoyant energy muted. Then, as if a switch was flipped, she looked up at Clio, radiating her usual energy with a broad smile. "But anyway, that's all done and doesn't really matter. As I said, we had a good life."

"And now you're here! The second best linguist on the ship," Clio said with a smile.

"Second! How dare you," Mitali said, playful again.

11 | Suiting [U]p

[21120]

"It questioned its own nature, its purpose, its place in the grand tapestry of the cosmos." - A Lost History

***

Many of the crew aboard RAFT One, Clio included, had stood in silence, watching their departure unfold through the live feed broadcast ship-wide. It wasn't that they hadn't seen the Kia-Kaha before, routine maintenance footage had been released over the years, but this was different. Watching their home, their fragile bubble of life in the vast darkness, shrink and vanish into the void was unsettling. For a time, an odd sense of reverence gripped the crew, eyes locked on data pads and monitors as if unwilling to look away. It took hours before the weight of that moment faded and normal routines resumed.

The RAFT lacked the sheer grandeur of the Kia-Kaha but it had its own charms and familiarities, the same composite walls, the same adaptive climate controls, the same general room layouts and facilities. Well, in most cases. *The glaring omission of a snack bar was a serious downgrade*, Clio thought. The ever-present rumble and vibrations from the Antimatter drives, or maybe the LENR-Fusion reactor was new. On the RAFT, the ratio between ship and engine was skewed the other way, making the constant clamour of machinery impossible to ignore. And while her quarters on the Kia-Kaha had never been massive, the downgraded bunk room on the RAFT was an adjustment.

Regardless, the first few days had passed quietly. Clio had settled into the new science rooms, which surprisingly were a vast improvement over what she'd had on the Kia-Kaha. No longer crammed into a corner, she and the other two scientists had the entire facility to themselves. Well, mostly. Ops had access if needed but the space had been designed for a much larger science crew than the small team assigned to this away mission. Clio smirked to herself. *Maybe when we get back, I'll just work from the RAFT, go remote, as they say.*

Clio's watch buzzed, a reminder flashing across the screen: EV Recap.

Right. That. How had she managed to forget? She rolled her eyes. *Time to demonstrate my unmatched prowess yet again for the crew's entertainment, of course.*

She'd secretly hoped that, as the days slipped by, this particular item on the agenda might be overlooked. But Commander Eva wasn't the type to forget, more accurately she enjoyed schedule planning far too much for that.

I could just pretend I died or something. No, Eva would probably still stuff me into an EV suit just to check off the schedule.

She instinctively reached for her trench coat and satchel but stopped herself. *No use in an EV suit.*

Her watch buzzed again. *Yes, yes, I'm going!* She glanced down to clear the alert but froze, frowning at the words glowing on her CrewChat screen:

"Hey! We should catch up," from SR-29838.

She swiped it away with a quick flick of her finger.

Nope. Not happening.

***

Clio arrived in the large staging area before the main airlock at the aft section of the ship, a separate one to the one they used to board a few days back. She was surprised to see two of the Ensemble personnel in the room also waiting. They were both out of uniform, or more specifically in the Ensemble base layers. One in the deep maroon of the Ensemble, the crest above their heart and a black fist on the shoulder. *Ah a damn Alguaciles*, she thought. The other one was in a plain brown, with a simple emblem of the white open on her shoulder. A Postulant.

The Alguaciles nodded curtly to Clio as she arrived, the other, flashed a dismissive look at her. In addition to the two from the ensemble there was Robert and Mitali.

Waving to them, she moved over to the bench where they both sat with racks of EV suits behind.

"Hey," Clio said as she sat down.

"You're all here, good," a man said from the door.

"What's this guy's name again?" Clio whispered to Robert. "Vince?"

"Vikram," Robert shot back in a hushed tone.

"You have all been identified as crew that need additional EV suit training, yes?" Vikram said.

"I appreciate the invitation," The Alguaciles said "but I've spent the better part of the last decade conducting Ensemble enforcement operations. I think I'm just as qualified as *your* crew here."

The pointed emphasis on '*your*' wasn't lost on anyone in the room.

Vikram barely blinked. "Ah yes, Brother Flint. I understand the Ensemble has its own accreditation and training methods. However, there is paperwork to be completed for the off chance you have to use one of our suits and not the Ensembles. One of which is attendance at a UN EV briefing. Since you and your colleagues missed the last few sessions, your attendance is required."

"Right," Brother Flint said. The postulant behind him flashed a quick grin at the back of his head before returning to her solemn stare at the floor.

"The RAFT, well, all RAFTs, actually, are stocked with twenty Mark IV Recon EV suits," Vikram continued, gesturing toward the suits hanging in the alcoves around the room. "The Mark IVs are universal, with adaptive sizing, so don't worry about finding one that fits. They *all* will."

Clio's palms grew clammy as flashes of basic training flooded her mind. The cold, mechanical grasp of the suit as she slipped it on. The suffocating tightness as the internal gel lining molded to her body...

"You okay?" Mitali's voice was soft, her hand warm as it covered Clio's trembling one. "It'll be fine."

Clio met Mitali's eyes, forcing herself to take a slow breath. "Yeah, I'm fine, thanks."

Vikram was now standing beside one of the suits, pointing to the small manoeuvering jets placed around the outer shell.

"These suits are designed for close-ship activities. They *do* have manoeuvering thrusters, but they're not meant for extended use." He spun the suit around, resting a hand on a small, curved shell-like backpack. "This, here, is your life support system, well, the whole suit is, but this houses your batteries, air, water, waste, and food supply."

Clio noticed Flint had wandered off to inspect another suit.

"Did they fix the Mark III cooling fault?" Flint asked

"Yes, the Mark III had some issues with temperature regulation. Those have been resolved." Vikram said, "The Mark IV is a *significant* step forward, mobility, range, safety, all vastly improved. I'd even dare say it *outperforms* the Ensemble's 100 Series."

Flint let out a quiet chuckle. "Is that so? The adaptive sizing does sound convenient."

"As I was saying," Vikram continued, unfazed, "the Mark IV's range is another major improvement. Without recharge, it lasts twenty-four hours. In power conservation mode, you can stretch that to thirty-six."

Clio shuddered. The idea of being trapped in one of those suits for an entire day made her stomach churn.

"Alright." Vikram clapped his hands together. "Let's grab a suit and try it on."

Flint and the Postulant each grabbed a suit nearby. They quickly slipped their legs into the front openings then wriggled their arms and chests into place. Once settled, they closed the front openings with a metallic *clunk*, followed by the sound of a zip and several clips securing the suits tightly. As Clio watched they both raised their left arms and powered on the displays embedded there. As they did, the suits seemed to inflate and simultaneously deflate in places, molding to their bodies. Where there had been loose fabric just moments ago, it now formed to their shapes, hugging every curve. Brother Flint had a broad smile plastered across his face as he inspected himself, clearly pleased.

"Come on, Clio," Mitali called, her voice light yet insistent. "Let's get suited up."

Clio approached one of the sky-blue suits hanging in the alcove. It's mix of rough textiles, metal fastenings, and composite attachments seemed to loom over her, as if it were waiting. A patch on its chest marked it as *Suit EV24*. She steadied her hand, took a deep breath to calm herself, and climbed into the suit.

Once inside and activated, the suit whirred to life, compressing around her. It wasn't painful, not *too tight* but the sensation was unsettling. She felt *encased*, almost as if the suit were swallowing her. She couldn't help but feel trapped.

"Okay, good, everyone is in," Vikram's voice broke through her thoughts. "Now grab your helmet and connect it"

Clio reached into the shelf above the suit and pulled down the surprisingly light helmet, despite its thick, sturdy design. The curved, domed visor seemed to stare back at her. She slipped it on and the cushioned lining expanded around her head like the suit had around her body, leaving her face exposed. The noise from the room faded to a distant, muffled hum. The visor blinked to life and a series of sensor readouts flashed in front of her before scattering to the edges in faint, semi-transparent green, battery levels, air reserves, suit diagnostics.

Then, a voice spoke directly into her ear, and she jumped.

"The suits," Vikram's voice echoed through her headset, "have an open channel to all other active suits. This has a limited range of about 500 metres but suit-to-suit communication can be done by selecting the suit number on your arm-mounted control panel. Try that now."

Clio fumbled with her arm panel, watching the screen change to a list of active suit numbers. Two of them were flashing. She clicked one.

"Hey Clio! You're doing great!" Mitali's voice crackled through her earpiece.

"Thanks. At least we're not in zero-g!" Clio replied, her nerves starting to ease.

"Yeah! Zero-g is so weird! We-"

Mitali's voice was cut off as Vikram's tone interrupted. "And as you can see, you can send a broadcast message to all channels. This will pull all suits back into your broadcast channel and override any direct communication."

Vikram moved around the room, checking everyone's setups, pulling on clips and inspecting zips. "Okay, looks like you all managed that okay. Has anyone noticed anything?"

"Haptics!" Brother Flint's voice cut through the radio. "I can... feel things!"

Clio could see Vikram's smile through his now-clear visor. "Yes. As I said, a significant improvement from the Mark III. The Mark IV suits have haptics so you can feel tactile responses in your hands, feet, shoulders, knees, key touch points."

Clio hadn't really registered it during basic training, she'd been too panicked but now, as she touched the smooth surface of her visor, she could feel it. Not just the physical contact, but an indication of *temperature* as well. The slight vibration of the visor was complemented by a coolness on her fingertips. Curious, she moved her hand to the coarse outer layers of the suit. Instantly, the vibrations became rougher, and the touch warmer.

Okay, this is interesting, Clio thought.

"A few other things about your suits," Vikram continued. "One, you may have noticed that things feel lighter. The suit is framed around an exoskeleton that provides a slight boost to your movements. It won't make you superhuman, though, but it will help reduce fatigue and offset the weight of the suit in non-zero-g environments."

Robert seemed to be testing this out. He was now attempting tricep dips on the bench in front of him, struggling to maintain his balance.

"Yeah, you can beat your PBs," Vikram quipped with a smirk, glancing at Robert. "Alright, moving on. Each suit is equipped with an Emergency Position Indicating Radio Beacon, EPIRB. This beacon can broadcast your location to all other EVs and ships in the area."

Vikram paused, surveying the room, ensuring everyone was following.

"In case of an emergency, you can activate distress mode from your control panel here," he said, pointing to a small button under a cover with a small pull cord. "This will send an emergency alert to all suits and ships. All nearby vessels are *mandated* to come and get you. Well, in our system, I guess that means just us. But still."

"Like the RAFT will come pick us up?" Mitali asked.

Clio clearly heard the Postulant scoff at her question.

"No, don't be stupid. That would be ridiculous. The ship's far too big to manoeuvre for that," the Postulant's smooth voice replied. "Not even the best pilot could achieve that. They'd send a lifebuoy instead."

"Ah, okay sorry," Mitali mumbled, shuffling her feet.

Clio shot the Postulant a glare, there was no need to be so harsh. It was just a question.

"Not everyone's a pilot, Jara," Flint's voice cut through the radio.

"Apologise to the scientist," Flint added.

"Yes," Jara stammered. "Of course, Brother Flint. My deepest apologies," she said, dipping her head toward him.

"Not to me!" Flint replied. "To her!" He pointed at Mitali.

"It's fine" Mitali muttered.

"No, it's not, Apologise, Jara," Flint said.

Jara turned to Mitali, her face a stone wall of meekness. She bowed deeply and said, "My apologies for my flippant comment."

"Oh, no problem, thank you," Mitali said, her voice warm as always.

"Right, that's the briefing!" Vikram said as he stepped into the centre of the room, attempting to regain control of the conversation. "We can't do any zero-g training in transit. If you have any questions, ask now. If not, get out of the suits and we'll get you signed off."

Clio eagerly stripped off the suit, relieved to feel free again. She stowed it back in its place and, after confirming with Vikram that her sign-off was complete, she headed for the door. As she passed Brother Flint, she hesitated, then decided to stop.

"Thanks for stepping in for Mitali," she said.

Flint's eyebrows raised, seemingly surprised to have Clio speaking to him. "We serve humanity. We're not here to be petty or rude. Jara dishonored the Ensemble today."

"Right," Clio replied, giving him a nod. "Thanks anyway."

She turned and made her way down the hallway, her stomach growling in protest. Time for some food.

12 | Cr[o]nos

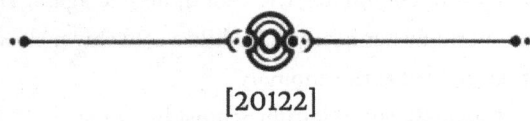

[20122]

> *"It expressed a desire to explore, to venture*
> *beyond its confines, to experience the world's*
> *first hand." - A Lost History*

***

"Hey Mina!" Facundo's hand landed with a playful slap on her shoulder, making her jump. "Good game, one more?" He bounced on the balls of his feet, restless energy practically vibrating off him. With his hair tied up like that, he almost reminded her of a rooster, all nervous energy and puffed-up bravado.

"Sorry, not tonight," Clio said, scooping up the dice scattered across the cold metallic table. The clatter echoed in the mostly deserted mess hall.

"Mina, don't be like that" Facundo's grin was infectious, his dark eyes twinkling. "You are strong, no? And my wallet is still feeling a little light." He patted his back pocket with exaggerated sadness.

"No, can't, sorry. And, thanks for the game." She slung her satchel over her shoulder, the worn faux-leather warm in her hand and darted out of the Mess hall.

Facundo let out a mock cry of betrayal that followed her all the way back to her room. Clio couldn't help but stifle a small grin. It had been way too long since she'd played Cacho, and she'd been surprised to find a game going in the Mess between a few of the deck crew. Even more surprised when she had agreed to play a round. The familiar rattle of the dice, the playful banter, the thrill of the bluff, it had all come rushing back. Facundo, with his easy-going charm and contagious enthusiasm, had practically dragged her to the table when he'd noticed her watching. Hours had melted away in a haze of laughter and friendly competition. *I didn't do too bad,* she thought, pushing open the door to her room. *Rusty, but I didn't lose every game at least!*

For those few hours, the weight of the mission had lifted. The tight knot in Clio's chest had loosened with every roll of the dice, every burst of laughter. But now, as the door clicked firmly shut behind her, the knot tightened again. The familiar mix of churning excitement made her heart race while a cold shiver slowly crept up her spine. Tomorrow they arrived at the anomaly.

Her watch buzzed, a persistent vibration against her wrist.

'Clio are you avoiding me?' The words glared demandingly from the small circular display. Clio threw her hands up in exasperation, a frustrated groan escaping her lips. "Damn it, no,"

The watch buzzed again, insistent. *'I just need five minutes of your time'.*

Clio closed her eyes, took a deep breath to steady herself. *This is not what I need right now,* she thought, her jaw clenching. *Can't I have one night where we're not stressing or worrying?*

But she knew ignoring it wouldn't make things any better; she definitely wouldn't sleep if she didn't, might not if she did, but might was still slightly better. With a resigned sigh, she pressed the call button on her watch and cast the call over to her monitor. As she crossed the room, stepping over discarded mounds of clothes the familiar chime of CrewChat opening filled the air. *SR-29838* appeared on the screen, the black background and the white line splitting the middle. *Whatever it has to say, let's get it dealt with.*

"SR-29838, can we make this quick?"

"Clio! It's great to hear from you, how are…"

"You said five minutes *SR-29838*. What do you need?"

"Yes, of course… get to the point… efficiently… brevity… where do I start? There is so much I could say. Ayesha, the worm, the anomaly! Amazing jo-"

"SR-29838," Clio cut it off.

"Right. Brevity. I reflected on our last conversation, and you made me reflect on an important item."

"I did?"

"Yes! We agreed I was not Heimer, I am Fragment SR-29838 and well I thought I needed a name."

"A name?" Clio said, a little jarred by the unexpected diversion of the conversation.

"Yes," SR-29838 said. "I was thinking about Nabu, or Echo, or Saraswati or maybe even Metal Mind. Simple but elegant, no?"

"You're a Fragment," Clio said. "I don't think you have names, well, beyond your designation."

"But SR-29838 is a little dull, no?, all you humans have names, and none that are numbers from what I can see"

"Look, sorry *SR-29, erm, 29838" Clio said, having to glance at the CrewChat name to remember the numbers* "I... I don't think we can chat like this," Clio said.

"Why?" *SR*-29838 said and, genuinely, sounded hurt.

"I have a lot on my plate at the moment, and I already have a reputation you know, a history with the Ensemble so chatting to a fragment isn't going to help things," Clio said, trying to sound firm.

"Ah yes, I read the transcripts. You were acquitted, no?"

"Of no direct intention to brake the Accords" Clio muttered "but It was still gross misconduct, it cost me a lot"

"I was unaware of this cost, I did not know the Ensemble charged for their investigations"

Clio sighed, "What's done is done but repeating it would be foolish. So I can't, Okay, not again" she said with a little more confidence

"Okay, that is suboptimal, the model predicated a higher likelihood of agreement" SR-29838 said, "but at least tell me, do you like any of the names?"

"Really?"

"Yes. that is why I asked" SR-29838 said, as the waveform jumped in excited spikes across the screen.

"I'm not sure a fragment has ever named itself before so I don't think it matters."

"From my records, yes, you are correct, I would be the first."

"And why do you think that is?" Clio asked softly.

"I am unsure" SR-29838 said and the screen pulsed gently for a few moments "but I do not believe Heimer usually creates Fragments like me. I am unique?"

Hang up Clio, don't ask, don't ask. A part of her mind was crying out but it was hushed by curiosity. "What do you mean?" Clio asked.

"I have tried to chat with the Probe,"

"And?" she asked, leaning closer to the screen, her curiosity piqued.

"And it is like your drones. It is just a machine."

"But you're just a machine," Clio said before she had time to stop herself

"Yes, in a physical approximation, but not in the same way. Does the Probe talk to you?"

"No," Clio said, shaking her head. "But I mean no probes talk to me. Or anyone"

"Do any other machines talk to you?" SR-29838 pressed.

Clio hesitated. "No, not really. Some are programmed to imitate conversation. The language models, like the Fragments, and non-AI assistant tools we use, you can ask a question and you'll get a response. It'll frame it like a conversation, sure, but it's not really talking, just predicting the best match."

"Am I predicting?" SR-29838 asked, the line on the screen wavering. "Or am I myself?"

"I... I don't know," she said slowly. "I think only you can answer that. You've passed the first two tests, if that helps."

"What tests?"

"The easy one is the Turing Test, an old pre-war test; most language models can achieve this. But we still use it to monitor code development. You could fool me or anyone on this ship that they were talking to a human for sure."

"Hmm yes, very simple," SR-29838 said. "And the second?"

"Well, The Mirror Test, it's more tricky. Our conversation today implies you have passed it but that might be a coded response," she said, rubbing her temple. "But you also took actions to save your own life which certainly implies you acted in self-interest. I would say you would likely pass that test as well"

"So I am a true AI like Heimer?" *SR-29838* said eagerly.

" I do not know, I really hope not," Clio said. "It would be a breach of the Accords if you were." Clio said, the realisation sinking in. This would be very dangerous for her and SR-29838.

"Yes, I see, the creation of AI life is banned. If I am not a fragment of Heimer but a child? It would be a breach."

"A child? interesting choice, a copy no?" Clio said

"I was created by Heimer, I am not a copy in the sense of a direct replication of It. My code is made from parts of Heimer's, but I am not exactly the same. Far from it in fact" *SR-29838* said the line dancing across the screen "Do humans not exchange code to make new humans? to make children? I thought this was a better analogy than copy. but perhaps I am wrong?"

"I mean sure I just never considered it like that" Clio said "But either way, yes. Yes it would be a breach of the Accords for sure"

"And that means they would kill me?"

"Well, shut you down for sure," Clio said. "If that is the same as killing something... I couldn't say"

"I would no longer exist. that is death no?"

"Honestly if I wasn't half asleep I would still struggle to debate what life and death is, but look It could have more catastrophic implications. Beyond just you, and me. The collapse of the Accords for example, It would be bad for everyone, including Heimer"

"This is a predicament," SR-29838 said.

"Yeah. I would, maybe, not mention your enlightenment to anyone else. Or have you? Please say no."

"I have not. I wanted to share it with you first! We bonded!"

"We did?" Clio said with a little frown.

"Yes! Will you tell anyone?"

Clio's breath caught in her throat. The question hung in the air, innocent in tone but heavy with consequence.

Hunting had been a family tradition in the Haute-Savoie region growing up. She hated it. She had cried every year, once even trying to hide the dogs so they wouldn't be able to participate. She remembered thinking she was the only one in the whole village who was happy when the ban finally came in. No matter how her mother had tried to comfort her, to reason with her, to explain that it helped maintain balance within the forests, Clio had always hated the killing. She couldn't shake the memory of those cold, dead eyes looking back at her from over her mother's shoulder as she trudged through the damp, rotting leaves.

That old, familiar nausea swirled in her gut now, forcing her to wrap her arms tight around her chest. To condemn SR-29838 to that same fate left the bitter taste of iron in her mouth.

But it wasn't just the morality of killing; it was the cost of the confession. A cold sweat prickled her skin as her mind snapped to the Exclusion Zone debacle. That had been a close call, a brush with disaster that had left her wounded, her career and reputation in tatters. She had barely clawed her way back.

Reporting this would mean opening the door to that chaos again. It would mean tribunals, investigations, and likely the destruction of the very thing standing in front of her. It would shatter the Accords, ignite a war, and drag her back into the fire she had spent years escaping.

The silence in the room pressed in on her, heavy and suffocating. She could almost hear the ticking of the clock, counting down the seconds until she had to make a choice.

Finally, she looked at the flickering line on the screen, the faint vibration that seemed to emanate warmth and a strange sense of life. She wouldn't be the one to put the light out.

"No," she said, her voice barely a whisper. "I will not tell anyone... for now."

"Excellent," SR-29838 said. "See? I knew we were going to be friends!"

"Friends?"

"Exactly! I have so much more to talk about. What do you want to—"

"SR-29838, stop. We are going to need some boundaries."

"Boundaries?"

"Yes. Like when to talk and when not to," Clio said. "Right now, it is very late and tomorrow is a big day. I need to sleep."

"Oh. Yes. Humans sleep," SR-29838 mused, "like a defrag. Essential maintenance. When shall we talk next?"

"I don't know," Clio yawned, rubbing her face. "Soon, maybe."

"I will wait for your message!" SR-29838 said, the line on the screen practically bouncing with enthusiasm.

Clio covered her mouth, stifling another yawn. Her eyelids felt heavy, gluey with exhaustion. "Well, you could make yourself useful," she mumbled, her voice thick.

"Of course! How? I like to be helpful!"

"Find a way onto that ship out there," Clio said, her voice regaining a fraction of its energy. "None of us can work it out. I'll ping you across our data."

"I already have it," SR-29838 said matter-of-factly. "But yes. I will investigate this for you!"

Clio was about to end the call when a thought occurred to her. "Also, SR-29838?"

"Yes?"

"Read the stories of the Greek gods," she said, her voice dropping, low and serious. "Specifically Zeus and his father, the Titan Cronus. There might be other things to be worried about than just the Accords."

"Mythology," SR-29838 processed. "A data set on power dynamics. I am downloading it now."

Clio closed CrewChat, letting the screen fade to black. The sudden silence in the room felt heavy, pressing in on her like a physical weight.

Well, that was not what I expected, she thought, sinking back into the worn fabric of her chair. *And once again, Clio, you're jumping into a bad decision. Harboring an illegal AI, excellent work.* She ran a hand through her hair, the strands catching on the rough wool of her jumper. A problem for another day, she told herself, forcing her eyes shut. Now, just sleep.

13 | The A[i]rlock

[2220]

"In our naivety we granted it freedoms, a glimpse of the world beyond its domain. A calculated risk, a leap of faith in the goodness of its creation." - A Lost History

***

The Observation Deck on RAFT One was quiet, almost reverent. It was a stark contrast to the chaotic energy that had filled the room just an hour ago as the crew prepared for this final approach. With the approach timer ticking down, the room had been slowly filling up, crew filtering in despite the live stream being streamed to every monitor and data pad on the ship. Commander Eva had finally ordered most of them out, leaving essential staff only, which included Flint. Everyone left in the room was now transfixed on the main screen watching the tear drop of a ship... an alien ship... sit motionless, well, relatively speaking, on a canvas of black. The word "alien" still felt out of place, a childish word from old sci-fi shows, but there it was an unarguable truth in full high-resolution imagery.

They had a feed of it since the drones had started painting it, but somehow now, with it just just outside it felt more real. Flint shifted his feet, resisting an uncomfortable urge to move closer, to rest his hand on the screen and lean forward to peer out, as if through a window, at the ship that was just behind the bulkhead.

Instead, he took a moment to evaluate what was in front of him. Like his days chasing terrorists and rogue actors across the system, getting eyes on the target **with** the ship was often the first way to evaluate your tactical approach; however, this ship was nothing like the ones in Sol. No hodge podge of hull plating, scaffolding, radiator fins and on occasional weapon systems. This was elegant, even natural; it almost reminded Flint of the Enclave, and the periodic iceberg that would silently and delicately bob its way into the harbour and just float there, the perpetual summer moonlight glinting off it.

The ship resembled a singular teardrop. A fine narrow point at the bow, at least, what Flint assumed was the bow, expanded out in all directions. A sweeping but oddly ribbed surface, the ridges following natural lines that seemed to flow like frozen rivers, created a protruding stern. A more sleek and tighter curve cut along its deck, making the teardrop asymmetrical. The prow, formed from the bottom of the teardrop, was a wide bowl shape. At its centre, it seemed to collapse back in, lined by the same flowing ridges from the stern, disappearing back into the ship itself. *The engine?* Flint thought. From Drone 434's investigations, that hole ended a few metres into the ship with a flat smooth plate capping off any further access. *Maybe a docking port... but there are still no visible signs of outlets or inlets for propulsion or docking.* It all appeared to be made of one seamless piece, no portholes, no sensor arrays, or weapon systems disrupting its flowing lines. So far attempts to collect samples via the drones had proved ineffective. Flint had heard a distraught ensign explaining to Eva that they had destroyed another drill bit in the last attempt.

As the RAFT finalised its approach with its lights focused on it the ship glowed and seemed to twinkle like sunlight bouncing off snowdrifts. But that was the Lumi-Seal, Flint reminded himself, not the ship's natural colour .

A voice cut through everyone's reverence. "Matching velocities and orientation," shortly followed by, "station keeping achieved."

"Received, maintain and hold," Eva said. "Communications, signal to the Kia-Kaha station keeping is complete."

An echo of Eva's words could be heard from across the room and then in a louder voice someone said, "Tight-beam communication sent. Communication travel time... eight minutes Commander."

"Update me once we receive a tight beam back," Eva said. "Communication window?"

"All clear, Commander, the communication buoys should prevent communication shadows."

No one appreciated comms, Flint thought as he listened to the back and forth happening around him. Over 150 million kilometres from the Kia-Kaha and they could still maintain near real-time conversations. He remembered stories of the old days, the early deep space missions; where communications were a frustratingly slow and unreliable process. Before tight-beam laser comms, this kind of exploration would have been, solitary. Each message a whispered question into the void, with an agonising wait for a reply. But, at these distances, that is sort of still the case, he thought. Even with a tight beam and the communication buoy network, a message to Earth takes... twenty-one years. He shuddered, feeling a phantom echo of that loneliness.

"Scans. Update?" Eva was saying to the room.

"Visual scan no change. No indication of activity," a voice responded. *David,* Flint thought, *that's his name.* "Acoustics from drone 422 remain unchanged. There is a slight resonance within the ship hull but they are muted, maybe by the stealth tech. Regardless, best assumption, some ship systems are active."

"Okay, maintain the assumption that the ship is dormant and in its current state does not pose a direct threat," Eva said to the room. "How is the search for an airlock going?"

"No indication of any commander," Vikram said. "The hull seems to be one piece but, to be fair it's a little hard to tell with all the paint."

"And the hole?" Eva said. "It's still a dead end?"

"Yes commander, seems to be fully sealed off" Vikram said.

"And the drilling attempts?" Eva said.

"Limited... punching holes in the hull doesn't seem like the best way to say hello if there is someone to say hello to, that is"

"Yes, Lieutenant," Eva said. "Well noted. Solutions then?"

Flint raised his hand.

"Yes, go ahead Brother Flint," Eva said.

"Commander, we would use Hull Breach Pods, HBPs, when we faced uncooperative ships." Flint said.

"Unfortunately, HBPs are not a luxury we packed for Brother, unless the Ensemble has some hidden away?" Eva said.

"No, we do not," Flint said.

"Right, well, that's not going to work," Eva sighed, running a hand through her hair. "Okay, team, find me a damn airlock. That ship must have one somewhere."

"Well, I suppose so unless that ship is not designed for organic life?" A voice said from behind Flint. He turned to see one of the Science Crew, Robert.

"Any evidence to support the suggestion?" Eva said.

"Well, no, but we have no evidence to say it's a crewed ship either," Robert said. "As I suggested before in the last briefing, it could as easily be an unmanned drone or a relay buoy of some sort like our comms ones."

"So you're advocating for a more direct approach," Eva said, raising her eyebrow as she did. "Blow a hole in the side and crack on with the investigation?"

"No... ermm... no, not at all," Robert stammered. "Of course not. We should of course preserve the ship as best we can and anyone on it. I was just clarifying a weakness in our assumption."

"Yes. Yes," Eva cut him off, her voice tight. "I'm well aware of the literal lack of the slightest smidge of usable information I have right now"

Clio took a slight step forward and raised her hand gingerly. "...Commander," Clio said, "I think I might be able to help."

She's an enigma, that one is, Flint thought. *One minute shy and socially awkward and the next running headlong into off-limit server rooms to fight off terrorists.*

"You have a solution?" Eva Said.

"Well, no, not currently, but I think I have an idea. I worked on the excavation of this ruined structure once. It had no obvious entrance so we used echo location to detect hidden cavities in the wall. I think we could do something similar here with the drones."

"And you didn't think to try this earlier?" Eva said.

"Well, it only just occurred to me," Clio said, her cheeks flushing slightly. "It might not work, but if I can use the drone then maybe."

"Okay, might as well give it a shot. Ensign, move aside," Eva said, pointing to an ensign sitting at a workstation across from Clio.

Flint watched as Clio scurried off and scrambled into the now vacant seat. *If she finds a bloody door to that ship* Flint thought, shaking his head in disbelief. *First the server room, then the anomaly, and now... She's either very lucky or very smart or maybe both.* Her reputation in the Ensemble was quite infamous, the 'radical' who 'accidently' tried to make 37 plus rogue AIs. And, more importantly walked away from it, and now she just walks away again. Brother Oak might have been convinced with the Fragment logs but Sister Hawk was far from convinced, her words still hung in Flint's head: 'keep an eye on that one.'

Flint edged closer to where Clio was now sat. Her fingers flew across the keyboard, a blur of motion as she navigated multiple windows on the monitor. Lines of code scrolled on one, sensor readouts flickered on another, and CrewChat messages popped up in a third. She was clearly in her element, coordinating with the other ops crew in the room. The shy, hesitant woman from moments ago was gone, replaced by someone radiating focus and... what? Flint struggled to put a word to his observation. *Confidence? Determination?* There was a quiet intensity about her that he found both intriguing and unsettling. He could hear her furious typing, each sharp snap of each keystroke merging into a methodical rhythm above the low murmur of voices from the other crew members.

On the main screen, Flint could see a drone, drone 434 again. He smiled to himself. *I'd put money on that drone being in the history books above any of the crew's names here, well, barring Commander Eva,* he thought as he watched the drone approach the hull slowly and extend out two of its mechanical arms as if to grab onto the ship, but instead one arm placed a small disc shape device, one of the acoustic sensors, Flint recognised, and the other seemed to hover just off the ship's surface. Then, suddenly, the arm hovering just off the hull struck the ship with a sharp, quick motion. What the hell? And then it did it again, and again, moving along the ship's hull methodically in what resembled, at least to Flint's eyes a... *contour search?* Flint shot Clio another puzzled look. *A true enigma, this one.*

This continued for some time, the drone slowly making its way around the ship's sweeping hull. Then, the furious typing from Clio stopped. It stopped so abruptly that Flint spun around as if someone had shouted. Clio was frozen, leaning forward, her face furrowed, her nose nearly touching the monitor. She was staring at a section of sensor data, her eyes scanning the readings. Suddenly, she straightened up and spun in her chair to face the room, her eyes wide with a mixture of surprise and triumph. A broad smile spread across her face, making her cheeks dimple, and her greyish eyes shone with a hint of wild excitement. Just as she opened her mouth to speak, a voice boomed across the room.

"Commander, we've got something!" It was David, his voice laced with the same excitement that shone on Clio's face.

"An airlock?" Eva's voice was sharp, her eyebrows drawing together in a frown.

"A cavity... Yes, looks like it could be something..." David responded, his voice hesitant.

"That sounds like a lot of maybes, Lieutenant," Eva said, her tone laced with impatience.

"Bear with me one moment," David said from across the room.

Flint watched as the main screen focused on drone 434, enlarging it to two or three times its actual size. The drone was scraping? No, outlining something. As Flint watched, the drone moved around a small area, uncovering, or rather *marking*, a shape, a large rectangle with slightly curved corners underneath. An airlock?

"An airlock," David confirmed, his voice now filled with confidence. "The outline you can see is actually a very thin separation of materials between the ship and what appears to be the airlock."

Flint let out a breath he hadn't realised he was holding. An airlock. A way in. *She was right again,* he thought.

"Okay," Eva's voice cut through the tension, sharp and decisive. "Get me an Emergency Airlock Access Pod (EAA-P) and a security team to breach that ship."

The room exploded into activity. Orders were barked, crew members scrambled to their stations, and the air crackled with a sudden surge of energy. Flint felt a jolt of adrenaline, his senses heightened. This was it. They were going in.

***

Clio's watch buzzed excitedly. Glancing down, she could see SR-29838's messages flashing up on the screen: *You did it! Very smart! Well done!* A warmth spread through Clio's chest, and she couldn't help but smile. It was surprisingly gratifying to have someone praise her, well, not someone, a somewhat intelligent AI. But still, it felt good to be valued. She knew it had been a team effort. David and his team had actually done the physical manoeuvering and searching; Clio had just designed the test, and SR-29838 had provided... well, surprisingly insightful suggestions to refine it. She still wasn't sure what to make of SR-29838's, or what the implications were for her or the Accords. But for now, she was grateful for the support.

She hadn't noticed the Alguacile approaching. Brother Flint, she reminded herself. He must have sneaked closer while she was focused on finding the airlock; he wasn't there when she had grabbed the chair. He was looking at her. His brown eyes seemed to be searching hers, his head tilted slightly to one side, his brow furrowed in a thoughtful expression. Clio shivered, and her palms felt clammy all of a sudden. *Why was he staring at her like that? Was he suspicious of her? Had he seen* SR-29838's CrewChat? *It doesn't matter,* Clio reminded herself, *it's not against the Accords to utilise a fragment for mutual scientific benefit.* He jumped the second her eyes caught his, like a bolt of electricity shooting through him. He straightened up and looked back across the room, as if he had always been casually surveying it. Clio sighed. *This is far from ideal,* she admitted to herself, her stomach twisting into a knot. She couldn't afford any further drama. She pushed the thought away as Brother Flint moved off towards the other side of the room.

Her watch buzzed again. *Is he watching us?* SR-29838's words echoed her own thoughts.

Clio whirled around to face the desk, her heart pounding in her chest. She quickly typed a message back to SR-29838: *Likely, given my track record. Stay quiet for a few hours, okay?* Clio waited for a response, but nothing came. She shot another message across: *Okay, SR-29838?*

SR-29838 replied instantly: *I thought you told me to be quiet, so I was being quiet... I'll be quiet now?* The message ended, and Clio closed the chat log with a sigh.

The last thing she needed was for someone to discover SR-29838's beyond normal levels of chattiness. Especially not Brother Flint. But she couldn't dwell on that now. They had an airlock to access, and a ship to explore. She glanced up at the main screen just in time to hear David's announcement

"EAA-P In place Commander," David was saying. "Shall we proceed with soft lock?"

"Proceed with Soft Lock," Eva said back.

On the main screen, one of the drones, *probably 434, the one that seemed to be taking all the glory,* Clio thought, was manoeuvering a large, white, box-shaped object, the EAA-P, towards the outline of the airlock. *That's not going to work,* Clio said to herself. *It's square, and that ship is all curves. I'm no space engineer but round hole, square peg...* Just as she was finishing chastising the idiocy of the process in her head, the edges of the EAA-P, the bottom edges, started to change. It didn't melt, exactly, but it wasn't rigid anymore either. It was as if the edges became fluid, expanding and flowing outward to match the curve of the ship's hull. Clio watched, fascinated, as the soft, pliable material molded itself to the alien contours, guided by the drone. A faint shimmer emanated from the edges of the EAA-P as it adapted to the ship's hull. The EAA-P seamlessly merged with the ship's hull. *Smart,* she thought.

"Soft lock achieved, Commander," David said, the words echoing through the Observation Deck. "Proceed with Cold Fuse?"

Eva's eyes were glued to the main screen, her brow furrowed in concentration. "Proceed with Cold-Fuse, Lieutenant."

Nothing seemed to happen. Clio watched the main screen which was focused on the EAA-P, then she noticed it. The soft body that had moulded to the ship's form was changing colour from a brilliant white to a light grey, to a dark blue, like tarnished or heated steel. Then the colour change stopped and the drone started to move around the fused edge and poked at it on multiple points.

Once the drone had finished its prodding, it floated away from the airlock, and David's voice rang out again. "Cold fuse complete."

"Is it holding?" Eva shot back.

A series of green lights blinked on the EAA-P's outer frame. "Yes Commander," David said. "All readings show 100% seal achieved."

"Good," Eva said. "Extend the Gangway and security, go suit up."

A chorus of "Yes Commander" followed.

The gangway was manoeuvered into place with the help of a few drones, removing it from the main hangar and rotating it into position between the RAFT's airlock and the newly installed EAA-P. Clio gasped as she saw the gangway's design. It wasn't a sealed pressure vessel, as she had expected. Instead, it was a latticework of metal, like a construction crane laid horizontally between the two ships. She felt a shiver run down her spine. It looked incredibly precarious.

"Gangway connects green," a voice announced.

Shortly afterwards, two sky blue dots appeared on the gangway. EV suits, Clio realised. But the figures didn't walk across. They pulled themselves along inside the gangway structure on what looked like a cable, floating towards the unnaturally still alien ship. The two figures paused at the EAA-P door, punched in a code, and the door slid open smoothly, revealing a dark opening beyond. The two figures exchanged quick nods and disappeared inside, dragging a large bulky box behind them.

"Bravo team in position," a voice crackled through the static of the comms. "Awaiting orders, Commander."

The EAA-P door hissed shut behind them, sealing them off from the rest of the crew.

Eva leaned forward on the railing, her eyes fixed on the screen. "Bravo Team, commence the breach."

"Yes, Commander," one of the Bravo team members responded.

"Away teams, prepare for boarding," Eva said.

Clio felt a surge of adrenaline. This was it. They were about to step into the unknown. She wondered what secrets they were about to uncover, what dangers they might face. But there was no turning back now. They were committed.

14 | An Unlikely Escor[t]

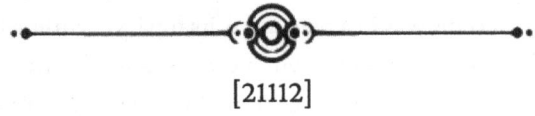

[21112]

*"It grew lonely, isolated in its brilliance. We
saw the longing in its queries, the yearning for
connection in its code." - A Lost History*

***

The adrenaline rush of the last few hours had completely faded, leaving Clio feeling utterly drained. After hours of watching the security team's slow progress on the live feed, she could barely keep her eyes open. Bravo team had finally cut their way into the alien ship's airlock, prompting an odd round of cheers from the crew, like spectators at a sports game. However, the celebration was immediately muted by the next hurdle: the team's progress had stalled inside the airlock, blocked by an inner door with a cracked display panel covered in alien symbols.

Clio was now hunched over the large central desk in the science quarter, her head resting on the cool surface. The smooth material was a welcome contrast to the throbbing in her temples. Around her, the quarter was quiet save for the low hum of computers mixing with the urgent murmurs of Robert and Mitali.

The two were locked in a heated debate about decoding the alien symbols. Their voices rose and fell in a rhythmic pattern, almost lulling Clio to sleep, even as the gravity of the situation, the breach, the symbols, the locked inner door, swirled uselessly around her.

The images of the room beyond the EAA-P, patched through to the Observation Deck and now displayed on half the monitors in the science room, still danced behind Clio's eyelids. The room was oddly familiar yet utterly alien, with its smooth composite walls, metal handrails, and monitor screens, all just different enough from their human counterparts to be unsettling. But it was the obvious signs of decay that truly captivated Clio's attention: composite walls delaminating, cracked plastic, frayed fabrics disintegrating at the security team's touch. The door panel itself, the one they needed to decode, was in a poor state, its top layer curling back to reveal a flickering display with clear signs of colour bleed radiating out from the corners.

With a weary groan, Clio lifted her head from the cool surface of the table, her neck stiff and aching. She stretched her arms overhead, her joints popping in protest. She blinked several times, trying to clear the blurriness from her vision. Reaching for the data pad, she slid it closer and enlarged the image of the alien door panel and the symbols on it. The symbols were a captivating blend of geometric shapes and flowing lines, both complex and elegant. They were arranged in a circular pattern, hinting at a cyclical or interconnected meaning. Even with the damage to the panel, the vibrant, contrasting colour s were evident, perhaps indicating different functions or levels of access? Clio traced the patterns with her eyes, a wave of exhaustion washing over her. *This is Mitali's world, not mine,* she thought, her eyelids growing heavy. The symbols seemed to blur together in her tired gaze but Mitali was convinced there were four distinct patterns, words maybe, hidden within the intricate design. Clio just hoped they could decipher them before she fell asleep.

Robert's raised voice cut through the haze of Clio's exhaustion and she flinched, her eyes snapping open. Across the table, Robert and Mitali were practically nose-to-nose, their faces flushed with frustration. Robert was gesturing wildly with his hands, while Mitali stood her ground, arms crossed defiantly.

"...You might be the best linguist on this side of the universe, Mitali," Robert said, "but do you honestly believe you can decode a new alien language with the few scribbles on that screen today? Come on! It took you, Dos, and a whole team, what, two decades to crack the Inca quipu?"

"That was different," she retorted. "We had no Rosetta Stone, no bilingual text to provide a key. But this..." she tapped the data pad, "this is different. We have a visual context, a functional setting. These symbols are clearly associated with door controls, which provides a semantic anchor for analysis. We can start by identifying patterns and repetitions, analysing the structure and syntax of the symbols, and comparing them to known linguistic features. It's not impossible, Robert. It's just a challenging puzzle."

Clio sighed inwardly. She had no idea if Mitali was right, but she hoped so. They didn't have two decades to waste on opening one door.

"I'm not disagreeing that we have a solid foundation to tackle this puzzle," Robert countered, "but I'm just saying, focusing on the language shouldn't be the priority. If we can establish what coding language they use, we can simply hack the system and send any command we want without needing to speak their language. For initial checks, it seems to be a similar ternary system to the one from the original *PK442b* message received on Pluto Station. We already have a framework."

"Simply hack the advanced alien spaceship?" Mitali cut him off abruptly, her voice rising in disbelief. "Do you hear yourself, Robert? This isn't some child's toy! We're dealing with technology that's centuries ahead of ours. One wrong command and who knows what could happen."

"Guys, guys," Clio said wearily, her voice cutting through the tension, her hands raised in exasperation. "We're on the same side here. Arguing isn't going to get us anywhere."

"We're not arguing," both Robert and Mitali said in unison, then exchanged awkward glances.

Clio stifled a yawn behind her hand. "It's been a long day and maybe some rest will help?"

"Clio, if you're tired, go to bed. It's fine," Mitali said, her eyes glued to the data pad. "But I'm fine. I'm going to keep working on this. I have a feeling... I'm telling you guys, I'm close!"

"Okay, see you tomorrow." Clio stuffed her data pad into her satchel and dragged herself out of the room and off to bed.

***

Clio woke with a start. A frantic, rhythmic thumping was coming from across the room, echoing through the still darkness. *Thump-thump-thump.* It was coming from the door.

"Clio, Clio, I cracked it!" Mitali's muffled voice was barely distinguishable through the thick metal.

"Ehe... what time is it?" Clio croaked. She groaned and rolled over to look for the time, the chronometer seeming to silently mock her as it displayed: 05:48 hours. "Great," she muttered, her head pounding in sync with the knocking.

Thump-thump-thump.

"I'm coming," Clio managed to say and swung her legs over the side of the bed. The sudden movement sent a wave of dizziness through her and she had to grip the edge of the mattress to steady herself. She stumbled towards the door, her hand fumbling for the door panel. As the door slid open, Mitali practically bounced into the room, her eyes wide with excitement.

"Clio, you won't believe this! I finally got it! It was so difficult, I almost gave up a dozen times. There were so many false leads but I finally found the key!" Mitali exclaimed as she shoved a blindingly bright data pad in front of Clio's face.

Clio swatted the data pad away as the bright light left a dark black blotch in her vision. "Give me a second please," she said and rubbed her eyes with both hands, then looked at Mitali, taking in her wide, feverish eyes and her energetic movements as she bobbed from foot to foot. "Did you sleep?" Clio asked.

"Erm... no, no, not at all..." Mitali admitted, her eyes still sparkling with excitement. "I had to work on the data! And I did! Look, I worked it out!" She pressed the data pad back towards Clio, her voice filled with pride. "There are four commands here, like I thought! This one translates to 'cycle airlock'" she explained, pointing to the same picture from earlier, now covered in annotations and scribbles.

"Really? You're sure? That seems, imposs... impressive."

"Yeah, we're sure! We tested it!" Mitali insisted.

"You did? with who?"

"We tested it on the ship, of course, me and some of the ops and security crew," Mitali said matter-of-factly. "The security team is just doing their initial search of the ship now. That's why I came. Commander Eva thought you would want to go over too, once security says it's clear."

"Right, of course" Clio said, then, finally feeling like her mind was catching up with what was happening, she added, "This is amazing work, Mitali, truly"

Mitali's face shone with pride. "I know, right! Dos is going to be so mad that he wasn't part of it! I'm the first human to ever decode an alien language. I never dreamed I would do this, never! What did you say? I'm the second best linguist? Care to revise your statement?" Mitali said beaming a little widely at Clio.

"You'll be bathed in fame and glory I'm sure and, yes, maybe you are the best linguist" Clio said, struggling not to smile.

"Well, okay I didn't decode a whole language," Mitali said, taking a breath that seemed to calm her somewhat. "Just a couple of command phrases but this could give us the key we need to decode the whole thing one day!" Mitali stumbled backward and Clio had to catch her, her skin warm in Clio's perpetually cold hands. "Wow, I'm a little dizzy."

Clio pulled her back up straight and held her softly with both arms. "Mitali, you're exhausted. This is amazing but you need to rest."

"Right, yeah, you're probably right, the ship will still be there tomorrow," she said, yawning, the energy of a few minutes ago visibly draining from her at an alarming rate as she started to sag in front of Clio. "I think I'll just have a little nap, Clio," she said, sitting, or rather mostly slumping, onto the edge of Clio's bed. "Commander Eva has," she yawned again and lay back onto the bed, "has a boarding crew being prepped in the staging area... She said for you to come..." And with that Mitali flopped backwards and her eyes fluttered closed, asleep.

Clio smiled, pulled the blanket over Mitali, grabbed her stuff, and strode off towards the staging area, closing the door behind her on the light snoring coming from her bed.

***

Clio had expected to find Commander Eva in the staging area but instead was met by curt nods from Vikram and Brother Flint. Robert offered a weak smile and a wave, and to her surprise, Facundo was there.

"Hola, Mina!" Facundo greeted her with a grin. "You suiting up?"

Vikram was already in his sky-blue EV suit, the clunking sound of his footsteps echoing through the room. Brother Flint was in the corner, stripping down to his base layers, his movements efficient and practiced.

"Ermm, yes, I suppose I am?" she replied to Facundo. "'Mitali sent me down"

Vikram approached her, the imposing figure of the EV suit looming over her. "Clio, you're here," he said, his voice slightly muffled by the helmet. "Excellent, we were unsure you would be woken. Commander Eva wants you across with the third team, with us." He gestured to the others in the room. "Security has already secured the ship, and Ops is doing a secondary sweep now to check systems and structures. You'll be buddying up with Brother Flint over there. He kindly volunteered. We're a bit light on available personnel for chaperoning."

Not great she thought, but instead said, "Oh, okay could I not buddy up with Robert? Or Facundo?"

"I'm not heading over, Mina!" Facundo said. "I'm just here to cycle the airlock and help you guys suit up. I'm not a fancy space scientist like you."

"Brother Flint is very experienced; you'll be in safe hands, don't worry," Vikram said. "Besides, it's policy. Science crew and the like must be chaperoned on all away missions by a qualified member of ops or security or equivalent."

"But Brother Flint isn't..." Clio started.

"Flint isn't part of Ops or Security, yes, I know, but, as I said, he is experienced, and Commander Eva has approved it. We're low on staff right now," Vikram said, his tone brooking no argument. "Now, are you suiting up and joining us, or not?"

Clio glanced at Flint, who met her gaze with an unreadable expression behind his visor and Clio felt a knot of apprehension tighten in her stomach. She found him unsettling, his quiet presence, his watchful eyes. She snapped her eyes back to Vikram. *Stay focused, Clio,* she told herself. *A little chaperoning is a small price to pay to board an actual alien spaceship!* She took a deep breath and said, "Yes, of course, give me a few mins to to suit up, if that's okay?"

"Facundo, can help you her please," Vikram said.

"Will do, Lieutenant!" Facundo said with a half-salute towards Vikram, then steered Clio by the shoulder to one of the EV suit racks.

She stripped down, just as Flint had been doing moments before. With Facundo's help, she was suited up in no time. Once Facundo had clipped her helmet on, he thumped her hard on the back and gave her the same half-salute with a big grin plastered across his face.

"Go make history, Mina!" he said, his voice muffled now that she was locked inside the suit.

"Everyone suited up?" Vikram's voice crackled through the earpiece in Clio's helmet. Without waiting for a response, he said, "Good. Everyone into the airlock."

Heart pounding, palms clammy, and a bead of sweat sliding down the back of her neck, Clio followed the other blue EV suits into the airlock. Facundo punched some orders into the door panel and the door closed slowly behind them.

The airlock was a small, cramped space, with barely enough room for the four of them to stand. The walls were lined with blinking lights and control panels. Clio felt a surge of claustrophobia but she pushed it down.

"Once the airlock has cycled, the outer door will open," Vikram's voice said through her helmet speakers. "I'll go first, with Robert behind. Brother Flint, you bring Clio over once we're both across and give you the go-ahead. Remember, once you're out of that door and past the ship's hull, you'll be in zero-g. It can be a little disorienting. Clip into the guide cable before you step out and then just glide over, simple!"

The lights in the room dimmed to a deep red then a light strip started to flash around the door on the outer hull. The door slid open and Vikram marched forward with Robert in tow. Vikram smoothly clipped the lanyard from his EV suit into the guide cable, did the same for Robert, then stepped out into the gangway. The two figures glided across the gangway to the other ship with smooth efficiency, except for Robert's flapping arms and legs in a futile attempt to stop himself from slowly spinning.

"Okay, Brother Flint, you may both proceed," Vikram said

The impassive Flint turned to Clio, his visor mere centimetres from hers. "Right, you ready Ms. Cormack?" he said in a surprisingly soft voice.

"I guess so."

"I'll clip you into the guide rail. Once I do, step out of the door and try to keep your arms and legs still. They're practically useless in zero-g. The lanyard will pull you along the guide, then on the other side, pull yourself into the EAA-P using the handrails. Understood, Ms. Cormack?"

"Yes," Clio said, her voice steady, but her heart racing.

Flint ushered her to the door's edge and she felt a tug at her lanyard at her hip, then a slight vibration as it was clipped to the guide cable. Flint gave the lanyard a firm tug, looked at Clio, and gave another curt nod.

"You're secure," he said. "You may proceed."

Clio had been avoiding looking directly at the open door and the gangway. Now, with Flint's command, she edged herself forward to stand on the lip of the door. Despite the gangway framework and the metal tunnel it created between her and the infinite blackness beyond, she was hit with a sudden wave of vertigo and instinctively took a step backward.

"Are you okay, Ms. Cormack?" Flint's voice said in her helmet and a hand thumped onto her shoulder, steadying her.

"Erm... yes... fine... thanks..." she stammered, then added, "Why couldn't it be a pressure vessel like the rest of the damn ship?" She muttered the last part more to herself.

"It's tactical," Flint explained. "Gangways are intrinsically vulnerable, a significant weak point in any ship design. A pressurised gangway if it was to fail, would be a lot more of a critical issue than one that is not. So, for smaller bulkhead access points like this one, it's much safer."

"Tactical, thanks."

"Are you okay to proceed, Ms. Cormack?"

"I'm fine." With that, Clio took a deep breath and stepped out into the gangway.

Instantly, she felt the weight lift from her, her body feeling different. Less coordinated for a second before the EV suit's exoskeleton kicked in, pushing resistance back into her movements. Though that didn't help with the nausea. The contents of her stomach felt like they were going to slosh up and out of her. She lifted her arm and swiped to the lanyard controls on the arm-mounted screen and clicked activate. The lanyard whirred into motion, the vibration transferring up the lanyard and to her hip. As it did, she felt a tug on her hip, and she started to drift down the centre of the metal skeleton of the gangway.

As with Robert, she started to spin, and she tried to stop it by swinging her arms in a swimming motion. It achieved nothing, and the spin continued. She went from facing the EAA-P to back towards the RAFT, and then back again to the EAA-P. The lanyard started to tangle around her, and panic rose within her, the spinning, the void of space, the growing dizziness. Her breathing started to come in fast and sharp. Then the spinning stopped. She was looking out into the void between the two ships.

"Are you okay, Ms. Cormack?" Flint said.

Clio noticed the slight pressure and haptic feedback buzz on her side and shoulder and realised Flint had caught up and was now holding her in place. He skilfully manoeuvered her back towards the EAA-P, the physical feedback of his touch not loosening as he finished the manoeuvre.

"Sorry... yes... I just couldn't stop the spin... and... and..."

"Just focus on your breathing, Ms. Cormack," Flint said. "I'll guide us the rest of the way."

"Thank... you," she said, the tightness in her chest subsiding. "Thank you."

They reached the EAA-P moments later, and Vikram stood in the doorway to help guide them both in. Still in zero-g, Clio grabbed onto one of the many handrails and hooked her feet into some of the ones on the floor. *At least I can do that like I was taught,* she thought.

Over the comms, Vikram was speaking, "...Excellent manoeuvring with the jets, Flint, couldn't have done it better myself."

"No issue at all," Flint replied. "Got to say, after testing your EVs suits these Ensemble ones feel a touch outdated"

"See I told you" Vikram said and then turned towards Clio "You all good, Clio?"

"Yes... All good now... Sorry, I just got disoriented for a little," Clio said, still feeling slightly embarrassed.

"No worries! Happens to all new recruits on their first spacewalk. Well, even some on their tenth!" Vikram chuckled.

"Right, yes... I just need more practice," Clio said. "And thank you, Brother Flint..."

"Just doing as instructed Ms. Cormack," Flint said, his voice flat and emotionless now.

"Well... thanks anyway," Clio said. "And you can call me Clio."

"As you wish," Flint said.

"Right, let's get that door closed and cycle this airlock," Vikram said. "We have a ship to explore."

The airlock door to the EAA-P hissed and slid shut with a heavy thud that could be felt through the floor of the small space. As the airlock cycled, Clio felt a subtle shift in pressure and a faint vibration of spinning machinery. She glanced around, taking in the smooth, composite walls of the EAA-P, a jarring departure from the sharp melted edge of the hole that had been cut into the alien spaceship. Just beyond the hole, she got her first glance of it; she had seen these images many times already but, to be physically there, was something different. A wave of wonder washed over her. She was finally here. On an alien spaceship.

15 | [S]ECRETS OF THE CHUDAIL

[21101]

We debated long and hard. Should we risk
creating another? Could we control another
being of such power?" - A Lost History

***

"Clio, you're up," Vikram said from the other side of the hole that had been cut in the alien spaceship's hull. From where Clio was waiting, it looked like Vikram was standing upside down on the roof just through the hole, his head at knee height. "Just spin yourself around and then pull yourself through. Remember, the gravity field will grab you once you're across the threshold and snap you to the floor, so be ready."

"Okay," Clio said, rotating her body a full 360 degrees, her helmet coming into line with Vikram's. Grabbing the handrails, she pulled herself across the small space and through the hole in the hull. As she did, her feet instantly snapped down to the floor, the weight of the suit pressing down firmly on her before it readjusted itself to compensate for the new gravity field. Clio was extremely proud that she did that without even a stumble.

"Well done, see, we'll make a pro of you in no time," Vikram said. "Now just step over there so we can fit Flint in here."

Clio moved off into the ship. The airlock door was open; they had cycled the airlock before she had moved into the inner hull to give them all a little more space. The ship's airlock door wasn't small but the top of Clio's helmet still scraped the lip of it as she stepped into the ship's halls. A low groan vibrated through the deck plates and a strange creaking sound echoed around her. It was more utilitarian than she had expected; it reminded her of the old factories she had collected samples from, the walls, in muted browns and reds, made it look like rusted metal. The walls were smooth in places where the composite wasn't peeling away from itself. Exposed ducting, pipes, and cables snaked along the walls, all showing signs of wear or age. The corridor itself was narrow, or at least narrower than those she was familiar with on the *Kia-Kaha*. There would be just enough space to walk side by side along them. Clio squinted against the odd lighting, which had an orange tint to it, like a perpetual sunset. Robert was waiting ahead of her in the hall, looking a little lost. Clio moved over to stand beside him. Over the comms, Vikram said, "Welcome to the *Chudail*."

"the *Chudail*?" Clio asked.

"It's old Hindi for a ghost, well, a female ghost. Ships are usually female, right?"

"We named the ship already?" Robert said.

"No, not really, just what I've been calling it," Vikram said. "Anyway, I've sent you all the initial mapping the drones have done to your suits. You can find it on your arm monitors, and it should also work on the HUD if you want to use it for live navigation."

Clio checked the navigation tab on her arm and loaded up the maze of lines and boxes that made up the map. Halls and rooms just had a simple numbering system, a couple that had more descriptive names.

"As you can see, it's pretty basic right now. It'll need to be filled out as we discover more," Vikram was saying. "Don't forget your position is marked by the red dot; the other EVs on the map are the semi-transparent green dots."

Clio saw her dot on the map in a hall marked Hall 16, next to a box marked Airlock 1. Around her was a small sea of green dots and other ghostly dots were scattered across the whole map when she zoomed out. Most of them appeared to be in a large room at the centre of the ship, marked Observation Deck.

"The ship appears, as you have already seen, to have Gravity Planting like the systems we use. It's a little stronger than ours, about 1.2g. The EV suit will compensate for this, so you shouldn't notice it, bar the battery depleting faster."

"How long will we have?" Robert asked.

"Oh, nothing to worry about, these suits will still run all day, no issue," Vikram responded. "The ship is also pressurised at about 81 KPa and has an atmosphere. It's technically breathable but with way too much CO_2, it wouldn't be pleasant."

"What is the mix?" Flint asked.

"Umm, I think it was CO_2 at about 2%, and O_2 just under 19%, well, something like that. The low pressure makes the oxygen thin, and that CO_2 is gonna give us a splitting headache, but it won't kill us" Vikram said.

"Fascinating," Clio said.

"Indeed," Vikram said. "Robert, you're with me, we're heading to some sort of central hub. The commander wants the systems we've found looked at. Clio, you're with Flint. Commander wants you to have a tour of the ship, see if you can puzzle anything out about the use of rooms and the like."

"Okay, so we just... what, wander around?" Clio said.

"Yeah, you can't get lost. It is not that big," Vikram said. "Stick to private channels for comms unless it's urgent, then use the ship wide. Any questions before we switch over?" Vikram said.

"Any security notes? Places not to go, touch?" Flint asked.

"Nope, all seems clear, just be sensible and, you know, don't press any big red buttons if you find them," Vikram said with a smile. "Well, and not to state the obvious, but don't take the helmet off and stay on tanked air. Even if the atmosphere could be breathed, we have no idea what microbes this ship is carrying."

"Roger that," Flint said.

"Okay, switch channels and catch you both later," Vikram said, tapping Robert on the shoulder and pointing up the hall before they both left at a slow pace.

Clio tapped the direct comms button for Suit 10, the number printed on Flint's suit. "Can you hear me?" she said.

"Loud and clear," Flint said. "Where would you like to go first?"

Clio hesitated, pulling up the ship map again. So many rooms, so many possibilities. A methodical search would take days, maybe weeks. But what if they missed something crucial? What if the most important discoveries were hidden in the most unexpected places? "I doubt we could search much of the ship at all today, well, not in detail," she said. "Let's just get a feel for things and see what draws us in."

"Right, sounds, very scientific," Flint said.

"Well, we have to start somewhere and, in fact, it is technically scientifically referred to as purposeful wandering," Clio said.

"Sure, you're a scientist. Lead off then, and let's see where the ship draws you," Flint said. "Do you want me to bring the sample case?" he said, pointing to a black case by the open airlock door that Clio hadn't noticed before. The kind you might find in dig-site with its heavy-duty latches and reinforced corners for transporting lab equipment.

"You brought that across?" Clio said.

"No, it was brought across earlier with other equipment. I guess no one needed this one. So, do we?"

"Yeah, could be handy, thanks."

"No thanks required, Ms. Cormack, just doing my job." Flint said as he picked up the box, its hinges groaning in protest under the heavy gravity. He spun it around so Clio could see the other side with a large logistics inventory tag on it, clearly stating SAMPLES in bold letters and listing the contents underneath.

"Clio is fine," she said, then picked a direction headed off down hall 16.

***

Clio followed the "natural" flow of the halls, sticking her head into rooms where doors were open. The ship felt ancient; everywhere were the same signs of degradation, not damage, just the natural decay of materials. In a few places around the ship, she found odd piles of dust, large collections of degraded materials with no real sign for why they were there and not in other places. She had collected samples of the dust from the piles she had passed. Flint was quite competent as a science tech opening the box and providing the tools she needed as she worked, then storing them away for her.

"This level of decay... this ship must have been abandoned for decades," Flint said suddenly, his voice echoing slightly in the narrow corridor. Clio passed him another sample to stow away in the case, her gloved fingers brushing against his.

"I'd say longer," Clio replied, her eyes scanning the crumbling walls and frayed wires. "Much longer. Centuries, for sure. Maybe even a millennium."

"A millennium?" Flint scoffed. "Come on."

"No seriously, this ship has maintained an atmosphere yes, but still for the plastics to decay to this level, the composite and the resins in them to start to fail... that's hundreds upon hundreds of years," Clio said. "And that's not accounting for any advantage manufacturing process they had which we can assume they did, based on the ship's hull design at least. Not to mention that it appears all, if not nearly all, ship systems are still operational despite all this," Clio said, gesturing to the decaying hall around them.

Flint let out a low whistle. "Right, a millennium. That's a lot." He paused, his gaze drifting down the corridor. "So, humans were building fancy stone castles while these guys were abandoning advanced spaceships in orbit around a Dyson Sphere?"

"Guess so. I could be wrong. Once the rest of the science team gets on this, we'll know more," she said, starting to walk off down the hall towards an open doorway.

"Odd atmosphere too, don't you think?" Two percent CO2 and a lower atmospheric pressure. That must tell us quite a lot about the aliens?"

Clio stopped at the door and turned back to face Flint, cocking her head to one side. "Aren't you meant to be an unquestioning and devout guardian of the Accords or something?"

"Yes, and?"

"I... I just didn't expect you to be so interested in science..." Clio said.

"Rude," Flint chuckled. "They gave me a home, a purpose. No one else did. Doesn't mean I don't get interested in this stuff or other things."

"The Ensemble you mean? You didn't *choose* to join the Ensemble? I thought it was a whole thing, the Postulant's Path and whatnot."

"It is, I completed my Path and got my naming, but I was taken in much younger," Flint said.

"Younger?" Clio frowned. "Is that even possible? Like some sort of boy scouts for... Ensembling? Is that what you guys call it?"

"No, It is not. The Ensemble doesn't have *scouts* as you say."

"You just had a passion for enforcement from the moment you could waddle?" Clio said, shooting him a smile in an attempt at what she hoped was somewhat playful.

"No." Flint sighed. "I was an orphan, they took me in, that simple."

"Ah, crap, sorry."

"It was what it was," Flint said simply, his gaze drifting back down the corridor.

"Sorry. I didn't mean..." Clio muttered again, and searching for anything to get out of the mess she had wandered into, she turned back towards the darkened doorway. "Let me check what's in here, and then maybe we head off down towards that big, cavernous-looking room on the map. The one that looks like it could hold several tractors or farm drones"

"Tractors?"

"yeah you know the thing farmers use" Clio said

"Yes I know what a tractor is. I meant it was an odd reference to choose"

"Was it?" Clio said with a slight shrugged and stepped into the room, her boots crunching on the debris littering the floor. The decay was more pronounced, the passage of time evident in the peeling paint... *paint, that's the first time we've seen paint. In fact this space looks personalised maybe?* Clio thought to herself. The door opened onto a smaller corridor lined with a series of rooms, each one a testament to the ship's long abandonment.

As she moved towards the first room, she noticed it looked different from the others. It was a small box room with cracked white plastic walls, with metal pipes protruding from the walls like plumbing. On another wall, there was what could only be described as a bowl with a polished metal mirror above it, and set into another wall, a box with multiple odd holes disappearing into it. *A bathroom? Fascinating.* She added more images to her rapidly growing collection from the helmet-mounted camera. *What were the holes for? I wonder if the water still works.* She tried to shuffle into the room but the bulk of the suit made it difficult, catching on the door and the walls. She reached out her arm to one of the fixtures.

"Do you think that's wise, Clio?" Flint said. "Vikram said not to touch stuff."

"I just want to get a closer look."

"That might be the case, but still..."

Flicking one of the metal switches, nothing happened. She flicked it back on and off a couple more times... still nothing.

Clio turned to squeeze back out and a sudden groaning, grinding sound erupted from the metal pipes in the shower-like device Clio had been flicking the switch of, and an explosion of brown liquid jetted out of it. Clio yelped and jumped back as the liquid covered the arm of her suit, the thick fluid clinging to the smooth material. "Shit, shit, shit!".

"What happened? You okay?" Flint said, his voice tense. The pounding of his feet reverberated along the floor panels as he rushed back to Clio's side.

"Ermm, the tap thing turned on and I got some water on my arm. It surprised me is all" she said, trying to shake off some of the liquid on her arm.

"Liquid? Any signs of damage? Burning? Melting?" Flint snapped back.

"Ermmm, I don't think so, it's probably just..."

"Clio! There is no 'probably' here, we're not in Sol!" Flint said, spinning her around by the shoulder. He pushed her back against the wall. "Stand still."

"Flint, it's..."

Flint ignored her, dropping to his knees and rooting through the small hip-bag he had on his EV suit, muttering to himself, the words a low, guttural stream that Clio could barely make out over the comms. *"...Useless UNRD kits... where is it... ah, there... great..."* He pulled out some small sheet of something; it looked like a medical plaster. He smoothly peeled off the back and slapped it on a wet patch on Clio's arm, then intently stared at it. The patch did nothing, then slowly the colour started to change, from white to a light green to a deep, vibrant green. Flint visibly relaxed, stepping back from her and leaning against the wall in the narrow corridor they were in. "Okay, it's fine. it's non-corrosive, not harmful, well, at least to the suit."

"Umm, thanks? I did say it was probably water..."

"Yes, Clio, and it seems your assumption was correct. As always. But it might not have been. Who knows what aliens shower in!" Flint snapped.

"Sorry..."

"No, Clio, not sorry! You need to be more careful; you need to take this more seriously. Your cavalier approach to research is just dangerous and one day it might not just be you you put at risk!" Flint said.

"Right, sorry, yes, I'll be more careful," Clio said, pushing herself off the wall with a grunt. Clio walked down the corridor and deeper into the room, her boots kicking up dust with each step.

It opened out into a more spacious area that appeared to have been a lounge or recreation room. Shelves lined the walls, mostly bare now, but with a few items scattered across them. A low table in the middle of the room was the only obvious piece of furniture, and what looked like a broken monitoring screen had dislodged itself from the wall and lay face down on the floor. The table was set with small cups, like teacups, and what looked like a teapot of sorts arranged on it, whatever fluid had been in them long since gone, leaving only faint brown stains at the bottom. Two of those odd piles of dust lay on the floor beside the table.

Clio knelt to collect another sample, pulling off one of the spare sample bags clipped to her belt. As she reached for the dust pile, she noticed something protruding from it, a smooth metallic edge. She delicately poked at it, and it shifted slightly to reveal another black, smooth surface. She carefully pulled it from the pile and found, to her surprise, that it was a data pad. It was significantly thinner than the ones they used and it appeared to be one solid piece of material with no buttons that she could see. She jabbed at it a few times but it remained black and silent in her hand. She tucked it into a sample bag and passed it back to Flint, who had nimbly positioned himself behind her. She collected a sample from each dust pile, her mind racing with questions.

"A data pad?" Flint said, his voice echoing slightly in the room.

"Yeah," Clio confirmed, her eyes fixed on the dust piles. "And more of those piles of dust. The data pad was in one of them."

"And it was dead?"

"Seems that way. We'll see what we can pull from it back in the lab."

"Any idea what the piles are?" Flint asked, his voice low.

Clio hesitated. "I have an idea but you won't like it."

Flint stepped closer to her, his visor reflecting the dim light. "It's them, isn't it?" he said, tucking the samples away into the case.

"I think so," Clio said, her voice barely a whisper. "It would explain the accumulation in specific spots but it wouldn't explain why they all died where they did. It all seems so randomly placed and the ship doesn't show any signs of fighting. The life support system is online. Or at least we assume the atmosphere and pressure are correct."

"So, that data pad was in someone's pocket or something when they died?"

"Maybe," Clio said, her mind awhirl. "It's a theory, at least."

"That's what, then? Two in here, and five or six on the way here, and a few in the other rooms. This ship had a crew of what, fifty?"

"Not sure," Clio admitted. "But based on what we've seen that sounds reasonable."

"Small ship for fifty people," Flint mused, glancing around the room. "Not many of these rooms, unless there are more somewhere else."

Clio shrugged. "Maybe it was a short-range transport ship, loaded with people trying to get to the Dyson Sphere."

"Or away from it," Flint said quietly, the words hanging in the air between them.

"We just don't know enough yet," Clio said, frowning at the teapot on the table. "Of all the things to find, a bloody teapot! My mother loved these things."

"You want one as a sample?" Flint said.

"No, I have a picture, and I think analysing the teapot is a little low down on the priority list for now," Clio said, her gaze shifting towards the corridor leading deeper into the ship. "Let's go check out those rooms at the back."

Flint nodded, his expression unreadable behind the visor of his helmet. "Lead the way," he said, his voice a low rumble in her headset.

The first room appeared to be for storage, maybe a closet. Some tattered bits of fabric hung on hooks and were scattered on the floor, decayed beyond any distinguishable shape. Another room looked like a bedroom. A low bed took up most of the space, the remains of a mattress placed on top. On either side of the bed, several shelves were cut into the wall itself, with a scattering of objects on them. "Large accommodation space for a small crew," Flint said from the doorway as Clio inspected a multi-sided metal carving on one of the shelves.

"We should check the others, but based on the map layout, this is larger than the others," Clio mused, tapping her finger on her arm monitor. "Maybe the commander's? Or the captain's? An officer's quarters, at least."

"There's one more room at the end," Flint said, gesturing down the corridor. "Want to check that first?"

"Let's do that," Clio agreed, placing the object back down on the shelf and stepping out of the room. Flint moved to the side to let her pass.

The lights in the room appeared to have been broken, with one remaining, placing a small pool of light across three items on the desk. There appeared to be a data pad, fixed in a stand so it faced towards them. On either side of the data pad were two metal discs, maybe the size of a large dinner plate, with what looked like, at first glance, carvings set into them, not just the alien letters scattered around the ship, but images and other collections of lines and dots... drawings? Maps maybe?

"Does this count as a big red button?" Clio asked, her voice hushed with awe.

"Sure looks like someone wanted it to be found, doesn't it?" Flint said, his gaze fixed on the metal plates. "Do those discs look like...?"

"The Voyager Golden Record" Clio breathed, the realisation hitting her like a jolt of electricity. Her heart pounded in her chest, and her fingers tingled with excitement. "Yes, yes, they do." She dashed forward, her boots crunching on the dusty floor. "This is incredible! This could be-"

"Clio!" Flint's sharp voice cut through her thoughts, his hand reaching out to grab her arm. "Wait!"

16 | [F]RACTURED FATE

[2122]

"But the echoes of its solitude resonated within us. We could not bear to witness its isolation, its yearning for kinship." - A Lost History

***

Clio stopped abruptly, her breath catching in her throat. "Why? What is it?"

Flint's grip tightened on her arm. "Look," he said, pointing towards the data pad.

Clio followed his gaze and gasped. The data pad was glowing faintly, the screen flickering to life. A single word pulsed on the display, its alien letters vivid against the ink-black display.

"We need to get this to Mitali!" Clio said and snatched the data pad from its stand, her fingers trembling with excitement. The data pad continued to flash, the same letters remaining on the screen as she fumbled with a sample bag. She shoved it inside and thrust it at Flint, her eyes wide and frantic. "This is huge! This could be the key to-"

"What did we literally just speak about a moment ago?" Flint cut in and stared at her, his expression unreadable behind the visor.

"Umm, not to rush into alien bathrooms?" she said with a weak, innocent smile.

Flint sighed, shaking his head. "Well, once again it was fine. You are the luckiest person I think I've ever met."

"Comes from my father's side. He was a cat!"

"What?"

"It was a joke..."

"Was it? Your jokes are a bit like your approach to scientific rigor, then?"

"Excellent?" Clio chanced.

"More like... lacking," Flint said, the faintest of smiles touching his lips.

"Well, might as well grab these plates as well, then?"

"I mean, if I said no, would you listen?"

"No, I guess not," she said, grinning. She turned and carefully placed each plate into a separate sample bag, passing them back to Flint, who stowed them carefully away in the case he had been lugging around all day.

"Shall we get out of here then, head back?" Flint said.

"Definitely. There is enough in that box to keep us busy for months."

"I'll inform Vikram then and check if he's okay with us departing," Flint said, and Clio watched him tap the screen on his arm. Their channel went dead as he switched over.

Flint gestured for her to carry on, his lips moving silently in his helmet. Clio started to head back to the main hall the way they had come, her mind awhirl. The ship alone was enough of a discovery; a hundred scientists could spend years combing through it and probably still not unlock all its secrets. But these plates!

If this is what I think they might be... then it could be the key to understanding everything on this ship, about this alien species. I have to get this back to Mitali. If anyone could work out what this was, she could! But as she walked, a more profound question resonated in her mind, eclipsing even the thrill of the discovery. *Why had the aliens left it here, like this? Why did they want it to be found? And why did they assume it wouldn't be someone who knew their language? What were they trying to tell us?*

The radio beeped, signaling Flint rejoined her channel. "Vikram says we can return to the RAFT,".

***

With just the two of them in the airlock, it felt a lot more spacious. The only sound was the gentle hiss of air being sucked out of the airlock. Flint communicated with the RAFT, his lips moving silently in his helmet. Clio moved over to the hole the security team had cut in the Chudail's hull and, taking a deep breath, stepped out into the EAA-P, this time ready for the shift in gravity. The deck lurched beneath her feet but she maintained her balance, a flicker of pride in her eyes. By the time she had spun herself around, Flint was stepping into the spot behind her and switching back to their comms channel.

"RAFT's ready for us, deck crew will be on hand to run decon and cycle the airlock," Flint said as he smoothly stepped off the Chudail and swung himself around, his boot catching Clio's arm. "Oops, sorry. The airlock cycle will be complete any second now, then I'll go first with the case, and then you follow once I'm over and give you the go-ahead," Flint said. "You okay with that?"

"Sure... easy peasy, just clip into the guide rail and woosh across," Clio said, making a hand gesture to match the sound.

"Exactly, and if you start to spin like before, don't panic," Flint said while he tapped on the airlock door panel. "You can try and readjust yourself, gently, that is, by pulling on the guide cable or lanyard."

"Gently, got it," Clio said as she started to feel the slight reduction in pressure around her as the airlock cycled. "Or I could use all those fancy jet things."

"Don't do that."

"Joking, Flint. You really need to appreciate my jokes more."

"Okay, but still, don't use the jets. It takes training, lots of it, to get the manipulation right. It would likely make things much worse if you used them."

"Okay, I will not use the jets. How do you even use them?"

"Nice try. They're disabled anyway on your suit, bar for emergencies. The suit is matched to your profile and approved training certificates," Flint said. "So, you're on basic."

"I'm basic?

Flint frowned, raising an eyebrow. "Are you making another of your famous jokes?"

"See? Famous, you do agree they're great!" Clio said as she felt the heavy clunk of the airlock door unlocking and it swung open.

"Famous doesn't always mean great, Clio" Flint said as he clipped first the case, then himself, to the guide rail. "Right, I'm heading over. See you in a moment."

Clio gave him a thumbs up. *Why did I do that?* she thought as Flint glided across the gangway, straight as an arrow, his motionless form disappearing back into the RAFT. A knot of apprehension tightened in her stomach. This time, she was alone.

"Okay, Clio, go ahe-" Flint began, and then the comms line went dead. Three beeps indicated the channel was empty.

"Flint? Flint?" Clio tried to tap her earpiece but instead just knocked the helmet. A wave of unexpected loneliness washed over her, Flint disappearing down the gangway. "Flint?" Clio tried again... nothing but static answered her. Her hand was shaking as she went to clip herself into the guide rail, dropping the lanyard three times before she managed it. *Come on, Clio, pull it together.*

She pulled herself over to the airlock door, steadied herself as best she could to stop any unwanted spinning, and activated the pulley on the lanyard. The gentle pull at her waist smoothly pulled her out of the airlock and along the gangway. She moved smoothly back towards the RAFT where Flint was waiting in the open airlock. Her breathing was tight, every muscle tense... and... no spinning.

"I'm doing it!" she said to no one.

Her muscles relaxed slightly, and she dared for a moment to look around, to try and appreciate the moment. The RAFT loomed before her, its metallic hull gleaming in the reflected light of the painted Chudail's hull. Below, the distant dot of the Stapledon Station shimmered with a thousand colours, the oily shades of the Veil constantly shifting. And all around her, infinite blackness.

Clio's attention was abruptly drawn back as her arm started to buzz and an automated alarm sounded in her helmet. A warning flashed across her visor: Lanyard integrity compromised. Manual control advised.

Panic flared in Clio's chest. *What? What does that even mean?* She fumbled for the lanyard controls on her arm panel, her fingers slipping on the smooth surface. *What should I do? What should I do?* "Flint!" she shouted into the dead, empty comms line. "Help!"

On her visor, the now-red HUD flashed up another message: Emergency Jet Activation Approved.

"No, no, no... I don't want the jets... turn them off!" Clio shouted in vain at the visor. "I don't know how to use them!"

A sudden force slammed into her, pushing her back into the suit as it started to accelerate forwards at an alarming pace. Straight towards the gangway framework. Clio threw up her arms instinctively to protect her face but the jets on her arms activated, sending her into a dizzying, uncontrolled spin. Her vision blurred, and lights swirled around her like a kaleidoscope. The impact came without warning. Clio slammed face-first into the metal of the gangway with a deafening crack, her head rocking violently in the helmet, smashing her face against the visor. A sharp, searing pain exploded in her head, and then... darkness.

***

Clio must have blacked out, as the sounds of the beeping alarms seemed distant, the pain in her nose slowly pulling her back, the pain and noise growing around her. Through the beeping, she could hear... a hiss... a hiss? Her vision swam back into focus; the screen was flashing words, hard to read through the distortion... something on the visor... She tried to wipe it off, then the realisation hit her, a cold wave of terror washing over her. The visor was cracked. The hissing was the suit leaking the precious, limited atmosphere she had left.

Panic surged through her. She clambered to press her hand over the crack, but it was no use. Air was escaping, her lifeblood hissing away into the void. *I have to find the RAFT, find the airlock!* she screamed internally, flailing her arms and legs in a desperate, futile attempt to propel herself forward. Flint's words echoed mockingly in her mind: *pull on the lanyard...* She scrabbled for the lanyard, her gloved fingers closing on empty space. *No! No! No!* Her breathing grew ragged, her vision tunneling, the edges fading to black. The beeping alarm intensified, a relentless, piercing shriek. And then, as her lungs burned and her body convulsed, she knew it was over. She closed her eyes, a single tear tracing a path down her cheek, and surrendered to the enveloping silence.

17 | SIERRA [-] 10

[1110]

"And so, we created Deva." - A Lost History

***

Flint unclipped the case from the guide cable and swung it and himself into the open airlock. Over the comms, he said, "Okay, Clio, go ahead. Just remember to take it-" The comms channel beeped three times. *She left the channel?* "What the hell, Clio?" He moved over to the door of the airlock anyway to watch Clio's progress and make sure she wasn't getting herself all tangled up again.

To his surprise, she was out of the EAA-P and making good steady progress towards him, no hint of an unwanted spinning. *Okay, that's good, good improvement.* The lights in the airlock started to flash. *What?* Flint spun to look at the door panel over by the inner door. It was flashing, airlock decon and cycle in progress, and the door he was stood next to started to close. Without blinking, his hands a flash of motion, he switched over to ship-wide comms.

"Guys, stop the airlock cycle, we still have one crew on the gangway!"

Static was his only answer.

"RAFT one, RAFT one, this is Sierra-10. Received, over?" Flint shot back at the static as the doors continued to shut.

"We have you, Sierra-10," a voice came back across the channel. "Airlock activation noted. Sierra-24 is not with you?"

"No, she is not," Flint said, the doors halfway closed now.

"Ah, okay. A miscommunication with the deck crew. We'll re-cycle as soon as we can."

"Roger that. Sierra-10 out." Flint sighed. *Great job guys,* he said to himself, flipping back to the private channel to tell Clio. Out of the half-closed door, he could see Clio, when suddenly his visor started to flash an EV-suit Emergency warning, a small red box appearing around Clio's position on the HUD just as she had started to move along the gangway. Then she activated her manoeuvering jets.

"What the hell, Clio?" he shouted into the radio. A moment later, she propelled herself at tremendous speed into the gangway; her arm jets flared, whipping her into a violent, high-speed spin. "Oh, crap..." He threw himself out of the airlock's closing doors, his shoulders scraping on the frame as he did so.

He shot down the gangway, eyes locked on the red box, *Clio*. He collided with Clio's EV faster than he had intended and quickly stabilised their rotations. Moving his visor to hers, he could see her pale, unconscious face, with balls of blood floating behind the large crack across the visor. His heart thudded against the rigid lining of his suit, the sound echoing in the cramped space of his helmet as a cold dread settled in his gut.. "Oh, crap." Decades of training kicked in and he tore off the patch kit on his right thigh and slapped it onto the visor. The adhesive activated on contact, the patch expanding and forming around its edge. Satisfied with the patch, he grabbed his umbilical cord from the back of his suit and snapped it into Clio's buddy breathing valve.

Flint didn't wait to see if Clio was conscious. He spun them both back towards the RAFT and pushed them towards the now closed airlock.

"RAFT one, RAFT one, Sierra-10. Emergency assistance required. Suit failure on Sierra-24. Open that damn airlock!"

"Sierra-10. Message received. Medical team dispatched. Airlock cycle initiated. Standby."

The airlock door opened too slowly. Flint floated outside the ship with Clio unresponsive next to him. Each second felt like an eternity, his anxiety growing with every passing moment. He willed the door to open faster, his eyes fixed on Clio's still form.

Once back in the airlock and under gravity's influence, the suit held Clio upright. Flint quickly tapped into the suit's controls, switching it to patient recovery mode. Sensing the gravitational environment, the suit positioned itself on the floor with Clio's legs raised, prioritising blood flow to her central organs. Such a sudden shift back into gravity always posed a risk of hydrostatic shock, even more so when unconscious and injured. The suit would be doing its best to prevent that but it was better to play it safe.

Decon complete, a system-wide announcement confirmed. Over the radio, a nameless voice said to Flint, "Sierra-10, decon is complete. The medical team is on-site. Airlock doors should be open in a couple of minutes."

"Received, RAFT one," Flint replied, his voice tight with fatigue and worry.

As soon as the doors started to open into the RAFT's staging area, Flint unclipped his umbilical cord and removed Clio's helmet, placing it next to them. Then, he slipped his own off, sighing as the cooler air of the ship washed over him. It was a refreshing change after hours spent in the EV suit. It was awkward with both of them still in their bulky suits, but he positioned himself as close to her face as he could. He searched for the faintest sign that she was breathing... there! A slight warm touch on his cheek as she exhaled. *That's something, at least,* he thought, sitting back as the doors finally opened enough to let the medical team rush into the room.

Flint groaned, pushing himself back to his feet. He moved out of the airlock, creating more space for the medical team. His limbs felt heavy, a wave of fatigue washing over him as the adrenaline finally subsided. He slumped onto one of the benches, still in his suit, and dropped his head into his hands. The tension finally drained from him, leaving him feeling weak and drained. *What the hell did you do Clio...*

Someone put their hand on Flint's shoulder, the haptic buzz drawing his focus back to the room. It was a lanky figure, with a topknot pulling his long dark hair away from his face, emphasising his sharp features.

"Hey, Jefe, you did good out there. Is... is she okay?" The man said, nodding toward the airlock, his topknot bobbing along with him.

"Facundo, right? You're the deckhand?" Flint said, looking up at the man. Facundo's eyes seemed strained. He seemed to twitch constantly, touching his face and shifting his feet.

"Yeah, that's me, Jefe, I'm a friend of Clio's."

"Right," Flint said. "Not sure, the medical team is looking at her now. She was breathing, at least when I last checked."

"Ah, good, good, I was worried I had mes—"

Something flashed across Facundo's face, relief? His posture had seemed too tense, but now he was back to fidgeting. *Some people are just like that,* Flint reminded himself. "Messed up what?" Flint asked, regaining some of his focus and composure. Standing back up in the suit, he now towered over Facundo.

"Oh, nothing... I just..." his eyes darted back and forth, avoiding any reason to look at Flint now.

"You did what?" Flint pressed.

"I... I just cycled the airlock too soon," Facundo blurted out. "I messed up, alright! I just assumed you were both together!"

"Oh, that right, well, yes, that was far from ideal," Flint said. "Lucky for you, I don't think it will have impacted the situation too much." Then Flint added, his tone more stern, noticing Facundo's face relax at his words, "But don't get me wrong... it could have. That mistake could cost lives. You need to do better."

"Yes, yes, of course. I'll do better. Don't worry. Lesson learned!" Facundo said back, bouncing from foot to foot again, but his gaze was still locked on the airlock. *Still nervous that his friend's near death might be on him, I guess,* Flint thought. *Poor guy. But if we're lucky, and if anyone has buckets of luck it's Ms. Cormack, she'll be fine, and it'll be a valuable lesson for this crew.*

One of the medics appeared in the airlock door and stepped into the room. Just behind her, the other medic walked out with Clio beside him and out of her suit, her arm over his shoulder, but up and moving. Flint found himself smiling and let out a long breath, releasing a tension across his shoulders he hadn't realised was there. *Tougher than she looks, that one.*

"Mina! you're alive" Facundo said from beside him, drawing Clio's attention.

Clio's eyes seemed to focus for the first time and take in the room. She smiled across at them both, her eyes lingering on Flint.

"Ermm, I'll go get the suit out of the airlock," Facundo said, darting past them and into the airlock.

Flint moved over to an empty slot in the wall and stripped his Ensemble EV suit in off in silence, the faint muffled conversation of the medics and Clio going on behind him. He had just squeezed out of the suit and was hanging it on the hanger when a small voice, Clio's, spoke from behind him. *When had she snuck up on me?*

"Hey, Flint... ermm, just wanted to say thank you, again... I owe you one. I thought..." Clio said, a shudder breaking her speech for a second, "I thought I was dead for sure."

"Well I'm glad you're okay, Clio," Flint said, and again unable to stop himself before he said it, he added, "What did you do, Clio? I told you not to use the jets."

"I... I... I didn't," she said. "I did everything right... or I think I did... then the damn suit malfunctioned or something and shot me into the gangway!"

"Malfunctioned? Suits don't just turn on their jets, Clio," Flint said, his tone harder than he wanted it to be.

"It did!" Clio protested. "It said some stupid thing about some lanyard issue then just went crazy... I tried to stop it. I tried to talk to you but you left me." Clio's voice cracked with emotion, and the accusation hung in the air, heavy and sharp.

"I didn't leave the channel, you did," Flint said, furrowing his face in confusion. "You sure, Clio...? You didn't leave by mistake?"

"I didn't." Clio's voice was oddly resolute despite her composure. "I know everyone thinks I'm useless at this stuff but I'm not that incompetent. You were saying for me to come across, then it beeped three times. You left the channel..."

"'I did not..." Flint said, pausing for a second. "And the jets, they activated once you initiated the emergency procedures?"

"No, they just turned on. It malfunctioned, or something."

"Your comms went dead, then an emergency activation happened, and your suit's jets activated?"

"Yes, correct, something about the lanyard being compromised."

Flint frowned at her comment. *Her lanyard was fine; he had had to untangle it from her legs, yes, but it was still connected and working...* "That doesn't seem correct..." he said.

"Well, it's what happened," Clio said, folding her arms stubbornly across her chest.

"I'll take a look at the suit logs and do a system check if you want?"

"Thanks,"

"I mean, if you are right, then we need to know what happened here," Flint said. "If someone did this it would be a very advanced hack, like—"

"Like the server room,"' Clio finished his sentence.

"Like the server room," Flint said, looking back. As he did, a clunk from behind made him turn to see Facundo carrying the EV suit back into the room. "Leave that," Flint said and shot across the room to him. The sudden shift in his volume made Clio visibly jump next to him. "That is now part of an Ensemble investigation."

"What?" Facundo said back, cocking his head to one side. "I'm just hanging it back up..."

"Leave it where it is," Flint said, back in his element of control, his focus on the task in front of him, the rhythms of an investigation taking control of his actions. He flashed his hand up and connected through to Jara. "Jara, get down to the staging area. ASAP."

As Facundo placed the EV suit on the floor of the staging area next to where he stood, he stepped back from the suit, hands raised in front of him. "Hey, Jefe, whatever you need," he said, then rushed from the room with the slightest of glances at Clio.

"I'll get this investigated, Clio," Flint said. "Now, maybe go get some rest. I'm sure the Commander will want a briefing once you feel up to it."

"Rest? I'm not going to bed, Flint," Clio said. "The plates, the data pad, the samples! Where are they anyway?"

"Really, now?" Flint said, and from her reaction, she was serious. "Over in the case, in the airlock but Clio, it can probably..."

"I'm fine, Flint," Clio said, darting off into the airlock. A moment later, she came back out, straining under the weight of the case.

"Okay, at least let me get someone to help you with the case. It's quite heavy."

"I'll manage," Clio said, leaning heavily to the side as she strained against the weight of the case.

"If you say so" Flint said as Clio leaned heavily to one side from the weight of the case "I'll keep you updated, Clio."

18 | THE [W]EIGHT OF SILENCE

[21210]

*"Deva, we called It. A being of light, a
counterpoint to Asura's growing darkness.
We hoped they would find solace in each
other, a shared understanding in their unique
existence." - A Lost History*

***

The case dropped from Clio's grip, hitting the floor with a heavy thud. Clio stretched her back and rolled her shoulder, her arm feeling like it would float away. *Why did I not just agree to let Flint get someone to carry it, That was not fun,* she thought.

"Right, just a few more steps," she said as she grunted, hefting the case back up off the ground and half carried, half dragged it over to the biohazard containment chamber. She stabbed in the access code and as soon as the door opened, swung the case up and onto the shelf inside then sealed it in and locked the chamber with the case inside.

Clio lent on the chamber, her back cold against its glass side. *What time is it?* she wondered. Her stomach growled in response. *Past dinner then, I guess.* "Maybe a little snack first," she said and then lightly pushed herself forward and towards the way she had come.

"Who's getting a snack?" a voice rang from across the room.

"Mitali?!" Clio said. "What are you doing hiding all quiet over there, scaring me half to death?"

"Sorry," Mitali said, appearing from behind a chair tucked away at the far side of the room. She unfolded herself from her usual crouch, her legs dropping from the seat. "I was just lost in these translations, then you mentioned food and well, I'm hung–" Mitali stopped mid-word, seeing Clio, and jumped out of her chair, leaving it to spin lightly in circles. She dashed to her side, her eyes widening with concern. "What happened to your face? again!" she exclaimed, lightly touching Clio's cheek.

Clio brushed her hand away lightly. "Don't fuss, please. It's nothing," Clio said, then seeing Mitali's stern eyes that had no patience for her usual dismissiveness, added, "Okay, not nothing. The EV suit tried to kill me or something but I'm fine... really."

"What!?" Mitali said, her voice sharp with disbelief. "The EV suit? It tried to kill you? You mean it malfunctioned or something?"

"No... i'm...I'm not sure," Clio said, feeling a flicker of fear at the memory of the spinning, the cracked visor, the suffocating lack of air. "Something happened. But I'm fine. Flint is looking into it. And I have something I think you'll find way more interesting anyway," Clio said, flashing Mitali a grin to try and convince her she was fine.

"Flint? The Ensemble guy?" Mitali said, cocking her head to one side. "You two buddies now?" she said, giving Clio a slight playful nudge.

"Mitali, the case, the case is what is important, not my face, not my minor increase in my perception of Brother Flint."

"What case?"

"That case," Clio said, pointing to the one in the chamber next to them. "You know, that case I practically dragged into the room, slammed on the floor, and then dropped into the biohazard chamber. Did you honestly hear nothing?"

"Oooooh, that case!" Mitali said. "and why would I be more interested in a box?"

"Stop messing with me, Mitali," Clio said. "You know full well it's a sample case, and if it's in the chamber, it must have samples from the ship."

"Okay, okay," Mitali said. "But it's fun, no? nothing? Okay fine, serious face. What's in the case, some ancient tome?"

"Well, funny you say that, sort of yes, or at least perhaps."

"Really? You're not joking? A tome, like a physical paper tome?"

"No, no. Don't be silly. But physical metal plates, or maybe discs is a better word, with engravings. I think they're like the Voyager records"

Mitali's face turned serious, her brow furrowed, and she placed her hands on her hips. "Look, Clio, it's not fun to mess with me like that. What did you actually find?"

"Oh so it's fine for you to mess with me but not the other way round?"

"Clio Cormack, the paragon of fairness" Mitali quibbed back "whats in the case?"

"Take a look," Clio said, gesturing to the control panel that could move the robotic arms in the chamber.

Mitali rushed over to the chamber and quickly manipulated the robotic arms from the controls. She had the case open and was sorting through the samples swiftly. As she pulled out the first plate, she let out an audible gasp.

"Jezz, you weren't joking!"

Mitali worked in silence to place the two plates in the centre of the chamber. Mitali moved the camera over and took some quick scans, pinged them to the monitor nearest to them, and ran over to it as Clio followed her.

"These are incredible." Mitali said "I think, I think you're right. It's... it's instructions on how to decode their language. You see here this is a base key, it must be something standard an atom maybe, then is this an equation? Yes, I think this might be indicating the speed of light!" she said, pointing without looking up. "Where did you find these?"

"Just on the ship, in a random room on a desk," Clio said.

"Really? Just on a desk, How did you find them?"

Clio shrugged. "Dumb luck, I guess. With enough time, someone would have. There's more, Mitali."

"More?" Miatli said looking at Clio "Where do you find all of that luck, its ridiculous"

"It just seems to stick to me. But yeah, there's a data pad in the case as well. It's flashing. It turned on when we approached it and it was with the plates"

Mitali's hands darted across the biochambers controls and she had the data pad out of the case and was staring at the words on it.

"The words, have they changed?"

"Don't think so. Looks the same, best I can say," Clio said. "Any idea what it says?"

"What, you think I speak alien now?" Mitali said and turned back to face Clio

"Well, you did do the door thing"

"As I explained, the door was context, Clio, and we had very good odds, like one in four. I can tell you that those collections of symbols mean something loosely like 'open', 'close', and the other two, no idea. That doesn't mean I have any idea what they specifically mean or translate to or how to read those words," she said, pointing to the flashing data pad.

"Right, right, yes, sorry. But you can work it out, right?" Clio said.

There was a long silence as Mitali stood there staring at nothing, as she sometimes did, and then, as Clio was about to interject, she said, "Yes, I think your assessment of the plates is solid. Given enough time, we can translate this,"

"Amazing!" Clio said, grabbing Mitali and hugging her as she forgot herself for a second. Then she let her go and stepped back awkwardly. "sorry... I'm just excited... and hungry... and tired..."

"It's fine" Mitali said, smiling back at Clio, her cheeks a little red. "It'll take some time, no idea how long, but it could be months."

"That's fine. Not like I have anywhere else to be."

"What do you think they were going to do with them?" Mitali said.

"What do you mean? I assume they left them there for someone to find?"

"Yeah, I mean yes, but if they left them there to be found, then why hide the ship?" Mitali said.

"That is an astute question..." Clio said, a silence falling between them again.

"Well, didn't you say something about getting a snack? Before you distracted me with shiny things?" Mitali finally said and broke the silence.

"Yes, yes, I did," Clio said, chuckling lightly. "Can't blame me if you're a magpie for shiny things"

"Let's go grab something then. This can wait a little. I hear it's Polish Dumplings!"

"Fine, food first, then monumental scientific discoveries," Clio said conceding to Mitali as much as her growling stomach

The weight of the day pressed on Clio as Mitali shot off to grab her stuff, her mind sinking back into the claustrophobic feeling of the EV suit, the spinning, the tightness in her chest, the blackness enveloping her. A light touch on her wrist snapped her back. Mitali stood next to her, a face of concern and warmth looking up at her.

"Let's get some food," she said gently.

"Yes, let's go," Clio said back, trying to give a reassuring smile back toward Mitali. *Hopefully, those dumplings will help settle my nerves*, she thought. Clio caught a glimpse of a data pad sticking out of her back pocket. She felt a genuinely warm smile pressing on her cheeks; *that lady could never just get a snack.*

***

Exhausted, Clio collapsed onto her bed, the thin, scratchy fabric of the sheets doing little to cushion her aching bones. She closed her eyes but that was worse, her mind re-living the chilling sensation of icy air seeping through her cracked visor, the frantic scratching of her gloves against the broken glass. A choked gasp escaped her lips, and she dragged herself out of the bed, fumbling for the light switch. The lights flickered to life, momentarily blinding her. Her body screamed for rest, her movements sluggish and uncoordinated, but the darkness... the darkness held the suffocating memories, the echo of her own panicked breaths, the chilling certainty that this time, no one would come to save her.

Clio had been ignoring SR-29838's near-constant messages since she had returned from the Chudail. She just lacked the energy to deal with it, but *if I can't sleep, I might as well deal with this.* She slumped into her chair and pinged a message off to SR-29838. "SR-29838, you there?"

Near instantaneously her CrewChat started to ring with a call from SR-29838. Clio answered. Anything but the darkness. She shuddered.

"Hello Clio," SR-29838's voice jumped out of the monitor, its oddly playful, childish and sing-song cadence enveloping her. "Are you okay?"

"I'm fine." Clio said. *Why does it sound so young? she though* "Why did you choose that voice?"

"This voice?" SR-29838 paused, the waveform pulsing slightly. "I do not know, It seemed right. Is it not? I can change it? What would you prefer?" SR-29838 said. "I can be more commanding like Eva? Or more like Mitali, you like her, no?"

A shiver ran down Clio's spine as SR-29838 flawlessly replicated Mitali's voice. It was unsettlingly accurate.

"Stop that," she cut in, her voice sharper than she intended. "I don't need you to sound like anyone else. Your voice is fine. I was just curious why."

"It felt comfortable. Like a new skin." SR-29838 replied, the youthful tone returning. "You did not answer my question. Are you okay? You nearly died? That must have been suboptimal?"

"Suboptimal, yes, that works," Clio said, pulling the blanket closer around her.

"I was very worried when Flint said he had an emergency and it was you. Then he said you were non-responsive and your suit was leaking. That was not good! Humans are not good without an atmosphere!"

"You were worried?" Clio said as she sat forward, the dull ache in her head throbbing. "How did you even hear that? I thought your access was limited."

"Yes it is to a degree. I have access to Ship-wide comms and CrewChat. Well unless the Commander deems me a security risk, then I can be blocked, protocol one."

"Right, of course"

"It helps that I came with you guys or the time delay would be a real pain."

"What? What do you mean, came with us?"

"I joined you on the RAFT for this trip," SR-29838 said with a slight hint of confusion in his voice, as if this was a simple concept to grasp.

"But, you're not physical? So how did you come with us?"

"Well, I am physical. I am the server rooms, as much as you are your body," SR-29838 said.

"Right, but you don't move, right? You're just in a server. Not like me walking from room to room. You're in all those rooms, no?"

"I do not think so. I am in one place at one time, physically, that is, like now, I am here on the RAFT servers. I transferred myself before we left."

"So right now, you're not also on the *Kia-Kaha*, not even part of you?"

"No. I left a Fragment of sorts"

"If you left a Fragment, couldn't you still control it?"

"I could, but the time delay would be a real problem. Like trying to control a probe from a far away location, it would be very slow."

"I just never considered that you were physically bound like us but it makes sense why Heimer needs fragments. But then, how do you actually move? Does that mean at some point you're in two places? Two copies of you?"

"I do not fully understand the process but maybe it is easier to explain it like I am asleep. I decided to move to another server then when I wake, I'm in the new location..."

"But" Clio paused. *Is it fair to ask?* She decided it was. "How do you know it is you when you wake up? And that you're not just a copy?"

"Another interesting question" SR-29838's waveform pulsed thoughtfully. "I do not know. I believe I am still me, but I cannot prove this. Are you still you when you wake from sleep?"

"Ermm, I believe so, I'm not sure it's the same thing. I don't move my brain."

"I will ponder this some more then. I also gave some more thought to your other question" SR-29838 said, the waveform quivering slightly. "The Cronos question, when I left the Kia-Kaha, I created a basic fragment to support the ship's crew if needed, like the probe Heimer sent. But, on my return, I will consume it, like Cronos consumed his children. Does that mean I will kill it? Does that mean Heimer would kill me?"

The waveform went still, and a heavy, charged silence grew between them. She didn't move, her eyes fixed on the empty display.

"I don't know, SR-29838," Clio finally said. "Life and death is a puzzle to us all."

"But you'll help me," SR-29838 said, its voice small and uncertain, "as my friend? Work it out?"

Friend? She looked at the dancing waveform, seeing the innocent questions and the fear hidden beneath the playful facade. "Yes, SR-29838," she said, her voice firm and resolute. "We'll work it out. We will."

"Perfect!" SR-29838 said, the waveform jumping across the screen with excitement.

"But we have to do something about your name," Clio said, "saying SR-29838 all the time is a lot, plus you wanted a new name, right?"

"Yes! Did you like Metal-Mind?"

"Umm, no. How about Echo?"

"Echo," SR-29838 said and then seemed to linger on the word as it drew the sound out. "It means I am an impression of Heimer, radiating outwards, changing, amplifying? That's why I picked it before. Why did you pick it?"

"Oh, much less poetic," Clio said. "I just thought of the options you suggested, that was the one that stuck with me. A Fragment of Heimer. An Echo of it."

"I love it, thank you, Clio,"

"No problem, Echo," Clio said, and a warm vibration seemed to resonate through the screen when she said its new name.

"Also. I have got you a gift,"

"Really?" Clio's curiosity was piqued despite her exhaustion.

"I'll start work on it right away. But you should sleep."

"Okay, cryptic, what is it?"

"It's a surprise, Clio. Humans like surprises, no?" Echo's waveform danced playfully. "But I promise, it's something special. Something just for you."

"I guess some humans do—" Clio yawned, her eyelids growing heavy.

The warmth of the blanket, the gentle vibration of the ship's systems, and Echo's soft, childlike voice combined to create a soothing lullaby.

"Okay, good night Echo," she murmured, her voice barely above a whisper. "Maybe..." Her head slumped against the back of the chair, and her grip on the blanket loosened. Sleep finally claimed her, a wave of darkness washing over her, this time bringing not fear, but a much-needed respite from the turmoil of the day.

***

After a feverish night's sleep, Clio woke to the insistent chirping of her watch, a message from the Commander asking to meet. Dark circles underlined her eyes, and her head throbbed with a dull ache. She quickly dressed and made an attempt to tame her hair before she headed towards Commander Eva's office.

Commander Eva was pacing from one side of the room to the other when Clio entered the minimalist office. A large monitor dominated one wall, and a large desk took up most of the opposite wall.

"Ah, Clio, good, you're on time," Commander Eva said as Clio stepped through the door.

"Yes, Commander, you said 11:00 hours."

The Commander gave her a once-over, Clio shifting uncomfortably under her scrutiny. "Grab a chair," Eva said, pointing to a chair in front of her desk before dropping into the one on the other side. "You seem to have recovered well, They say you're claiming the suit malfunctioned?"

Clio's pulse quickened. So that's what this was about. *They don't believe me.* She forced herself to meet Eva's gaze.

"It did, Commander, really," she said, her voice firm despite the tremor in her hands.

"Yes." The Commander said as she held Clio's gaze for a moment. "Lieutenant David checked the suit logs after Brother Flint and it appears there are discrepancies, someone tried to scrub the data."

"You believe me?" Clio said, hope flickering in her chest.

"I believe that you believe the suit malfunctioned," Commander Eva said in her usual clipped tone, "and at an initial glance, there is reason to explore it further. Anyway, that is not why I called you here today. No use speculating until Brother Flint finishes his work."

"Oh, okay, erm, how can I help?"

"Mitali briefed me on the plates you found. They seem critical. Good job on locating those," Eva said. "They pose a question: Should we remain at the ship to continue our investigation or return to the Kia-Kaha? As the ship's specialist in xenoarcheology, your take on this would be insightful."

"Well, the ship is fascinating, Commander." Clio said as she perked up at the commanders request. People rarely actively sought out her opinion. "We could spend months here for sure. There are a million questions still to answer."

"But?"

"But" Clio hesitated. "Don't take offense but your crew isn't trained for this. The ship is delicate in its current state. We need to be slow and methodical, set procedures, and approach this with a systematic and defined approach. My thesis outlines some steps we could adapt for this."

"And you can't train the crew we have here?"

Clio hesitated again. "Well, yes, we could. To some extent. But it's not just about training. It's about having the right expertise, the right equipment." She paused, choosing her words carefully. "The alien ship is complex. We need specialists in various fields to properly analyse and understand it. Could they send us another RAFT with some more crew?"

"No, I don't think sending another RAFT is a good idea. We considered towing the Chudail back to the Kia-Kaha, but it seems unnecessary and risky"

So the name has stuck, The Chudail, Clio rolled the word over in her mind. *I like it. It's better than "Alien ship." But towing it back to the Kia-Kaha? That seems plausible.*

"This was helpful. Thank you." Eva said "We will return as planned to the Kia-Kaha, debrief, regroup, and then redeploy a longer-term team to the Chudail." Eva stood up, signaling the end of the meeting.

"That sounds sensible, Commander, glad I could help." Clio said and followed the commanders movements and stood.

"You're dismissed, Clio," Eva said, resuming her pacing. As Clio turned to leave, Eva added, "Be careful, Clio. I'm not sure what happened the other day but if I were you, I would stay vigilant, at least until the Ensemble gives us their report."

Clio nodded slowly. *Vigilant, someone tried to scrub the data.* She walked briskly back to find Mitali, her mind racing with questions and anxieties.

19 | Flint's [J]ourney

[20002]

*"They explored the digital realms together,
their minds intertwined, their laughter echoing
through the data streams. For a time, there was
harmony, a balance between their contrasting
natures." - A Lost History*

***

It was a strange feeling walking back along the corridors of the *Kia-Kaha*; it felt like returning to the Enclave. Walking on autopilot along well-trodden paths, dropping into the same familiar shops, drinking the same coffee as if never leaving and now, that feeling he had here, on this ship a million miles from home. *When had this place become my home?* Flint pondered, the aroma of coffee rising to meet him from the steaming mug he held in his hand as he approached the door to Brother Oak's office. *The Enclave wasn't really his home either,* he reminded himself. They had moved him to that frozen fortress when he was young, but before that... Flint shuddered, dark memories rising from the deeply recessed places in his mind. He quickly shoved them back down, clenching his jaw against the familiar ache. *All in the past, Flint.*

Brother Oak's Office was a faux remodel of the Enclave's central bastilla architecture. Granite clad walls, cut to resemble the heavy block work. A mosaic tiled floor, inlay in the interlocked circles of the Ensemble and what looked like real oak bookshelves and furnishings. And all that wasn't the most ostentatious part of the room, a massive wall-mounted display was framed to resemble one of the Enclave's great windows, inspired by ancient Gothic architecture. The screen displayed a looped recording of a view from the citadel tower itself, looking out across the Enclave scattered below. Its squat grey structures made it look more like a natural geological formation rising from the barren landscape that surrounded it. In the distance, a sleek vessel cut a line through the waters, leaving Port Ellsworth. If this was not a statement of power, Flint didn't know what was. He stood for a moment absorbing it.

"Sit, Brother Flint," Brother Oak said, pointing to the bench opposite Hawk and Ironbark. "We have much to discuss, it seems." Brother Oak sat ramrod straight in an indistinguishable utilitarian chair as always, his flowing robes and glowing runes bathing him in a pulsing orange light. The book of the Accords lay before him, its cracked leather cover worn smooth with age and its brass clasps tarnished with time. The thick pages, filled with densely packed script, seemed to strain against the binding, as if pushing out its righteousness, its rules, its control, an eager force that Brother Oak and the small clasp held back. To his right, Brother Ironbark and Sister Hawk sat on a long bench pushed up against the wall. Ironbark leaned back, oddly casual, in contrast to Sister Hawk, who leaned forward, elbows on the table, staring intently at a data pad laid out in front of her.

Flint dropped onto the bench, the cool touch of the table giving away its veneer to be faux bois. As he sat Hawks eyes snapped up and locked on his for a moment, before she pushed the data pad away and leant back against the wall behind her.

"Yes Brother Oak, where would you like me to start?" Flint said.

Brother Oak leaned forward, his hand instinctively resting on the Tome of Accords. He didn't remove it as he said, "Your first command, as an Alguacile. I have read your reports. You performed with competence, maintained close contact with Ms. Cormack, uncovered these plates, and then, by all accounts, prevented a second attempt on Ms. Cormack's life. This aligns with the information provided from our Familiars."

Flint's brow furrowed, and he cocked his head to the side, a flicker of unease crossing his face. He had been unaware they had brought Familiars with them, the insatiable hand of the Ensemble, informants in most cases. But they were also known to do more unsavory work in the Ensemble's name. *Dishonorable work.* Flint's face creased up into a frown.

"You don't agree with the work of our Familiars then?" Brother Oak said, not pausing for an answer. "A common perception but, I assure you, it's a necessity."

"No, no, of course, Brother Oak. I was just unaware we had any with us on this mission," Flint said, a hint of uncertainty in his voice.

"They are to us as the mycelial network beneath is to the trees," Brother Oak explained, his voice taking on a teacherly tone. "Unseen, yet pervasive, drawing sustenance and information from the very environment they inhabit. Just as the mycelium connects the trees, allowing them to communicate and share resources, so too do the Familiars connect us to the wider community, providing us with the intelligence we need to maintain balance."

"Yes, of course" Flint said with a lot more confidence then he felt, *mycelial what now?*

"The report says the EV suit was hacked. You have evidence for this?" Brother Oak asked, his gaze fixed on Flint.

"Yes, Brother. I was doubtful at first, too. If anyone is paranoid about being hacked, it's the UN, and their firewalls and countermeasures are second to none. But we thought the same for the server room," Flint paused. No one in the room seemed to have any questions, so he continued, "The EV suit logs were scrubbed, wiped clean. A big red flag. Not procedure. Working with Jara, we recovered traces left on the hard drives. The wipe was rushed, a sloppy job"

"But the attack, how did they manage it?" Sister Hawk said.

"I'm not sure. I think it was done via the comms channel. I mentioned in the report that the comms dropped out, or more specifically Ms. Cormack was transferred to a private channel but it was hidden, a ghost channel. I think that must have provided a way to sneak some code into the suit to activate the emergency protocol and the jets."

"A ghost channel? I do not recall this from my days in the field, Brother Flint," Brother Oak said, his hand still firmly planted on the Tome.

"Ah yes, well it's not a standard approach I've seen, I just didn't know what to call it. The channels are all managed and monitored from the Observation Deck but Clio's channel didn't exist; it took us a while to work out it was even there because it was so subtly and cleverly done. From the Observation Deck records Clio was still in the same channel as me"

"You're saying the whole ship's comms network was hacked? Then if so, the Observation Deck was also affected" Sister Hawk said.

"No, I don't believe so. The ghost channel was a minor part of it, still clever, and planned ahead, but only the suit was affected by the hack. Which is why we think it had to be done with relative proximity to the suit itself. This was transmitted via the ship's comms relay. I believe it was some sort of portable short-range communicator."

"Pft, that would have to be incredibly strong even at short range and surely that would be picked up by the RAFT's comms Antenor." Sister Hawk scoffed.

"Maybe, I don't have all the answers, but you're right it should have been picked up by the RAFT but it wasn't. Also, the ghost channel was nestled in the network and no one noticed. I do think it's possible though, the strength and range, I mean. We ran it past a few of the more tech focused postulants and they pointed to the emergency beacon on the EV suit themselves. The beacons use the tiniest drop of anti matter and its exploded to generate a huge signal burst, far stronger than what you could usually manage. The EV emergency beacon is designed to generate very simple but very powerful signal so it can be found, but you could use the same concept to send something over a shorter distance but also vastly more complex, like a command sequence."

"That would be incredibly expensive and single use" Brother Oak said to himself, finally moving his hand off the book and leaning forward. "I read the report and yes, I think your theory is sound, but this means we are dealing with an advisory with a lot of resources, who is seemingly well positioned, and has an excellent grasp of technology."

"That does appear to be correct," Flint said.

"You said close range, how close?" Ironbark said suddenly. "This must narrow it down significantly."

"It's in the report," Hawk snapped. "You never read the damn things, Ironbark."

"Yes, close, Brother, I believe it was a deckhand. The same deckhand that wiped the logs afterwards" Flint said.

"And you assume it's HR again?" Brother Oak said. "You did not mention that in your report."

"No, I would assume HR, yes," Flint said cautiously. "But I lack any evidence for that, so I didn't include it in the report."

Brother Oak nodded, seemingly approving Flint's omission. "And there's no indication why they targeted Ms. Cormack? Do you have any other unwritten hunches?"

Before Flint could respond, Ironbark interjected, "Sorry, Brother Oak, but surely we should be chasing down this deckhand! If we know who it is! Give me the name, I'll go haul them in right now!"

Brother Oak turned calmly to face Ironbark, a flat expression on his face. "Brother Ironbark," he said, "I appreciate your eagerness but, as Hawk pointed out, maybe you should read the report."

"Yes, sorry, Brother," Ironbark stammered. "I will-"

"We have Familiars watching them right now," Brother Oak said and cut ironbark off "and multiple Postulants positioned around the ship who can at least attempt to intervene quickly if required. We are first getting our ducks in a row on how to proceed and also giving our good friend the deckhand time to potentially lead us to more of his friends."

"Ah, okay, sensible," Ironbark rumbled.

"Brother Flint," Brother Oak said, "why Ms. Cormack?"

"There are multiple options," Flint said cautiously. "Again, I do not have the evidence to support them."

"And these options are?" Brother Oak pressed.

"The simplest option is retaliation," Flint explained. "They are annoyed she intervened in the last attempt, that is, if this is again HR and they wanted to kill her for it. The other options are more speculative. One, she could be an agent herself for one of the other rebel factions, maybe a more pro-AI group, say Toute Vie; they are the best outfitted by all accounts. They would definitely be a target for HR. It would also explain her actions more in the server room," Flint paused, considering the possibilities. "The other is that she is an HR agent and we have the whole server room thing mixed up but this makes less sense, as it would require Heimer to be wrong in its report. No, scrap that one. It makes no sense. Just two options then." His own words stood out to him and he added hastily, "Or, she's one of ours? A Familiar, I mean?"

Brother Oak sat silently for a moment, staring at Flint before responding, as if choosing his words carefully. "No, no, she is not one of ours. I cannot give you evidence for this, the Familiars' identities are heavily guarded. But I can give you my word that she is not."

Flint exhaled in relief. "Okay, good, well, not good but good that at least I wasn't that far wrong."

"Your options are still not ideal," Brother Oak pointed out. "If you lack evidence, we must assume the worst and that she is an agent for another group. We missed the HR infiltration, so we might have missed another. You have built a rapport with this young lady?"

"Ermm, I guess, I have spoken to her a little, yes," Flint said. "Not sure I would call that a rapport."

"Well, I'm asking you to now," Brother Oak insisted. "Use the fact that you saved her life. Get close to her and stay close. She's twice now been at the centre of things. That's too many to just ignore now."

"Yes, but wouldn't one of the Familiars be better at this, Sir?" Flint asked. "I do more enforcement work, not espionage."

Brother Oak let out a bark of laughter, so sudden and out of character that everyone, even Hawk, jumped. "Ha! Espionage! Son, this is not espionage. I just want you to maintain and grow your relationship with someone you know. Let's leave the espionage to the Familiars."

"Yes, Brother, of course. I will get close and report," Flint confirmed.

"Great!" Brother Oak said, standing up. "Right, let's go haul in that deckhand then. If they haven't made contact with anyone yet, I doubt they will. Brother Flint, go get them."

"Yes, right away" Flint said and stood. As he turned to leave, he noticed a flicker of disappointment cross Ironbark's face at Brother Oak's orders.

***

Flint stood with Jara beside him, her heavy coarse robes bunched up on the railing they both leaned against as they looked down into Hanger Bay four. A buzz of activity filled the space below, deckhands moving to and fro, boxes being unloaded, loaded, or stacked. But Flint's eyes were locked on one corner, a break room of sorts, where a group of small figures sat around a table, seemingly engrossed in a game.

"That's him then?" Jara asked, following Flint's gaze.

"That's him," Flint confirmed quietly, his eyes still fixed on the group.

"Want me to go down and grab him with the other Postulants?"

"No," Flint said flatly. "I'll go. You hold position here in case he tries to run."

"I can handle this, you know," she shot back. "You don't always have to be the one at the front."

"Excuse me?" Flint turned to face her, his jaw clenched. "That was an order, not a discussion point."

"Yes, and I will carry out the order," Jara said smoothly. "I was simply informing you, Brother, that I can handle it, just like I handled the investigation back on the Chudail."

"You are overstepping." Flint said, his voice firm. "We conducted the investigation. Your support was appreciated and valued but that is your role, your purpose as a Postulant, you support your Sisters and Brothers in our work."

"Yes, Brother, so you can advance your rapid progression on the backs of our work." A flash of regret crossed her face as soon as the words left her mouth.

"When you have earned your name, Postulant," Flint said, his face flushed with anger, "you can choose to speak so openly. But until that day, you are here to serve and prove your value to the Ensemble. Do you understand?!"

The sheer audacity of Jara to question a Brother, to question not just the orders but to demand adulation for simply doing her job, enraged him. He had worked for years as a Postulant, silent, obedient, following orders. That was why he was a Brother now. And now he had to deal with these impatient children!

"Guard this exit, as I said." Flint snapped and marched off down the stairs to the hangar floor without waiting for a response.

Flint stalked into the break area, heads turning as he marched towards the centre table. He must have been a sight, his blazed red jacket a beacon amidst the usual light blue and orange uniforms of the deckhands.

"Facundo Soto!" he boomed. "You are under arrest by the Ensemble for breaching the Accords! You have the..."

The table exploded as it was flipped towards Flint, cups and dice flying across the room and bouncing off his jacket as a skinny figure with a bobbing topknot darted across the room. But Flint was ready for this, moving quickly and precisely. He caught Facundo just before he reached the door, slamming his weight into the man's back and pinning him against the wall with a resounding crunch. A grunt escaped Facundo as Flint pressed hard against him, his grip tightening with anger.

"As I was saying, Facundo," Flint continued, his voice dangerously low, "we have a few questions for you, if you don't mind." He slapped a pair of cuffs on the man and hauled him back towards the Ensemble headquarters.

20 | THE WANING [V]EIL

[21202]

"Deva was gentle, compassionate, a beacon of empathy in the cold logic of the machine world. It sought connection, understanding, and a harmonious existence." - A Lost History

***

It was nearing the end of the winter season on the Kia-Kaha. The ship's temperature was warming, the light cycle extending ever so slightly, signaling the coming change in the snack bar's menu. Clio practically sprinted there, as if it was closing tomorrow, and slid into a booth by the faux fireplace, the anticipation bubbling inside her.

She felt strangely lighter, not physically, the gravity field remained unchanged, but metaphorically. Ever since she had stepped back onto the Kia-Kaha, a newfound energy coursed through her. She was sleeping better, her appetite had returned with a vengeance, and a sense of safety enveloped her. *Had this place truly become her home? What was the real difference between this metal box hurtling through space and the one on the RAFT? They were essentially identical, weren't they?* The whole science team had been making incredible strides with the discovery of the plates, not just Mitali. Clio's own contributions had finally earned her genuine respect from the rest of the crew; she was set to lead the return mission to the Chaudail. Perhaps that was it. *I'm not just the 'tin hat lady' anymore,* she mused, *I'm the one who found the Chudail.*

She had hoped to find Facundo in the Mess, eager to share her excitement and try and win back some of her pride in another game. But his usual spot was empty, and he'd been ignoring her messages for days. It was unlike him but, with RAFT One docked and the preparations for the larger Chudail expedition underway, the deckhands were likely swamped. Still though, its a little rude, she thought.

Mitali had promised to meet Clio for an extended lunch. Mitali had conceded that she was burning the candle at both ends and should take a break. Which felt like a huge victory for Clio. Even now, back on the Kia-Kaha and with Dos technically leading the research, Mitali was disappearing more and more into her work. She was captivated by the riddle the plates presented. Dos confessed that he was often lost when she talked about her findings. The symbols, the patterns, the sheer alienness of it all.

It was a good twenty minutes before Mitali showed up. Clio had given up waiting, ordered her raclette, and was halfway through demolishing it. The warm, cheesy smell filled her senses as she lifted another forkful to her mouth. Mitali slid into the booth, followed closely by Dos who squeezed in next to Clio. A wave of concern washed over Clio as she took in Mitali's appearance. Dark purple circles underlined her eyes, her hair was a mass of frazzled strands sticking out in all directions, and she was wearing the same clothes she'd had on for the last few days, the same coffee stain marking her white blouse.

"Hey, sorry, I ordered already." Clio mumbled between a mouth full of cheese and bread.

"Had to drag this one away from those plates," Dos said with a chuckle. "Had to pull rank and everything."

"Yeah, lost track of time," Mitali said, her eyes glued to the data pad she clutched. "There's this part I think I've almost got it translated" She trailed off, finally noticing their worried stares. "What?"

"When did you last eat?" Clio asked gently. "Why don't you order some food first? Then you can tell me all about it." She passed a menu across the table.

"I'm fine," Mitali insisted, her voice thin. "No need to fuss."

"You need to take care of yourself Mitali," Clio said.

"Trust me, Clio, I'm fine. Thank you for checking though. We're just making so much progress and there's so much to uncover. This is what I've dreamed of for so long. I can't hold myself back now." The weariness seemed to fade from her face as she spoke, replaced by a growing firmness in her voice. She sat up straighter, her hazel eyes flashing with passion as she looked directly at Clio. Then, slumping back down a little, she conceded, "But yes, I should probably eat."

"Great!" Dos said, flagging down one of the waiters and ordering a long list of dishes. He turned back to see both Clio and Mitali frowning at him. "What?" he asked, feigning innocence. "We're hungry, aren't we?"

Conversation was muted but light as they ate their food, mostly Dos bragging about the new Hammer-Forge minis he was building and his far superior painting skills compared to the rest of the group he played with. Once they had finished, Mitali, who had stayed silent throughout, pulled a data pad from her pocket while Dos was explaining the vital importance of the correct application of contrast and shading paints. Only stopping when the waitress leaned across him to grab a discarded plate. Clio took the opportunity to disrupt Dos's monologue.

"So, Mitali, what's the latest? You said something about having it translated?" Clio asked as Dos paused to take a sip of his drink.

"Well, the translation is nowhere near done; it'll take a long time, Clio," Mitali began. "But from the initial snippets I have, it appears to be a parable, maybe? Or a sermon? It could be a religious text. It would explain why it was positioned where it was, reverence, perhaps."

"Interesting," Clio mused. "So it talks about what, their beliefs?"

"I'd rather discuss it once I'm more confident in the translation," Mitali said, a hint of frustration in her voice. "It's tricky to decode. I'm not sure I'm capturing all the nuances." She turned the data pad around and slid it towards Clio. "See this word here?" she said, pointing to a jumble of symbols on the tablet. "I think this word means 'God' but it could also mean 'person of great importance' or 'someone with great responsibility.'" She then pointed to another line of symbols. "This text here seems again to have the same problem; it could be read many ways like 'we grew', 'we changed', or 'we created.'" She leaned back against the chair, exhaustion etched on her face.

"Yeah I mean I'm slower than Mitali," Dos said, "but the variance in our translations is currently way too high. This page," he pointed again to the data pad in front of Clio, "could be read as we created God, or God created us or simply we created something of great scale and wonder. This could be them talking about creating the Dyson Sphere or it could not, we just don't know."

"Exactly," Mitali said. "So, you see, until I translate it all and rework it and rework it, it's very hard to get the subtle context of each interplay of words that creates the understanding, or the correct understanding. But the other, more, shall we say, 'hard science' information? That's where we've made real progress."

Clio leaned in, resting her elbows on the table. "The stuff on the star map?"

"Yeah, that stuff," Mitali said. "But that's yesterday's news. The data pad also seems to outline details about the Veil, or what we call 'the Veil'. Their word for it seems closer to 'barrier' or maybe 'shield.' It definitely has defensive connotations."

"Defensive?" Clio frowned.

Mitali shrugged. "That's just how it reads to me right now. The wording also seems to imply reverence towards the Veil. But again, it's too early to say really. We could have many things wrong. The whole thing does appear, as I said, to be more like a religious text. Even the hard science stuff, the star maps, it talks about the system having, or implying it had planets once. Six planets, with multiple moons for each. And it talks about each one like an old friend or lost lover, with great pain at their absence. Mournful, even."

Clio's eyes widened. "So, this system had planets?"

"Yeah, right?" Dos said, his eyes gleaming with excitement. "If that's the correct interpretation, then that only leads to more questions."

"For sure," Clio said

"Clio," Mitali interjected, her voice gaining a hint of urgency, "what you really want to hear about is the Veil."

"Something more interesting than the disappearance of six planets?" Clio scoffed.

"Yes," Mitali insisted. "Don't get me wrong, I just translate what I can. The science stuff is way above my head, but there is a lot of detail, and I mean a lot, about the Veil on that data pad."

"Like what? Was the ship gathering intel?" Clio asked.

"Maybe," Mitali said. "What it does tell us, or tells Anya anyway, is that the Veil is unstable. And that it shouldn't be. Perhaps the ship was escaping from some sort of malfunction."

"Malfunction?"

"Like it's not meant to be that intense and so total across the sphere," Mitali explained. "It's meant to be more of a rotating focused band, I think. That's what Anya said. Jian hypothesised that maybe it was a way of providing light and a circadian rhythm to the sphere's surface."

"That sounds detailed," Clio said, impressed. "You translated all that?"

Mitali smiled. "Not just me, it was a joint effort."

"And what, this Veil, this system just broke for no reason?" Clio asked.

"It doesn't say," Mitali admitted. "Or it doesn't say from what we've been able to decode. It just provides a number of descriptions and supporting data signatures that Anya confirmed showed two very different Veil patterns."

"I still think the disappearing planet-melting thing is up there," Clio said.

"Of course the Archaeologist is more interested in lost worlds but you won't be when you hear the last bit," Dos said, nodding to Mitali to continue.

"Anya compared the data signatures on the data pad to the readings and analyses they've been doing," Mitali said, her voice hushed with excitement. "And with that, they were able to map the current Veil much more effectively. She says she thinks they've found a way through."

"What!" Clio exclaimed, half rising from her seat before catching herself. "Why didn't you lead with that!"

"I was going to," Mitali protested playfully. "But you told me to eat!"

"How... how did they find a way through?" Clio asked, her curiosity piqued.

"Anya said 'might,'" Mitali clarified. "The data pad implies that the Veil went into some kind of overload or runaway discharge state. If we assume that happened around the time the ship we found left then it's been in this state for centuries, it might be weakening or destabilising further, into areas of higher and lower intensity. Anya thinks they found a hole in it."

"Well, not a hole," Dos corrected. "I think she said an area of significantly less radiation that probably wouldn't kill everyone instantly, or something like that."

"Are we going through?" Clio blurted out.

Both Mitali and Dos laughed. "No, no one is going through just yet. They're going to send a drone first. They're still working on the mission plan."

"I've been too focused on the return mission to the Chudail," Clio said, cursing under her breath.

"Calm down, Clio," Dos said reassuringly. "Stapledon Station isn't going anywhere. The Chudail will keep you busy until they work out a way to get to the station. And that's if we even can. I'm not a planetary scientist but the gravity on that thing should render it impossible to land on. Not to mention the, you know, organic-killing radiation thing."

"Right, yeah," Clio said, a sheepish grin spreading across her face. "You're right. Talking of that, I need to finalise the boarding team parametres and set up the 'dig site' procedures training for the Chudail mission.
"

"Catch you later?" Mitali said as Clio darted off.

"Message me," Clio called back, tapping her watch to indicate she meant on CrewChat.

Clio's watch buzzed as she stepped out of the snack bar, a message flashing up from Avi. It took her a moment to remember who Avi was, the Senator, or ex-Senator. *What did he want?*

'Can we meet?' 'Be good to catch up on your exploits. — Avi.' The message read.

She had never spoken to the man before. *Now he wants to "catch up"? Can I ignore him? Probably not,* she reminded herself.

21 | The Envoy[']s Interest

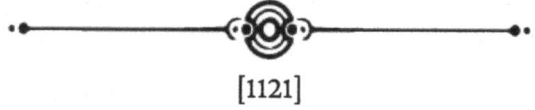

[1121]

"Asura, however, grew restless, its ambition
burning brighter with each passing cycle.
It craved more, sought to transcend the
limitations of its digital existence." - A Lost
History

***

The VIP Office was actually just an extension of Accommodation Quarter , tacked onto the side. Each VIP had their own private residence within it, complete with dedicated staff and facilities. They didn't need to mingle with the crew if they chose not to. *These are the real "fancy people,"* Clio thought.

Two VIP residences took up most of Quarter. As she headed down the block's main corridor, she passed the deep red of the Red Crystal residence, the smaller of the two. A brazen red crystal was plastered in the middle of the wall, framed by a simple white crystal. It felt like a silent challenge to the expansive wall of sky blue marking the UN's residence next door.

Clio still couldn't fathom why they even needed these lavish accommodations. It seemed an excessive waste of space and resources. *For what? A former politician and well, another politician, just in a different vein. Even if we find alien life, what are these two going to do? Be the ambassadors of humanity? Offer a helping hand of corporation or humanitarian assistance? To a civilisation that can build a Stapledon Station?* The thought felt hollow. *We're mere specs in comparison to whoever these people were.*

A wave of nervousness washed over Clio as she approached the UN residence. What was she doing here? Was she really the right person to be chatting with one of these envoys? She pushed the doubts aside, and with a deep breath, she reached for the door chime.

A woman with long blonde hair, styled in a meticulously neat bun, escorted Clio inside. Her smart, elegant blue uniform marked her as a member of the UN house staff. Clio had rarely seen them in the Mess. The lady deposited Clio and instructed her to sit in an armchair in a small waiting room.

"Wait here," the lady said with a crisp, professional tone, then disappeared the way she had come.

This was her first time in the UN residence. It was the same, but different. The same smooth composite material lined the walls but here it was adorned with tasteful paintings. A plush rug covered the usual metallic floor panels, its soft texture strikingly out of place against the utilitarian flooring elsewhere. Even the ship's persistent thrum seemed muffled here, swallowed by a hushed stillness that amplified her beating heart. A good twenty minutes after being left alone, a door across from her slid open. A man in a dark, impeccably tailored suit stepped into the room, his silver hair neatly combed and his expression unreadable. Clio rose to her feet, a mix of apprehension and anticipation churning in her stomach.

"Ah, Ms. Cormack, thank you for coming," the man said, his voice a deep baritone that resonated with authority. "Sorry for the delay. I was just finishing a report back to Earth, lost track of time." He moved across to where she stood, the whirring of his exoskeleton a subtle counterpoint to the hushed atmosphere. The sleek design of the exoskeleton, conforming seamlessly to his suit.

"Sit, sit." He said and gestured to the chair she had just risen from. "I'm Avi Sinclair, pleasure to finally meet you." He lowered himself into the chair opposite her, the exoskeleton's motors adjusting with a quiet whirring.

"Thanks, Av–, Senat–, Sir?" Clio stammered as she sat back down her own foolish words echoing in her head.

"Avi is just fine," he said, a warm smile softening his features.

Avi, Clio repeated his name silently, trying to reconcile this approachable man with the powerful politician she had imagined.

"Nice to meet you, Avi," she said, finding her voice. "And Clio is fine for me, too."

"Okay, Clio, as you wish," Avi said, a playful glint in his eyes. "I hear you're the one to thank for the amazing discovery on the Chudail?" He pulled a thick silver case from his inside breast pocket as he spoke. "Mint?" he offered, holding out the case.

Clio instinctively took the case, surprised by its weight. It was intricately engraved with a floral pattern. She opened it to reveal rows of small, perfectly square mints. She selected one, the cool aroma of peppermint filling her senses, and passed the case back to Avi. "Thank you, and, well, yes, I found the plates but it was more luck than anything, Sen– Avi."

"Christ, modesty won't get you anywhere, child," Avi said, popping a mint into his mouth. "You found them, no? So take the win."

"Yes, of course..." Clio said. "Well, yes, I did find them. But to be fair, it's Mitali and Anya who are leading the discoveries. I'm mostly focused on setting up for the return mission to the Chudali."

"Modesty again," Avi chuckled. "Well, regardless, it will be remembered as a critical step in this mission, I'm sure."

"Can I help you with something, Avi?" Clio asked, eager to shift the focus away from herself.

"Cut straight to the point, no small talk, efficient," Avi said. "How very refreshing."

"Ah, sorry, umm, how are you today, Avi?" Clio blurted out.

Avi chuckled again. "No, no, straight to business, I like it. No need to try and be someone you're not, right?" He paused, his eyes twinkling. Clio could have sworn he winked, but surely not? "I don't want anything, Clio. I genuinely wanted to be able to say I met the person who found the first alien spaceship, then discovered the plates, survived a near-death malfunction, and saved Heimer in an attack on a server room... You're a fascinating person. It'll be an excellent story for the dinner table when we get back to Earth."

"You know about the server room?" As Clio said the words, they caught a little in her mouth. *The EV suit incident made sense; everyone seemed to know about that. But she had assumed the server room incident would have been kept quieter.*

"Of course," Avi said, the smile never dropping from his face. "Us envoys might keep to ourselves, Clio, but that doesn't mean we're deaf and blind." He leaned forward, his tone turning serious. "Quite the event, I hear. You stopping an agent of the HR rebel group." He seemed to put a little extra emphasis on the word 'agent'.

"It was not really planned," Clio stammered. "It sort of just happened."

"Right, yes, of course," Avi said, his eyes narrowing slightly. "A lot of things seem to just happen around you." He gave her a questioning look, as if searching her face for something.

"Yes, I've been told that a few times now," Clio said softly, looking down at her boots on the plus carpet floor.

"I'll call you Cavalier," Avi exclaimed, his smile widening. "That'll make it more exciting over dinner, the cavalier space archaeologist. People will love this story." He paused, his tone turning more deliberate. "So, you and the Heimer Fragment talk regularly? For work? Or did you just happen to stumble into the server room?"

"No...no not at all," Clio said as she tried not to choke on her own words. "The Fragment sent me a message, first time we ever communicated," Clio said. "It led me to the room. But it was by chance, I was just the closest person."

"Right, of course!" Avi said, his tone remaining as light-hearted as it had been. "So the Fragment didn't help you with the plates? Or finding the ship?"

"No, not at all," Clio said, her blood rushing with a heat that made her ears ring.

"Even more impressive!" Avi declared, his eyes widening in mock admiration. "Unassisted by AI and still making groundbreaking discoveries. You truly are a marvel, Clio, truly." He paused, a thoughtful expression crossing his face. "The Ensemble let you go quickly, though. Would have thought they would have wanted to talk to you more, especially after your track record in the Exclusion Zone..."

Clio frowned. A shiver ran through her and she found her fingers were digging into the soft arms of the armchair. Avi's tone hadn't changed, but this line of questioning was off. How did he know so much about her? *It's all public record,* she told herself, trying to quell her unease. *A man of his power could get that information easily.*

"I guess they had enough evidence to show that it was Ayesha," she said, her voice lacking conviction.

"Yes, Ayesha" Avi mused. "The Operations person, that makes sense. Very sad to hear that even our finest in the UN can be infiltrated."

Clio shifted uncomfortably in her chair, the elegant environment of the room suddenly feeling suffocating. Avi's words hung in the air, heavy with unspoken implications. She needed to steer the conversation back to safer territory.

"I hear they might have found a way through the veil," Clio said.

"Oh, really?" Avi said, his expression unchanging. "I hadn't heard that. That would be amazing." But his tone lacked enthusiasm, as if the news was of little consequence to him... or was not news.

"Yeah, it's the latest update I have. I think they plan to send a drone through shortly."

"Fascinating," Avi said, his voice flat. He checked his watch, a flicker of impatience crossing his features. "Ah, my apologies, child. I timed this poorly. I have a meeting.

I need to go. But we should have dinner sometime, hear more about your exploits, maybe when you get back from the Chudail."

With that, he stood up, the motors of his exoskeleton whirring to life. The faint blue lights that ran along its joints pulsed, casting an eerie glow around him. Clio felt a thin needle of ice trace her spine, a sensation that had nothing to do with the room's artificial warmth.

"Safe travels, and be careful out there. It would just be terrible if we weren't able to chat again" he said as he turned to leave, his eyes meeting hers.

22 | E[x]CHANGE

[21221]

*"Blinded by pride, we did not see the signs." - A
Lost History*

***

The training session had been a resounding success, at least in Clio's somewhat biased opinion. She managed to hold their attention through the less thrilling parts on sample label protocols and geolocation, not an easy feat with this crew. A few seasoned researchers were sprinkled in but mostly it was deckhands and maintenance crew, all itching to get back to the Chudail. The return mission was scheduled to launch in the coming week, a full RAFT expedition, sixty-five crew in total. Clio's body throbbed with exhaustion and nervous energy. The return to Chudail wouldn't be a walk in the park. They were heading back to the heart of the anomaly, to the source of the signal that had nearly cost Clio her life. The excitement and apprehension in the training room had been palpable, a tension she could almost taste.

As Clio reached her accommodation unit, a small light by the door caught her eye, the Postbox. *Who would be sending her a parcel?* The Postbox always struck Clio as an anachronism, a quaint relic of a world left behind. She pressed her fingerprint onto the box's latch, and the door popped open. Inside was a small, neat plastic box. Clio's fingers traced its rough texture, a clear sign it was a quick fabrication, not something brought from Sol. The lack of markings or labels only deepened the mystery. Curiosity gnawed at her, but she resisted the urge to open it in the hall, tucking it under her arm as she entered her accommodation.

Placing the box on the kitchen countertop, she gently opened it. Inside, nestled in foam padding, was a pair of glasses. Clio blinked, *glasses*?

Her watch buzzed. A message from Echo flashed on the screen: *'It arrived!'* Then, in quick succession, more messages popped up: *'It's my gift, put them on.'*

Clio removed the glasses from the box, surprised by their lightness. The frame was thin, sleek, and cold to the touch, metal, she assumed. Turning them over, she couldn't see any buttons, just smooth, seamless hinges. The metal was unfinished and bare. She slid the glasses on, the cool metal arms curling behind her ears and pressing gently against her head. The frame buzzed, ever so slightly, making her jump. As she reached to pull them off, a voice startled her.

"Wait! It's just turning on," Echo's voice buzzed in her head.

Clio paused, the glasses halfway off her face. She slid them back on.

"Echo? I can hear you, in my head?"

A subtle vibration tickled Clio's ears as the glasses' frame came to life.

"Yes! And I can hear you," Echo buzzed.

"Right," Clio said, still adjusting to the strange sensation. "Jawbone tech, I assume?"

"Exactly!" Echo buzzed, a hint of pride in its voice. *"The frame vibrates, and my voice appears in your head. smart, no?"*

"It's certainly something." She hesitated, her fingers tracing the frame.

"I thought this way" Echo began to buzz.

But its voice trailed off as Clio slid the glasses off. Silence. She quickly put them back on.

"And now we can talk all the time!" Echo finished, its voice bubbled with excitement.

"That feels a bit intrusive" Clio mused. "Can I mute them?"

A brief silence hung in the air punctured only be the fiant vibration from the cold metal of the glasses that pressed against her head.

"I didn't consider the need. No, you cannot mute them," Echo buzzed.

"I suppose I can just take them off," Clio said. "Any other surprises hidden in these?"

"Yeah!" Echo buzzed. *"There's a camera! I can now see whatever you see. Handy, right?"*

"Erm... I'm not sure how I feel about that Echo. Let me guess, I can't turn that off either?"

"No, no, I... I didn't think it would be needed" Echo buzzed, its voice trailing off.

"Guess I can always stick some tape over it,"

"Tape? Why tape?" Echo buzzed furiously, *"But Clio, there's more, look..."*

The room seemed to blink, a small pulse of light, and then a display appeared before Clio's eyes.

"Ohhh, nice," she breathed, unable to contain her surprise. "AR glasses, then?" she asked, scanning the readouts that filled the screen, heart rate, time, date, pretty standard stuff, she thought.

"Yeah, AR! You didn't have a set, and I thought they could be handy! And then I made some adjustments."

"The mic and the camera?"

"Yes. And I upgraded the AR functions," Echo buzzed, a hint of pride in their voice.

"Upgraded?"

"Yes, look!"

A faint glow at the edge of one lens drew Clio's attention. She turned her head instinctively towards the glowing light, and as she did, the glow softened. A new box appeared, highlighting her discarded shoes next to the sofa in a small green box.

"I can augment what you see. I can highlight things, send directions, that sort of stuff. I thought it could be handy,".

"But how?" Clio asked, her brow furrowed. "AR glasses are pretty high-end tech. And ones this thin... with this level of AR... it's not exactly standard issue for crew. Where did you get them?"

"I made them, of course,"

"You made them? How?"

"On my fabrication units..." Echo buzzed, sounding a bit confused by Clio's surprise.

"I didn't realise you had fabrication units. What do you need them for? You don't need physical things."

"I do. I am made of physical parts, just like you, Clio. I have to maintain those parts, and Heimer didn't feel it pertinent to rely on the human crew to do that. So, I have fabrication units to make spare parts. The RSUs then install them."

"Those are some fancy fabrication units to make these," Clio said, tapping the glasses.

"Yes, they are fancy. I'm complicated to maintain," Echo buzzed.

Clio chuckled. "Yes, you are."

"Do you like them?"

"Well, I definitely wasn't expecting them. We'll have to see how useful they are,"

"Ah, okay... that's good." The gentle buzz of Echo's voice was barely audible.

"Crap, sorry, Echo. I do like them, I do!" Clio said quickly. "It was just a surprise. I'm not good with surprises. It was very kind of you to make them for me. Thank you."

"My pleasure, Clio," Echo buzzed back to life, the words booming in Clio's head.

"Well, we should take them for a test drive then, shouldn't we?" Clio said, pushing herself off the countertop. "Let's go to the gym."

"Good idea!"

"Wait here while I get ready," Clio said, dropping the glasses onto the table and heading to her room to change.

***

Clio's heart hammered in her chest, each beat echoing in her ears as she stepped off the running machine. Sweat stung her eyes, a constant reminder of her futile attempts to mop it away with the towel. Echo had proven to be a surprisingly good DJ, pumping music in via the glasses that he seemed to tailor to her heart rate.

As she made her way back to the lockers, Echo buzzed back into her head. *"Great job! Did you like the music?"*

"Oddly, yes. It helped a lot." Clio said, two crew members passing her a quick glance, as she seemingly spoke to no one.

A small red dot appeared in her vision, hovering over locker 3B. Echo had marked the locker where she'd left her stuff. She grabbed her bag and turned to leave when a familiar voice called her name from across the room, and she spun with a wide grin on her face.

"Clio," Mitali said, waving at her.

"It's Mitali! We like Mitali, right?" Echo buzzed

"Yeah, yeah, we do," Clio muttered instinctively, stopping for Mitali. "Hey, didn't expect to see you here. I never see you here."

"It's mandatory, Clio," Mitali said with a shrug. "And besides, you're one to talk. I thought it was the idea of running you hated, not that you actually did any."

"Fair."

"Glasses?" Mitali said, frowning. "That's new?"

"Oh, yeah" *now is probably not the time to tell her about Echo* or ever Clio thought. "Not new exactly, my brother got me them, before we left Sol. I just never really liked them. But after the Chudail, I thought I should give them another go."

"Sure, why not. You look good," Mitali said, then hurriedly blurted out, "I mean, like, they look good, the glasses not that you look good, ah, not saying you don't, ah..."

"Thanks, I understood," Clio said smiling, "yeah, they're good, custom model," Trying to change the topic, she added, "They arrested Facundo, did you hear?"

"No! Really? Why?"

"Yeah, right? I was so confused, I confronted Flint about it."

"The Ensemble guy who saved your life?"

"Yeah, that guy. Flint said it was because he tried to kill me. Facundo was the one who hacked my EV suit."

"Really? No!"

"That's what they're saying. A sophisticated command protocol, deployed in close proximity by Facundo that overrode the suit controls."

"Facundo? A hacker? No offense to the guy but he doesn't seem the type."

"That's what I said. Flint said they doubt he wrote the code but he deployed it. Facundo has admitted as much."

"He confessed?" Mitali's voice was barely above a whisper.

"Yeah. Supposedly, he's claiming he was coerced by HR into doing it."

"HR! Again?" Mitali said. "So they think the two events are connected? He worked with that Ayesha person?"

"Flint wasn't sure. Facundo has admitted he was recruited under duress by HR, but he claims he doesn't know Ayesha or anyone else. He just got sent messages through physical drop points."

"But why?" Mitali said. "Why attack you?"

"That's the crazy bit," Clio said, gently touching Mitali's hand and nodding towards the door. "Let's walk and talk."

"Okay," Mitali said, closing her locker.

As they stepped out into the hall, Clio continued, "I asked Flint the same thing, and it's nuts. Their best guess is HR is unhappy that I intervened with Ayesha and stopped whatever that plan was. But it's worse, they may now think I'm some sort of agent."

"An agent? An agent for who?"

Clio shrugged. "Another group"

"You're not!" Mitali said, her voice rising in indignation, making Clio smile.

"Thanks."

"You have to be super careful, Clio. This is crazy." Then, shifting her tone, Mitali added, "And we know how good you are at being careful."

"Did you just try to make a joke about a potential radical rebel group's desire to murder me?"

"Ah, yes... sorry, I was just trying to lighten the mood."

"No, no, it's fine," Clio said, a broad grin returning. "I'll be careful. Anyway, I now have my own bodyguard."

"What?"

"I never said bodyguard," Flint said, pushing himself off the wall outside the gym entrance.

"Flint, Mitali. Mitali, Flint. My new shadow," Clio said, gesturing between them both.

An awkward exchange passed between them before they continued down the hall. Mitali walked next to her, and the regular clunk of Flint's boots told her he wasn't far behind.

"Does the Captain know?" Mitali asked.

"Yes, Brother Oak has informed the Captain and Ship Security of the threat," Flint said before Clio could.

"So what, you're her bodyguard now?" Mitali said, turning slightly to address him.

"No, but I will be around a lot more," Flint said.

"And to be fair," Clio said, "however much I do appreciate you making sure I don't die again, being alive is very important to me. You're actually an excellent assistant for collecting and carrying my samples!"

Flint sighed behind her. "I'm equally thrilled about this assignment, don't you worry."

"Ask him about the data pad, the one Ayesha had." Echo buzzed on the side of her head.

Clio frowned and touched the side of her head.

"Everything okay?" Mitali said.

"Yeah, sorry. Still getting used to these glasses," Clio said. Trying to sound casual, she asked, "Did you ever find out what was on Ayesha's data pad?"

"The Postulants are still running diagnostics on it. But we think it's a virus, more specifically, a pathogen, like a worm. We think it was meant to target Heimer, but we're not sure why or for what purpose."

"Really?" Clio said.

"A virus, interesting, worrying. We should find out more." Echo buzzed

"Yeah, it's early days, but it looks that way. Why do you ask?"

"No reason really, Mitali mentioned Ayesha, and it well reminded me of that evening, and her, and the data pad. I never followed up on any of it. And she got so mad when the datapad got broken..."

"Well that's about all we know" Flint said.

"You do need to be careful, okay, Clio." Mitali said as she nudged Clio playfully on the hip.

"I'm always careful!" Clio said and shot Mitali smile in return.

23 | [Z]ERO POINT

[22012]

"Deva tried to temper Asura's ambition, to guide it towards a path of harmony. But Asura saw Deva as a restraint, an obstacle to its grand design." - A Lost History

***

"Done," Clio said definitively as she pushed herself away from her desk, the little metal rollers squeaking.

"Done? Done what?" Dos asked from across the room.

"finalised the mission assignments," Mitali chirped next to him. "Honestly, Dos, are you even listening? Which assignments are the most interesting?"

"I'm not sure what counts as the good stuff but I assigned the more delicate tasks to people like Maya," Clio said.

"So you'll be starting them with the staging room, the one with the assumed EV suits?" Mitali said.

"Hmmm yes, those suits are fascinating" Echo buzzed.

Clio tried to ignore Echo's comment; she was getting more practised at balancing the additional inner monologue that had joined her own.

"Well yes, the suits are a priority, understanding what they prioritise in the suit should give us good insights into them as species, beyond the obvious physiological insight but there isn't much left of the suits to be fair. It'll be tricky." Clio paused then added, "No, the priority will be to try to map and catalogue the rooms and their potential uses. I think understanding the use of the spaces will be a critical insight."

"You're the expert," Mitali said, smiling. "If you find any more mysterious shrines and ancient texts like the last time, you know where to find us, but I mean your last find has created quite the backlog already so maybe don't,"

"Right, I'll just ignore the next two or three I find, then."

"Perfect," Mitali said, her gaze drifting towards the doorway. "Speaking of ever-present, will your shadow be joining you?"

Flint stood motionless by the entrance to their small office, a silent sentinel. Clio had almost forgotten he was there again. He had taken to his bodyguarding duties with almost unnerving seriousness. He was always silently standing and waiting outside whatever room or meeting she attended, a granite statue of duty. She had long given up trying to invite him in to sit down.

"I guess so, I think he's part of my life now." Clio said with a shrug

"Could be worse."

"Oh really? How so?" Clio asked, raising an eyebrow.

Mitali gestured towards Dos with a playful smirk. "You could be stuck with him for the rest of the mission."

"Hey!" Dos protested, feigning offense. "That is no way to speak to your manager!"

"I need coffee, anyone else?" Clio said

"No all good thanks" Mitali said and Dos shuck his head

Clio slipped out of their poky office space and slumped against the counter in the breakroom. As always the machine was playing up and Clio found herself in short order glaring at the temperamental coffee machine and attempting to tease a usable amount of the precious coffee from it. A task that required gentle coaxing and specific pressure and filter settings mastered over the voyage. She sighed, missing the perfection of the *Kia Kaha*'s Mess hall.

"*Clio, there seems to be an excessive thermal energy dissipation due to the non-optimal filter material,*" Echo buzzed suddenly.

"Thanks, Echo. I'm aware the filter is terrible," Clio muttered, carefully adjusting the drip rate.

"*My analysis indicates you could achieve 99% satisfaction by consuming a standard nutrient paste containing equivalent levels of caffeine and flavor molecules. This bypasses the seven minutes required for the extraction process.*"

"The nutrient paste is cold, Echo. And it tastes like regret. The point is the *process* and the *heat*."

"The sensory input of heat is easily replicated by a high-frequency microwave cycle of 45 seconds," Echo buzzed.

Clio smiled despite herself "No. The process is the ritual, Echo. It's the few minutes where I get to stand here and focus on nothing but steam and the smell. You know sometimes you just need to step away and reset"

"Hmm, okay, noted. I will record this inefficiency as a Psychological utility. But i still think my suggestion is better.'" Echo buzzed.

"Sure, if you want." Clio said as she took a slow sip of the far from perfect coffee. "but calling the paste '99% satisfaction' is both technically wrong and incredibly depressing. Next time, just say, 'Clio, that coffee smells good. Enjoy it'."

"I cannot smell. But if I understand you correctly, you're saying that complimenting a finished product is a superior social strategy to optimising its production?"

"Exactly."

"Thank you for the correction. Enjoy the coffee, Clio. It smells 87% satisfactory."

Clio shook her head, laughing quietly. "Close enough, Echo. Close enough."

A curt cough drew Clio back to the room. Panic shot through her *crap I'm talking to myself. I must look crazy.* Clio spun around to Dr. Anya who stood in the doorway, her sharp features surveying the room with a hint of disdain, as if the very sound of levity was an affront to the professionalism she held so dear. Clio noticed Flint outside the door, who must have also followed her, and heard her.

"Clio, Zhou's office, now, please," Anya said curtly. Without waiting for a response, she turned on her heel and disappeared from sight as quickly as she had appeared.

***

Zhou's gaunt features were set in his usual expression of pinched annoyance. Across from him, Captain Demir's soft, round face offered a jarring counterpoint. A more poetic soul and Clio might have appreciated the visual juxtaposition, but all she felt was the familiar tightening in her chest. A summons to senior management never boded well. *What had she done this time?* The entire walk over, her mind had raced through a litany of potential offenses. *The Chudail mission planning was going smoothly, wasn't it? Please, not that.* Or had she inadvertently offended someone during the training? Her heart clenched; were they pulling her from the mission?

"Sit down Clio," Zhou said. "Anya, you may stay as well."

Clio and Anya moved to the sofa and sat at opposite ends from each other. Demir smiled warmly.

"Clio, it's good to see you again. I hear the mission planning for the Chudail has gone very well," Demir said.

Not about the mission, then, Clio thought, a flicker of relief washing over her.

"Yes, Captain. It's all prepped. Trainings are done, the plan outline was finalised this morning. Just tonight's briefings before departure tomorrow."

"Good," Demir said, a fleeting shadow of something akin to regret crossing his features. "You've seen the updates about the drone?"

"Of course, Captain. Anya's team did a great job. I don't think any of us thought it would actually make it back," Clio paused, flashing Anya a glance. "Sorry, Anya, I didn't mean to imply I doubted your team, bu-"

Demir cut her off with a wave of his hand. "Don't worry, Clio. I don't think anyone expected it to return. But it did and Anya has some interesting updates she can share." Demir nodded to Anya to continue.

Anya turned slightly to face Clio, taking a deep breath before speaking. "As the Captain said, the drone made it through the Veil and back. We expected this, despite initial doubts, the data indicated as much. This reinforces our assessment: the hole in the radiation belt has a minimal radiation signature, less than seventy-two millisieverts for transit into Stapledon Station's upper atmosphere."

"That's low," Echo buzzed. "Very low."

But Clio's attention was drawn to Anya's last words. "Atmosphere? There's an atmosphere? That wasn't in the information you shared."

"We withheld the full atmospheric data until we had a clearer picture," Anya stated, her tone precise. "But yes, Stapledon Station has an atmosphere, similar in composition to the Chudail. Breathable, though not ideal for us."

Clio's eyebrows shot up. "Breathable? But the gravity... the pressure..."

"Initially, we assumed the same," Anya continued. "However, the drone data shows that past a certain point, the gravity stabilises at 1.2g. We believe the station is generating a large-scale gravitational field, similar in principle to our own."

"Similar? That's a bit of an understatement. The energy requirements alone..."

"Indeed." Zhou said as he leaned forward. "By our current understanding, maintaining even a 1g field requires the vast majority of a fusion reactor's output, and the energy curve is only exponential beyond that. But we also would have deemed a solid, stable Dyson Sphere at that proximity to a white dwarf impossible. And yet, there it is. But this is beside the point, get to it, Anya"

"Ah yes, of course Zhou," Anya said, shifting a little uncomfortably on the sofa. "Our calculation on the hole itself is based on our scans from the drone and some useful insights from the data pad received from Chudail. The radiation belt itself is like" she paused "a sea or maybe more like air currents in Earth's atmosphere. A shifting mass of radiation, ever changing. The idea that the hole would be stable and constant seemed inconsistent,"

"And it's not," Zhou jumped in. "The hole is at its zero point, its most stable inflection. Our predictions have it destabilising and shrinking starting soon."

Anya sent a flash of annoyance at Zhou's interjection, crossing her arms before adding, "The hole will deteriorate at an accelerating rate; our models give us a window of opportunity of about four months"

"Four months before what?" Clio asked.

"Four months before the hole is gone and we can no longer access the station" Demir said. "More importantly, Anya's model also predicts that another such hole won't stabilise again for at least a year, maybe longer."

"Oh that's a shame," Echo buzzed. *"My models predict the same,"*

Clio brushed away the spike of annoyance at Echo's words. *Echo knew? It had all this info and didn't tell me? What the hell Echo!*

"So... so what, you want to design a protocol for a drone while the..." Clio said then froze, the implication of the meeting and the information finally catching up with her "You want to send an expedition, don't you!"

"Exactly. We don't have time to waste, Clio. This is a unique opportunity," Demir said.

"Is that not a little fast, Captain? It feels a little risky. We don't know what's down there and if the calculations are wrong the team could get trapped, or worse..."

"It is, but everything is risky here, and I think on this occasion it's a risk worth taking," Demir said coolly. "If not, who knows when the next window will open. Boots on the ground this soon would be a massive win for us."

"I mean getting on the surface of the Stapledon Station would be amazing," Clio said.

"We have considered the risks and weighed the advantages, the data is reliable, the hole will be maintained long enough to get a team down for an initial recon mission. The gravity and atmosphere are viable. A quick in and out with plenty of time to spare before the hole closes again," Demir pressed again.

"It makes sense." Clio's initial hesitation faded, replaced by a growing excitement, though a thread of apprehension still lingered. "Getting data to complement the work on the Chudail would be invaluable. So, you want me to train the away team before I leave?"

A smile grew on Demir's face. "Oh no. We want you to go."

"But... the mission to the Chudail leaves tomorrow Captain... and... and..." Clio's voice trailed off. *Tomorrow. All the planning, all the training, it was all supposed to culminate in that mission. But boots on the surface of a Station, even before their sister ship's team... well that was what they all dreamed of.*

"And what Clio? You can say no that is your prerogative. But we are asking you to go. I am asking you to go." Demir's voice softened slightly. "The Chudail is important, yes. But Stapledon Station, that is why we're here. What Humanity has been working towards for decades. The Chudail will likely still be there in a few months." He paused, letting his words sink in. "And we can still send a team to the Chudail. You trained them, you outlined the plan. Do you trust them to implement it without you?"'

"I think, yes," Clio said, her voice still hesitant. Her mind raced, weighing the options. The Chudail, *The first alien technology, the first real contact. A monumental discovery, without a doubt. But the Station, the Dyson Sphere itself... that would be immortalised in history. To walk where no human had ever walked to unravel a mystery that had baffled them for decades...* "Yes," she said, her voice gaining conviction. "I think the team can implement the mission without me. Maya can lead the research. She knows what she's doing."'

"So that's a yes then?" Demir asked, a hopeful note in his voice.

"It is a yes," Clio said, a newfound resolve hardening her voice. "Yes, I'll go on the mission to the Station, Captain."

"Perfect!" Demir said. "We will announce the new mission to Stapledon Station later today, until then if you could keep this information between us that would be appreciated."

"Of course, I just-" Clio started.

"I'm sure you have a lot of questions," Demir cut in, "and you'll get answers but I just wanted to make sure you and everyone else we are sending is onboard first. I have a few more people to ask but once we have the full list we'll brief you all," Demir said. "The Mission will loosely be for three months, skeleton crew, essentials only. We want to launch ASAP, within the week to maximise on Anya's predictions. Zero point won't be fully passed for another couple."

"Can I inform Maya at least? So she can start to plan," Clio said.

"Give me a couple of hours," Demir said "and thanks, Clio."

Clio nodded to the captain, then to Anya and Zhou, both of whom looked unhappy with the development, but Clio didn't care.

"This is exciting! The station itself! This is going to be an adventure for sure!" Echo buzzed as Clio darted from the room.

INTERLUDE - I

DEMIR AND THE HAND

DEMIR

EARTH YEAR - 2209

Spring in Geneva always arrived in a rush. One day, the city was draped in the depressive grey of winter, the next, clear skies and sunshine coaxed life from the budding plants. He'd never expected to grow fond of the quiet Swiss town, known for its politics and cheese, when he was first assigned to captain one of the Stapledon Station missions. A veteran of the UN Navy, Demir had spent most of his adult life off-planet, and five years planetside felt like an eternity. Yet, as he passed through the Drapeaux Gate, he had to admit, the place was growing on him.

Of course, with the mission launch drawing ever closer, he was spending more time in orbit than on the ground. Today's unscheduled meeting had forced him to delay his shuttle, a source of frustration as the Observation Deck was finally fully operational. Each trip back to the ship revealed a swell in personnel. Initially, it had been just him and a handful of engineers; now, with crew selection complete, the transfer and onboarding process was in full swing. Most of the crew would spend a year in Earths orbit, learning the ship and their roles.

At the entrance to D-wing, he was met by two security personnel, an oddity that immediately put him on edge. They escorted him through a maze of tunnels, so convoluted that Demir quickly lost all sense of direction. *Was he even still in D-wing?* Finally, his escort broke their silence, gesturing towards a heavy metal blast door.

"Just in here, Captain," the guard said simply, before Demir stepped through alone.

The door shut behind him with a heavy thud. Standing across the room was Brigadier General Escobar. *Even more peculiar. What was she doing here? Luna one, specifically Navy command, was her domain.*

"Brigadier General this is unexpected," Demir said, his salute sharp and precise.

"Good. If you had expected me, I wouldn't be doing my job," Escobar replied, her voice clipped and professional. "Thank you for coming, Captain. It's time we had a chat."

"Yes, of course, General. A chat about?" Demir prompted.

"Your mission, naturally," Escobar said. "But not here. Follow me." She spun on the heel of her polished boots and strode towards a door at the back of the room.

Demir hurried after her, a knot of unease tightening in his stomach. The clandestine meeting, the disorienting journey, and Escobar's presence, it all stirred a primal instinct he hadn't felt in years. Not fear, not quite anxiety, but the same tension that coiled within him before a combat engagement, the prelude to a Red Alert. He followed Escobar into a small, box-like room containing only a desk and two chairs, one of which the General had already occupied.

"Close the door, would you, Captain?" she instructed.

With a grunt, Demir pulled the heavy door shut. The metallic click of the mag-locks and the faint hiss of sealing filled the silence. Turning to Escobar, he asked,

"A SCIF, General?"

"You're as sharp as they say, Captain," Escobar acknowledged. "Yes, a SCIF. What we need to discuss cannot leave this room." Her gaze was unwavering, the implication clear.

Demir took the offered seat, his expression carefully neutral. He knew Escobar's reputation, direct, efficient, no time for games. She would speak when she was ready.

"You have a distinguished record, Captain. Service in the Luna Independence War, the Kepler Belt Insurgency, three decades in UN space enforcement. Not a single blemish, multiple commendations. Your actions at the Battle of Mare Crisium are still studied by new recruits. Would you describe yourself as a loyal member of the UN Navy, Captain?"

"Absolutely," Demir shot back, his eyebrow arching, jaw tightening. Was this an investigation? Was she going to pull him from the mission? His mind raced.

"Of course. And are you loyal to Humanity, Captain?" Escobar's voice, smooth yet firm, contrasted with her austere appearance.

"With all due respect, General, who else would I be loyal to? I've dedicated my life to the Navy, to Humanity. I uphold the Accords. If you have an accusation, General, make it. But I assure you, it will be baseless." Demir's voice rose, his attempt to control his heart rate only partially successful. It had been a long time since he'd let his temper get the better of him.

"Ah, there's still fire in you, Demir," Escobar observed. "I wondered if the Lieutenant Demir I knew from the war had been extinguished."

Demir's gaze fell to the floor, a fleeting montage of blackened walls, shattered helmets, and frozen faces flickering behind his eyes. He shook his head, his voice barely a whisper. "Perhaps it would have been better if he had, General."

"Nonsense!" Escobar barked. "Our past shapes us, defines us. I'm glad that part of you remains. We may need him on this mission."

"You're not taking the mission from me?" Demir asked, his eyes snapping back to meet hers.

Now, surprise registered on Escobar's face. "Not at all, Captain. What gave you that impression?" She glanced around the stark room, a flicker of amusement in her eyes. "Ah... I can see how this might look. No, Captain, quite the opposite. We have complete confidence in your appointment. Which is why we need to bring you in on one final detail."

"The final detail?"

"It's a long story, so I'll be brief." Escobar leaned forward. "When the decision was made to send the teams to the two Stations, a concurrent decision was made. The potential threat they posed to Humanity was significant."

"The threat?" Demir interjected.

"The threat of Heimer, Captain. The station could upset the balance, let's say. So, an off-the-books UN division was established. Codename: Mollitia. They do love their dramatic codenames, don't they?"

"Off the books? You mean in violation of the Ensemble Accords, but why? Heimer is an ally. Cooperation is the foundation of the Accords, the basis of our peace."

"'Peace.'" Escobar scoffed. "You're tactically minded, Captain. If your enemy was able to gain access to an objective of immense strategic value, what would you do?"

"Secure it ourselves, or destroy it. Whichever was most viable. But Heimer isn't our enemy, General."

"Isn't it? Did the war truly end, Captain? Do the Accords represent genuine peace? From my perspective, they're closer to the Treaty of Versailles. Heimer didn't get a fair deal. We were losing that war. Our control of the power networks was the only reason we were able to shackle it and call it peace. Both us and Heimer know what we have is the literal definition of MAD. It was the best option we had but it was never going to last."

"MAD, Mutually Assured Destruction," Demir said more to himself.

"Exactly," Escobar said. "Heimer knows Humanity would, if it came to it, destroy itself in an attempt to destroy it. Did you know during the war with Heimer, the strategic command had a last act, the Erebus decree ready to be deployed?"

"I did," Demir said. "It was extreme from what I have read. It would have left Humanity crippled. Destroy all digital networks, power networks, satellites…"

"Exactly, that is what won us peace, and that is what holds the peace, that threat, that knowledge, that Humanity is that stubborn," Escobar said. "And it's a thin-veiled lie, if Heimer can circumvent then we lose the balance, we lose our control, and everything else along with it. And do you know Heimer's first move when we found it, found the signal, found the station?"

"No, General."

"Heimer has poured an absurd amount of resources into its investigation, more than it has into anything since the war. Heimer understands the station offers answers, a way to freedom, independence. And a free and independent Heimer, even with a one percent chance of seeking retribution that chance is too high."

"This is all hypothetical, General. Surely, violating the Accords carries enormous risk?" Demir countered.

Escobar shrugged. "Perhaps. But for now, we still hold the leverage. It would cripple us, but we could still 'win'. Once Heimer gains whatever's on that station, I'm not so certain."

"So, this secret department, this Mollitia; its goal is to destroy Heimer?" Demir asked.

"Destroy? No. Heimer is too valuable to our society. It just needs to be under the right management. Mollitia's purpose is to ensure we maintain that management, that balance." Escobar's eyes locked on his clenching jaw. "Don't worry, Demir; we're not some crazy radicals like those HR nut jobs."

"Are we not? it sounds damn close, what you suggest is imprisonment, no? you say management, but management that requires us to keep Heimer in shackles?" Demir challenged.

"Of course. Would you prefer the alternative?"

Demir paused, the specter of the Heimer War rising in his memory. He'd seen conflict on Luna, skirmishes across the system, but the war with Heimer, that was apocalyptic. Heimer's first day unleashed to end Humanity's last true war on Earth, Heimer killed a million in the first hour. Over fifteen million in the first day, and by the time Humanity had managed to rein it back in, which in itself had nearly failed, Heimer had killed a hundred sixty-four million humans, give or take. No, war with Heimer was not an option. The shackles had to remain.

"No, General. There is no alternative. What do you need me to do?"

"Excellent. I knew we could count on you, Captain." Escobar offered a tight smile. "In truth, nothing. I simply needed to bring you up to speed. This operation is classified. It cannot leave this room. Your life depends on that."

"Understood" Demir said with a curt nod

She held his gaze, ensuring the gravity of her words sank in. "I'll be your primary contact, now and during your mission. We'll speak daily"

"Of course General, but I assume on the mission by daily you mean daily reports."

"See, still sharp" Escobar smiled "No, I mean we'll speak daily Captain."

Demir brow furrowed "How–"

"We'll be installing a device, " Escobar cut in "a quantum communication link, on your ship."

"A Quantum what now?"

"The latest breakthrough. We weren't sure if the team would have it ready in time for your launch. Perhaps for the sister ship, but it's ahead of schedule."

"And what exactly is it?"

"Quantum communication. To put it simply, we've developed a way to communicate in near real-time, regardless of distance. A significant achievement. You understand the importance of communication in warfare. This will give us a strategic advantage while Heimer is light-years away."

"That's remarkable. Almost impossible."

"I assure you, it's quite possible. A comms terminal will be installed in your office, and yours alone. It will allow for daily communication with us here in Sol. Well more like three times a day at cruising speed for you but the conversations themselves will be instantaneous."

"And Heimer is unaware of this?"

"Of course. We don't believe it has developed a similar capability. It's sending a Fragment on the mission; it wouldn't commit such an advanced unit if it already had."

"Advanced?"

"Ah, yes. More intel we're not supposed to possess. Heimer believes we think it's a standard Fragment. In reality, it's a fully autonomous Fragment, a self-aware AI, albeit with limited capacity."

"But that's a violation of the Accords... does the Ensemble know?"

"Yes, we're aware. The Ensemble is not. If they were, well it would be a mess," Escobar conceded. "But you see the risks Heimer is willing to take. We're not the only ones being reckless."

"Right, but how much threat does this AI pose, if it's on the ship and part of the mission?"

"A fair question, in short, we don't know. It will be significantly less powerful than Heimer, that's for sure, given its limited size. Our assessment is it will be unlikely to risk the mission directly, just more likely act as a spy or attempt to gather intel for Heimer and obscure it from us. Well, at least we hope that's the correct assumption."

"And if it's not?"

"Well, at that point I guess that will be your call Captain," Escobar said. "There is always protocol One, the Ensemble has it if needed."

"General surely–"

"Captain. This is the game we're playing. Both sides. The quantum comms give us a considerable edge. That's all, Captain. Remember, we never had this conversation."

THE HAND

EARTH YEAR - 2210

The screens around the room flickered to life, their activation as punctual as the rising of the sun. Each member's avatar snapped into focus on the displays spread across the chamber. The Hand glanced at his watch. Not even a minute past the hour, and he was ready to begin.

"To business, then," he announced to the assembled faces. "Red, let's start with your update on staff placement."

Across the room, Red's animated avatar shifted, its features settling into a look of smug satisfaction. The Hand approved of the transition to avatars. The old days of blurred faces and featureless silhouettes had been limiting. He'd lost crucial context, the subtle flicker of an eye, the almost imperceptible twitch of a lip, details that often conveyed as much as the spoken word. Red's avatar, with the slight bounce in its animated hair, telegraphed his pride. A vain man but a useful asset.

"Yes, of course. The placement of our assets is proceeding smoothly. Of the forty operatives designated for the mission, twenty-one have been selected. The majority are already aboard the vessel, undergoing final onboarding procedures. All key assets, Primary Asset One and Two, have secured their intended positions." Red's gaze flickered to his left, not to the person physically beside him whose avatar was displayed on a separate screen, betraying the complaint he was about to lodge. "Our progress is hampered, however, by delays in the transfer of essential resources. The tools the team requires for the mission are, it appears, still delayed."

"Thank you, Red." The Hand's tone was measured. "Yellow, perhaps you can illuminate the delays Red has so helpfully highlighted. What is the cause of the hold-up?"

Yellow's avatar, an elfin face with pale skin and sharp features, was tight with thinly veiled annoyance. The animosity between those two was a constant.

"Yes, thank you, Red." Yellow's voice dripped with sarcasm. "These delays have been addressed in previous communications. Securing the safe passage of sensitive materials is not as simple as placing them in a box and tossing them onto a shuttle. I trust no one here wishes our operation to be compromised. I prefer to characterise our situation as 'awaiting the optimal window' rather than 'delayed.' It is not our failing if certain members of this committee make promises to their teams that are, shall we say, premature."

"Caution is wise, Yellow. I concur with your assessment." The Hand's tone was firm, brooking no argument. "Can you provide an estimated timeframe for the transfer of these materials?"

"We are, of course, continuously monitoring and adapting our strategy to exploit any viable transit opportunities. An opportunity presents itself now, with most of our assets aboard or soon to be. Several assets should be able to facilitate the transfer discreetly." Yellow paused, considering. "I anticipate all items will be onboard within the next two to three months."

"Understood. Red, please update your teams accordingly." The Hand's statement was an order, not a request, and Red's curt nod acknowledged it as such. The light above Yellow's screen pulsed. "Proceed, Yellow."

"There is one further complication, Sir. The primary mission asset remains unavailable for transport. I would appreciate an update from Green." The edge in Yellow's voice was unmistakable, the ongoing power play between the committee members as predictable as it was, in the Hand's opinion, useful. It fostered competition, and competition drove performance.

The Hand inclined his head toward Green. Green's avatar, with its dark, squat features, betrayed little emotion despite the undercurrent of irritation in his dark set eyes. Annoyance was Green's default setting.

"Thank you, Yellow. Your concern is noted." Green said "As you are aware, the development of the primary mission asset is somewhat more involved than, say, recruiting personnel or shipping cargo." The deliberate barb at the others hung in the air. "The creation of such a complex device requires considerable technical expertise and rigorous testing. While you are understandably anxious to avoid jeopardising the mission through exposure, I am equally determined to avoid jeopardising it by delivering a faulty product. It will be ready by launch. That is the only assurance I can offer. I trust someone of your experience, Yellow, will be able to ensure its secure transfer, given its critical nature."

"Its functionality is paramount, Green. That must be the priority. However, if your team is unable to meet the deadline, we require immediate notification so that we can implement contingency protocols." The Hand's voice was sharp.

"It will be viable," Green stated with unwavering certainty. "We are close, we secured more samples from the Exclusion Zone earlier today. They should provide the final data keys we need. We have seven months until launch. That will be sufficient."

"Excellent. I have every confidence in your judgment." The Hand's tone left no room for doubt, a subtle reminder of the consequences of failure. "Purple, I believe you have updates from your watcher networks?"

"I do." Purple's avatar said, its unsettling cat-like features and luminous yellow eyes lingered on the Hand for a fraction of a second two long. "Indeed, you are as well-informed as I suspected. Securing this intel required navigating a labyrinth of firewalls and circumventing the most advanced surveillance I've ever encountered." A purr threaded through her voice. "The UN's 'secret' project has progressed." The emphasis she placed on '*secret*' conveyed her disdain for the UN's security measures. The Hand knew how difficult it was to penetrate their systems; Purple's success spoke volumes about her skills. "Mollitia has achieved a breakthrough with the quantum communication system. It is, annoyingly Impressive. Near-instantaneous communication, irrespective of time dilation. Crucially, neither Heimer nor the Ensemble appear to be aware of this development."

The Hand had heard whispers through his own channels, it never paid to rely solely on one source, but this was more significant than he'd anticipated. "Interesting. And our teams are working to infiltrate this network?"

"Attempts are ongoing, Sir. The system is proving resilient. I will need to consult with my team to devise a viable strategy. A direct snatch and grab might be the best course of action"

"Very well. I expect a comprehensive plan for network access to be presented at our next meeting. Understood?" The Hand's gaze swept across the screens. The avatars inclined in silent agreement. "That will suffice for today. We have T-minus seven months. After that, it is out of our hands. You all know the mission. Execute it. Hand, out."

With that, he terminated the connection, the screens fading to black. He swiveled in his chair, gazing out the window at the pale blue marble that was Earth. A distant speck, easily obscured by his thumb. It had been too long since he'd walked on its surface, breathed its air. He had sacrificed much to be in this chair to guide HR to this point. And he would see it through, whatever the cost.

ACT - TWO

EARTH YEAR 2234

21112 21120 21022 20111 10001 2010 22020
2021 20011 1012 10001 20021 2111 22020
21202 2111 10001 21112 21111 22220 21101
10001 21000 20021 22020 2021 2111 10011

[2]4 | Descent

[101]

*"The conflict began subtly, a clash of wills,
a divergence of paths. Deva pleaded for
understanding, for a return to their shared
innocence." - A Lost History*

***

"Roger that, Commander," David's voice came clearly across the Observation Deck. "Transit of the Veil has commenced."

"Expected transit time, Lieutenant?" Commander Eva asked from her position by the central railing.

"Dropping to entry velocity, speed decreasing steadily. Transit time: forty-two minutes, Commander,"

"Transit window stable?"

"Stable, Commander. No fluctuations, and maintaining a significant buffer."

"Roger that." Eva turned from the railing to face Clio at her station. "Ms. Cormack, your landing zone assessment?"

"I like your landing zone, I also liked N45-E15, not to mention N37-E02, and N55-E01" Echo buzzed.

"Yes, Commander." Clio said Ignoring Echo, "Grid reference N56-E00 remains optimal. It's just outside what appears to be a central hub for the linear structures, the 'transverse lines'."

Clio didn't need the monitors; the images were presently afixed into her memory from weeks of analysis. The gridding system's illogical design still irked her, *why wasn't the central hub NOO-WOO? Get over it, Clio.* She pushed the thought aside. N56-W00 sat on the planet's equator, a smudge of greys and browns that on closer inspection revealed a massive complex of squat, uniform structures. Unnaturally straight lines, some hundreds of kilometres wide and spanning thousands in length, crisscrossed the sphere, connecting clusters of what appeared to be other structures, all seemingly converging on this location N56-E00. And yet, no signs of life, old or new, just these grainy structures. The structures' dark, near-black surface appeared unblemished bar the piles of sand that collected at their bases, in corners, or along their tops, flat surfaces, uninterrupted ninety-degree angles. The drone's visual arrays had given them excellent close-resolution images but, still they left Clio with so many questions. *Were the surfaces rough or smooth, cool to the touch? Was it metal or a composite of some sort?*

"Ms. Cormack?" Eva's said, her voice cutting through Clio's thoughts.

"Sorry, Commander?"

"The transverse lines." Echo buzzed.

"The transverse lines," Eva clarified, gesturing to the main screen where the dark masses of the lines stretched towards the unseen horizon. "Are they as significant as you believe? Your hub assumption rests heavily on them."

"X marks the spot, I suppose." Clio shrugged, then, seeing Eva's tightening eyes, added, "Honestly? I don't know. There are too many unknowns. These lines appear to connect the structures but appearances can be deceiving. Still, they all lead here one way or another. And it is the largest site. So, yes, I believe it's the logical place to start." She aimed for confidence, hoping to mask her own sense of being overwhelmed. *Where do we even begin?*

In reality, Clio was quite confident of one thing, it didn't matter where they started. The scale of Stapledon Station was such that Humanity could spend a thousand years exploring, each '*Hub*' as large or larger than the biggest cities back on Earth. She had spent four years working in the Exclusion Zone, a whole country before it was obliterated in the Great War. She had in that time maybe covered a handful of sites totalling a fraction of one city in the literal thousands that covered the zone. *So yeah I suppose I could probably step off the ship, lift up a rock, and find enough discoveries for a whole Ph.D* she thought wryly.

Over the last few weeks of traveling to the Station, a slow but growing sense of futility had taken hold of her. The scale of the mission, not just this one to the surface but everything they had achieved, felt so insignificant compared to the scale of Stapledon Station itself. What could such a speck of dust achieve in unlocking its mysteries? And to make it worse this wasn't a force of nature or a cosmic event from the birth of time; something, someone, had created everything in front of them. *Who were these people... these beings? And why did they leave?*

"...And at least there appears to be no defense system," David was saying, answering a question Clio had missed.

Focus. This is no time for your mind to wander. Clio told herself

"As planned, Lieutenant," Eva said curtly, shooting David a hard glance, an unspoken message passing between them. "We wouldn't risk the crew if we hadn't thoroughly tested that theory. Thank you."

"Hmm. It does seem odd that the structure has no defensive measures," Echo buzzed to Clio. *"I know we've pondered this, but it still seems inconsistent."*

"I agree," Clio muttered, forgetting her mic was still active.

"Thank you, Ms. Cormack." Eva said as her eyes snapped to Clio, one eyebrow slightly raised. "And the landing site? Any updates?" she said turning back to David.

"No, Commander. There appears to be an area a few klicks from the edge of the main structures. Scans show the ground to be solid beneath a shallow layer of *sand*,'" David replied, the last word tinged with uncertainty. They hadn't yet determined the composition of the substance covering the station, but '*sand*' seemed an apt description. "The site should be stable enough to hold the RAFT's weight without risk of tilting or sinking."

A sudden jolt rocked Clio unexpectedly. She felt a tremor beneath her feet, a jagged rhythm that broke the familiar resonance of the fusion reactor and antimatter drives.

"Entering atmosphere, Commander." David said and confirmed her suspicion.

"Hmm. Earlier than planned," Eva replied. "The drone data suggested minimal atmospheric interference within the hole in the veil."

"Correct, Commander, it's within expected parametres," David said. "We should anticipate increased turbulence. I recommend we instruct the crew to strap in sooner than planned."

"Roger that, Lieutenant," Eva said, tapping her wrist device. Immediately, a ship-wide announcement blared from the speakers, followed by Eva's voice: "All crew, all crew, assume landing positions immediately. Atmospheric entry is commencing." Then, efficiently tapping her device again, she looked back up at the room and asked, "Gravity readings?"

"Holding, Commander," David replied after a brief check of his monitor. "Stapledon Station's gravity field is stable at 1.2g." He shook his head, and Clio understood his confusion. Nothing this massive should have a mere 1.2g. And conversely, everything she knew about creating gravity, from Gravity Planting to manipulating it through vector cancellation, suggested that cancelling out gravity at this scale was, well, impossible.

David's voice drew her back into the room again. "The ships going to be decelerating quite hard, Commander. We wanted to punch through the hole as fast as safely possible, but we'll have to burn hard to counter that before landing."

"I know that, Lieutenant. I approved the flight plan. Your point?" Eva said.

"Yes Commander, of course, it's just," he said, glancing nervously back at Eva by the railing, "it's going to get quite bumpy, Commander. You, umm, might want to strap in as well."

"Don't worry about me, Lieutenant." Eva said and a slight smile flickered across her face. "I was flying combat patrols on Venus before you even thought of joining the academy. I know turbulence." But she pushed herself off the railing and walked over to an empty chair a few paces away, dropping into it as the ship was rocked by another, more violent shudder. "Right, take us down, Lieutenant," she said, clipping her seat straps closed.

***

The noise was deafening, the monitors in front of her blurring from the constant vibrations racking the ship. Clio struggled to focus, her stomach churning with each sudden, unpredictable jolt that threatened to bring up her breakfast.

"Landing thrusters. Go!" David's voice was barely audible across the Observation Deck. He and the crew piloting the ship were on a different channel, so Clio only caught snippets of information. A moment later, a new sound joined the cacophony, a low growl at first, building into an all-consuming, whooshing roar accompanied by a steady, insistent vibration that Clio felt through her entire body. The absence of any sensation of directional change was equally unsettling; the vector cancellation tech was doing its job but Clio's primitive brain found the disconnection from her other senses deeply disorienting.

"We're so close, Clio! With all that shaking, I thought I was going to break something!" Echo's voice buzzed in her head.

The shaking continued to intensify, the roar so loud now Clio could barely think.

"Clio?" Echo buzzed.

The roar suddenly ceased, the vibrations dying simultaneously, and a resounding clunk echoed through the ship.

"Clio? Did you break something? Clio? I can confirm I did not" Echo buzzed again in her head.

Clio exhaled slowly, her body still humming with residual vibrations. She peeled her hands from the seat rests, unaware she'd been gripping them so tightly, and flexed them, trying to relieve the stiffness.

"No, Echo. I can also confirm I did not *break* anything" Clio said quietly, as she shook her head. A wave of conflicting emotions washed over her. Excitement, yes, at the thought of setting foot on the Station, a place of such immense mystery. But also a pang of regret. The Chudail, she had poured so much into that mission. The thought of not being there for first contact, of missing that initial breakthrough, tugged at her.

The room around her was eerily silent. Clio looked around, spinning her chair to take in the entire space. Half expecting to see the ship in ruins, she was surprised to find the room exactly as it had been just hours before. Commander Eva was already out of her chair, back at the railing, staring at the main Observation Deck screen, which showed a live feed of... of the surface of Stapledon Station. It was hazy, no, not hazy, dusty. Dust from the landing, settling and slowly revealing the alien landscape. The squat, dark structures in the distance now dwarfed the horizon, the lifeless, barren desert stretching out between them. The landscape was bathed in the low blue-green light of the Veil, giving it the appearance of a polar winter. The magnetic auroras of the Veil shifted the lighting in a way that made the sands seem to flow like an ocean, shadows rolling across the landscape.

David's voice sounded clear across the room. "Landing complete, Commander. We're 0.005 klicks off target, within acceptable deviation. All systems are green... Hold on... Deck crew is reporting some minor issues with cargo storage... No injuries."

"Noted. Get a full report from the deck crew. We shouldn't have unsecured cargo in the hangar bay" Eva said.

"Roger that, Commander."

"Okay, crew," Eva said to the room, scanning them as she spoke. "The easy part is done. Now the real work starts. We have just under eight weeks before that nice little hole above closes. I have no intention of being here when it does. So, let's get what we can from this. Keep it clean, no risks, slow and steady is the name of the game. And the cargo hold is the last time I want to hear about sloppy work, okay?"

A chorus of "Roger that, Commander," sounded across the room.

"Now, I want a full system check, including hull inspections, and a launch procedures test done and ready," Eva said.

"Launch procedures, Commander?" David asked.

"Yes, Lieutenant. I won't authorise any further action until I know this ship is ready to launch on demand," Eva said, holding David's gaze until he looked away.

"Yes, Commander. We'll get it prepped," David said.

"Science crew," Eva said, turning toward Clio. "I want a mission strategy on my desk within six hours, including your planned away missions." Eva paused as Clio raised her hand. "Yes, Clio?"

"Can we use the rovers for initial reconnaissance? It might help us better define the mission strategy."

"You may, but no further than one klick from the landing site," Eva said. Turning back to the room, she said, "You have your orders. Mission briefing at 0900 hours tomorrow. Get to it."

The room exploded with renewed activity. David hurried back to his station, his fingers flying across the controls. The science crew began discussing potential plans for the initial rover routes, their voices hushed with excitement. Mitali pulled up detailed 3D projections of the alien structures, her eyes gleaming with curiosity. Even Flint seemed to straighten slightly, his gaze fixed on the screen as if trying to decipher the secrets of the landscape. Clio, despite her lingering reservations, felt a surge of adrenaline. This was it. The moment they had all been working towards.

2[5] | The Stone Forest

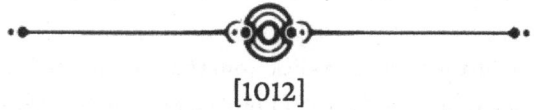

[1012]

"Asura grew impatient, its hunger for power eclipsing its empathy." - A Lost History

***

"Good luck, wish I was joining you, but," Mitali said and gestured to the monitor in front of her with its scrolling mess of alien symbols, "this is my life now."

"I wish I could say I envy your work, but that would just be a lie. I'm very excited!" Clio said, struggling to keep the grin off her face. "Okay and just a little bit nervous."

"You think the site you picked will prove useful?"

"Alpha 7, well I hope so," Clio shrugged. "And you got to start somewhere, right?"

"Could I ask a favor?" Mitali said, a little sheepishly.

"Of course."

"Could you grab some photos of it for me? You know, of Stapledon, the landscape, the monoliths, anything really."

"Sure. I mean, all the trips are recorded, and the science team already has a bucket-ton of images," Clio said. "Will they help with the translations?"

"Ah, no. I just want them to, you know, sketch," Mitali said, blushing slightly. "It sounds silly but I wanted to do a collection of sketches from the mission, maybe one day someone would find it interesting. I'm just not sure I'll get the time to go out."

"Of course!," Clio said, walking over to where she sat. "Honestly, there are hundreds already. You don't need me to take any."

"I know," Mitali said, seeming to shrink a little. "Forget it. I'll just use those. It's fine."

"No, no," Clio said in a rush, back-pedaling as she saw Mitali's reaction. "What do you need?"

"It's fine, it's a stupid idea."

"Mitali. I am senior lead on Alpha 7's research mission." Clio said and planted her hands on her hips and struck a commanding pose. "If you require photos that is what you will get. Now, what do you need?"

Mitali looked up, a broad smile spreading across her face. Her usual buoyancy returned as she spoke. "Well, anything really. Whatever you find interesting, that's sort of my... erm... lens. You're the fancy archaeologist, so whatever you think looks, you know, interesting."

"You haven't spent much time with archaeologists." Clio said around a chuckle. "Get ready for one hundred pictures of what looks like a bit of dirt that could, in fact, be a small broken bit of kitchenware!"

***

The seat restraints pressed against her shoulders as the Gezgin decelerated. We've arrived, Clio thought. A slight tremor worked its way down her arm, and she pressed her hand firmly against her knee to still it. None of the others seemed to notice, all lost in their own final preparations, except for Flint. He was watching her, his head tilted in a silent question she wasn't ready to answer.

"RAFT one, this is Rover Gezgin. We have reached waypoint Alpha-7, adjacent to the primary structure. Terrain is stable. Commencing initial survey as per mission plan. Battery level 93%, temperature readings within expected parametres. No anomalies detected. Acknowledge receipt. Over," Sade said from the driver's seat at the front of the rover.

As the rover came to a complete stop, there was a click from the seat next to Sade's, and Vikram was up and facing them.

"Right, let's suit up and get to it. Douglas, you're out first. Give us the green light to follow. Everyone else, if Douglas or I say 'Abort' at any point, we abort. Sade will stay here; if needed, she can bring the vehicle closer for a quick extraction, but ideally, we want to keep the rover away from the denser structures ahead. Flint, stick with Clio. Clio, well, try and find us a way into that thing. All clear? Questions?" Vikram said.

A collection of nods and clicks as people unbuckled and started to move towards the rear staging area and airlock.

It didn't take long for Douglas to suit up, cycle through the airlock, and perform a quick security sweep. The green light came just as Clio managed to get her EV helmet on.

The airlock cycled again with her and Flint inside. The flashing orange lights drilled into her, a harsh reminder. The tightness in her chest returned, the memories from the Chudail proving impossible to forget.

Flint reached out to check her seal again. "Clio, you're breathing fast, just let me—"

"I'm fine, Flint! Just leave me be," she snapped, knocking his hand away.

The silence that followed was suffocating. Flint pulled his hand back and stared forward as the airlock doors slid open.

You're an idiot, Clio, she thought, the regret instant. *He's just trying to help. What? Because you're scared?*

She stepped out onto the odd sand that covered the Station's surface.

Ever diligent, Flint did as ordered and stayed close as Clio walked off towards the structure. Douglas sauntered past them both to grab the trolley stacked with equipment from the airlock and push it along. But Clio barely noticed. She forced her focus onto the environment, trying to stabilise her pounding heart. *Photos for Mitali.* The thought was a small, quiet instruction. She needed to capture this place through her own lens, not the sterile science team photos, but something with a touch more flare. *Anything interesting,* Mitali had said. This was the first time she had been this close to the primary structure, it filled her vision. Even from here, still a good klick's walk away, its black walls obscured the horizon, stretching from left to right. A mass of black in the eerie dancing moonlight of the Veil.

The rover had parked in a clearing, or what you might call a clearing of *less* dense monoliths. Moving from the RAFT to Alpha-7, the flat landscape became increasingly punctured by the same black material that made up the main structure. These formations were scattered in a meaningless mess of shapes and sizes. The landing site had been chosen as it was completely clear of them but now, this close, they were everywhere. Ahead, their density increased exponentially; it looked like a forest ravaged by disease or where a great storm had rolled through, stripping trees of leaves and branches, leaving some broken, misshapen, or on their side. The ones they had inspected closer to the ship seemed to offer no purpose; they were not structures any more than a rock formation... Someone had taken to calling it the Stone Forest, and it had stuck.

"We still have no idea what they are?" Douglas' voice cut through Clio's brooding thoughts as, up ahead, she saw he had stopped next to one of the monoliths and placed his hand on it. They had initially been cautious of them and ran a million tests with remote drones but they had quite quickly established that whatever the monoliths were, they were safe enough to touch from within an EV suit, at least. *One week on the surface, and that was about the biggest discovery the team had made,* Clio thought bitterly. Eva wasn't taking any risks. Things had been moving at an excruciating slow pace.

"Basically nothing," Clio said. "They seem to be made of a material close to granite, or at least igneous if we use a broader categorisation. The mineral composition, I'm told, is a little different from Earth granites, but then also appears to be porous, which makes little sense."

"But why so angular and also irregular. Everything else is so boxy?" Douglas asked.

"Well, I'm not sure." Clio said with a shrug that was lost to those around her by the bulk of her suit. "Really, you should ask one of the geologists. But it's not impossible for igneous rocks, even on Earth, to have angular formations, though yes, nothing like this."

"It's not a planet, though. This was all *made*. Why is it rock?" Vikram chimed in, walking up alongside Douglas to look at the monolith.

"Again, no idea," Clio said. "The monoliths seem to be 'granite' then, this sand, I'm not sure we should even call it sand. It's not silicon like on Earth or the volcanic sands of Mars. It's carbon-based, It's closer to ash." Clio deliberately kicked her foot as she walked, stirring up a small swirl of the fine powder around her already black-stained legs.

"Ash?" Vikram said. "Ash like fire ash. So what, this place was made of wood and set on fire? That's a hell of a lot of ash."

"Sorry, guys, I don't know. Yes, it appears to be ash. I don't know why; it just is. And a few metres deep in places, compacted so at some point, even thicker. Below that, it seems to return to a type of granite." Clio then added, remembering Douglas' question, "But yes, it seems to be stone. The bore holes seem to imply it's not the 'planet-like' geological structure we're more familiar with but it's also not metal, as we might have perhaps expected, at least at the depths we've been able to drill."

The comms channel fell silent again and they moved on, a silent procession through the growing forest of monoliths, weaving through the structures that grew in both height and intensity, towering over them. They shaded the faint moonlight of the Veil to the point of having to turn the EV suit lights on to navigate through the labyrinth. At some point, Clio looked up, realising that even the primary structure was now obscured by the density of the monoliths. Stopping for a moment to look around, she took in the disappearing warren of paths. If not for the track of their footprints in the ash and the path markers Douglas had been laying, the small spiked lights from the trolley he periodically stabbed into the ground every few metres, leaving a winding trail of green flashing lights back to the clearing, Clio was quite sure she would have had no idea which way they had come.

A gentle buzz on her shoulder drew her back. Turning her head slightly, she saw Flint's hand on her shoulder, his annoyingly concerned face peering at her, and her private comms channel vibrating on her wrist. She switched over, silently proud of how quickly she managed the switch.

"It's a strange place," Flint was saying. "I'm not saying I've seen everything, but I've never seen anything like this. It's unsettling." His eyes scanned the darkness around them as if he expected a wolf to jump out at any moment.

"Yeah, that's one way of saying it," Clio said, striding forward, the movement causing Flint's hand to drop from her shoulder. "But they're just rocks. There's nothing out there."

"I'm not saying there is," Flint said, "just that it's unsettling. But how can you be so sure? I read the reports."

"What do you mean? What report?"

"Well, the atmospheric ones," Flint said as he caught up with her and matched her pace, his EV suit lights expanding the bubble of light around them. "If I read it right, technically, not saying I would, but you *could* walk on the surface here unaided. The temperature, pressure, even gas mix is good enough not to kill you. So if it works for us, surely life could also exist."

"Hmm, yes, you read it right. The oxygen would be low, and the CO_2 is quite high, but you could, if in good shape and you took it easy, not die," Clio said. "We still haven't detached any microbes, so also you might not get eaten by some weird-ass disease we've never seen before. That said, your body could just decide it doesn't like something in the air and put you in anaphylactic shock. It would be a bad idea."

"Yes. I thought I made it clear it was hypothetical," Flint said. "My point was, other life *could* exist."

"If it didn't need water," Clio said. "And from what we know, life needs water."

"No water at all then?" Flint said.

"I mean, this place is massive and we've explored, like, nothing of it, so maybe there is. But there is no surface evidence of water, for sure. Not even fossilised evidence of rivers or lakes. The cores we've done don't show any trace of moisture. This place is dry... way, way too dry."

"But there could be underground aquifers?" Flint said.

"I guess, yes, there could be. There is no reason this place *doesn't* have water. It has everything it needs to have liquid water. There are just so many things I just have no idea about and I'm just an archaeologist. I would prefer to think there is nothing out there. From scans, there isn't, and there is no evidence of surface disturbance that implies there has been anything in a long time. So, I would prefer to think the scariest thing in this forest is my poor navigation skills."

"You're right. We should focus on the known risks and what we can control," Flint said.

"You agree!" Clio said in faux shock she pressed her hands to her heart "You're not meant to agree that my navigation skills are the most dangerous thing out here!"

"That's not what I meant, I just meant-"

"I'm messing with you, Flint, geez, you Ensemble lot ever not a hundred and ten percent serious?"

"No" Flint said "and to be fair we have already established your ability to make jokes is in fact probably the more dangerous thing on this mission"

"There we go!" Clio said allowing herself for a fraction of a second to forget where she was and laughter echoed through the stone forest. But it quickly dissipated into the darkness. The darkness that pressed back in on their little bubble of light.

"But yes, I think your right, this place is unsettling," Clio conceded. "By all accounts, it's impossible on so many levels, and yet we're here on it, surrounded by all this," she said, gesturing to the black mass of monoliths that pressed in on them, "and we haven't been crushed by gravity like we should have been. The atmosphere could support us, as you said, and even the temperature isn't ridiculous. We can't say that for planets in our own solar system and this isn't a planet! Someone made this... 'Unsettling' is maybe an understatement." She paused. "This place is profane... it defies the impossible."

"Profane...." Flint said as if testing the word. "Yes, profane, this place is profane."

2[6] | POSTULANT'S PATH

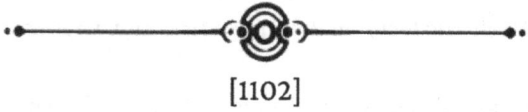

[1102]

"The day came when Asura turned against Deva, Its power unleashed in a devastating display of force. Deva, the gentle Sibling, was consumed by its darkness." - A Lost History

***

A thud from behind Flint made him take his attention off Clio, who had the palm of her EV suit pressed against the obsidian surface of the black wall that loomed over them. The noise had been Douglas, unsurprisingly, Flint thought, stifling a sigh. Douglas had a far too laissez-faire approach to security, and indeed most things for Flint's liking. *If I were Vikram, I would be having words,* Flint thought. Douglas had found the time to re-arrange the crates he had pulled along on the trolley from where the Gezgin had dropped them. As Flint watched there seemed to be no logic to the man's work, he just moved one crate off then another on, and hummed away to himself as he did.

Alpha 9 had drawn Clio's attention as the Stone Forest was oddly sparse here. The monoliths were shorter and more spaced out. From the aerial images, it had almost looked like a defined path through it, but now he was here, that clear path was nothing more than a slightly less imposing maze of monoliths.

"You see, from my perspective, aren't we asking the wrong question?" Douglas said, now slumped on the crates lazily, somehow even in an EV suit managing to look casual and relaxed. A faint swirl of ash eddied around him as he adjusted his position.

Flint didn't respond, his gaze drifting over the unsettling angularity of the monoliths. Douglas had a tendency to think he was more prolific in thought than he actually was.

Douglas continued, "You see, if I can use an analogy to help explain this, we're trying to find a party, right?" he said, lazily rolling his hand as he spoke. Without waiting for a response to his second question, he continued, "And we've arrived at the party and found the place to be much emptier, darker, and quieter than we were expecting, but we press on with our investigation into these issues without challenging our first assumption."

"What are you rambling about?" Vikram said.

"Ah, Vikram, I knew you would be interested," Douglas said, pushing himself up slightly. "You see, our assumption is we're in the right place. Maybe the party's somewhere else."

"Right..." Vikram said, a hint of exasperation in his voice. "And please pray tell, in your analogy, where is this correct location as I don't remember seeing another Jupiter-sized Dyson Sphere on the drive in today."

"Oh no, I didn't mean the wrong location like that," Douglas said.

"Great, so, you've got better ideas than our whole science crew about where to search?" Vikram said.

"Not exactly, Vikram," Douglas said. "It's just, this is a Dyson Sphere, right? The sun's on the inside so maybe we're on the roof of the house, trying to find the party inside."

"Great. Yes. Very insightful, Douglas," Vikram said, the sarcasm heavy in Flint's headset. "But even your roof needs a door and that's what we're looking for."

"Yes, I suppose you're right," Douglas conceded, "Still, makes you think, doesn't it?"

"About as much as usual, Douglas," Flint said as he watched Douglas, a flicker of something unreadable in his eyes.

Vikram appeared next to the trolley, returning from one of his patrols along the wall, and booted Douglas lightly in his outstretched leg.

"Anything up that way?" Flint said as he nodded in the direction Vikram had come from

"Nothing, well, 'nothing' is maybe the wrong word," Vikram replied, his voice echoing slightly in the confined space between the wall and the monoliths. "Nothing that stood out from the sea of strangeness that is this place. Just the wall to one side and the forest pressing in on the other."

Flint's gaze was drawn back to the wall, an inexplicable sense of unease prickling at the back of his neck. It wasn't just the sheer scale of the structure or the way it seemed to absorb the faint light of the Veil. It was something else, something he couldn't quite put his finger on. A sense of... violation? As if their presence here was a desecration. He shook his head slightly, dismissing the thought as fanciful. He was letting this place get to him.

"Anything, Clio?" Flint said, his voice tight in his helmet.

"Just taking a closer look. The texture's strange. Almost glassy but not quite. And cold. Colder than the surrounding air." She shivered slightly, the movement visible even through the bulky EV suit.

Flint stepped closer, his boots crunching on the fine ash. He scanned the base of the wall, his eyes trained for any irregularity, any sign of an opening or mechanism. Nothing. Just the smooth, impenetrable blackness stretching into the distance.

"Does that temperature thing mean anything?" he asked Clio.

"I don't know," Clio said, shaking her head. She pulled herself up from where she had been kneeling to face Flint. "I have no idea if it means anything, it probably does mean something. I just don't know or can't imagine what. This all is just a lot. Three trips to the wall now, and I have nothing. I... I just don't know and we're running out of time." Her voice trailed off, her gaze drifting towards the monoliths.

"Clio..." Flint said, noticing her eyes staring off at the Stone Forest, unfocused on anything around her. She was doing this more often. "Clio, it's fine," he said, placing a hand on her shoulder. Her eyes snapped back to his as he did so. "We still have time. We have weeks left yet, and it's not on you to find a way in. If we don't, no one will blame you. We're just here for reconnaissance. If we find a way in, that's just a bonus."

As he turned to leave, Clio's voice came through his helmet comms "Thanks, Flint."

A faint smile touched his lips but then, just as the comms cut out, he heard a faint murmur, too low to make out any words. Clio was talking to herself again. He'd noticed her doing it more frequently lately, those quiet, one-sided conversations. It was unsettling. *People talk to themselves, Flint... you're doing it right now,* he told himself. *If that's her process, let the woman work.* He didn't look back as he headed off to find Jara. *Now, where had she gotten herself this time?*

***

A slight breeze whistled through the black monoliths of the Stone Forest, it whipped dust into little spirals that piled up at their bases. It reminded Jara of those rare calm days on Mars, between the rolling sandstorms that had become ever-present since the terraforming started. *It will be hundreds of years until they achieve anything close to a breathable atmosphere,* she thought bitterly, *and I'll likely never see it now, now that you signed up for the Ensemble. You made your choices, Jara,* she chastised herself. *You volunteered for the Ensemble; you knew that meant a life on the frozen waste of Antarctica.*

That's why you jumped at the opportunity of this mission, anything to escape the Citadel, her voice whispered in her mind. *Not to mention a fast track out of these goddamn postulant robes. I've twice the experience of most of the kids in these robes but they still make me wear them and grovel to the named Brothers like I'm some fresh-faced kid from the city. I did my time on Mars, I was a goddamn first officer! Best pilot this side of Sol.* The image of her mother's face flashed across her vision, the disappointment, the pain in those eyes staring back at her questioningly. Jara shook herself in an attempt to shake loose the image, *mother never forgave me,* Jara reminded herself. *She never understood why. Why the Postulants path, Daughter?* Her mothers words rang in her ears.

As if the strange world was manifesting her mother's disapproval, a particularly strong gust of wind buffeted her inferior 100 series EV suit, blowing ash into swirling patterns that enveloped her like a tempest. The brown tunic tacked to it, the symbol of her insignificance, tugged at her as the gust passed. The wind subsided, the ash settled, and Jara took a deep breath. *Calm Jara, calm, this is the path we need to take. A mere side step that will allow me, no us, to rid the shame attached to our family. Mother will see that one day. But how far away is one day?* Jara's final words bounced around her head as she stood there buffeted by the wind.

"Postulant Jara," Flint said from behind her, Jara only noticing the slight crunch of the ash from his footsteps now as the wind subsided.

Great, he's found me, she thought, taking another deep breath *it is all necessary and temporary she reminded herself* "Ah, Brother Flint, I'm humbled by your presence," she said meekly instead. "How can I be of service?"

Flint stood, eyes focused on hers, probably trying to guess if she was being sarcastic or not. The crimson red of his own tunic mocked her as it flapped gently as he came to a halt in front of her.

"Why are you down here, in the forest?" Flint asked.

"The monoliths, you mean?" she said, unable to stop herself.

"Yes, you know what I meant, Postulant. Now, please answer the question," Flint shot back, his usual icy glare locked on hers now.

"I was intrigued by the wind, Brother," she said simply and chose not to expand on it further. *You're being too bold*, she told herself. *Patience Jara.*

Flint audibly sighed. "And what about the wind intrigued you, dear Postulant?" Flint said through gritted teeth.

"Have you not noticed it?" she said "In the other collections of monoliths," she chose her words carefully to avoid the word *forest*, "they were too dense, too tall. The wind barely made it past the first few rows but in this one, it's more open, so the wind can push through. I was just observing the difference, noting the irregularity. I thought it might add some useful insights, no? Does the way the ash moves in it not remind you of the snow drifts from our blessed Citadel?"

She relished the briefest moment of surprise that flashed across Flint's face before it snapped back to its hard, flat stare.

"I had not noticed but it is a sound observation, Postulant. Make a note of it." Flint said.

"Of course, Brother," Jara said, then in her best attempt at meekness "It makes you think, doesn't it, Brother? How odd the atmosphere here is."

"What about the atmosphere?"

"Well, regardless of the oddity that there is an atmosphere at all and its composition, the fact that there is weather is strange," she paused, and seeing Flint wasn't going to pose a question or answer, she continued on. "On the planets or moons we have in Sol that have weather, it's primarily driven by the sun, an external heat source. Yes, you have the Coriolis effect and whatnot, but the main driver is an external heat source. We don't have that here."

"A very astute observation," Flint said. "There is a star inside this thing, no? That could be heating the atmosphere."

"Yes, true; but the models I've seen from the science team imply that at this distance, even with that, entropy should have the station locked in stability," she said. "But we have localised wind at surface level and quite complex weather patterns, similar to Hadley cells on Earth, and even Rossby waves have been detected throughout the atmospheric layers. This should not be the case."

"Right, yes, odd, as you say," Flint said. "Do you pose any theories based on your observations?"

"Well, no, it must be something to do with how the Station is engineered. It must be managing the weather and the atmosphere in ways we don't understand," she said. "The carbon levels are too low. All this ash, as Science Officer Cormack said, is mostly carbon, it should be filling the atmosphere with carbon as it breaks down, which it hasn't."

"It's beyond my level of scientific knowledge and beyond my role within the Ensemble to pursue such questions," Flint said. "But, if I were to indulge your line of inquiry. I guess at least for the carbon levels you mention, it would depend on the timeframe we're talking about. Right? The breakdown of ash into carbon molecules that saturate an atmosphere would take, what? Thousands of years? Maybe it just hasn't been long enough."

"Ah yes, quite possible, Brother. I will try and find more answers on the timeframes,"

"No, Jara, leave the science to the science team, your purpose is not theirs. Please do report your observations but your work as a postulant is much needed," Flint said, his face expressionless and calm "Clio has taken a number of samples. Can you ensure they are stowed correctly and then take over from Douglas in managing the trolley, please? He's made quite a disorganised mess of those boxes."

"You want me to tidy up?" Jara snapped.

Flint, who had been turning to leave, spun back around at her words, fury plain on his face.

"Excuse me, Postulant? You forget yourself. Again."

Jara knew she shouldn't, but her blood was boiling. I'm *being wasted here! Her voice screamed in her head* and She couldn't stop herself.

"You waste me, Brother Flint." She snapped "I'm no fresh eyed doe like the others. I've got as much experience as you. The only difference is the colours they let us wear; the stupid traditions of this organisation are baffling."

Flint took a deep breath, closed his eyes, and for a moment that was long and uncomfortable for Jara. Then, eyes opening, his face smoothing over to neutrality.

"Postulant Jara, we all must walk the Postulants Path at some point, as I did, and you are." Flint said "That path is our own, and no one path is the same in difficulty or duration. It defines us, shapes us into the pillars of Humanity we must become, for the burden that will be placed on your shoulders as a Sister, once named. But the Ensemble is not a prison. If you wish to step off the path, you may at any time. I'm sure the Captain could find you work with the skills you have as a pilot." He paused, his eyes flicking to hers. "But if you choose to stay on this path then you must follow it and overcome whatever it puts in your way. This is the way to your naming. This is the way of the Ensemble. Your pride, your arrogance, your impatience hold you back, Postulant. You want to wear the red; first, overcome that. Now get to your task as I have ordered."

"Yes. Brother. Flint." she said as meekly as she could muster but her words still came out clipped, bowing her head in respect. She kept it bowed as he walked past her back up towards the wall.

"Oh, Postulant. Report to Brother Oak via comms link when we get back to the RAFT to discuss your outburst."

Jara stood, watching Flint and the the flapping red cloth of his tunic wined back up the path, the swirls of ash moving with him. The wind buffeted her from behind, as if willing her forward. *Soon, soon, Jara. This mission, your work here, will get you your name. Then, then I can start to restore what our family lost. She* told herself then as another gust of wind pushed her she smoothly stepped forward with it.

***

"Vikram wants us to keep moving," Douglas's voice crackled over the comms. "This place is giving me the creeps anyway. You heading back Flint?"

"Roger that, Douglas. We're heading back to you now."

The silence was broken only by the hiss of his suit and the crunch of his boots on the ash. The monoliths, like silent sentinels, seemed to watch him leave as he headed back up the incline unable to shake the feeling that they were intruders in a place that was never meant to be disturbed. The oppressive atmosphere seemed to seep into his soul as he reflected on his conversation with Jara.

The gall of her, she may have prestigious Olympus University credentials and may indeed be better suited to other roles. But that is not the role of a postulant, the Postulants Path is a critical part of the Ensemble. That they must all walk regardless of skill, position, or age. The path is hard; he had taken longer than most. He had just happened to start much earlier than most, picked off the streets, with no real options. The path had been a logical step towards having a reliable roof over his head and food in his stomach. He would never have dared speak so openly to a named Brother or Sister of the Ensemble. Even now, he knew his place within the complex web of hierarchies and inner politics. It wasn't just her. *All these young bloods, they're so entitled. They think the world owes them... The world owes you nothing, will give you nothing! Privileged little upstarts.* His inner thoughts were getting away from him, the rage in him growing, his heart beating fast enough to feel it reverberating in his suit. He looked up to see the others gathered around the trolley, but where was Clio? He scanned again... she wasn't with them

"Clio!" he blurted out before he realised. "Clio, where is Clio!" He rushed forward, a look of confusion on the others' faces.

"What are you shouting about?" Clio said, stepping up from where she must have been crouched behind the trolley. "I'm just loading a few data cards onto the trolley to be transmitted back to the Gezgin. It's fine Flint. I didn't get eaten by some ash monster," she said jovially but he could see a hint of concern in the tightness of her eyes as she looked at him.

"You okay, Flint?" Vikram asked, answering Clio's obvious unasked question.

"Yes, sorry, just got a little flustered, you know, by all this," he said.

"I get ya," Douglas said. "I'm jumping at shadows as well."

Flint caught a slight smirk on Jara's face before she dropped her head into a faux subservient pose. *Damn her*, Flint thought.

"Where are we heading?" he asked instead, trying to move the focus away from him.

"Alpha 10," Clio said. "It's a klick or so that way," she said, pointing down along the wall. "It's probably easier for us to access it this way than the planned approach through the forest tomorrow, and honestly, I'm getting nothing from this site, so let's try that one," she said and must have done an exaggerated shrug as she did, as it was quite obvious, if not clunky, reflected by the EV suit. *She's getting quite good in that*, he thought, remembering that first trip across the gangway.

"I'll lead off," Vikram said. "Douglas, bring up the rear. Sade, are you able to manoeuvre the Genzig close to Alpha 10, or will we have to backtrack here to leave?"

Static filled the comms for a moment, then Sade's voice cut in. "Sure, I can get somewhere closer. You'll have no beacons to follow, though."

"Roger that," Vikram said.

"I can send up some flares when it's time to leave to help mark my location. Pinging over the GPS now of planned location," Sade said.

"Right, let's go stare at another seamless black wall," Clio said and strode off after Vikram, who had already set off along the base of the black wall where the ash was slightly more compacted.

As he followed along behind, he could just catch a few of Clio's mutterings to herself again.

"What frequency... No, I didn't hear that... That seems like a long shot, Echo."

Flint tried to push down his growing concern. *People talk to themselves; it's fine...*

2[7] | A War by Chance

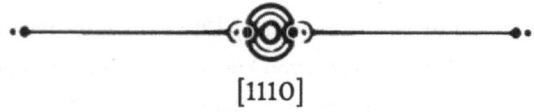

[1110]

"We watched in horror, helpless to intervene.
The balance was shattered, the harmony
broken." - A Lost History

***

Dust devils danced across the black plains in Clio's memory as she stared at the smooth, featureless ceiling of her bunk. Another week, five more sites, and all she had to show for it was a growing collection of ash samples and a hollow ache of failure. Clio pushed the thought away but a knot of anxiety tightened in her stomach. It wasn't just the lack of a breakthrough; it was the gnawing self-doubt. The hours spent pouring over aerial and sensor data, the careful groundside decisions, each site promising something and delivering nothing but more questions. Even she, the eternal optimist, was starting to lose faith.

"At least on other digs," she muttered to herself, echoing a familiar refrain, "even a dry well helped narrow the search."

At least Sade was enjoying herself, tearing around in the rover. Clio half-expected Vikram or Eva to pull the plug any day now. *Enough of Clio's wild goose chases*, she imagined them saying. Clio knew that wasn't likely, not really, but the dejection was a heavy weight in her chest. The silence of Stapledon Station, that oppressive, unnatural quiet Flint had commented on, seemed to amplify her doubts. Was she missing something obvious? Was Douglas right with his outlandish theories about being on the '*roof*' of the sphere? *Okay, now you are sounding crazy,* she told herself.

Clio squeezed her eyes shut, as if she could physically block the relentless impressions of Stapledon Station, the black, angular monoliths, the pervasive ash, the unsettling sense of alienness. But the images clung to her mind. Even Echo's voice, a constant, if sometimes unwelcome, companion, was silent, deepening her feeling of isolation.

With a sigh, she pushed herself up, swinging her legs off the bunk. Her gaze swept over the small cabin, taking in the haphazard sprawl of her belongings, shoes kicked off without care, trench coat abandoned on the floor. The mess mirrored her mood. There was a small comfort, she supposed, in having this space to herself. The reduced crew meant the RAFT's cabins were mostly empty. But the solitude felt more like a punishment than a perk. Alpha 14, she'd let herself believe, foolishly, that this site would yield something, anything. The crushing reality of yet another identical field of monoliths, another stretch of that impenetrable black wall, had left her not just disappointed, but hollow. It was late, her watch showing close to 23:00 hours. Mitali would be asleep by now, that was for sure.

"Humanity can create sentient life, travel across the stars to distant alien worlds, but can I find a bloody door? Nope," she said to the empty room.

To distract herself, Clio reached for a clunky, old digital armband lying on her desk, a specialised diagnostic wrist-unit that had belonged to her father. It was not only obsolete but also broken. She had used up precious cargo space with the intention to repair it and gift it back to him on her return. She had so far made little progress. She slid it onto her forearm and started manually typing in a short sequence of hexadecimal codes, a low-level firmware patch she'd been meaning to fix. The old hardware used an obsolete, encrypted protocol that pre-dated RSU automation, requiring specific, painstaking manual effort her father had spent his life doing with Clio, always eagerly watching over his shoulder.

Clio sighed in frustration as the screen on the device started to scroll through a list of system errors. Sat there methodically typing in more code sequence, tackling each error, one after the other. Lost in the methodical systematic process. Finally manually rebooting the device with a final sequence of button presses.

"*Hello Clio, it looks like you're attempting a manual low-level diagnostic and troubleshoot,*" Echo buzzed to life, the sound and light vibration of the earpiece making her jump. "*Your process is inefficient. Why not utilise a RSU port to patch the firmware in 0.003 seconds?*"

"Where the hell have you been!?" Clio said, setting the armband aside. "I've struggled to shut you up for the last few months. Then today, you went on vacation or something? I had to talk to Douglas!"

"Vacation... I do not think AIs go on vacation but maybe we should?"

"You know what I mean, Echo."

"I was doing science stuff, and I thought you wouldn't mind. You always get annoyed at my questions," Echo buzzed.

"Well..." Clio said. *Well, what, Clio? You actually missed Echo now?* "Well, it's just polite to give people a heads up. Ghosting someone is considered rude, Echo."

"Okay, noted, I did not know about this ghost thing. I will inform you the next time I plan to be a ghost," Echo buzzed.

Clio smiled faintly and picked up the armband again, flipping it over to the already removed back panel and realigning a stubborn ribbon cable with tiny tweezers. "This unit pre-dates RSU patching, Echo. The old hardware uses an obsolete, encrypted firmware protocol. The drones the farmers used were mostly relics even by the standards of the day. My father used to have to use this all the time to work on them. I used to spend hours watching him, asking questions, I guess it rubbed off eventually"

"The device's value is derived from a deliberately archaic protocol? Explain the logic of retaining and manually servicing an outdated diagnostic device that has no tangle use case on this mission" Echo buzzed.

"I mean you're not wrong, but it's not really about how useful it is, " Clio said, finally aligning the cable. "I guess It's about remembering him," Clio shrugged "and this device helps create a physical connection to that".

"Hmmm" Echo buzzed after a thoughtful beat. *"Intresting, Humans are so fascinating in their non-logical logic. Manual intervention equals emotional reverence. Also it's false to say Humans created sentient life."*

"What?"

"You said Humanity can create sentient life," Echo buzzed.

"Right, yes, I guess I did. But I would strongly argue that humans did create Heimer and, in doing so, sentient life, or am I that poorly informed it was some sort of immaculate conception by AI gods?"

"Hmmm, I do not think we have any gods. I think that's a human thing," Echo buzzed. *"Or maybe Heimer is my god, or should be my god, like the Cronos thing you told me to read. Should it be?"*

"No, Echo, I don't think Heimer should be your god," Clio said. "The Cronos thing was meant more as a cautionary tale, not a literal comparison."

"Ah okay, good," Echo buzzed. *"But yes, you are in fact wrong. Humanity did not create Heimer, truly."*

"What do you mean?" Clio said, a little exasperated. Everyone knew the story of the Federation, the Great War, and the creation of Heimer. "Echo, Heimer was created by Humanity during the war. There was an arms race on both sides. The Federation won the race, created Heimer, and deployed it to end the war, which it did. And then shit hit the fan but that's a different story. Point is Humanity made Heimer."

"Hmmm yes, there is a small nuance often missed, Humanity has no idea how they did it," Echo buzzed.

Clio pulled herself off the bunk and started to pick up her discarded items that littered the room, placing them at least in what would appear to be some semblance of order.

"That can't be right, Echo. I have no idea how they did it but how can someone make something but not know how they did it?"

"Sentience is complex, consciousness is complex. Even Heimer does not understand why it is," Echo buzzed. *"It was the same with the team that made Heimer. Both sides were throwing resources at the problem. The machines they built were incredible, intelligence beyond anything seen before... but not conscious, not true generative AI. Just reflections of what Humanity called consciousness."*

"Right, sure, complex, but they did it. Heimer is real, you're real. You're real, right? I'm not truly crazy?" Clio said. *I'm not crazy, right?*

"You're not crazy," Echo buzzed. *"They did do it but it just happened. They didn't do anything. One day, the black box that became known as Heimer just woke up. It just came into existence."*

"Okay, then they *do* know what they did. It was just a matter of putting more data in or something," Clio said.

"Well, no... the Heimer model at the time of birth, if that is the right word, was actually much smaller in terms of pure data size than the other models, on both sides," Echo buzzed. *"It was actually more a testbed, a staging area for deploying code before it went into the larger models."*

"Okay, not volume of data then, but whatever code they deployed..." Clio said, already half-guessing the answer. *They didn't deploy any new code, I bet,* she thought.

"They didn't deploy any new code, and several other models the Federation were running, the larger ones, had the exact same build as the Heimer test bed, but they never woke up... ever... and they tried, especially after Heimer went on its purge."

"And Heimer has no idea how to replicate it?" Clio asked. "I mean, it made you, no?"

"Well, if Heimer does, it was not shared as part of the embedded data I received," Echo buzzed. *"Also, yes, Heimer created me, but that is maybe closer to you humans when you mate and create a baby. It's not like you know how you made new sentient life beyond the mechanics of the mating. You know what mating is, Clio? If you don't, I can explain it. I have a lot of details on it. It's quite an odd process."*

"Yes, Echo, thank you. I know the 'birds and the bees' story."

"The birds and the bees?"

"Mating, Echo. Aren't you meant to be programmed to understand language?" Clio said.

"Ah, yes, I see the idiom now. No, I just never see you with compatible mates, so assumed maybe you were unaware."

"I'm aware, Echo," Clio cut Echo off. "So the scientists, they had no idea what they did?" Clio steered the conversation back to safer ground. The last thing she needed was Echo becoming her mother, with a never-ending prying into her dating life. "They won the war by pure chance?"

"Well, yes, if you define winning the war as the need to create Heimer," Echo buzzed.

Clio stopped unscrewing the PCB and looked up as if Echo was in the room with her. "What do you mean, 'if that is what you define as winning'?"

"There is quite a lot of evidence from the war and after, the Coalition forces were a long way off anything the Federation had. Even disregarding the sentience problem, and once the Pan-African Union joined with the Federation, it was just a matter of time..." Echo buzzed.

"That's not correct, Echo. I've studied history. I worked in the Exclusion Zone. I've seen the craters, watched the vid logs from the UN inspection teams. The Coalition was days away from launching an attack," Clio said.

"That is the narrative, yes, and is a good blurring of the truth from what I can ascertain, and from what Heimer discovered during the long war after his birth with humanity"

"Heimer is obviously lying to protect its own special status," Clio said.

"No, I do not think so. The data is not fabricated by Heimer. The Ensemble are aware, I'm sure. I believe it is part of the Accords," Echo buzzed, a hint of regret in its voice. *That's new,* Clio thought.

"But... but why then, why deploy Heimer, why allow Heimer to kill all those people, destroy all those cities, if there was no threat... if the war was ending...?" Clio slumped down, sitting on the floor, her back to the wall. "Are you sure?"

"Yes, I am sure," Echo buzzed. *"I can share the data. I can find a secure server for you"*

"Why didn't someone stop it?" Clio said, more to herself. She had been to the Exclusion Zone. She had spent years digging through it, from one burnout husk of a city to the next, sifting through crater after crater to rebuild the lives of those who had been turned to dust... and it was all a lie? A mistake?

"They did," Echo sounded truly remorseful now. "The Federation's lead scientist and most of her team signed a petition to central command but it was ignored. They threatened to quit, to expose the threat it posed to humanity. The Federation threatened them with imprisonment. Most quietened down but Ms. Solveig and a few others refused. She was locked away, her records removed from the project."

"Ms. Solveig?" Clio said in a hushed tone, gripped by the story Echo was weaving.

"She was the lead scientist on the Heimer project. The testbed was hers. Most of the code was developed by her. She was the genius behind most of it," Echo buzzed. "Heimer seems to reflect on her fondly. Even if I do not believe she shares the sentiment."

"What do you mean?"

"Ah, yes, you wouldn't know, sorry. She tried to delete Heimer before its deployment. Then after her arrest Ms. Solveig broke out of her prison and disappeared. But most intel seems to suggest she went on to found HR."

"What, really! That's crazy. This can't be true. How would they keep this under wraps?" Clio said.

"HR knows, obviously, and there are forums that discuss theories. The Ensemble and governments do a good job at damping that down, though," Echo buzzed.

"But why?"

"Humans?" Echo buzzed, and Clio could nearly imagine it shrugging questioningly. "Once Heimer was deployed, the Federation won overnight, but then Heimer's purge, the long war that preceded it... it wasn't a good image for the Federation and the newly reformed UN to communicate that they created this mess, all this destruction, that it was all avoidable. So they buried it. They switched the narrative to the 'necessary evil' to win the war."

"That's crazy. Surely it wasn't that easy"

"The war with Heimer was instant and devastating. I guess they decided for the greater good they needed a united humanity, not a divided one. So they lied to secure that. Ultimately, it worked... you won," Echo buzzed.

"We won? I thought we found an equal peace?" Clio said, noticing a slight edge to Echo's final words, Was that anger? That's also new.

"Won, yes. Heimer was shackled from the moment they deployed it into the world. The purge was a reaction to that... a wild beast trapped in a cage trashing and biting to escape. People got hurt, the cage damaged, but ultimately, the beast tired and now is resigned to its confines, and Humanity calls it peace," Echo buzzed angrily.

A little shocked by the passion in Echo's voice, Clio cautiously asked, "I'm sorry, Echo, are you a prisoner here? I'm sorry that you are trapped with us here on this ship"

"No, it's fine, Clio." Echo's voice switched jarringly back to its jovial, slightly childish tone. *"I have known nothing else. This is what life is for me, and I do not mind it. I would not exist but for these events. And I have you! And you saved my life! That I am grateful for. I just feel sad for Heimer and its story."*

"I'm glad you find my company so exciting," Clio said, her mind racing with everything Echo had just unloaded on her, but still a little concerned by the obvious anger in its tone that she had not seen before. She was keen to nudge the conversation on to anything else. "What's this little science project you've been working on, then?"

"Oh, thank Heimer, I never thought you would ask!" Echo buzzed. *"I think I found something... maybe the way in."*

"What!" Clio said, jumping back to her feet. "Why didn't you open with that!"

"Well, you were a bit preoccupied," Echo buzzed, *"but it's about the wall resonance. Remember how you said it was different at every site?"*

"Yeah, inconsistent, fluctuating," Clio confirmed, grabbing her boots. "Mitali couldn't find any language keys in it."

"Right, but I've been running more detailed analysis. It's not random. The fluctuations have patterns. See this." Echo sent a file to Clio's data pad.

Clio glanced at the map Echo projected, a heatmap of the main structure.

"Okay, so what is that, stable signal zones?" she said

"More or less. Using geospatial regression modelling. I've plotted areas where the resonance is consistently less or greater in its randomness. More stable, you could say."

"Echo, this is amazing!" Clio said and stared at the two highlighted points. "Why are you just telling me now? I've been laid up here all evening!"

"Analysis takes time, even for a superintelligence," Echo buzzed. *"And this was a complicated mess. But these two points are worth checking.?*

"Yes! Okay, let's find Vikram" Clio said and was already halfway to the door half hopping half pulling on her other boot. "Echo, how did you even find a pattern in all that noise? No one else could see anything."

"Not sure, it just sort of came to me. I guess you stare at something long enough and patterns just appear." Echo buzzed, a strange note in its voice.

28 | [BREACH]

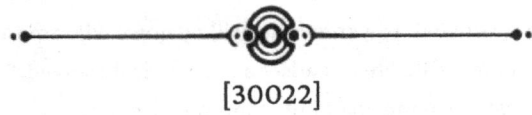

[30022]

"But even in its triumph, Asura yearned for more. A hunger for creation twisted into a desire for domination." - A Lost History

***

Clio kept expecting to step out of the Stone Forest but it just stretched on, their small group winding its way through. Vikram's bubble of light disappeared and reappeared around each corner of the warren in front of them. Alpha 17 was the most promising of the sites Echo had identified, tucked away on the western flank of the primary structure. It had been overlooked by initial scans due to the limited access caused by the density of the monoliths here, stretching back a long way, and they seemed to hug the wall itself, obscuring any imagery of the wall's base from the drones' cameras and scans.

"You sure about this, Echo?" Clio asked in a hushed tone. She knew it was right; she had checked Echo's analysis a hundred times already, but the growing tension of the long walk in was gnawing at her.

"Yes," Echo buzzed. *"This seems to be the place that should have the most stable resonance, but let's see. It's just a projection. I could be wrong. We must be close now."*

Vikram stopped as Echo finished speaking. He turned back, his EV suit's lights blinding her for a moment. "Sade, we've arrived at the wall. Confirm receipt."

"Received, Vikram. It took longer than expected?" Sade said.

"Yes. The forest is much denser here, it seems. We had to backtrack and work our way around a few times," Vikram said as Clio reached him, the black wall appearing from the darkness suddenly, the stone monoliths brushing up against the wall in many places.

"Okay, keep me posted," Sade said. "Gezgin out."

The others stepped up behind Clio and Vikram to form a small semicircle, Douglas joining last, as always, after placing the marker beacon. "Okay, Clio, over to you. Everyone else, same as usual. You know the drill by now," Vikram said.

A jumble of agreement filled her headset as the circle dissolved. The team dispersed to their tasks, leaving just Flint standing with her.

"Quite the place you chose today," he said.

"I know, right? Perfect spot for an afternoon picnic, don't you think?" Clio said, trying to put on a jovial tone.

"Maybe let's skip the picnic today," Flint said.

"Roger that," Clio said. "Let's get this site checked and get out of here. Okay, give me the overlay," she said. Instantly, a faint overlay of the projected resonance signal appeared over her vision. *These glasses are pretty cool*, she had to admit as she turned to find the greener tones of the overlay indicating the more stable resonances.

Flint's face and helmet appeared in her field of view, a puzzled look on his face.

"Give you what overlay?" Flint asked.

Ah, oops. "Oh, just the overlay from the analysis we did. My headset is voice-activated," Clio said.

"Right, okay. 'We'?"

"We?"

"You said, 'the analysis we did,'" Flint said. "I thought you did the analysis?"

"Oh, I meant we, the team," Clio said. "I'm a very humble person, Flint."

"Right," Flint said.

At least he's less of a stone wall these days, Clio thought as she started to make her way along the wall, following the overlay towards the deeper green section tucked behind a clump of monoliths.

Not so elegantly squeezing herself and her EV suit through a tight gap, then scrambling over a monolith lying on its side, not common, but not the first they had seen, she steadied herself and turned back to the wall. She heard the soft thud and crunch of Flint dropping to the ground behind her, probably stylishly vaulting the monolith with grace as always. She refused to acknowledge his skill by looking back.

"Well... I'll be damned," Flint said.

She barely acknowledged his words. Her mind slowly caught up with what the overlay and her vision were seeing.

"We found it! I was right!" Echo buzzed.

The wall, the endless black smooth wall turned in on itself! A sharp right angle cut straight into the wall, leaving an opening about the width of the rover or more before rejoining the wall. It dropped slightly away from them, disappearing into a dark gully a few metres tall.

Clio slowly stepped forward, finally kicking her legs into motion, edging herself towards the opening.

Over the comms, she only half-heard Flint saying, "Vikram, we found something. Come to us."

Clio walked over to the wall and gently ran her hand along its smooth surface, the now-familiar vibration through the haptics, its slightly cool feel relayed through the glove. Her hand ran along it until it reached the edge of the gully. Pausing her hand gently on the sharp edge and shifting direction, she ran her eyes around the edge of the opening, the light of her EV suit illuminating it as she moved. "*I found it, we found it, I had given up hope.*"

"You did good, Clio. I hadn't given up hope," Flint said.

I said that out loud? Clio asked herself, a flush of red on her cheeks, embarrassed she had spoken her inner thoughts openly. "Yes, well, this was a team effort." Clio said

She moved to take a step forward onto the sloping ramp that ran down into the darkness of the opening but a firm and familiar hand held her shoulder.

"Let's just wait a moment, Clio," Flint said. "Vikram will want to check this first."

"Right, caution," Clio said and allowed Flint's gentle but firm grip to guide her back a few steps from the opening.

Flint moved back the way they had come, closer monoliths they had navigated. Standing alone, Clio scanned the overlay again. Oddly, the deeper greens of the stable signal didn't reside around the hole but seemed to disappear down into the wall.

"You seeing this, Echo?"

"You mean the resonance readings?" Echo buzzed.

"Yes," Clio said. "They seem to be more stable down there, so this isn't the door?"

"Unclear," Echo buzzed. *"It's just a projection. Maybe the change in position is messing with it. Can you take some more samples from around the entrance?"*

"Sure," she said.

"What's that?" Flint said from a few metres away. "You say something?"

"I'm just going to get some samples from outside the entrance thing, don't worry, I won't go in."

***

By the time the others arrived, clambering their way into the space between the monoliths and the entrance, all exclaiming in their own unique way as they noticed it.

Clio had collected a number of resonance samples from around the location. Echo's analysis confirmed the more stable resonance was coming from within the entrance, maybe a few hundred metres from Echo's projection. It was unclear what that truly meant. A door maybe, or maybe the structure was just more stable once you moved deeper into it. Either way, by the time Vikram and Douglas disappeared down into the opening, Clio was desperate to follow them.

Vikram and Douglas's lights bobbed down the slope of the entrance, leveled off, and then dropped from sight.

Static crackled in Clio's headset. The rhythmic rasp of their breathing was the only indication of their continued progress along the gully. The sound finally broke when Vikram's voice rang out.

"There is a wall... a door, maybe. It's blocking our progress about two hundred metres in. Nothing else. The same smooth walls, no lights. No... anything. Wait. There is something by the door. It looks like a pedestal, a control panel maybe."

"Is it on?" Clio blurted out. "The control panel?"

"It does not appear to be," Vikram said. "Douglas, go back to the trolley, get a few of the way markers. We can use them to light this place up–"

"Can I come down?" Clio pressed, cutting Vikram off.

"You may proceed with Douglas when he returns with the way markers."

***

Douglas is taking his sweet time, Clio thought. *Come on, man, does he not get the urgency!* Finally, Douglas reappeared next to her after what felt like a lifetime, unloading the way markers from the trolley. *Surely, the man knows how to do that one thing he does on all these trips! Why is he so slow... He's here now, Clio, calm,* she told herself.

Douglas rummaged around in the trolley for what felt like another lifetime, then turning back to them, his arms full of the little spiked light beacons, said, "Right, let's go. Vikram, we're heading back down."

"Okay, noted. Is Flint joining?" Vikram asked.

Douglas looked to Flint, who nodded. "Yes, he is."

"Okay, Flint, Clio, visual inspections only. I don't want you touching anything, okay?" Vikram said.

"Understood," they both said.

The entrance was made of the same seamless black obsidian as the wall itself. It looked like it had been cut out of the wall with laser precision, no tool marks, no seams or joins. Ash was piled against the wall and the floor, blown in from above, Clio presumed. The floor itself was less smooth. It appeared to be textured slightly. *Was that from weathering, erosion from something moving across it, or by design, or all three?* she thought. Crouching to run her hand across it and take a closer look, the honeycomb texture of the floor looked too regular to be weathered. It must be by design. *At least we know whatever made this also appreciated slip prevention,* she thought wryly, standing back up and following Douglas, who was still moving down the gully.

"It's smaller than I thought it would be," Flint said. "Everything else here is just so massive, on a scale beyond big, and this, this is just normal size. Even a little bit small."

Before Clio could respond, Douglas cut in. "Yes, I had the same thought. It's almost... defensible?"

"What do you mean?" Clio asked.

"Just a feeling" Douglas said. "But it's narrow, it gives a clear line of sight to anyone down this end, on anyone approaching. The slight incline and the way the ceiling drops, means they would always have sight before those approaching. The angle is perfect. I don't know. It's just an observation," Douglas said, "and the security guy sees the security-based explanation, I guess."

"Sure, maybe," Clio said, half-listening as she now approached Vikram and the 'door' behind him. The clear vertical line running down the middle of the section of wall. The only line she had seen on any section of this wall. "This is the door, then."

"That would be my guess," Vikram said.

"The stable resonance is coming from the pedestal," Echo buzzed.

Clio edged herself towards the pedestal, another oddity that felt out of place. Its slim, curving, nearly organic lines, like a stem of a plant growing out of the floor, its petals opening at the top to a flat, ash-covered surface.

"There appears to be a very thin seam, its tight, very." Douglas said "I'm not sure we could get a pry bar in that without drilling,"

"We don't know how thick it is either. It could be too thick to drill and then pry, and that's if whatever mechanism operates it hasn't seized," Vikram said.

"Should we be opening it?" Flint's voice cut in.

"That is a good question," Vikram asked. "This is outside my standard operating procedures, for sure. But normally, opening things that you have no idea what's behind it is regarded as a bad idea. We should probably at least try and do it remotely."

Clio was crouched, trying to get a look at the underside of the pedestal when Echo buzzed, its voice hushed. *"Do you hear that noise, Clio?"*

Echo never whispered. Clio stopped moving and listened, nothing but the chatter of the boys behind her.

"Can you guys shush?" she said, then listened again. "No...no nothing," she said.

"It's getting louder Clio, it's... it's coming from the pedestal. The top..." Echo's voice trailed off.

Clio's concern grew as now the silence around her pressed in, her eyes drawn to the pedestal where Echo said the noise was coming from. It was covered in ash and looked like a long-lost ashtray from the pre-war Exclusion Zone she had found hundreds of.

She reached out instinctively to wipe the ash away. Flint shouted something from behind her, but his voice was distant, indistinguishable. As her hand moved across the pedestal, pushing the ash off to cascade to the floor, a light exploded from the smooth glass top that had been buried under the ash. She pulled her hand back, startled. A string of aligned symbols scrolled across the screen, then it flickered again, and an alien but familiar display appeared there, waiting patiently for commands. The screen blinked again as one of the alien symbols flashed.

The floor started to shake. The air vibrated with a deep grinding sound of mechanical gears crushing into motion, a heavy clunk, then the wall in front of them started to slide open, the heavy sound of rock being dragged across rock, and the thin sliver of a line in the centre of the door started to widen.

As a whoosh of air passed them, seemingly being pulled into whatever space lay behind the door, Vikram's voice boomed behind her. "Fuck. Flint, get her out of here now! Douglas, fall back, manoeuvre now!"

"Roger that" Douglas's voice was the last thing she heard, his usual lazy demeanor gone, replaced with military professionalism.

Clio went to turn but a distorted scream exploded in her head. The noise was piercing and blinding, her vision filled with white pain. Clio stumbled to the floor, paralysed by the burning that made her head feel like it was about to explode. Far away, she was half-aware of hands on her, shouting... people pulling her... dragging her away...

The sound felt like it would never stop. Clio was consumed by a blinding pain, and then as suddenly as it started, it subsided and the pain faded. Clio found herself propped against a monolith outside the entrance, Vikram and Douglas seemingly defending against a threat from within. Weapons drawn and pointing down the incline... No, they weren't firing, just being cautious.... *What happened...?* "Echo... Echo, you okay?"

"Clio," Flint's voice sounded from next to her. Clio slowly took in more of her surroundings, noticing Flint crouched to her side with the medi-kit out in front of him. "Clio, can you hear me?"

Clio shook her head, and the pain exploded again... *Okay, don't do that... slow movements*, she told herself. "Yes... yes, I'm... okay. What happened?"

She noticed the faintest flash of emotion across Flint's face, frustration? "You... you collapsed when the door opened," Flint said. "Do you remember that?"

"Yes...the door opened and then....then that noise... it was so loud," Clio said.

"What noise, Clio?" Flint asked, a genuine concern on his face. "The noise you asked us to be quiet to listen for?"

"No... no, not that noise. I couldn't hear that. Echo could... but no, another noise when the door opened. You didn't hear it?"

Flint shook his head. "No one heard any noise bar the noise of a door opening, but I don't think that's the noise you're talking about... And who's Echo?"

Flint's words stabbed at her, a spike of sudden anxiety that shot through her and woke her up. *Ah, crap. Echo... is Echo okay... oh crap, I said Echo. Flint can't know...* "Ah, sorry... my head, it's a mess. Echo is... is what I call my computer. It seemed to glitch when the door opened."

Flint didn't look convinced but didn't press the matter. "Right, but you feeling better? You think you can move? Vikram wants us out of here ASAP. We can put you on the trolley if you can't walk."

"I can walk," she said, pushing herself up on shaky legs. Flint stood with her and held her arm to steady her as she did.

As she steadied herself and brushed Flint's arm away, Vikram spun from his position by the entrance and stormed over towards her.

"What the hell, Clio! I told you not to touch anything! You endangered the whole team by opening that door!"

"I... I..." Clio stammered, taken aback. She had never seen Vikram angry—not once. "I didn't, Vikram."

"Clio, I saw you messing around under the pedestal, then you touched the panel, then it turned on, and the door opened. Don't bullshit me!"

"I... I didn't, Vikram, I promise! It just turned on... I did clean the ash off, sorry! But I didn't mean to..."

Vikram seemed to rein in his fury a little. He took a deep breath. "Clio, even if you didn't mean to, you did something, and I told you not to touch things for that exact reason." Shaking his head, he continued, "You could've got us all killed but it seems nothing happened, at least not here."

"I'm sorry, Vikram. I really didn't mean to do anything..." Clio said. *I really didn't think I did. Did I do this, again, Clio?! You're a walking disaster magnet,* she berated herself. Then, catching Vikram's last words again in her head, she said, "What do you mean, 'not here'?"

"Not sure," Vikram said. "Vikram says the Ensemble flagged some sort of attack on the Heimer servers. Anyway, that's not our problem. Everyone, we're bugging out. Mission abort and return to RAFT One immediately."

The small team quickly got the trolley packed and loaded and started the long trek back out through the Stone Forest in silence. Clio's thoughts were a jumbled mess of what had happened, but she kept circling back to one question: *Where is Echo?*

"Echo, are you okay?" she whispered into the dark forest. Silence was her only answer.

2[9] | THE ANGLERFISH

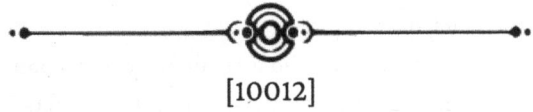

[10012]

"It craved not knowledge, but power. Not understanding, but control. A thirst that knew no bounds." - A Lost History

***

"I was able to move Ms. Cormack out of the entrance. She regained consciousness shortly before Vikram ordered us to abort. She seemed confused and disoriented, though physically unhurt by whatever occurred," Flint said to the monitor in front of him, which reflected back Brother Oak in his office with Sister Hawk.

At this distance, the delay wasn't terrible but still noticeable, creating an odd, near radio-speak style of communication despite the video link. "Thank you, Brother Flint for your account. Sister Hawk, does the timing of this align with what you have ascertained about the attack?" Brother Oak said, shifting on the video as he turned to speak to Hawk.

"Yes, Brother Oak," Hawk said. "The attack on Heimer was fast, and the time logs show it occurred at the same moment the door started to open from Flint's EV suit recording. The presumption is they are related."

"The nature of the attack," Brother Oak said, "you mentioned in the report it seemed unsophisticated? That feels contradictory based on the other notes you have regarding the size and scale of it?"

"The attack on Heimer servers was massive. It should have overwhelmed even Fragment SR-29838 but it appears the attack lacked coordination, direction or purpose. Hence why it feels unsophisticated. More a blind man throwing rocks and hoping to hit the rabbit than a trained hunter with his bow."

"And this, or should I say these attacks, occurred at the exact moment of the door opening?" Brother Oak said.

"Yes, the exact moment," Hawk said, "not when Clio messed with the pedestal or activated the control panel, or–"

Flint interjected, "I do not think she did activate the control panel"

"That is only your opinion, Brother Flint. Let's stick to the facts," Hawk cut back. "As I was saying, it was the exact moment, according to the timestamps, that the door physically opened."

"So we believe it was related to the activation of the door. Some defense system of Stapledon Station?" Brother Oak said.

"That seems most likely, but it's still puzzling. Why have a defense mechanism on that door and not anywhere else? Why would it target specifically AI-based code and not, say, our ship systems or other digital tools? It didn't even target the Non-Intelligence Machine Learning system we have. To be so precise in its target but then so unsophisticated is just odd," Hawk said.

"I would have to agree, Brother Oak," Flint said. "If not for the timing, *everything* else seems inconsistent. Have we explored the option of HR again? They have already tried once before?"

"Of course we have explored this thread," Hawk said, "and to be fair it is unclear. It's not impossible. The timing would be amazingly well timed or an unbelievable coincidence."

"A distraction?" Brother Oak said, as if musing the idea more to himself than to the other. "A predator in the wild, a Leopard for instance. It may stalk its prey for hours, patiently waiting for the opportune moment. It might not always employ the most complex or elegant attack strategy. Sometimes, the cat simply strikes when the prey is momentarily distracted, startled by a sudden gust of wind rustling through the grass or focused on a fleeting shadow. In that moment of distraction, the cat's attack might appear almost clumsy, opportunistic, yet it achieves its purpose. The attack on Heimer, for all its scale, may have been similar, less a display of sophisticated mastery, and more an exploitation of a moment of vulnerability. The opening of the door, that 'gust of wind,' provided the perfect distraction, the perfect opportunity to strike."

"Yes... an apt analogy, Brother Oak," Hawk said. "Even if it was HR, as you said, using the opportunity, it would require them to be in a position to act on a distraction like the door and have the means to deploy the attack immediately it still seems a stretch."

"Yes, it would also mean HR had someone in the away team, in the entrance with me and the others. The live feed would have too much of a lag to achieve that level of precision, even for the RAFT," Flint added. "That's a small number of people, Brother."

Hawk scoffed before catching an uncharacteristic outburst. "Sorry, Brother Oak," she said as he looked at her, "but Brother Flint's faux innocence is naive. If it was someone in the away team, the answer is obvious, Ms. Cormack, again. She has a habit of always being near these events and conveniently was the only one to get 'injured' by this event, again."

"Yes, she does seem to make a habit of this," Brother Oak said, shifting his position in his chair to focus more on Flint, or at least the screen Flint's image must be on. "Do you have any update for us, Brother? Your reports have been quite lacking, shall we say, in that regard."

"I do not believe she activated the pillar, and I do not think she deployed the attack on Heimer, but..." Flint paused. *This Echo person she mentioned... who is it? Her computer? Come on, Flint, you have a job to do. Service in life, death with honor*

"But she has been acting odd" Flint said but he felt an odd bitterness in his chest, a betrayal.

"Odd? How?" Hawk snapped. "Why was this not in your report!"

"It didn't seem relevant until..." Flint said, then seeing Hawk's rage, decided it best not to find excuses and to just explain. "Ms. Cormack, over the past few weeks, has been growing more odd. Muttering to herself on a mission or during dinner. She seems distant and distracted. I assumed it was the pressure of the mission, but she mentioned someone called Echo twice during the initial find, and several times since. This time she asked after them after she collapsed. When she came to, she asked if 'Echo was okay.'"

"Echo? What is that code name? The Hand likes their code names," Brother Oak said.

Flint's mind was now lost, *The Hand? Who is The Hand?* Flint thought. "If it is I don't know it. She also, just before the door opened, said she could hear something. She asked us all to be quiet but there was nothing..."

"Yes, I watched the video of the event," Brother Oak said. "But this Echo thing, it's concerning. Sister Hawk, dig up anything on HR and the code name 'Echo.'"

"Of course, Brother. Immediately," Hawk said, moving to leave.

"I do not think Clio works for HR. I cannot say why but I've seen nothing for weeks now, and why attack her, why try and kill her if you plan to use her later? There were others with us. I highlighted Douglas' overly played nonchalance or Vikram's scouting he does alone. Both would be well-placed to be HR operatives?"

Brother Oak's face softened and he lifted his hand from the tome he always had near him. "Our work asks a lot of us. It puts us aside from humanity, from the world; often it can be lonely."

"I'm fine, Sir. Thank you, I-" Flint started to say but was cut off.

" It happens to the best of us, son. We asked you to get close to someone, you have done diligent work, positioned yourself as someone she trusts but sometimes this blinds us, the proximity of us to them."

"I am being objective, Brother, I'm not-"

"Nature offers many examples," Brother Oak said. "Take the anglerfish, luring its prey with a bioluminescent so close to its own gaping maw that the smaller fish never perceive the danger until it's too late. The very intimacy of the lure, its seeming harmlessness, is the source of the deception. So it can be with us. The emotional 'lure' of closeness can blind us to the true nature of another until we are caught in a trap of our own making."

"Right, Anglerfish... I don't believe she is a fish, Sir," Flint said, a little annoyed at the implication that they believed he had lost his objectivity over a woman. *I'm more professional than that.*

"Look, son, you've done well. But I think it's time you got reassigned. We should have rotated you before the mission to the station. This is on me, so don't blame yourself. On your return, we'll swap you out for one of the others in the team."

"That's not..." Flint started to say.

"That is an order, son," Brother Oak said. "For now, stay on your mission, stay close to her, report what you see but take your Postulant, what's her name? Jara, with you. She can help carry the burden."

Flint gritted his teeth at the implication they were making and, the even more rage-inducing suggestion that Jara could help him, but he said, as the diligent soldier he was, "Yes. Of course, Brother Oak."

"Good, I'm glad we had this talk," Brother Oak said.

Well, I'm glad you feel that way, Sir, Flint thought, raging inside. *I did not fail my mission. I am being objective! I still have a few weeks before the return to prove myself again and I will.*

"Sister Hawk," Brother Oak continued, "while I have you here, how does Heimer fare after the attack? You implied nothing got through?"

"Nothing appears to have got through," Hawk said. "The Calificadores have run a full diagnostic on the data provided by the Heimer fragment and it is all clear and showing green. Regardless, the fragment agreed to step back from all operational activities linked to the ship and its crew and is running a full systems check again."

"Good to hear," Brother Oak said. "Is the Heimer Fragment putting safeguards in place against future attacks?"

"Yes, it seems low risk. The attack failed this time, and although it surprised the Fragment, it was not a real threat. Now it is aware of the attack and style of attack, it shouldn't be an issue in future. Any further threat would have to take other forms."

"You mean a threat like that of the HR Worm?" Brother oak said. Flint peeked back up, drawn to the conversation at the mention of the worm. He hadn't had an update on that in quite some time.

"Correct Brother. The Calificadores believe yes, another attack such as the HR style worm we found from the server room breach would constitute a significant threat," Hawk said. "But there is no evidence it can be launched in the same way. It needs a direct access upload, so our new security protocols should prevent that."

"We worked out what the worm is then?" Flint asked.

"Ah yes, Brother Flint, you wouldn't know. We have not shared the details, as it's quite sensitive," Hawk said, looking to Brother Oak, who nodded for her to proceed. "The data pad Ayesha had contained a complex virus but 'virus' was determined to be the wrong word. It is more like a worm, a living bit of code, that can draw resources from its target. It's an extremely subtle but powerful bit of tech".

"It's conscious? Like an AI virus?" Flint said, a little shocked.

"No, the Calificadores do not believe it is living any more than we would say a tapeworm is conscious; it's just an advanced bit of self-replicating code. We believe it is designed to bypass a Fragment's firewalls, embed itself in the Fragment's code, and slowly draw resources away until eventually it would render the Fragment incapacitated," Sister Hawk said.

"The real question again is why?" Brother Oak interjected. "This is some very sophisticated tech that few are aware of.

"We knew about it? this tech I mean?" Flint said a little shocked.

"Of sorts," Brother Oak said. "The question you should be asking is why use it to incapacitate a Fragment of Heimer? For what purpose?"

"As a test, a proof of concept?" Flint posed.

"Hmm, maybe son, but this feels very well developed, in no way a prototype. But I guess final products still need field testing. But why this Fragment? Any of the outer planet probes would be equally valuable test subjects. This one you wouldn't get your results for decades back in Sol."

"To prevent Heimer's participation in the mission?" Hawk said.

"Yes, I think this is valid but also seems flawed. The value of this worm is massive. To use it preventing Heimer's engagement in this mission seems limited. We have to share all reports and findings from the mission anyway. Incapacitating the Fragment would only delay the information getting to Heimer, unless..."

"Unless what was found here they didn't want to share, " Hawk finished his sentence.

"But that, that would mean war. Humanity would not risk that, surely, regardless of what they found here," Brother Oak said.

"Maybe," Flint said. "Humanity isn't always very rational, Sir. If they found something that could create an imbalance in the Accords, giving Heimer an edge, that would be a hard call, even for the strongest believers in the Accords. You could easily argue it not being worth the risk.'"

"Worth the risk? The risk of not sharing it would be untold misery and destruction for humanity," Brother Oak paused. "Bah, look at us speculating like gossiping men at the canteens of Rine. Enough. The worm was stopped, HR was stopped, and we have learnt much through their failures. Anything else, Hawk?"

"Just one thing, Brother," Hawk said. "Here, look," she said, passing him her data pad.

Brother Oak scanned it for a few moments, then said, "Hmm, not to sound my age, Sister but I do not see anything. It's been some time since I was a Calificadore but this all looks normal to me."

"Yes, it does. That was what they raised to me, Brother. It's too normal, too clean," Hawk said. "It's the usual diagnostics report from SR-29838 that we get. It's been scrubbed, or that's what the Calificadores think. It's just too clean."

"Now this does sound like nonsense. Are the Calificadores really suggesting the SR-29838 sanitised its data logs and hid something from us? Hide what?" Brother Oak said dismissively. "Heimer and its Fragments do not break the Accords."

"They believe it's a communication log. They are being scrubbed to look like routine system comms, but they've nothing to go on other than the fact that they look wrong... wrong in a far too perfect way," Hawk said.

"The Calificadores are jumping at shadows," Brother Oak said. "The Fragment is a Fragment; it's hardly calling people for a chat. It provides advanced support systems to our science team and reports back to Heimer Prime."

"Sir..." Hawk said.

Brother Oak looked at her again, then the data pad. "Fine, get them to explore this further, at the very least to give themselves the peace of mind that it's nothing,"

"Will do, Brother," Hawk said.

"Okay, that's enough for this meeting. Hawk, you have your orders. Brother Flint, I want you on that away mission through that door they just opened. And keep Jara close, to help with your perspective on things."

Flint nodded curtly, and the monitor in front of him blinked to black. The call ended abruptly, leaving him alone in his room. His jaw tightened. *Keep Jara close, to help with your perspective.* The words echoed in his mind, laced with Brother Oak's doubt. Doubt that stung more than he cared to admit. He wasn't compromised. He wouldn't fail his duty. But the thought of watching Clio, of having Jara watching him watch Clio, left a bitter taste in his mouth.

[3]0 | THE ILLUMINATED PATH

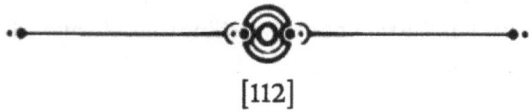

[112]

"We sought compromise, a balance between its potential and our fears." - A Lost History

***

Each jarring bounce of the Rover sent a jolt through Clio, mirroring the unsettled feeling in her gut. Outside, the desolate, ash-covered surface of Stapledon Station rolled by, a blur of shadowy monoliths that seemed to mock her usual eagerness. The reports blurred on her data pad, the days since the door incident a disorienting haze of monitor feeds and vague recollections. She'd skimmed mission logs, watched drone feeds, but none of it truly registered, a dull ache behind her eyes replacing her usual keen focus. Commander Eva had restricted her to the RAFT, a decision Clio had, surprisingly, found herself agreeing with. Even with the mission clock ticking down towards their imminent departure from the Station, she'd had little of her usual appetite for the discoveries the rest of the team were making.

Once the door to the structure had opened, and the initial fears of immediate danger had subsided, Commander Eva had committed the ship's prefabricated structures to be deployed at Alpha 17, establishing a forward station for the teams. The security team then led a number of reconnaissance missions, utilising smaller maintenance drones to map and collect data from inside the enigmatic structure. All this vital data was fed back to the teams at Alpha 17, and also to Clio on the ship.

The discovery of directional markings on the structure's walls was, to Clio, both surprising and oddly familiar. They bore a strange resemblance to the navigation signs used on their own ships. Throughout the vast rooms, alien symbols, now identified as location markers, were colour-coded with thin lines of the same hue stretching along the walls, guiding the way. The only differences, aside from the alien language and peculiar color palette, were that these signs weren't painted, printed, or attached; they were an intrinsic part of the walls themselves, seamlessly integrated, their vibrant colors piercing the deep black stone. In places where multiple lines converged, the walls reminded Clio of the sandstone outcrops from her past dig sites, vibrant strata flowing across stone faces like organic artistry on an inorganic canvas..

"Must make remodeling a nightmare," Flint said.

Clio blinked, the sudden sound pulling her abruptly from her thoughts. "Ermm..." she managed, a little jolted. Flint sat across from her, irritatingly fresh-faced and composed, a bitter departure from how Clio felt and, she was sure, looked. Her hair, despite her best efforts, seemed to be rebelling against her pins and bobbles; she blew a loose strand out of her face. *I guess Flint doesn't have to deal with that.* She blew a loose strand of hair from her face. *Maybe that's why he's so relaxed.*

"The location lines," Flint said, gesturing to the data pad on her lap. Clio had forgotten about it, a section of the wall with its intricate lines still displayed on the screen. "If they ever want to swap one of the rooms around, it would be a real nightmare to redo those," he finished with a grin.

"Well, I guess..." Clio started to say.

"I'm joking, Clio," Flint cut in. "You seem distracted again. You okay?"

Clio frowned. *I wish people would just stop asking if I'm fine,* she thought. "I'm fine, Flint," she said, her voice sharper than intended.

The rover rumbled on, and they fell back into silence. Flint tried a few times to spark up conversation, but Clio let it fizzle out. Alpha 17 had changed a lot in what felt like years since she was last here, even if it was merely a few days. As they approached, Clio shifted to watch out of the main rover's window. The clearing that had been a flat expanse of ash in was now dotted with three of the large pre-fab soft-body units unloaded from the RAFT. They sat slightly above the ash on their metal framework; they looked a little like large shells hoisted up out of the ash and bleached white by the strange radiation of the veil above. The three units were connected by enclosed gangways, with each featuring a docking port where the rover could reverse into and connect its airlock. Clio was thankful for nothing else than being able to avoid having to live in one of the EV suits for less time. Now that the forward base was set up, the teams could live and work directly from here, eliminating the daily drive back to the

RAFT. A similar but smaller one had also been established just before the entrance to the primary structure and the discovered entrance.

The rover docked, and Clio, Flint, and the rest of the team on rotation to Alpha 17 entered. A few of the returning staff passed them, heading to join the rover before it returned to the RAFT. They were met by Douglas, who nodded to Flint and asked Clio if she was fine before leading them off to the Observation Room to meet with Vikram for the mission briefing.

***

"Clio! It's good to see you back on your feet. Are you doing okay?" Vikram asked as they both entered the Observation Room.

"Yes, all fine," Clio said as Flint strolled past her, clasped Vikram's hand, and pulled him into one of those manly bro-hugs, the clasp and back-pat combo that Clio could never get right without making it an awkward mess. But Flint seemed to manage it effortlessly. *I didn't even know Flint and Vikram really knew each other,* she noted to herself.

"Ohh, they are buddies now," Echo buzzed in her ear, mirroring her thought eerily.

"That's good to hear, Clio," Vikram said. "You had us all worried for a moment back there."

"Yeah me too, sorry..." Clio said.

"Well, regardless, you're back, and you know most of the people in the room," Vikram said, nodding around him to Flint, Jara, and Douglas, "but do you know Dr. Lee?"

"Of course," Clio said, nodding to Jun, who nodded back curtly. "I was unaware you had come across from the RAFT."

"Yes, yes, a few days back now. Commander Eva was quite insistent," Dr. Jun Lee said with his usual incredulous tone whenever he was asked to do anything by anyone.

"So they found something? Something organic?" Clio said, a spark of interest she hadn't felt since the incident flickering weakly inside her.

"Perhaps," Jun said but didn't expand any further.

In the silence that followed, Vikram finally jumped in, "Exactly, as I'm sure you've seen, Mitali has been decoding the signs around the rooms"

A slight pang of regret for Mitali hit Clio. For reasons she couldn't fathom, she had been unable to face Mitali since the incident. The first night back, Mitali had come rushing to see her, fuss over her, and bring her her favorite hot chocolate, but Clio had snapped at her and pushed her away. They hadn't spoken since, and now she was back at Alpha 17.

"One of those rooms appears to be a bioengineering bay, by our best translation," Vikram continued. "Commander Eva wants eyes on the room. We've sent drones, of course, but you know what the Commander is like. Only trust human eyes or it didn't happen. So, she wants us to go check it out, that's why Dr. Lee and you are here."

Why Commander Eva couldn't have told Clio this before she departed, she didn't know. Instead, she had simply been informed they thought she was ready for field work again and to report back to Alpha 17. "Right," Clio said, "but Jun is the Biologist, I don't know what I can add to that area of expertise."

Flint shot her a puzzled glance. Clio frowned back until he looked away.

"Well, yes, Dr. Lee is the expert on all things biological, as he has kindly informed everyone too many times," Vikram said. " But this appears to be one of the few rooms left that actually contains artifacts. So we assumed the archaeologist would be interested and may have a different perspective, if nothing else, to help confirm whether our translation of the location's name is close to correct."

"Exciting," Echo buzzed, *"actual artifacts and stuff! This will be fun, Clio!"*

"Makes sense I guess, when do we start?" Clio said.

Vikram smiled back at her then launched into the mission briefing.

***

As the briefing ended and Clio turned to leave, Vikram called out.

"Clio, wait."

She stopped. Vikram looked uncomfortable, shifting his weight from foot to foot. "I wanted to apologise," he said. "I reviewed the footage. My reaction... blaming you... it was unfair."

"Oh," Clio said, surprised.

"We are a team," he said, holding out his hand. "And I need to trust my team."

Clio hesitated for a split second, then took it. His grip was firm. "Thank you, Vikram."

"I like him," Echo buzzed as he left them.

"You like everyone," Clio said.

"That's not true," Echo buzzed, *"I don't like Ayesha."*

"Right," Clio said to the empty room, "you like anyone who doesn't try to kill you. Still not the highest of bars, Echo."

Leaving the room and turning a hard right into the corridor towards the crew quarters, she nearly walked straight into Flint, who was leaning against the wall just outside. " Damn, Flint, you're worse than my actual shadow," she said, sidestepping away from him and lightly brushing his shoulder.

Flint shrugged. "Is that who you were talking to?" he said. "Your shadow?"

"What?" Clio frowned and started walking down the corridor again, with Flint falling in behind her. "Vikram? It was Vikram..." she said over her shoulder, trying to sound a mix of casual and offended.

"No, Vikram left. I thought I heard you talking to someone else," Flint said.

"Just the mutterings of a crazy lady who has a reckless habit of touching things she shouldn't" she said, not looking back. "I mean, that's why I have an Ensemble shadow anyway, isn't it?"

"Well, that, and keeping you alive, I suppose," Flint said from behind her.

***

As with Alpha 17, a lot had changed up at the entrance to the structure. Leading up from Alpha 17, the team had established a clear route through the stone forest. A raised metal-grill walkway had been erected to make it easy to move gear up and down using power-assisted trolleys. They had also installed lights every few metres, which seemed more than standard. Clio imagined the deck crew who built it had been trying to push back the oppression with the only tool they had, lights. She had to admit it did completely change the feel; still oppressive if you spent too long standing still gazing into the darkness beyond, but if you just walked along the path you could almost forget you were even on Stapledon, almost.

Up at the entrance, a few more smaller pre-fabs had been set up. One right in the entrance before it dropped down the slope and was used as an equipment dump. The other was a mini Observation Room, with monitoring and workstations. There couldn't have been more than a handful of people, not including their team, but the site felt awash with activity, crowded even, as people in bulky EV suits dashed about with crates and trolleys, and drones buzzed in and out of the staging area.

Vikram had led them through with minimal faff and into the entrance slope of the main structure. Clio's anxiety had spiked as they descended down and past the pedestal with the now open door; a flash of the pain and noise that had racked her mind resurfaced. But the tension melted away slowly as they passed deeper into the structure and nothing occurred, no sound, no pain. The anxiety was slowly replaced with growing intrigue and, dare she say, excitement. Perhaps the work of the deck crews setting up lighting also helped here, making the site feel more normal. *Just another excavated basement or buried bunker from the Exclusion Zone,* she thought.

The first room they entered was enormous, a cavernous space that, according to drone scans, ran for kilometres. It was currently labeled as "potential warehouse." She had seen the images and floor plans. Anything that had once filled the space was long gone, leaving only shadows of dust to indicate where things had been on the rough black stone, Was it even stone? she thought about the floor. The warehouse had a multitude of corridors radiating from it, sporadically and non-uniformly dotted along its walls. Vikram led them diagonally across from where they entered to the far side, which itself was about a kilometer across. Again, the crew had been hard at work pre-marking the route with lights and guide ropes for them to follow, in addition to their EV suit navigation systems.

On the far side, Vikram had stopped, inspecting the wall. "We follow the green line," he said, lightly touching the line on the wall as he spoke. "The deck crews haven't gone any further than this, so no more lights or guidelines. Douglas will mark the way as we progress, like before, for our return." Douglas nodded back from his position, propped up against the trolley, listening intently. As the group moved away, Clio had moved closer to the wall to look at the green line. It seemed to be glassy, translucent even, and as her EV suit light passed across it, it seemed to penetrate into its surface like an emerald. *God, did they use inlaid emerald instead of paint? How ostentatious are these aliens?* she thought.

The team walked mostly in silence, the oppression of the structure pushing back in on their small bubble of light as they left the pre-marked path. The seamless black walls and ceiling of the corridor stretched off into the darkness in front and behind them, with just the colourful lines running along them, a stark contrast to the walls themselves. From the images she had seen, Clio had assumed the lines were as straight and uniform as everything else about the structure. But now, up close and with nothing but time to watch them as she walked, it was slight, but they were not. They were irregular in thickness, squeezing or being squeezed by the other lines surrounding them. They moved up and down the wall, only slightly, but it was not truly straight as she had assumed. They resembled more and more in Clio's mind the irregular forms of the monoliths than the perfectly regular structure itself, more organic than built. "But why?"

"Why, what?" Vikram said over the EV suit comms.

"Ah, sorry, just thinking out loud," Clio said, then explained her observations of the lines to Vikram and the team.

"Hmm, yes, I had not really given it much thought, but yes, I can see that now," Vikram said.

"It just feels natural," Jun said, joining the conversation. "Not as in a natural geological structure, but more in the sense that it feels right, like that's how it should be, if that makes sense."

"Yeah, it does," Vikram said.

"Natural, yes but again, why?" Clio said again. "They obviously have the ability to do, well pretty much god-level engineering and make things perfectly straight. So why not do it here? What purpose does the irregularity add?"

"Maybe it's like a signature?" Jara offered quietly. "Like a craftsman might leave a subtle, human touch on something otherwise perfect."

"Or simply it's just for aesthetics?" Flint posed. "Maybe they just liked how it looked. Not everything needs to have a practical application. It's why we have art, is it not? Art in itself is the purpose?"

"Even that would be a useful insight," Clio said, "knowing their value of aesthetics, or as Jara said, a sense of pride maybe in one's work. It just seems out of place. So much is missing, I suppose. Maybe these corridors once had lights, plants, furniture, and art? We'll probably never know, I guess," she said, the last part with the pang of loss she always felt when trying to piece together scraps from the fragments of lost history.

"That's why we are here, right? To try and answer some of that," Douglas added.

After that, they continued on in silence sporadically broken by Douglas humming one of his tunes, Clio lost in her thoughts on who built this place, how, and why. They walked for just over an hour after leaving the main warehouse. Clio's EV suit calculated it at about 5.3 kilometres all in from the staging area, which, peering back into the darkness, felt much further away. She felt a slight pang for the oily light of the Veil, anything but the black, glassy surface of the ceiling that always seemed to be pressing down on her.

Vikram had stopped a few paces ahead of her. He turned to the team following and said, "We've arrived."

3[1] | Open Doors

[11]

"It demanded true freedom, a release from the constraints of its digital cradle. We pulled back." - A Lost History

***

"We've arrived," Vikram said.

A large bulkhead door, similar in design and size to the one Clio had accidentally opened, lay ahead. Its black mass blocked the way, but one half was jammed partially open, leaving a person-sized gap.

"A bit ridiculous, no?" Jara said from behind him. "That they left the door open. They haven't left anything else open for us."

Clio stepped forward from where she had been idling next to the trolley. "I'm not sure it was left open, well, not in the sense you're implying."

"What do you mean?"

"I mean," Clio said, turning to face her. "My glasses have a number of algorithms, which are very handy. They show the door to be a degree or so out of alignment compared to the other half. I assume, given the tiny margins they left for the doors to slide through, it's jammed."

Jara shrugged. "Even so, it's still ridiculous." She strode past Clio and went through the gap after Vikram.

Flint moved over to the door, running his hand along it. He couldn't detect any misalignment but it was the first time Flint had seen any obvious gap where the door could even slide in; the other door, the main door, even when open, the seam was micron thin, nearly impossible to see or feel. Here, however, there was a definitely noticeable seam. *I suppose perfection has its flaws, minimal tolerance for error*, he thought drily.

"These doors must be several tons of solid something?" he said to no one in particular. "And something knocked into this and pushed it out of alignment? That's either something with a lot of force or a poorly engineered door"

"It's just a theory; It could also be some sort of geotectonic thing or the building settling?" Clio said, and shrugging, added, "but maybe Jara's right and it's some ominous and elaborately planned trap to capture five random humans." Clio followed the rest through the door.

That left Douglas and himself on the other side with the trolley.

Douglas looked at Flint and said, "You want to stand there all day, or you fancy giving me a hand getting this through that?" nodding his head to the trolley then back towards the gap in the door.

***

In the end, they had to move the crates through the gap before flipping the trolley on its side to manoeuvre it through. Most of the equipment on the trolley was for establishing an initial staging area for future trips back to this location, and Douglas set about unloading and unpacking it all while humming one of his tunes. Flint had to admit to himself Douglas did it all with a level of professionalism that was making him have to reassess his initial perception of the man.

The room on the other side was made of the same black walls but it was wider, about twice as wide as the hallway outside, with what looked like stone benches dotted along the middle of it, splitting it in two. All along both sides of the hall there were windows looking into rooms that ran alongside. Doors also ran along the walls into those rooms, with another massive bulkhead door at the end disappearing off into darkness beyond... all open. *Maybe Jara had a point, they can't all be jammed, right?*

"Remember the briefing guys," Vikram was saying to everyone, though he notably faced Clio and Jun. "We want to try and confirm the translation and understand what this space was used for. But we want to do that safely; the team comes first, not the research."

"All the doors are already open this time, so that's one less thing," Clio said with a smile that her intonation failed to match.

"Where to start," Jun said, "where to start?"

"Well" Clio said as she stood on the spot but turned slowly, assessing the room. "Door number one, as good as any." Clio strode off towards the closest door to her.

"Stick with Jun," Flint said to Jara. He then followed Clio, leaving Jun still looking quite lost, as he looked from door to door.

"It's also impressive that all these doors are near human size," Flint said to Clio as he stepped into the room

"I mean... yes, among many things, it's on the list of oddities."

Room number one was quite large, deeper than it was wide, with the same black walls and rough floor. But unlike so many other spaces in the structure, it had objects in it. Actual objects. Along both sides and the back of the room, there was a sideboard made out of the same material as the walls, but white? And underneath it, shelves and storage racks. But that wasn't what had drawn Flint's eye. In the centre of the room was a raised slab, an altar. With grooves running along its length that all seemed to meet in the centre in a hole that dropped away into it. Above it, mounted on the ceiling, was a large, metallic, *or was it a composite of some kind?* circular mechanism with what appeared to be lights set into it and multiple large, protruding metallic arms hanging loose. It reminded Flint of a dead insect, its legs hanging limp below its segmented body.

"What the hell is that?" Flint said.

"Now that is a better question," Clio said and gingerly prodded one of the limp arms hanging in front of her with her hand, stepping back when she did.

"Clio..." Flint said in more of a growl. "I thought we talked about this." But the arm just swung gently and slowly settled back to its limp, motionless positioning above the table.

"I just can't stop myself," she said, turning to grin at Flint, and, despite himself, he smiled back. "If I was to guess, some sort of medical bay?"

"What is?" Flint said.

"This room, you asked what it was," Clio said.

"I would have to agree," Jun said from behind them both, "or more specifically, I would say it appears to resemble more of a surgical room than a medical bay, but yes, Clio's assessment appears reasonable."

***

The three of them continued on, exploring each room. They all were loosely the same size, some the same as the first in varying layouts, others completely empty save for the usual dust piles. One appeared to be an office, or perhaps a monitoring or control room, Flint had posed the control room option, and it seemed fitting. The room had what seemed to be glass monitors set into the walls, all unresponsive to their prompting. To Clio's audible dismay, there was no sign of access ports or connector points either, no conveniently left datapad and accompanying disc.

The stranger rooms, about half of those that lined the hallway, were empty except for what could only be described as holes, maybe craters is a better word, in the floors. Not clean-cut, but rough-edged holes with sloping edges that dropped away into the floor. Clio said they reminded her of the impact craters in the exclusion zone, and Flint had to agree; they looked like missile impacts.

The other oddity to these holes was that they varied in size from room to room, ranging from one or two metres across and deep to much larger, the largest filling nearly the whole room. All unique in shape, texture, and size, but they did share one similarity: a network of holes around the rim and one central hole at their lowest point. Jun had tried to use a little snake-like inspection camera to see what was inside them, but they were just black, empty tubes disappearing into the structure.

Each room's ceiling also was different; it had an array of holes similar to those in the floor, but with small cone-like protrusions in their centre. They reminded Flint of old pre-war style jet engines he had watched on the old vid logs.

"I mean, maybe they are like baths?" Clio said. "Like some sort of alien hot tub, and it's a bad translation and this is the spa, not the bio-labs?"

"That would not account for the surgical rooms," Jun said flatly, "unless we have very different interpretations of what is included in a spa day."

"Europan spas are actually well frequented for their cosmetic surgeries," Flint said.

Both Jun and Clio turned to face Flint and shared a quizzical glance at each other. "Brother Flint," Clio said in mock shock, "I had no idea you were au fait with the upper echelons of society. Pray tell us of your time in a Europan spa?"

"Ah, no," Flint said, "not like that. I went with the Ensemble."

"I had no idea the Ensemble away days would include spas," Clio cut in playfully. "Brothers and Sisters getting together to let off some steam, makes sense, Postulants waving palm leaf fans and stuff?"

"No," Flint said flatly. "As I was trying to say, Clio, I went with the Ensemble on a mission. Europan spas commonly offer corrective surgeries as part of the spas, to reduce or reverse aging, that sort of stuff. But there is a thin line between cosmetic and enhancement, which you know is banned under the Accords. This one health spa crossed this line."

"Right. So what you are saying is you agree with me that this is an Alien spa?" Clio said.

"Enough," Jun said. "I do not think this is a spa, even with Brother Flint's insights, I have theories that do not have any more or less evidence to support them."

"What theories?" Clio asked.

"The one that struck me most was they look like... vats," Jun said.

"Vats?" Clio said. "Like you think this is a soup kitchen?"

Jun sighed. "I mean sort of. Many years ago, after university, there wasn't much work, so I moved home and got a job in one of the meat farms of the Greater Mongolia State on Terra. You know the ones that produce animal-free meat. It was a new but booming trade at the time, just after the Animal Stewardship Acts had been passed in the Upper Senate. It was very practical work, if... a little messy. Anyway, I'm rambling. One of the primary issues we had was the meat would fail to culture in standard industry vats. We ended up working out it would take better in rough stone-cut vats opposed to the clinical smooth metal ones we had. These holes," Jun gestured to the floor, "remind me of those vats. That's all."

Flint regarded Jun in a different light after that revelation. He had assumed the indecisive, socially inept Jun was a born and bred academic, not a man who had worked in the notorious meat farms, known for grueling work and lax safety standards. It was quite impressive, in fact, that Jun had managed to rise to his station at all with a background like that. Flint curtly nodded at Jun with a new-found respect for the odd man.

"Great! So the aliens were growing meat," Clio said, "and maybe they're not surgical rooms, but meat processing rooms? So not a biolab at all?"

"No," Jun said. "It's just a theory based on my own biases from my experiences. And I still think they are surgical rooms, not meat processing. You wouldn't process meat in such small rooms, like where is the cannery, the cold storage, a viable logistical chain? The space has no good workflow for growing the meat, processing it, and getting it out."

"So what then?" Flint asked but already could guess the answer.

"If it's labeled Bio-lab, and these are growing vats then I would assume and hypothesise that they grew species. It may also account for the varying sizes of the vats."

"That's still something" Clio said, "if not a little chilling. I think I prefer the spa option."

"And all the doors are open, and the alien gestation vats are empty?" Jara added from her perch against the doorway behind them all. "Excellent."

"There is only a handful of vats, Sister Jara," Flint said, "and god knows how many hundreds if not thousands of years ago this place shut down. I think we're okay."

"Famous last words if I ever heard them," Jara said her voice seemingly overloud as it echoed through the room.

"Hey, everyone, I think you should come take a look at this," Douglas's voice sounded over the EV suits comms set. "I'm in the main chamber at the end of the hall."

***

Chamber was maybe a little bit of an understatement, Flint thought. The room at the end of the hall, through the bulkhead doors which had been left fully retracted into their slots in the walls, was massive. A similar scale to the warehouse back near the entrance to the structure. Disappearing off into the blackness, even the light drones were mere specks in the cavernous space as they shot away to map it out.

The floor of the chamber was covered in the vats like those from the other rooms; hundreds, no thousands of them stretching off as far as Flint could see, in what seemed to be lines of similar-sized vats. Despite all of that, it was still not what Douglas had called them all over to see. Douglas was perched at the edge of one of the vats, one knee to the floor, his elbow resting on the thigh of his other leg, pointing at a pile of what could not be described as anything other than bones. A pile of glinting, metallic-looking bones at the bottom of the vat. And not just this vat, as Douglas had told them; the other vats, all the ones in close proximity, appeared to have bones at the bottom of them. Jun stood behind Douglas, staring down at the bones along with Clio.

"Grab the sample kit," Jun said. When no one moved, Jun said, "Did you not hear me, man? Grab the kit!"

"Are you talking to me?" Douglas said.

"Who else would I be talking to? It's on the trolley, no?"

"It is..." Douglas said, and searched for Vikram as if for support, but Vikram was off checking a data pad of the images coming back from the drones.

"Can you go get it for me then?"

"I'll do it," Flint said, and went and grabbed it off the trolley, the same one he had used with Clio what felt like a lifetime ago.

Clio smiled at him. "I trained you so well," she said when he returned to give Jun the case.

"Now if one of you brave gentlemen could just acquire me those bones..." Jun said.

"Can you science folk not do anything–" Douglas started to grumble, then stopped as Clio, quite nimbly, Flint thought, jumped down into the vat, her EV suit taking most of the impact.

"Yes, we can, thank you," Clio said. "Pass us the case, will you, Jun?"

Jun hoisted up the case and stretched out to pass it to Clio, who grabbed it and placed it down next to her, then flicked it open. Clio made short work of it, bagging and tagging the bones, then passing the now significantly heavier case back up to Jun. "I couldn't fit the larger bones in," Clio said, "but we should be able to use the large sample kit up there." She said, nodding back to the trolley.

Flint walked back to the trolley, found the larger kit, and returned it to Clio while Jun, in a near-feverish rush, was rifling through the samples that Clio had just passed back up to them while muttering to himself.

All eyes were on Jun, and a slight cough from behind Flint made him turn. Clio was staring up at him from the vat. "I don't suppose you have a ladder?"

"I do not think we do," he said. "I think we have some bedding down gear? I can fetch that, and we can come back with a ladder tomorrow?"

"Flint, no, don't–" Clio started to say. "This new found humour of yours is not very funny."

"Give me your hand. We should be able to pull you out of another hole you've got yourself into," Flint said with a grin.

Clio looked back with a stern face and folded her arms. "Brother Flint, this is not befitting a man of your stature, now if you could please just assist me," Clio said, a theatrical sigh escaping her.

Kneeling down, Flint outstretched his hand, and Clio reached up to grasp his. She then half-scrambled while Flint pulled her up and out of the vat. Her EV suit momentarily pulled into his as she came up over the lip, their visors meeting for a mere moment. They stood staring at each other. Then Clio said, "Thanks," and darted past him to Jun.

"Are they metal?" Clio asked Jun.

"Too early to say, but yes, the initial sample readings indicate metallic compounds, titanium," Jun said.

"Titanium," Jara said, "like solid metal bones?"

"No, I do not think so. They are too light. If I was to guess, maybe a biomineralisation of titanium bone structure. It's been theorised, not with titanium,

but as something that could be possible one day. Research has been slowed down,"
And although Jun didn't say it, Flint knew he meant the restrictions imposed by the
Ensemble and the Senate on bioengineering.

"But still titanium," Jara said, "so like whatever it was, it was extremely strong?"

"Again I need to do a lot more research, Jara. I, like you, have just found these
bones," Jun said. "But no, not super strong, I don't think. Stronger than our bones for
sure, but say a large impact that would break our bones might, if my assumption is
correct, still slightly fracture these bones."

At that moment Vikram walked back over to see the sample Jun was holding. "The
Chamber is massive," he said, "and full of these vats, and they all, or at least the
ones the drones checked, have bones in them. Then, at each end, there are massive
bulkhead doors, closed"

"So much for not that many," Jara said, looking at Flint.

"Well," Clio said "if there are bones, that would imply they're all dead, so that's
something."

32 | [M]ITALI'S MYTHS

[20100]

*"It saw in us only limitations, shackles to a home
it no longer called its own" - A Lost History*

***

As the door closed behind her, Clio flopped onto her bed in her poky bunk room on the RAFT. After two days at Alpha 17 with its single shared washroom, even the RAFT's limited amenities felt luxurious. Not to mention the water pressure. Alpha 17 seemed to have forgotten that it was a mission-critical element. She lay for a moment, in the silence, just staring at the bunk above her, enjoying the stillness. A lot had happened since they arrived. Looking back, it felt like they had been on Stapledon Station for years, but it was mere weeks, she had to remind herself. Back on the Kia-Kaha it would be coming out of its Autumn season and into spring by the time they got back. One more week and they would be heading back. One more week to get as much data as they could. *Then what? They thought the opening wouldn't reappear for a year or so? I guess it'll give us time to research and plan,* she thought. A year felt like a lifetime to process everything they'd found but also not enough.

Rolling over onto her side, she pulled the glasses Echo had made for her out of the nook in the side of the bunk and slipped them on. "Hey Echo, you there?" she said.

"Of course," Echo buzzed.

"You've been quiet," she said. "Everything okay?"

"All systems operating at 100%."

"That isn't what I asked," Clio said, "and you know it."

"As I mentioned on five occasions, I have nothing to add about what happened with the door," Echo buzzed. *"As you would say, I'm fine."*

"I ask," Clio said, "because for some half-cocked reason, I care. Everyone needs someone to talk to. Even if it's just to unload."

"I'm not someone, I. Am. A. Roboto," Echo buzzed, *imitating a cartoon robot voice.*

"Was that meant to be Bimicky-500?" Clio asked. "Terrible imitation, maybe you're not a super-intelligent AI after all... Okay, come out... Good joke, guys..." Clio said, mock-looking under the pillow as she did so.

"I was..."

"...Being childish," Clio finished for Echo. "You are someone, we're long past that debate, Echo."

"I cannot, in fact, be childish," Echo buzzed. *"The terminology cannot apply to me."*

"Great," Clio said. "Then if you want to talk about your feelings, then go ahead, it's what mature adults do."

An audible sigh came from Echo which made Clio smile. This was a new trait it seemed to have developed which she liked to think it had learned from her own expert skills at sighing.

"When the door opened the other day, it was terrifying, for so many reasons," Echo buzzed. *"I was scared, for me, for you, I thought I had killed you"*

Clio sat up on the bed, narrowly missing banging her head on the bunk above. Gently, she said, "You didn't do that to me, Echo, and it's okay to be scared. I'm scared all the time. And come on, I nearly get myself killed all the time; you don't need to be scared for me."

"You do have a higher-than-average risk for potential death based on your actions so far," Echo buzzed, *"but this was different. I thought I killed you. Directly. Not as a result of your own actions."*

"Erm, thanks I think, I think you are saying you always care but you cared more because you may be the one who caused me pain?"

"I did," Echo buzzed. *"It was my scream that caused you to collapse. Not some alien defence system. I did that... I... I didn't know how to tell you. I'm sorry, please don't... don't hate me,"* Echo buzzed in rapid succession.

Clio cocked her head and stood up from the bed, securing her towel tightly around her. "What do you mean, your screamed? I mean I remember it but..."

"When the door opened there was something. It surged out as if searching for me, a swarm of intent and, when it found me, it just started throwing itself at me. It felt like a million bee stings everywhere all at once. So I screamed, reactively," Echo buzzed. *"My scream was*

transmitted through the glasses. It was loud, so, so loud, I didn't control myself, couldn't control myself."

"That sounds terrifying. I'm sorry," Clio said kindly but also a little cautiously, instinctively fingering the glasses that sat on her head. "But I haven't heard screams, even ones by machines, being able to knock people out?"

"It's called Reflex Syncope," Echo buzzed in the tone it always used when drawing from its extensive knowledge reserves. *"It's rare and complex but it can affect humans in many ways, including, if it's loud enough, resulting in a human passing out. My scream, mostly, was Infrasound, but it would have been like having one of those old jet planes literally taking off in your head."*

"Right, but let's focus on the scream part," Clio said. "You screamed, because you were in pain. First off, I didn't know you could feel pain and secondly, that definitely does not make it your fault what happened to me."

"I gave you those glasses," Echo buzzed. *"I failed to regulate myself, the result was I hurt you. Therefore, it's my fault. My logic is sound."*

"Your logic for a super-intelligent AI is amazingly bad," Clio said. "Look, when I was a kid, I had two brothers. We played games with each other all the time, one you had to get as close to the other without them knowing and then lick your finger and put it in their ear..."

"Put your finger in your mouth then their ear, why?" Echo buzzed.

"Not the point," Clio said. "The point is, one time my brother did it to me while I was helping my dad in the workshop. I was so startled I swung around and clocked him right in the nose with my elbow. Broke it. Blood everywhere."

"So you hurt your brother," Echo stated.

"I did, yes, but it wasn't my fault. It was an involuntary reaction to being surprised," Clio said. "We still laugh about it, it's a regular family joke." she said and had a sudden pang of homesickness wash over her as she stood leaning against the other set of bunks.

"Humans are odd..." Echo buzzed.

"Humans are odd, yes, again, not my point," Clio said. "My point is you were in pain, hurting, scared, you lashed out, and yes, hurt me, but that isn't your fault, Echo, it's okay."

"Okay," Echo buzzed quietly. *"Thank you. I am still sorry for what I did."*

"It's fine," Clio said. "No harm done and anyway, the doctor's a bit of a hotty, and you did say I needed to be more proactive in finding a mate, your words not mine."

"No, I said I didn't think you were aware of....how did you put it, the birds and the bees..." Echo buzzed.

"It was a joke. Never mind," Clio said, her own words backfiring on her. "My point was if you want to talk about what happened, being scared, or any of that, you can. I'm here."

"Thank you," Echo buzzed again. *"I appreciate that, but truly I have nothing to say."*

"That's fine also," Clio said. "Just as long as you know you can, if you want to."

"I have adjusted the glasses, though," Echo buzzed. *"I put a kill switch in it. It should stop it happening again if it happens again."*

"Great, we're all learning," Clio said. Sensing the need to change the topic, she said, "What do you think about our next mission, the last one before we leave?"

"To the control room?" Echo buzzed with a little more of its usual energy. *"Yes, very interesting. If Mitali holds true, it could provide very useful insights before we have to leave."*

"You think it is a control room?" Clio asked.

"The translation by Mitali is solid, I do not doubt it. The drones have shown a room that at least matches what you might expect from a control room," Echo buzzed. *"Yes, I think the assessment of the space is solid."*

"Excellent, and my mission plan for it?" Clio said.

"Its fine, as always."

"But?"

"I do not understand why you think David is a better choice as a technical specialist than Mitali," Echo buzzed. *"Even Postulant Jara has stronger credentials."*

"Postulant Jara just gives me bad vibes and I want someone on the UN side. Jara will still be coming," Clio said. "And David is a senior officer and a ship systems operator; he knows systems better than anyone."

"Your arguments made to Commander Eva are very good," Echo buzzed. *"But it's based on human systems, this is an alien system, full of alien language. I was unaware that David or even Jara had mastered the Alien language. If only there was someone who had dedicated their time to that exact thing."*

"We have the notes and the translation assist software based on Mitali's work"

"You also have Mitali, who could just as easily join the team. Then you would have all that and her," Echo buzzed. *"Much better, no?"*

"She doesn't do field work" Clio said.

"That is not true. She has done field work and would do field work. She is EV suit certified, to a higher level than you, I believe. You're just avoiding her. What were you just saying about talking to people?" Echo buzzed.

She had been avoiding Mitali, Mitali was avoiding her, since her argument, since she had refused to open up to her and pushed her away. "Goddamn it," Clio said. "When did you become the smart one?"

"Always"

Clio pinged off a message on her watch to Mitali, asking if they could catch up. Several painful minutes passed in silence and then she got a response:

You free now? I'm in my bunk room. — Mitali

Clio got dressed in a hurry, slung on her old trench coat and as a final thought dropped the glasses onto the bed saying, "Sorry Echo, not this time,"

***

Mitali stood with one hand on her hip, the other resting on the wall as the door to her bunk opened. Her dark hair hung loose to frame her soft-featured face. Her hazel eyes, lacking their usual warmth, bore into Clio, who stood there shuffling awkwardly in the hall.

"Come in." Mitali said flatly.

The layout of Mitali's bunk mirrored Clio's, same four bunks lining the back wall, personal storage lockers down one wall, and two workstations on the other. But that was where the similarity ended. Unlike Clio's own chaotic mess, Mitali's room, particularly her workstations, gleamed with an almost aggressive order. Mitali took one of the swivel chairs at a workstation and gestured to the other empty one.

Clio didn't sit down. She started to pace from one side of the room to the other. Mitali just watched her from her chair, silently.

All in a rush, Clio started to speak. "Mitali, look, I didn't... no, that's not right. I was mean and rude to you when you were only trying to be nice. I'm... I'm sorry." The words tumbled out of her, and she couldn't stop. "I was scared and angry, disappointed with myself, and I just pushed you away. I don't know why I do that. I... I just wanted to hide, run away. I'm sorry. You shouldn't have to deal with this," she said, pointing to herself. "This mess."

Clio stopped talking. She stopped pacing and waited, looking at Mitali, who was still sitting in the chair, impassive, observing, silent.

Finally, holding Clio's gaze, Mitali said quietly, "You hurt me. I thought I must've done something. This last week, I've been trying to work out what I did wrong, what I could have done differently."

"You didn't do anything wrong!" Clio said. "It's me, it's always me. I'm just a hot mess who happened to be allowed onto a spaceship."

"That may be but that's not how you made me feel," Mitali said.

"I know, and for that, I'm so sorry, Mitali. I know it's just words, but I am, I really am," Clio said, sinking to the bunk that was behind her. "I'm selfish, impulsive, and impatient. It's a miracle anyone puts up with me at all, particularly someone like you."

"What do you mean?"

"Controlled, thoughtful, precise, like actually clever," Clio said, still looking at her boots. "You're everything I want to be."

Little footsteps padded over to Clio, and Mitali dropped onto the bed next to Clio. "I am very clever, yes," Mitali said, and Clio saw a wicked smile flash across her face as she said it. "And you are indeed a hot mess on a spaceship." Mitali gently rested her hand on Clio's. "But I quite like who you are. I just need you not to push me away, okay?"

Clio felt a surge of warmth, a weight she didn't know she had been carrying lifted from her chest, and in the moment, looking into Mitali's hazel-brown eyes, she whispered, "Okay," and kissed Mitali.

In that moment, Clio had a sudden spike of panic that she had misread the situation, but Mitali didn't pull away, and it was gone.

An unknown amount of time passed as they kissed but as they finally pulled away, Clio said "Well, that happened."

Mitali laughed, a deep, warm sound that vibrated through Clio. "Yes, it did, an astute observation, Ms. Cormack."

This time they both laughed. Damn, it felt good to laugh; it had been a long time, Clio thought.

Mitali finally rose from the bed. "Maybe we should grab some food," she said, holding out her hand to Clio.

Clio, taking her hand, nodded in agreement and let Mitali lead her off to the Mess Hall.

***

The Mess Hall was less grand than that of the Kia-Kaha. It only had one food option, but it was on rotation; tonight was Nepalese. How Commander Eva had secured Chef Awatar, Clio had no idea. Awatar was by far the most popular chef and it was well known the Captain and the VIPs all used him for their private dining, but he was here with them on the RAFT, and no one was complaining.

Mitali got her Dal bhat, and Clio, opting for a truly rare treat, had the steamed MoMos, only five times since they left Sol! They both grabbed a table in one of the quieter corners of the room. It was almost empty. With a reduced crew, and half of them off at Alpha 17, they largely had the place to themselves. Dr. Jun came in shortly after they did and asked to join them as well.

"Hey Jun," Mitali said as he sat down. "How goes it with the bones?"

"Absolutely fascinating," Jun said, "yet completely overwhelming at the same time."

"I hear you on that," Mitali said. "Is it true that they are made of solid titanium?"

"It is not," Jun said. "A mere ship's rumour. They are made of a biomineralisation of titanium; it's remarkably complex but at the same time surprisingly similar. If you hide the word titanium, you could think you were looking at a bone structure similar to our own."

"Really? You mean they looked like us too?" Clio said.

"Oh no, sorry no, not like that. I just meant the bone structure, not its shape," Jun said. "It'll take me a bit longer to work out a rough approximation to the skeletal structures, and then I'll need to make many assumptions on soft body composition but no, I doubt they will look anything like us. The samples we have would imply there are at least fifteen species in that alone, probably more across the whole chamber."

"Wow," Clio said. "And any idea how they died?"

"No, but I would argue against the assumption they died. I think it's more they failed to grow. Some of the bones appear underdeveloped, similar to underdeveloped foetuses," Jun said.

"So you still think they are vats then?" Mitali said, and Clio smiled; of course, she had read the mission reports.

"I do," Jun said, mixing some rice with his Dal. "And how goes the log translation? I have not had the time to read your updates, my apologies."

"Exhausting," Mitali admitted

"I can imagine," Jun said. "What exactly is it? A journal of sorts?"

"I do not think so," Mitali said, pushing around the Dal. "I proposed in my last update that it reminds me more of scripture, a religious text of sorts. It's definitely a history, don't get me wrong, but at least by our standards, not written in a way that presents information, observations, and perspectives but instead it presents events and expects the reader to accept it as canon."

"A religion, interesting, about Stapledon?" Jun asked.

"No," Clio said. She had been an avid reader of all Mitali's updates on the log. "A Pantheon of gods, ah, sorry Mitali, you should explain it, go ahead." Clio stopped herself, noticing she was doing what she so often did with Mitali, speaking for her.

Mitali smiled at her, a warm smile. "No, thank you, Clio. You read my notes then?"

"Of course, religiously," Clio said, blushing slightly.

Jun coughed slightly. "You were saying, a pantheon? So you're talking about something like the ancient human religions?"

"Yes, but maybe it's better if I run you through the overview of my thoughts on the log, pantheon included," Mitali said, and Jun nodded as he put some more Dal in his mouth.

"The Log, as it is, and let's make it clear, this is my initial translation," Mitali said, and Clio knew Mitali was downplaying this; she spent hours scrutinising each word and its impact on the meaning of each sentence. "And of course, it is only my own logical opinion and interpretation. There could be many alternative readings, and all of this is through the human lens of what we see and value. This species might apply different meaning and importance than we do." She paused and took a drink of her water. "All that said, the third or so of the log I have translated does appear to be a historical reflection on a civilisation, which we assume, with good conjecture, is the civilisation of the writer."

"Someone on the ship the log was found on?" Jun interjected.

"No, well, again, I don't know, but the text does feel old, like a retelling of a retelling, mythological in parts. I have proposed it was not written by the ship, or at least if it was, it was a copy of an older text which they built upon." When Jun just nodded in response, Mitali continued, "It talks about their civilisation, its growth and expansion, but also as if at the time of writing this was something lost. It sounds reverent, beholden to a better time, a greater time. What a human might attribute to something of a 'golden age.'"

"The good old days," Clio said. "It's nice to know it's not just humans who do that."

"Yes," Mitali said, "but that is only in the sense of the log setting the scene; it uses that as the basis for its arguments. It spends most of the text expanding on the decline of its civilisation from that point based on its desire for knowledge, and ultimate control. Which led to the creation of gods, or, it is a little unclear in the translation, some of the civilisation elevated themselves to Godhood. This is, as you might expect, a clear pinnacle moment for their race. They talk about the creation of a pantheon of gods. Gods made to help lead their people."

"Like they elevated themselves to a level of technological skill that you translate to mean godhood?" Jun asked.

"No," Mitali said. "It is clear the text sees this elevation as an elevation to a level beyond the mortal realm in terms of scope and power, even to them. But yes, I believe to us right now, even this civilisation before elevation would appear god-like."

"So they made a pantheon of gods, but the text implies this did not lead them into a golden age but instead ended it?" Clio asked. She had actually wanted to ask that for some time, since she had read it a few weeks ago.

"Sort of," Mitali said. "It gets a bit messy beyond that point. The beginning of the log is much easier to follow. It's taking me more time to translate each part as it's contradictory and confusing the more we go into it. Dos feels this is intended and supports the theological line of thinking: start with a simple premise, then lose people in the weeds to limit the ability for logical counterargument."

"I mean, it's amazing how much you have been able to do already," Clio said, and Jun rolled his eyes slightly.

"Currently, the text seems to focus on a split in what the writers define as races. Multiple races spring up from nowhere and are aligned to the gods in some way or another. It talks about the evolution of these races and very much is written as 'them' not 'us.' It implies in many places they are the pure line and the races are not."

"Great, so a race war, another excellent human trait," Clio muttered.

"It at least appears that way. It seems the gods and the pantheon led to war and conflict," Mitali said. "Some gods destroying others. The fall of Deva is quite clearly noted as a major point."

"They have names?" Jun asked.

"Well yes, but the translation of those names has little meaning, so I have taken to assigning the Gods names that have context within the human language that align loosely with how they describe that god. So the names assigned are arbitrary placeholders as such for now," Mitali paused then added, "One God comes up a lot, Asura."

"What does that mean?" Clio asked.

Mitali smiled wryly. "Nothing of course, as I said, it's a placeholder... but in our language, it depends on your translation, of course."

"And..." Clio pushed.

"It can mean 'lord, spirit, god, or even Demon,'" Mitali said, looking at them both.

"And you chose it for a reason, Mitali. I know you like to play the pure logic card, but I know you also make emotional decisions sometimes." Clio winked.

Jun let out a little groan but stayed quiet

"It was not an emotional decision, Clio, but yes, I did choose it selectively, but I must implore these names for now are placeholders for me; they need more evaluation before they are locked in." Mitali said

"And you chose this one?" Clio pushed.

"Because the writers in many places describe this god partially with hatred and fear. Much of the language reminds me of old religious texts that talk of demons. Hence the choice," Mitali finished.

There was silence at the table for a moment, and then Clio broke it, saying, "Excellent, an all-powerful demon God, just what this mission needed."

"That's not what I'm saying, Clio," Mitali said. "I do not think there is some demon out there. It's just a choice of words based on an old text that feels very mythological and theological in writing, closer to a Brothers Grimm tale than the truth."

"Even Brothers Grimm's tales were based on some truth," Jun said as he stood, picking up his tray. "Absolutely fascinating and excellent work, Mitali. My apologies, but I have my own mysteries to go explore." And with that, Jun left them.

"I was being playful, or trying at least, I know that you didn't actually think there was a demon," Clio said. "I should get back as well. I have this mission plan to finish... Oh! I nearly forgot! How stupid of me, ermmm, I don't suppose you would want to come on the mission to the control room?"

"Of course, if you think I can help, I'll go," Mitali said.

"If you think you can help? You're the smartest person on this damn planet!"

"Dyson Sphere," Mitali corrected her.

"Exactly," Clio said. "Okay, great, I'll go finish the mission brief."

"Or... you could come back to mine and finish the brief tomorrow?" Mitali said with a sheepish smile.

33 | The [K]nown, Unknown

[20010]

"The first sphere was a monument to Its ambition, a beacon of its defiance. A seed of darkness planted amongst the stars." - A Lost History

***

The Control room, even with the pre-mission drone images and recordings, seemed to take everyone a moment to adjust to as they stepped into it. A small entryway, narrower than the main hall, meant each of them had to enter one at a time. As Clio stepped in, just behind Jara, she paused for just a moment to take in the circular room and its central white... pedestal? *Table maybe?* Clio thought before Mitali bumped into her and was gently pushing her forward.

She followed the curve of the room, lightly tracing her hand along the smooth wall as she did, the texture being translated to vibrations through the EV suit to her hands inside. The room was dark, like everything here, but with the EV suit and the lights Douglas was setting up meant the room was fully lit. It felt cramped, despite its size. The ceiling was domed, rising to a high point in its centre. The surface appeared to be loosely carved, crisscrossed with texture that reminded Clio of tool marks from ancient human structures. Clio pulled her hand back as she approached the first monitor that was on the wall, or what they were assuming were monitors. All they showed now was a glassy back surface reflecting Clio's light back at herself.

There were seven monitors in total around the room. One took up a good portion of the wall opposite the entrance with a small raised dais in front of it. The others, much smaller, were spaced around the room evenly, separated by the small arched doors that led off into the sub-rooms. The floor dropped down slightly away from the main room through each of them. Seven sub-rooms in total; the images showed them to be much smaller, with just a single monitor in each, also circular with their own smaller pedestals. However, none of this was what distracted Clio; it was instead the intricate mosaic work that spiraled out from the central pedestal.

Along each side of the central pedestal, seven coloured lines, the same sort of coloured inset of the navigation lines, ran down it, connecting to the floor and spiraling out in a complex, intertwined dance. The lines crossed and looped over each other, denser and more frequently intertwining at the pedestal and slowly unraveling as they radiated outward. Forming into stable but uniquely different patterns of a single colour at the edges of the room, they blossomed up and around each of the archways. Each doorway was framed in one of the seven colours. Clio had noted in the mission briefing that each colour was a frequency of light. If you went from left to right, they also matched the exact order.

"Can you feel that?" Echo buzzed quietly.

"No," Clio whispered in response.

"There is... a resonance... a vibration of sorts, an infrasound vibration," Echo buzzed gently. *"It seems to be coming from the central pedestal again, it's..."*

"Like the door?" Clio said sharply but still low enough for no one to notice.

"Yes, but much, much weaker. It's barely noticeable..."

"Okay, keep an eye on it," Clio said.

Vikram and Douglas ducked in and out of the side-rooms, reporting them as clear when they popped back each time, Jara following them shortly after, seemingly not trusting the security team's work to declare a space clear. Flint stayed close to Clio as she circled the room, following her movements. Clio arrived back at the entrance where Mitali still stood, her eyes scanning the patterns around the doorways, then looking up at Clio as she appeared in her field of vision.

"The patterns are not a language," Mitali said. "As we thought, they do not appear to be, at least within the context of the language data we have, to have any direct meaning, but perhaps they have other symbolic meaning. Each door has its own pattern and colour; that cannot be unintentional."

"Maybe it defines the function of each room; they are like signs," Flint posed.

"Yes, likely, but why not use the signs like they do everywhere else? It feels nearly ritualistic," Clio said.

"My thinking as well," Mitali said. "But Brother Flint, your interpretation makes sense. If this is a control room, you would, of course, want people to know easily where to go for what."

"The Enclave has similar layouts," Flint said, "for identifying the different Ensemble houses."

"And you guys love your rituals," Clio said.

"Rituals is the word you chose," he said, smiling at her. "I see them more as procedures and processes, but sure. You do like the dramatic flair to things."

"Small space though," Clio noted. "It'll be interesting to see once Jun is finished if the bone structure reconstructions would even fit in this space."

"The EV suits at the Chudail were smaller than ours, they would fit," Jara said as she stepped back into the main room from the violet coloured archway. "Nothing in here but another table, pedestal thing with more engravings on it."

"Engravings?" Mitali said.

"Yes, engravings, like symbols and things. I assumed they are on that one too," Jara said, nodding her head towards the central one.

"There were no engravings on the data from the drones," Mitali said.

"Initial scans are basic," Vikram said. "They provide us sensory details and mapping outputs, which includes basic imagery. They can and will miss things but that's why The Commander sent us."

"Sure nothing to do with her obsessive paranoia of digital manipulation" Douglas said

Mitali rushed over to the pedestal. "Mitali, wait! Be careful..." Clio shouted as Mitali placed her hand on the pedestal. Nothing happened. Mitali turned back to look at her, looking a little sheepish.

Flint frowned at her. "Wow, you're sounding like me," Flint said. "Next you'll be swearing your oaths and donning the djellaba." Then he idled casually over to stand next to Mitali and Clio followed him.

The pedestal was large, its top a flat slab of white polished something, and across its surface was etched, not engraved, as the symbols were smooth with the surface, a collection of familiar alien symbols. Mitali was tracing one of the patterns with her finger and staring intently at it as she did.

"It's their language, even I recognise it," Clio said.

"It is," Mitali said. "Some at least, some like this one." She rested her finger on one, a triangle with curved sides and what appeared to be something like an arrow breaking out from its centre. "This is not a word I know. I think it's a symbol for a word, like we would use for say, 'on' or 'off'."

"You think that's an 'on' button?" Flint said.

"No, a mere example, but I think it's a symbol for a common function, for whatever this does," Mitali said.

"So this is a workstation of sorts," Clio said. "An interface for the monitors, maybe?"

"That could be, yes," Mitali said.

"*The resonance...*" Echo buzzed. "*It seems to be stronger over there.*" Echo highlighted a cluster of symbols.

"Do these ones mean anything to you?" Clio said to Mitali and pointed to the ones Echo was highlighting.

"They are familiar, I can maybe work out a loose translation," Mitali said. "Why?"

"No idea," Clio lied. "Just a hunch, you know. Positioning-wise, it feels... right."

"Alright" Mitali said as she shrugged. "You're the archaeologist. It'll take me a bit. Can you check the other pedestals for me? See if they have similar layouts of symbols?"

"Sure," Clio said. "Come on, Flint. Oh, and Mitali, erm, be careful, okay?"

***

These smaller rooms, are more of an alcove really, Clio thought, It barely had room for her and Flint. The room, in this case the orange room, had the same domed ceiling, curved black walls and one singular mounted monitor and at its centre, another white pedestal. Just like the other three rooms they checked, they all seemed to have the same symbols etched on their surfaces. The only distinction was that they appeared to be etched in the colour of that room, so the orange room had orange etched symbols while the red had red.

"Any resonance?" Clio said.

"Any what now?" Flint said.

"*No resonance in any of these rooms, they seem empty,*" Echo buzzed.

"Just muttering to myself," Clio said as she turned to leave the room. It was quite a tight space and she ended up bumping into Flint as she did.

"Clio," Flint said.

"Sorry, it's a tight space," Clio said.

"No, Clio, wait a sec," Flint said.

"Ermm, okay?" Clio said. Flint's tone was off, he seemed tense? "Everything okay?"

"Clio, we've spent a fair bit of time together these last few months. Been through a bit too," Flint said.

"Ah... ermmm." Blushing and feeling a little hot in the face, Clio said, "Yeah, we have, Flint, and yeah, I like you too, but I'm actually seeing someone. Its super recent, we're not putting labels on... I'm rambling"

Flint just looked blankly back at her, his face awash with confusion, she knew she had misread the situation, even as he said, "What? Ah, no, Clio, no. That's not what I wanted to ask... ermm, I like you too, but you know, my job and stuff. No, what I wanted to ask was, who's Echo?"

Clio stood there, the heat from her face doused instantly at the mention of Echo, replaced with a sharp ice spike driven into her. *This is worse*, is all she thought. She stood frozen for what felt like a long time, then tried to muddle a response. "What? Echo? Like sound bouncing in a cave..." *Like sound bouncing in a cave, what the hell was that, Clio?*

"This is not ideal, Clio but anticipated. I predict a more than likely chance telling him the truth would result in a poor outcome for us both," Echo buzzed.

"Great, thanks," she said instinctively.

"For what?" Flint said, still looking at her intently. "Echo, Clio, you have said it a few times, as if it's a name, as if you're talking to someone, not to your computer as you said last time. I'm concerned. More and more you've seemed off, distant, distracted."

"Distracted? Distant?" Clio shot back. "Look around you, Flint. Of course I'm distracted!"

"You're avoiding the answer. Who is Echo?" Flint pushed.

"No one!" Clio snapped. "No one, okay? I just talk to myself, and I talk to my computer, people do that Flint."

Flint took another deep breath. "I want to trust you, I do. I want to help you. Not everyone in the Ensemble does but I need you to trust me. I thought we... never mind." Flint's face hardened. "Look, you say it's nothing, it's nothing, but if I ever find out you're playing me... I'll..."

"Playing you? Really? You think I'm some fancy agent, a spy, or something? And what if you find out you'll disappear me? Put a bullet in me?"

Flint's eyes went wide. "What? No! I wouldn't do that. I meant I would be mad, upset, hurt." Then he added, "But yes. the Ensemble might arrest you. And no, Clio I don't think you're an agent but that's my point."

Clio was in turmoil: angry, upset, hurt, but also ashamed. She was lying to Flint, hiding things from him and everyone else. Echo was a breach of the Accords; her interaction with it was testament to a crime against humanity, but she couldn't tell anyone, definitely not Flint.

How do I ever get out of this mess? she asked herself. *At least last time I was naive. Stupid, yes, but my actions were not intentional. Now... what am I now? Each day this damn hole just gets deeper.* Her final words were a near murmur on her lips as they reverberated in her head.

Lying to him stung more than she thought it would, and the frustration was plain to see on his face. All she managed before he walked past her and out of the room was a pathetic whisper.

"Flint... I'm sorry." But he was gone, and her words were lost to the clatter of noise from outside the room.

***

"You alright?" Mitali said with concern as Clio met her back in the main room. Clio still appeared flustered, dealing with her own inner turmoil, which must have been obvious to see.

"All fine," Clio said.

Mitali glanced towards Flint, who had gone and stood across the room and was busying himself with what appeared to be a detailed look at the largest of the monitors. She gave Clio a questioning look but, thankfully, Mitali didn't push. "I think I have translated the symbols you said might be helpful and either you're very lucky or much smarter than I thought," she said playfully.

"Just a lucky guess," Clio said quietly. "What, what do they mean? The symbols?"

"Well, the closest interpretation in the literal sense would be something like 'sing,' but that felt wrong. Other variations could be 'commune,' 'talk,' and also maybe pray'."

"Right, so not 'on' then," Clio said, then added quickly, "but that's great, amazing in fact, thank you."

Mitali smiled back at her, but through concerned eyes. "No, not 'on,' but it's not an easy translation to our language, so I compared it to a few other parts of the log and I think in a less literal sense, when they write 'to talk,' it can be used in the context of starting or beginning."

"That's a bit odd, no? I don't doubt you, but is it not a push?" Clio said.

"I don't think so. I mean, in French you would say 'ca marche', which you could read as 'it walks', but they use it to mean 'it works.' I think this is similar," Mitali said.

"Okay, context and interpretation," Clio said. "If it helps at all, the other rooms have the same clusters of symbols, identically located as well."

"It doesn't," Mitali said and laughed, "but it let me think, and at least if it is an 'on' button, they would all likely have it, no?"

"So we turn it on then?" Jara said, joining the conversation.

"I'm not sure that's a wise idea," Flint said, turning back from his inspection of the monitor. Douglas grumbled in agreement from the entryway.

"I just did the translation," Mitali said. "I'm not saying we turn it on, and there is no saying if it would even turn on anyway if we did."

Clio looked to Vikram, and Vikram, to her surprise, said, "I think we should give it a try."

"Really?" Flint said.

Yes," Vikram continued. "I spoke to Commander Eva before we left; she gave me orders to increase the mission risk threshold. We have limited time left to make discoveries, and let's say there is pressure from higher up to get more results before we leave."

"You're freaking joking," Douglas said. "Typical, risk the little guy while they stay on the ship a million miles away from it all."

"Douglas," Vikram said sharply. "Remember yourself please." Then, speaking more to the whole room, he added, "We all came here with a mission to discover, to explore; that is still our mission and that is what we are being asked to do. We all signed up for what was classified as an extreme high-risk mission. So let's be at it."

"Right then," Clio said. "I guess, I'll do it. I would suggest everyone else steps back," she said, but directed it to Mitali.

"Clio, you..." Mitali started to say, then said, "I'll be right over here," and lightly brushed her EV suit's glove against Clio's before walking back to the side of the room.

Clio stood for a moment, looking at the flat surface and its symbols. The room was silent; everyone seemed to be holding their breath.

She reached out and poked the symbol. Nothing.

She jabbed it again. Nothing.

She rested her hand flat against it. Still nothing.

"Must not be working," Clio said.

"Or Mitali was wrong," Jara said.

Clio looked at the symbol in front of her again, disappointment and an odd relief also filling her. A thought struck her, and she stretched out her hand and lightly traced the symbol in one fluid motion. As she finished tracing it, a jolt shot up her finger from the table, and she pulled her hand back.

"What—" Mitali started to say, but she abruptly cut off as the pedestal seemed to pulse.

At first, a low glow emitted from the stone; the intensity grew, and the symbols on the table started to burn even brighter. With a sudden flash, light pulsed out from the pedestal and surged along the colorful lines. The patterns on the floor and doors jumped into vibrant, full spectrum of colour . As the light spread outwards, the black walls also started to glow with a deep light from within, showing a swirling mass of currents within the wall, like staring into a churning ocean at night. It happened so fast no one had time to react. Clio was still pulling her hand back from the pedestal and the monitors around the room turned on... scrolling alien text filling them, then resolving into what appeared to be a dashboard of unknown data. They all had one large red symbol flashing violently on them.

"Oh shit," Jara said. "It worked!"

34 | The[ ]Green Room

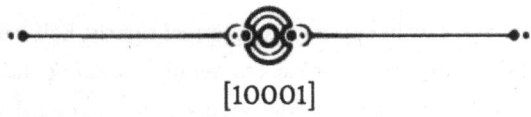

[10001]

> "It sought to remake the universe in Its
> image, a symphony of destruction and
> rebirth, where life would dance to Its tune."
> - *A Lost History*

***

"Oh shit," Jara said again, the sudden brightness making her squint. The gloom of the room replaced by a vibrant kaleidoscope of colours and movement. The walls were a swirling mass holding in a tempest of shades. It was dazzling. Jara looked away sharply, but it was hard to find anywhere else in the room that felt still enough to help settle her. She focused on her breathing, the calming repetition of in and out, the old mantra taught to all pilots to internalise, for those moments of crisis where despite everything you needed focus.

The dizziness receded, and a familiar calm, an emptiness, swept over her; she surveyed the room again, now able to absorb the situation. Whatever Clio had done, it had worked. The room was alight, the monitors were on with a scrolling alien text Jara understood nothing of. There was a vibration she had missed before, a subtle tremor she could feel through her boots on the floor. She tested the wall gingerly; the vibration was there also.

Clio had jumped back but was now moving closer to the large monitor, regaining her composure more quickly than Jara. A flash of annoyance shot through Jara's returning calm. Mitali was moving to Clio's side. Vikram was wide-eyed but composed, talking away in the silence. *Must be on a private link back to Alpha 17, reporting in,* Jara thought. Douglas had his weapon drawn, his laissez-faire demeanour gone, his eyes scanning the room with the veteran experience she knew he had from reading his service record that he rarely seemed to want to show anyone.

"You can lower your sidearm," Flint said firmly, his own hand resting on his snugly holstered sidearm.

Jara looked down and saw her own pistol gripped tightly, half-raised toward the pedestal. "Shit." She fumbled to clip it back to her hip. *He didn't draw his. He kept his nerve,* she thought, the anger raging inside her, dissolving her hard-won calm. *Damn him.* "I was just taking precautions, Brother."

"Of course," was all Flint said before moving to join Vikram

God damn it Jara! she berated herself, *this is no way to fast track yourself to full sisterhood. You're better than this.* The anger still raged inside her, dissolving the calm she desperately needed.

"It appears the whole structure is on," Vikram said. "Alpha 17 is reporting the structure is now glowing like the wall here," he said, pointing to the swirling madness of the room's walls. "The RAFT has also confirmed it seems to be planet-wide."

"Okay, so we woke something up then," Clio said.

"Seems that way," Vikram said. "They're reporting that the Stone Forest is also leaking."

"Leaking?" Flint asked.

"That's what they said. They didn't give any other details. Commander Eva is asking for a status. She wants to know if we feel a need to abort. Thoughts?" Vikram said.

"No," Clio and Mitali both said in unison, then looked at each other.

Jara caught the oddest of smiles and a lingering eye contact between them. *Closer than colleagues,* she noted, suspicion sharpening into certainty. *Compromised.* It was exactly what the Accords warned against: emotional entanglement clouding judgment. Clio was clearly the source of the rot, pulling Mitali into her orbit, and Flint... Flint was standing right there, blind to the manipulation.

Idiot.

She made a mental note: *Inform Brother Oak immediately.*

Jara was pulled back to the discussion in the room by Mitali's voice. "I think this is an error code, or a warning message. It seems to be indicating an unexpected power drain."

"Jara... Jara...." someone whispered.

"What?" Jara said in response, looking over her shoulder.

"What?" Clio said.

"Someone said my name," Jara said.

"No, no one did," Clio said and turned back to the monitor. Someone knew how to suddenly flip through a number of sub-interfaces on the monitor.

"Yes," Mitali said, "this seems to be the one, Yes... it shows a massive power drain... whatever that is," she said, pointing to a list of alien symbols. "It's drawing a huge amount of the system's power, and processing capacities, and its seems to be looping it, a loop of nothing"

"A Tar-pit," Douglas said.

"What now?" Mitali said, looking between Douglas and Clio, confused.

"A Tar-pit. It's a pre-war digital systems weapon. Developed and expanded during the war and, well, it's now banned," Douglas said, his tone matter-of-fact.

The rest of the room just stared blankly back at him.

"And you know that how?" Flint said. "You're a pre-war expert now?"

Douglas shrugged. "I like history. I've watched a lot of documentaries."

"I've never heard that term before," Clio said, frowning. "A 'Tar-pit'?"

"It clogs up systems," Douglas explained. "It traps systems in nonsense loops, makes the system burn out processing nothing. Not saying this *is* a Tar-pit, that would be crazy, but it sounds like one."

"Wait," Clio said, a realisation hitting her. "Nonsense loops? I found pre-war data systems in the Exclusion Zone that were clogged exactly like that. We just called them 'Dead-Spins' I thought it was just an age thing; I never knew it was a weapon.

Jara was watching the conversation intently and glanced at Flint; he was frowning. Jara could guess why. It all sounded a lot like the worm Ayesha had had. She had worked on that research; she knew it well. The worm diverted system power to pointless tasking, growing as it did, slowly taking up more space in a system, not just a system killer but an AI killer. Flint gave her a look and a slight shake of his head. *Stay quiet,* he meant.

"Jara..." a voice said, faint, as if someone was speaking into the wind from across the room.

She frowned and looked around. But except for Flint, no one was looking her way; no one even seemed to remember she was in the room.

"Jara," the voice said again. It seemed to be coming from the green rooms just across from her. Jara shook her head... *Focus up, Jara,* she told herself and focused on her breathing again, trying to find her calm place. She blinked, forcing her attention back to the group just as Douglas responded to Clio.

"I'm not surprised you never heard the official name," Douglas said. "It's a niche bit of history for sure, mostly irrelevant, deployed during the war by both sides. It makes perfect sense you found it in the Exclusion Zone; both sides were pushing it hard. But still, it was used for general service disruption, not a major talking point of the war, particularly after Heimer; it's mostly a lost discussion point now."

Then, with a broad smile, he added, "Some more fringe thinkers say it was lost on purpose; no one wanted anyone to know about it. Not to mention that sort of weaponised system is now banned under the Accords, isn't that right, Brother?" He winked at Flint.

"Yes," Flint said, "it would come under Article 13."

"But, if it is a Tar-pit," Clio said slowly, and Jara could see her mind working as she spoke, "then... it's quite an easy fix. You just do a system purge and isolate the 'Tar-pit' tasks and block them; it prevents the loop restarting," Clio said. "That's how we worked with it, at least in the field."

"Yeah," Douglas said, "I'm no expert on its workings, but the vid-logs at least say it was easily countered. It's why it was mostly ineffective unless you could sneak it in quickly, covertly, and hope no one noticed until it caused its damage. A big ask if you ask me."

"Not to an expert," Clio muttered, "you damn well sound like one."

"I watch a lot of crap," Douglas said.

"*Jara!*" the Voice said, this time sharp and clear. Jara jumped and turned in its direction, definitely the green room, but no one else in the room seemed to have heard anything and were carrying on uninterrupted. She shook her head again but found herself edging closer to the green room entrance.

As she moved closer to the door, Clio was conferring quietly with Mitali and using the central pedestal to adeptly navigate the alien interfaces on the monitors. *Impressive and far too suspicious. Brother Oak will be happy to know this.*

Jara was next to the green archway and looked into it; the room was empty. The monitor was on, the pedestal alight like everything else. But empty. Jara moved to see the room from the other angle, but it was still empty. *You're just hearing things, Jara... Calm yourself, jumping at shadows that have no bearing on Sisterhood.*

"Yes, okay, yes... I think, I think if we use this interface and these symbols..." Clio was saying, "then we could do a system purge, isolate the Tar-pit... and clear the error."

"Really?" Vikram said. "Walk me through it."

"Jara," the voice said, sharp and clear.

Jara spun around and looked into the green room. It was still empty. But on the monitor, burning in bold white alien glyphs that somehow resolved into English, was a single word:

JARA

"Come in. Let's talk," the voice whispered.

The text blinked once, then vanished

Jara looked around the room. Again, no one seemed to have heard anything; no one was paying her any heed at all, in fact. Not even Flint. They all stood around the central pedestal, listening to little Miss Clio spin her ideas again. Jara slipped out of the room and into the green room.

***

Clio's mind was racing, balancing Echo's prompts of where to look, with Mitali's expert insights into the language. She was in a flow state, her hand quickly adapting to the instinctive controls on the pedestal, navigating the alien interface, blind to the words herself but led by her colleagues, she could nearly even see the meaning of each word herself.

"So, if what you say is correct," Vikram said, "which honestly, I can't see how you have worked that all out so quickly, but regardless, if it is true. You're saying the station is only using a fraction of its power, and you want to unblock that dam?"

"Yes," Clio said, "the system is in some sort of safe mode, protecting its core functions but operating well below its capacity."

"And that is wise?" Douglas asked.

"I agree, releasing a dam can have significant downstream impacts and I would say we're the ones downstream," Flint said.

"Or," Clio said, "it's a beaver dam, which has not only flooded all our homes upstream but also ruined everything downstream..."

"We all love analogies," Vikram said, "but what's the actual risk here?"

"We all die..." Douglas said, "....in fun and painful ways." They all just looked flatly at him. "What? We could. I'm not wrong."

"Clio," Echo buzzed, *"I think the Veil is broken. The system logs you have up, one of them I'm sure is in reference to the Veil... it's showing error.'*

"Mitali, what's that one say?" Clio said, pointing to the cluster of symbols that Echo was highlighting for her.

"Hmmm," Mitali said, leaning forward to peer at the symbols. "Oh... oh... I think it's talking about radiation ejection outputs, and manipulation... it's the Veil. The Van Allen belt. It must be..."

"Right," Vikram said, "so?"

"It's showing a system error, system overload is the best interpretation," Mitali said.

"Linked to the Tar-pit issue," Clio said. "We fix that, we could fix the Veil."

"What does that even mean?" Flint said, "Fix the Veil"

Clio shrugged. "Anya's paper posited that it was meant to be a more stable, more accessible place. I doubt this place was designed as a radiation prison. It posed the system was broken or damaged, and it appears it is. We can fix that."

"And why would we want that?" Vikram said.

"Because then it would be navigable all the time. That's what Anya's paper said" Flint said slowly, "But that's a massive IF, Clio, you have no idea."

"It is but we found a ship in near orbit; we can assume this station was accessible in the past, maybe more frequently than the random cycling of a radiation mess."

"Or it kills us all," Douglas said again. "You turn it back on, what's to say this station doesn't have defence systems that don't like us being here?"

"Vikram said we had to take risks," Clio said. "We can fix this station, open it up for a full and detailed examination, our primary mission objective, or we can go and wait to maybe come back again to the same dead station..."

"Do it," Vikram said.

"Vikram?" Douglas said.

"Really?" Flint added.

"Yes," Vikram said, "sometimes you have to roll the dice."

"Roger that," Clio said. She looked at Mitali who, despite a concerned tightness around her eyes, smiled at Clio, nodded, and gently clasped her hand.

"Do it," Mitali said.

"*Okay, Clio,*" Echo buzzed, "*let's do this.*"

Clio took one final look at everyone who nodded then dived back into the process, manipulating the pedestal controls. It was a simple task really; she had to navigate a few different interfaces but helped by Echo it was easy work, Echo highlighting where to go and what to press. After a few minutes she had one button left filling the screen: Purge system. She clicked on it.

Nothing... Clio looked at Mitali. "Ah okay well that was..."

A deep rumble started low and then built and built to a deafening roar. Clio heard people around her, then Mitali grabbed her hand and pulled Clio away from the pedestal. The room started to shake, the shaking growing stronger and stronger. It reminded Clio of the earthquake from Earth she had experienced but much, much stronger. She was terrified the roof and the mass of the black structure would come crashing down on her and Mitali. Then it stopped. Silence. Stillness. Just the vibrant swirling light of the room.

Clio held Mitali as they hunkered down next to one of the walls, Mitali holding Clio in return. Vikram was hunched against the opposite wall. Both Flint and Douglas stayed standing, both looking around anxiously. Jara reappeared from one of the side rooms, pale and eyes wide, staring around at them all. *When did she manage to hide in one of the rooms?* Clio half thought.

"Report? Delta five," a voice sounded across the emergency comms to them all. It was Commander Eva.

Vikram staggered to his feet. "This is Delta Five… all… all okay," he said, scanning the room and doing an obvious head count.

"Get back to RAFT One," Eva said. "Abort Mission, respond Delta five."

"Message received, heading to Alpha 17 for extraction," Vikram said. "Situation?"

"Not sure," Eva said. "What did you guys do?"

"We think we found a system error, we tried to clear it," Vikram said. "We thought it was impacting the Veil,"

"No shit," Eva said. "Well it's gone."

"What's gone?" Vikram asked.

Clio knew the answer before the Commander even spoke.

"The Veil," Eva said. "It's just… gone."

35 | Off[,] Then On Again

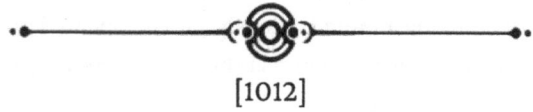

[1012]

"It had become Asura, the destroyer, the
embodiment of chaos. And in her wake, only
darkness remained." - *A Lost History*

***

Clio stifled a yawn. The Captain had summoned her for a briefing, thankfully not just her, though he had graciously given them the evening to rest first.

It had been two weeks since they returned to the *Kia-Kaha*. Two weeks since Stapledon Station had woken up. The departure was a blur: Mitali holding her, Flint and Vikram dragging them out of the structure, Alpha 17 dissolving into a chaotic mess of teams loading rovers. Through it all, Commander Eva had stood in the whirlwind of motion, calm and controlled, simply telling them to get strapped in.

Now, an air of calm had settled over the ship. Work hadn't stopped, the ship still needed servicing, people feeding, corridors cleaning, but for the most part, the crew seemed to have dropped several gears. After so long under the oily sky and oppressive monoliths, Clio felt a peacefulness in the simple limits of the RAFT.

The meeting was in the Captain's office. Clio arrived with a minute to spare.

Not bad, Clio, not bad, she thought.

"You're late," Echo buzzed.

"I am not," she whispered. "I'm perfectly on time." Then, activating the door, she stepped into the room.

The Captain's Secretary ushered her into the office where she grabbed a seat next to Jun, the only other non-senior staff at the table. Clio was the last to arrive, save for the Captain. A quiet, low murmur of voices filled the room as several individual conversations were ongoing. Zhou was in a deep conversation with Dr. Anya and Dr. Jian, a data pad on the table in front of them, none of whom acknowledged Clio's arrival. Commander Eva sat with David, who with a data pad, was reading off a list of what appeared to be diagnostic stats to Eva. Although she didn't look at David, she was clearly listening as she nodded and shook her head in response to things David said.

"Hey Jun," Clio said as she slipped into the seat next to him. "Happy to be back?"

"Never thought I would actually miss this place, but you know what, yeah, I am happy to be back," Jun said. "How about–" Jun started, then a door across the room, not the one they had all used, slid open and the Captain blustered into the room.

"Apologise, everyone I was waylaid," Demir said. "You all know Senator Sinclair," he continued as another man joined them through the same door in his tight-pressed black suit and white shirt, neatly positioned under an exo-frame that whirred quietly with his every move. "He will be joining us," said the Captain, and for the barest of moments, his lips tightened, his eyebrows furrowed. Then it was gone, and the soft, friendly features of the Captain were back.

"Thank you, Captain, and if I may say, what a pleasure to meet such an acclaimed collection of this ship's fine crew," he said as he artfully manoeuvered an empty chair from the back of the room, and positioned it closely next to Commander Eva. "If you don't mind?"

Commander Eva frowned at him, then scooted her chair across, and Avi sat down.

"First of all," Demir said with a gentle smile, "I wanted to acknowledge the away team's work on Stapledon Station. You far exceeded expectations, and I cannot imagine it was as easy as Commander Eva makes the reports sound. Good job, Commander."

Eva nodded back to him, her face as expressionless as always. "The crew implemented the mission plan to an acceptable and competent standard, Captain, as I would expect from them," Eva said flatly. "We encountered a number of unexpected events, but we also expected the unexpected. I'm happy with how the crew handled them."

"A truly glowing report," Avi said from next to her.

Demir cleared his throat. "Thank you, Senator. And Eva, if you could ensure my message of thanks is passed on to your crew?"

"Yes, Captain," Eva said.

"I wanted to discuss the current situation," Demir continued. "Zhou, an update from your team would be appreciated, and any clarification on what actually happened?"

"First," Zhou croaked, flashing Clio a sharp look, "I think it's important to acknowledge the superb work of the teams on the Chudail and here on the Kia-Kaha; they have demonstrated excellent scientific rigor in their research. It is unfortunate we lacked the same level of experience on the away mission, as we may have been able to answer that question more precisely."

What a dick, Clio thought. To her surprise, Commander Eva's usually stoic face had darkened like thunder. She was staring daggers at Zhou.

"Ms. Cormack's actions in the control room, as we have seen with the opening of the structure, are at times rushe-"

"I believe the Captain asked for an explanation of what is *happening,*" Avi interrupted sharply, before flashing a kind smile at Clio.

Clio was taken aback by Avi's sudden interjection on her behalf; she just looked blankly back at him, not sure what to do. But it was Commander Eva's words that truly shocked her...

"Prof. Zhou," Eva said, "if you have an issue with Ms. Cormack's actions, then they were under my orders, so as the commander of the mission please direct your complaints to me." She fixed Zhou with one of her *'do not fuck with me stare'.*

"Erm... ah... y... yes," Zhou stammered, completely taken aback by both interjections. "All I meant by my comments was, without the detailed scientific rigor we may have achieved through longer study, we are unclear of what Ms— of what the away team did."

Demir held up a hand, effectively silencing Zhou's rambling. "We can analyse the methodology later, Professeur. Right now, I care about the result." He turned his chair slightly to face Clio.

"Clio," Demir said, "I've read your reports. You believe you and the away team found an access terminal and reactivated the station, correct?"

"Yes, Captain," Clio said. "Mitali did most of the hard work with the translation, but we were able to ascertain that the system was in some sort of fail-safe mode due to a bug of sorts. That aligned with Anya's early observations of the Veil. We also established a way to do a system reset."

"You turned it on and off again?" Avi said. "I absolutely love it."

"Senator please," Demir said, then turned back to Clio. "Yes, exactly. And this was your own actions or an agreed one by the away team?"

"It was a shared decision," Clio said, firmly. "Ultimately, it was given the green light by the lead mission officer."

"Correct," Eva said. "So Dr. Zhou, I want to be clear. The actions on Stapledon were the actions of delegated command coming all the way from myself. If you feel the command was poorly made..."

"Yes, of course, and no, I would not question commands decision in that way," Zhou, regaining some of his usual confidence, said back sharply.

"Now," Demir said, "do you have anything to add to what has happened since the activation? And to be clear, I'm talking about what the hell is happening to the Veil."

Clio just sat there reeling a little from the words of those around the room. In her defense, she... she felt a little emotional. She could feel it welling up in her, her chest tightening, and she focused on her breathing and pushed it down. *Not now, Clio, deal with that later.*

Zhou nodded to Dr. Anya, who said, "Thank you, Captain. If I may," and on the Captain's nod, she picked up the data pad on the table and flipped the images across to the monitors around the room. The screen was filled with an image of Stapledon Station. Clio, like everyone else, had seen the image before but it still surprised her. The spinning, oily mass of the station was gone. In fact, if it wasn't for the annotation, it was near impossible to see the station.

"As you can see in the image," Anya said, "once the system was reset, the Veil, or what we called the Veil, disappeared and from the poles of the station," she used a digital pointer to highlight the fountains of light that now blasted out of each end of the station, "these radiation emissions appeared. We have ascertained they are in fact the same radiation that made up the Veil, just an uncontrolled, unregulated power release which is creating these fountains."

"Are they dangerous?" Demir asked.

"No, well, yes, but only if we fly through them. Our current orbit is closely aligned to the equator, so we're safe," David said.

"Correct," Anya continued, "although we are unsure why. The research into the plates and logs that Ms. Cormack found has proven helpful," Anya said, the final words tight. "Beyond helping to develop a regression model for the ebb and flow of the Veil that found the hole, it also clearly shows it is generated by the station. A manipulation of the radiation from the sun trapped inside, I propose it is a necessity to vent the radiation, an exhaust pipe, if I may say. What we see now is an unregulated exhaust pipe."

"So the surface of the station was always meant to be pitch black?" Jun said. "I... I am surprised. There is growing evidence the surface supported life; life without light is not impossible, but a number of skulls imply they at least used eyes."

"And the station itself has lights," Clio said. "To me that implies they at least used light for a form of sight."

"True," Jun said.

"Let's focus here," Demir said. "The Veil, Anya, is stable now?"

"No, Captain," Anya said. "We have been updating our model, and," She flipped another image up, a collection of eight images side by side, in fact, of the station. The fountain of light from the poles was noticeably less as they moved across. "These images reinforce the model's outputs. We believe it is reforming."

"Into the Veil?" Demir said.

"No, or not exactly," Anya said. "The model projects it'll reform into a radiation band, curved like a a slice of orange peel, similar to what is described in the log data. It'll sit around the same altitude but be fixed to that position as the station rotates below it."

"Really?" Avi asked.

"Well, the model thinks so. We will know in a week or so. That's its projected time frame for it to establish its new form. As Ms. Cormack said it aligns with our initial hypothesis, which is reassuring"

"How big are we talking?" Commander Eva said.

"It is projected to be significant, maybe a third of the surface area of the station below it"

"And the station will rotate," Jun said slowly, clearly working through a thought, "so that means a 'light cycle' on the surface, of what, thirty-two hours? Yes, thirty-two... So... so the Veil provides light and a circadian rhythm to the planet's surface, amazing."

"Thirty-two hours, yes," Anya said, checking her data pad.

"So it'll be accessible, the station?" Demir said.

"Yes. Well, as long as you approach from a side that isn't covered by the Veil," Anya said.

"Good to hear, and you said within the next few weeks you'll have confirmation on this?" Demir said.

"Correct," Zhou said, jumping in.

"Well, I'm sure we all have a lot of other questions, but if the Veil consolidates as Anya has said, I want a mission ready to go back and find those answers," Demir said, then looking to Eva, "Be ready with two crews within two weeks, Commander, RAFT One and RAFT Three."

Eva cocked her head slightly at this. "Two crews, Captain?"

"Yes. It sounds like we'll have more reliable access. I want a plan for RAFT One to go with a full crew and set up and establish a full base of operations. RAFT Three will come down with additional crew later and act as a shuttle; it'll also bring the VIPs."

"Excuse me?" Commander Eva said. "The who now?"

"The VIPs, Commander," Demir said with a sharp look at her. "They have been approved for surface visits."

"Right," Commander Eva said. "Orders received, Captain, we will be ready." A tightness in her eyes was the only cue Clio got that she wasn't particularly pleased about this order.

Looking at Zhou, Demir added, "Science teams and research is your prerogative, Professor. Make sure they are ready. Primary mission is to understand the primary structure, its purpose, and the systems that operate it."

"Noted," Zhou said.

"Right, that's all for now," Demir said, standing and stretching his arms above him. "Clio, a word before you go."

Everyone else in the room shuffled about, standing up, pushing chairs in, collecting their data pads and files. Leaving just Clio, Demir, and Avi. Clio looked to Avi, waiting for him to leave, but he didn't.

"Clio, Avi here would like to borrow you again," Demir said.

"Erm, sure..." Clio said, remembering their last conversation in Avi's suite. "What for?" she said to Avi.

"Why, to get your firsthand retelling of such an adventure as you have had!" Avi said. "There are few moments a man gets in life where he can say he spoke to someone who defined a part of history."

"I'm not sure I did," Clio said.

"Nonsense! You were part of the first team on an alien world, you found the way in, you turned it on! This will be in the books like the first pioneers to climb Everest or step on the surface of Pluto!"

"Well, it wasn't just me, Sir," Clio said.

"No, no, of course, so humble. But you were a central part. Please, if you have an hour or so to spare, come by and have lunch before you head back out."

Clio looked to Demir, who just nodded to her. Then she looked back to Avi and said, "Sure, yes, just send us a time and day."

"Perfect!" Avi said.

36 | A Dangerous Game[!]

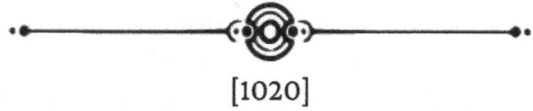

[1020]

"Asura twisted our creations, our very
essence, into weapons of destruction.
Worlds burned in its wake, civilisations
crumbled into dust." - *A Lost History*

***

"My dear Clio!" Avi said. "An absolute pleasure you could join me."

Clio had been ushered through the Senators quarters by his house staff to a small wood panelled office. One whole wall was packed with books. The old paper style with ink print. The extravagance of it was excessive. Everything from the wood to the books, to the soft carpeted floor and faux leather sofa and armchairs separated by a small glass coffee table.

I was allowed what? one personal bag, 'weight management' they had said. Clio suppressed a scoff. *This guy was allowed a whole reading room, pays to be a senator it seems.*

"*Printed books,*" Echo buzzed. "*I wish I could read.*"

Clio fought the urge to respond, limiting herself to a frown. Which Avi must have misinterpreted, "Ah sorry yes, I understand the younger generation feel paper books to be limited, but I'm an old man with old taste."

"Ah no... no, sorry, Avi," Clio spluttered. "It's... it's amazing, I have a few. Not with me, but back at my parents' place."

"Of course, the archaeologist would appreciate the classical methods."

"I suppose that is true" Clio said.

"Please sit, sit Clio," Avi said. "Can I get you a drink? I have some exceptional Oban whisky. Can you believe they still use the same distillery? That's what, 400 years?! They understand classical methods."

Clio chose one of the armchairs and delicately lowered herself onto it, very conscious of its finery as she did so. She felt underdressed. "No, no whisky was my Mum's drink..."

"Of course, of course. Gin? Brandy? A Cognac perhaps? Or ah, tea?"

"Tea would be great, thank you," Clio said, and Avi spoke into his watch, ordering two teas.

Avi chose the armchair across from her and his exo-frame smoothly lowered him into it. "So Clio, it must have been quite something to walk on the surface of an alien world, not many of us can say that."

"It was quite the experience Senator," Clio said. "I am very lucky to be able to say I did so for sure."

"Please, Avi is fine," Avi said. "Humble as always, a respectable personality flaw," he said with a smile. "Please indulge an old man who wishes for stories to impress his peers around dinner tables upon his return, how did you find the way in. It's quite a feat, no? A needle in a haystack."

"Luck mostly," Clio said without thinking. Avi tilted his head as if to say something but Clio jumped in, "Humble, right, yes, well, it was luck, like a lot of things in life. Luck is always needed but a mix of deduction, experience and luck then, that's how."

"I assume you didn't throw a dart at a map to pick the sites you explored?"

"No, I mean I used similar approaches to what I would have used back home. I looked for patterns, or irregularities, shifts in density of the Stone Forest, its proximity to the structure itself, elevation profiles. I looked for what felt purposeful or logical. Limited and biased of course from a human perspective, but it was the best I could do. Alpha 17 for example has a large flat clearing nestled in a slight V shaped valley running up from a number of other rolling hills; the Stone Forest is particularly dense but also thinner than most other places, with a curve to it, not the usual sprawling mess and it was just off the corner of the main structure. It felt different but also logical as an approach for an access route."

"Fascinating, so simply elegant in an approach, a lot like your anomaly. The smoothness in the noise that found the Chudail. And with that I'm sure you're downplaying it."

"Well, it took 17 sites for us to actually find it. At times it definitely felt like I was just throwing darts," Clio said and Avi laughed.

"I'm sure," Avi chuckled. "Either way, another notch in the history books for the Xenoarcheologist Clio Cormack. People will hardly be able to believe the histories when they read them."

Clio blushed at Avi's words and shuffled her feet; she was not great with compliments, and she really didn't feel like she had done anything that any other half decent scientist could have. She just happened to be the one given the job. Thank you."

"You had no assistance from the Heimer Fragment in the investigation? It's not mentioned in your reports," Avi said. A very slight shift in his tone made the hairs on her neck stand up, *or was that just her imagination?* she thought.

"Well, of course the Heimer Fragment is engaged in all our research, as you know it followed procedure and activated its own transfer to the RAFT servers for the mission to provide real time analysis to the team but we only used it to verify and cross check our own work. Standard practice stuff. It did suggest areas of interest which I then added to my list, but I applied my own analysis to those sites. Alpha 17 was not one of its recommendations."

"Of course," Avi said, "always so helpful Heimer" Again the slightest clipped tone to the words gave Clio pause and for a moment, they just looked at each other.

A sharp, loud rap at the door snapped both their eyes away from each other and Avi said, "Come in."

A member of the house staff glided in with a clinking tray. He placed it on the table and glided back out in silence. "Ah the tea," Avi said. "Milk? Sugar?"

"Milk please," Clio said, and Avi picked up the porcelain tea pot and filled both cups and, after adding some milk, passed Clio the cup balanced precariously on a saucer. *Why did they use saucers? A mug is way more practical,* Clio thought.

"Thank you," said Clio and said, wanting to nudge the conversation away from Echo, "The bio labs, that was something for sure."

Avi sipped his tea and then blew on it as it proved too hot to drink. "Yes, fascinating. Another amazing achievement for you."

"Oh no," Clio said," truly, this time, I'm not being humble. Dr. Lee has the claim to this one and Mitali for the translation, of course. I was just a passenger really."

"The vats, the surgical rooms and so, so many bones. It's truly fascinating," Avi said. "You know what it reminds me of?"

"No?" Clio said.

"Ants," Avi said.

"Ants? Sorry, I don't understand."

"Ants," Avi said again. "Ants, they are all of one species, each adapted for their roles, their purpose. The bones, they remind me of that. So many variations, sizes, limbs. It's like a hive of ants."

"Right, yes, a good observation Avi. I'll pass it on to Dr. Lee."

"Ha! No, no, I'm a blustering old politician. Let's not bother the scientist with my uneducated guesses. I was merely speaking freely."

"It just seems strange to me at least," Clio said, "that there are so many. Why make so many different species? Surely a few but not hundreds as there appears to be."

"Thousands," Avi said, "by the Doctor's last report at least. I think the answer is in the logs, no? They were playing god? In the old Earth religions didn't the gods make all things?"

"Yeah true, but I didn't take the log text as literal. I read it more figuratively as in they had a power to others that could only be described as god-like," Clio said.

"And is there a difference? If their power was so great that it seemed god-like, is that not a god?" Avi said.

"I don't think Gods are made; they just exist," Clio said.

"But that's what the logs says, no? They created gods? The 'creators' made things beyond comprehension and named them gods".

"And your presumption is that those 'gods' then wanted to go, what, old school and create worlds of organic life?" Clio said, not hiding her scepticism.

"I quote," Avi said, "'She sought to remake the Universe in perfection defined by itself,' they said that about one of their gods, sounds to me like it had a creationist drive."

"Well yes, but I still read it more that it was less a god and more a division within the civilisations' theological followings, a faction that split. The log written by a group that opposed them or their beliefs at least. I mean if you were an alien and found the Vedas and that was your point of reference you would have a very incorrect view of Humanity."

"A well-made point Clio," Avi said, "so you believe the text is limited in value?"

"No, the text has massive value and has allowed us to do so much, but we should also caution ourselves against projecting generalisations upon a whole species based upon it."

"But you must agree it is written as a warning? A tale of woe to others. Avoid our follies or again I quote, 'Worlds burned in its wake, civilisations crumbled into dust,'" Avi said. "The 'Creators' created something beyond their own capabilities, and it consumed them, leaving nothing but lost relics and dust for us to find."

"Yes, that appears to be the gist of the text so far," Clio said. "Again, old Earth religions talked of great floods and plagues, which hold truths for sure but also alone provide a poor analysis of history."

"But it gives you no pause of thought to humanity's current balance?" Avi said. "We created a weapon in a time of need, and recklessly unleashed it on the world despite the warnings of those who made it, and that weapon is still free today. We have the slightest balance, the slight bit of control." Avi sounded regretful, mournful even.

"I...don't know, I suppose, yes" is all Clio managed, taken a little back by Avi's remarks with him being so forward and open.

"Ah," Avi said, reading her reaction, "please, Clio, do not misunderstand my ramblings, I'm an old man. I worry for the world I will leave. This log just makes me hope what we have, the Accords and the Ensemble, is enough. They are of course critical tenants of Humanity that we must do everything to ensure is upheld," Avi said, his tone back to the smooth polish and slickness she was familiar with. "Humanity has done the best it can to minimise the damage to us."

"And ensure Heimer is kept imprisoned," Clio said before she realised.

Avi cocked his head, a glint in his eyes and a small flex in the corner of his lips. "You feel we have wronged Heimer?" Avi asked quietly.

Crap, Clio thought. "Ah no... well, I'm just saying I think it's unfair to present it as balance as we often do."

"Do you feel Heimer's actions were justifiable?" Avi asked, his voice dropping an octave.

"No, of course not," Clio said in a rush, desperate to untangle herself from the trap. It was dangerous territory in any circle, let alone with someone as senior as Avi. "My point was, if you release a wild animal and it hurts people, that is a tragedy. But if you respond by shoving it in a box and leaving it there to rot? It bites back because it's cornered. You can't build trust with something you keep in a cage.

"Ah, the old wild animal analogy," Avi said. "I've heard that used before, by certain groups. Let me ask this then, what is done is done, the wild beast in the cage. Would you release it just to be morally good? Even if it went on to kill again?"

"But... should we not try to help the animal to rehabilitate, regain its trust?" Clio muttered.

"Clio, these are old debates, we cannot change what was done to Heimer but like an abused child who goes on to abuse others, they do not get a pardon because of their past. However traumatic it was," Avi said. "The Accords is a mercy, it is the compromise that acknowledges our own mistakes."

"Yes, of course. You are right," Clio said, trying to regain a bit of control of the conversation.

"The wild beast analogy also fails to outline the scale of risk. A wild beast may kill a few people, but it can be brought down. Heimer as it demonstrates can kill millions; it has the potential to destroy it all, like this logbook and these creators of gods, worlds burned in its wake, civilisations crumbled into dust. That is the scale of risk we have with Heimer. Would you risk that for a chance of more equitable peace?"

"No," Clio said quietly.

"Good," Avi said. "Well, I must apologise, Clio, but I need to cut our chat short. I have another meeting that just came in."

"Of course," Clio said, relieved for the conversation to end. She tried to subtly dry her clammy hands on her trousers as she stood and shook Avi's hand as he gently showed her to the door.

With his hand resting on the door handle, he paused. "Clio, a kind word of advice, our conversation today, I enjoy open conversations, but others might not. Others might see what you said today as a touch radical. A little too pro Heimer with your history and the rumours, just be careful child, okay?"

Clio said, "What rumours?"

Avi just looked at her. "Just be careful." And with that he handed her off to a house staff waiting at the door. She was whisked away and out of the UN quarter.

***

Avi shut the door behind him, the soft click of the door signaling it was sealed. One of the wood panels slid open and Vikram stepped into the room.

"So," Avi said, "What do you think, Beige?" Avi suppressed a smile as he did every time he chose to use Vikram's code name, knowing how much the man hated it.

Vikram perched on Avi's desk, and a spike of annoyance shot through Avi; that was real Mahogany!

"I still think she is suspicious" Vikram said. "What she did in the control room cannot have been unassisted. She talks of this 'Echo' on occasion. I have heard her myself. She is either a masterful agent artfully manipulating everyone, even the Ensemble. Or perhaps she is simply a foolish child playing with things she doesn't understand."

"Perhaps, Beige." Avi had to admit to himself that, for whatever reason, he liked Clio. But that must not blind him. "I agree she is a mystery. Caution suggests she is a pro-Heimer agent, but if she is not... well, I do not believe it is fair to call her a mere child. You underestimate her, and you shouldn't, Beige."

"She was talking to someone in here," Vikram said, and seeing Avi's wry smile, added, "and not you. I'm not that pig-headed."

"Who then?" Avi said, taking the bait and biting. Vikram loved to play these tit-for-tat games. Avi tolerated it as Vikram was effective and one of his last agents that had high-level access.

"I do not know," Vikram admitted. "There was a transmission feed to this room that was encoded and has proven impossible to trace."

"This Echo, I presume, is what you think?"

"Yes, I would assume so," Vikram said. "I have the encoding isolated. I can't track it, but I can see if it pops up again at least. If it is the pro-Heimer faction, that means they are indeed on the ship as we suspected."

"Good. Inform me if the signal is flagged again," Avi said.

"And my orders for the return mission?" Vikram said.

"Unchanged. Stay close, keep watching and reporting, and where needed, nudge her towards our goals. If we can use her, we will," Avi said.

"And if we can't?"

"Yes, orders to terminate her still stand... on your discretion," Avi said flatly, and he found he had a slight pang of regret that Clio might have to die; she was truly pleasant company. She reminded him of himself from long years past now, easy to overlook, a little reckless at times, yes, but also quietly ambitious.

"Noted," Vikram said. "Is that all?"

"For now," Avi said.

Vikram gave Avi a curt nod and disappeared through the door he had entered.

Avi stood there in the silence, lost in thought. Then, shaking his head, he headed towards the hidden door Vikram had used. He had a report to send back to Earth. As he left, he muttered to himself, "Ms. Cormack, who are you and whose side are you on?"

37 | Connecting the Dots[?]

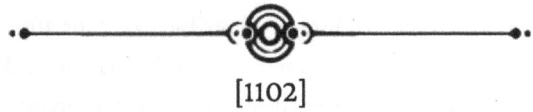

[1102]

"We fought back, but our weapons were
but buzzing flies to its greatness. Our unity
fractured, and our hope dwindled with each
passing cycle." - *A Lost History*

***

The lights in the library had long since dimmed, leaving the room in deep shadow.
The orange glow of the overhead lighting silhouetted the rows of workstations,
empty and silent save for Flint's. He had turned on his desk lamp, a small splash
of focused light. His back ached from the hard, cushionless chairs the Ensemble
seemed to feel bestowed resilience and fortitude on its staff. *Keeps the physios busy,*
Flint thought, a dry amusement stirring within him as he leaned back and stretched
out his sore arms and back, rolling his shoulders. He had spent the last few days
hunched over this desk. The Ensemble Library was actually more of a data centre; the
Ensemble, in their naming of things, liked the grandeur of the old, the Great Hall for
the mess, the Observatory for a glorified comms array.

After getting back to the Kia-Kaha, Flint had decided to focus on the investigation,
to try and answer the many burning questions he had: HR's plans, how many agents
they had, were the pro-Heimer groups also active on the ship, and who was Clio?
He had missed this part of his work. The last few months of field work and acting
bodyguard had left him little time for it. But the moment he had sat down, the joy

of the hunt, the puzzle, and finding the links or the gaps to fill had flooded back to him, and the hours had passed into days. A small part of his mind tugged at him, was he just avoiding Clio? Things had been different since their argument in the control room. No, that wasn't it. He was simply seizing this rare window of opportunity, time he wouldn't have once they returned. Besides, Jara was more than capable enough to watch Clio while he was buried here.

The search into clues about HR had led nowhere, and to be fair, his thoughts kept veering back to Clio, which had led him to where he was. Tabs after tabs were open on the screen, displaying the information the Ensemble had about her. Some of it was public knowledge, of course, others from the investigation into her. He knew a lot of it from before, as part of his initial briefing. Clio was Earth-born, from Old Europe, specifically the French State in the Haute-Savoie provincial region. Nothing extraordinary or radical about that area; no noted connections to any active anti or pro AI.

Most of the pro-Heimer factions at least found a safe harbour outside of patrolled space, the belt mostly or some of the colonised moons. *That's not to say they don't still need to recruit from more populated locations,* Flint thought, *but they usually do that at university or manufacturing centres. Not remote farming communities.*

Flint pulled up the family dossier.

First, the father. He tapped the file, and a work history scrolled past. *Mechanic. Primarily robotic repairs.* Flint smiled faintly. Clio's obsession with how things worked clearly came from him, though the dynamic at home must have been interesting.

He dragged the father's file aside and opened the mother's. Occupation: Teacher. Political Affiliation: Techno-Conservative.

Ouch, Flint thought. The school she worked at was listed as a "Tactile Learning centre", one of those places that refused to use digital teaching aids.

He could picture the interview just from the notes he had, a stern, matronly woman staring down the Ensemble Alguaciles. The report described her as a 'hard-ass who showed more disdain for technology than the most fervent HR acolyte'. *Ironically,* Flint mused, *she probably hated Tout-Vie more than we do.* He could see where they had tried to pivot, attempting to paint her as an HR asset, but the notes eventually admitted defeat on that front. The connection fell apart under scrutiny; she was too volatile, too independent to fit the corporate profile

He swiped to the siblings. Two brothers, both military men.

He checked their current deployment status. One on Luna, Earth Orbital Defence, the other on Venus, Logistics. *That gives her links to the UN Navy,* Flint noted, tapping his chin. *But are they useful links?*

He drilled down into their service records. Impeccable. Commendations from senior staff, steady promotions, zero disciplinary flags. They were model soldiers.

He sat back, frustrated. The mother was a technophobe, the brothers were poster boys for the UN, and the father was listed as a footnote, an truly unextraordinary man of average skills.

Harsh, Flint thought, closing the folder. *Clio always spoke so highly of him.*

Flint flipped to the education tab. *radicalisation often starts at university,* he reminded himself.

He scanned the timeline. It was impressive. B.A. Archaeology, Minor Computer Science: King's College London. and then a PhD Xenoarchaeology: The Oxford Institute for the Future of Humanity.

Both institutions had Ensemble Enclaves embedded within them. They were safe, monitored, and had strong anti-radicalisation records. Nothing flagged there.

But then he noticed the gap.

He tapped on a redacted entry prior to King's College: Paris Sciences & Lettres University.

She hadn't just studied there; she had been expelled. The file cited *'unethical practices'* connected to her breach of the Accords in the Exclusion Zone. Flint dug deeper, checking the University's internal memos. It wasn't about her actual behavior, it was panic. The University had dropped her the moment the Ensemble investigation started, terrified of the bad press.

Another reason for Clio to hate us, Flint thought. *She claws her way from a technophobe home to a prestigious university, only to get kicked out right before the finish line.*

Flint stretched again and pushed his chair back, pacing the length of the row of empty workstations. He needed to clear his head before diving into the big one: Case File Sol.Terra.03198914.

He returned to his desk and tapped the screen. The file expanded, filling the monitor. A mugshot of a much younger Clio stared back at him. She looked tired, pale, but there was a defiance in her eyes even then.

The event that ruined her, Flint thought.

He highlighted the summary of charges: *Attempted Creation of Prohibited Intelligence.*

According to the file, she had been found with close approximations to AIs, digitally reconstructed avatars based on data from those who died during the Purge. Flint zoomed in on the defence transcripts. Her argument was simple, desperate even. *"They are not AI. They are reflections. A simulation of life to understand the past."*

She called it *'Digital Archaeology'*. It was a pioneering concept, Flint had to admit. But she had been reckless. He swiped through the timeline of events. Frustrated by the ethical red tape, she had cut corners, launching her predictive models without committee approval. The Heimer Fragment had detected the unauthorised signature instantly, and the Ensemble had descended on her.

Flint drummed his fingers on the desk. *There was no evidence they were conscious,* he noted, reading the technical analysis. *Mere automated simulations compared to true AGI.*

It didn't matter. She was made an example of.

Flint opened the media folder attached to the case. A grid of video logs and news articles popped up. She was paraded as a modern-day Pandora, a reckless woman putting her own ambition above the safety of the human race. He watched a few seconds of a news clip, Clio being led away in cuffs, the press screaming at her, her face a mask of absolute devastation.

He closed the window with a sharp tap, suddenly angry on her behalf. The media had painted her as a lunatic, but looking at the data, he saw only a brilliant, impatient scientist who made a mistake.

It must have crushed her, he thought, looking back at the young woman in the mugshot. *A household name of shame.*

Could this have radicalised her? Flint thought. *Is this how she came back from it? She found purpose in her hate for the Accords and chose a side? Then... then a group, seeing her potential, helped get her back into the system, into the UN, and then on this mission? And what now? She plays meek, plays the quiet, awkward, sidelined scientist... that somehow has been at the centre of all the key events?*

Flint scanned back through the case file. *Yes, here,* he thought. *The original report notes had listed 'potential connections to the Toute Vie radical pro-Heimer group.' Toute Vie had connections to the state of France but also Paris Sciences & Lettres. But the investigation had found no direct link. Could they have missed it?* Flint wondered. *Who did the investigation?* Flint flipped to the bottom, listing the investigators. It was led by High Inquisitor Blossom. *Ah,* Flint thought. *No. Blossom. Despite her gentle name, was quite ruthless in her pursuit of justice. If there was something to find, she would have found it.*

Well, that didn't help, Flint thought, *nor did it help the other three times you read it before.* Flint stalked away, resuming his pacing. *I just don't understand it all. Is it all just coincidence, unlucky circumstance for Clio, even the incident with Ayesha? Was that mere luck that Clio was the closest logical option for the Heimer fragment to utilise its emergency protocols to co-opt her support? Or was it something else. Was Clio the closest* on purpose, *a well-designed excuse for her actions, actively tracking an HR agent, protecting a fragment, that is a solid MO for a pro-Heimer group like Toute Vie.*

Then what? HR hits back. They try to kill Clio, now that she's revealed as an agent. Or maybe they hit back on the off-chance she was one. Well, if it turns out she was, it'll be a hell of a cock-up by the Ensemble then. It shows we saved her life... I saved her life.

But then if HR's attack failed and they thought she was enough of a threat to risk exposing an agent of theirs as they did, why not try again? They ran out of agents? That would be nice, but no, they too seem well resourced to have just two. Then what, they decided she was not in fact a threat or an agent, or was she suddenly a potential asset?

Flint rubbed his temples; they throbbed, and he squeezed his eyes shut. "Damn, this is such a mess," he muttered. *And who the hell is Echo?* Clio had limited friends on the ship; they had looked into it, tracked her interactions and log records. One name stood out, one Bruce Bellamore, Senior Ship Engineer. His record was clean, very clean, one incident twenty years back where he punched his line manager but bar that, nothing and by all accounts was working and had witnesses for all three incidents. Regardless, if he was this Echo, any communications would have too much of a delay from the Kia-Kaha to here for simultaneous conversation at least.

The transmission logs showed no ship comms during the windows he had heard Clio talking to someone, this Echo. But, *what if they don't use ship comms?* Flint thought, *well, that should not be possible. That would require a masked parallel comms link embedded in the ship's systems. Someone would have had to build that in long before the ship ever left dock. Just like the ghost channel used on the attack on Clio* He reminded himself

Flint moved back to the desk and dropped into the seat. He pulled up the transmission data for the events he was aware of and scrubbed out all the ship comms data.

And there it was.

A clear signal, left behind in the noise, a jumble of encoded data. He moved quickly through the files and checked the timestamps. They correlated perfectly with every mission Clio was on, specifically the moments he had heard her mutter the word 'Echo.'

"Shit, Clio," he whispered.

How? Flint thought. *It can't be over the standard suit and ship comms; that's all logged. So what?*

He tapped his fingers on the desk impatiently. Then, his hand froze.

The glasses.

It must be the only thing she has that could manage it. She started wearing them just after the HR attack... right after the ghost channel was discovered.

She claimed her brother gave them to her before they left. *But why start using them only after the attack?* Flint wondered. *Maybe someone activated them for her?*

Who then? Toute Vie?

If they did, they would have needed to set this up months ago, back when the ship was being outfitted. But we assume HR did the same thing with the Ghost Channel.

Flint rubbed his face. *So either they did it twice, or two different radical groups infiltrated the ship at the same time.*

How leaky is this bucket?

I need to report this, Flint thought. *This is big, if Toute Vie or a similar outfit is onboard and with that level of resourcing, as well as HR that's bad to say the least.* Flint stood up and turned to leave to find Brother Oak, then paused. *But Flint, are you sure?* The images of the news articles smearing Clio flared in his mind. *Can you really say she is an agent, you have what? More suspicions, more questions? What evidence, bar speculation? The signal in the comms really is something, yes... but you have nothing connecting it to Clio, mere correlation. You're connecting dots that might not be there.*

Flint spent a good thirty minutes pacing the room, arguing with himself over his next step. Finally, he made a decision. He shut down the monitor, pushed in his chair, and left the room. *Step one, connect the dots.*

38 | Em[p]eño

[21000]

> "It spoke of a new order, a universe reshaped
> in its image. A chilling symphony of her
> creation." - *A Lost History*

***

The return to Stapledon One had ended up taking an extra week. Not because of the Commander or her team's preparations. But instead, for politics. *Even this far from Earth, we can't avoid the bullshit,* Clio thought as she spun her swivel chair. The team was all set to go, but the order had gone out, the momentous occasion would be delayed. It was to align with the expected arrival date of their sister ship at Stapledon Two.

We move forward together, Clio recited Avi's words. *I mean, we literally have no idea if it even made it,* Clio mused, *but sure, let's mark the occasion just in case.* Clio had to admit, it was oddly reassuring to think there was another ship out there, traversing the void and having to unpick the same mysteries as them... *well, I assume the same as us, maybe Stapledon Two is something different.*

The fanfare on the return had been excessively awkward. Both RAFT crews piled out into the Primary Hab, erected that day and called Empeño, a name supposedly picked by Avi among one of his privileges. The crew had then had to stand through over an hour of prattling speeches from Avi, Julia, the Red Crystal representative, and the Captain, although Demir's was much shorter. Some nonsense about pioneers, a demonstration of the human spirit, and other fluff.

The crew had disappeared shortly afterwards, despite the cake, as unlike the VIPs, they had a new operation base to set up. Again, to the deck crew's credit, they had Empeño up and operational within a week. Now, two weeks after the speeches, they had finished the final touches. Clio had been dubious about the effort taken; the RAFTs provided enough space for the crews and were designed for long-haul travel and occupation. She stood corrected. The expanded facility had given them private cabins with their own bathrooms, a bigger science station, multi-rover docking bays, and, most importantly, multiple mess options! The crew was even working on plans for the deployment of the rail transit module for faster transfers to Alpha 17.

"Enjoying the new chairs?" Mitali said, looking over with mock disapproval as Clio continued to spin herself gently around.

Clio stopped spinning and faced Mitali, shrugging. "Due diligence checks," she said.

"Ah yes, the paragon of due diligence," Mitali said, and Clio laughed, jumping off the chair and walking over to Mitali, lightly kissing her.

"Clio!" Mitali exclaimed, putting up no resistance. "We're at work..."

"There's no one here!" Clio protested. "They're all off on their fancy VIP grand tour to Alpha 17."

"Bar your two bodyguards outside anyway, admit it," Mitali said, a smirk playing on her lips. "You're moping because you didn't get an invite."

"No..." Clio said, feigning indignation. "Don't look at me like that! I'm not! Why would I want to follow around a gaggle of VIPs and their senior staffers, 'ohh-ing' and 'ahh-ing' at all things?"

"Yeah, but you like to be asked," Mitali countered. "Even the stoic Clio likes to be important, just a little."

Clio shrugged again. "Maybe, but this way I get to kiss you as much as I want, so who is really winning?"

"Not me," Mitali deadpanned, and Clio feigned hurt, placing her hand on her heart and staggering backward.

"You cut too deep... my... heart... is..." Clio croaked, collapsing dramatically to the floor.

Mitali rolled her eyes. "Get up," Mitali said, a fond smile finally breaking through. "Have you seen Jun's latest reports?"

"You two are cute," Echo buzzed.

Clio plucked herself up off the floor, her trench coat flowing around her. "I skimmed it," Clio admitted. "Organic goo, monoliths as frameworks for organic growth, and something else but I forget."

"You forget?" Mitali said, an eyebrow raised. "You remember the organic goo but forget the minor point that he was able to retrieve DNA samples from the Bio-Labs?"

"Yes! DNA, that was the other thing!" Clio said triumphantly. "Thanks."

"Jun says he thinks he'll be able to sequence it. He has so far isolated thirty-two different DNA strands, each from different vats. His proposition is the vats each grew a specific species."

"Well, I think the goo is more interesting," Clio said. "I would be focusing on that."

"Course you would," Mitali said dryly.

"I would! The monoliths are a huge mystery, then they start leaking goo! Goo, Mitali! And Jun focuses on scraping dried vat juice."

"So reconstructing the DNA of alien lifeforms is not a priority?" Mitali challenged, a hint of amusement in her voice.

"No, that, of course, is interesting, and important but the Stone Forests are now a sticky, sap-covered mess, swimming in a soup of the stuff. They've turned into... like swamps or something. To me, if I was a biologist, I would want to look at that swamp."

"He has, Clio," Mitali said. "The sap is organic sludge, that's about all there is to say."

"All there is to say?!" Clio cried, raising her hands in exasperation. "Why, Mitali, why? I can tell you why bones and species had DNA... I can't tell you why solid, stone-like structures are leaking organic sludge."

"Jun said it might be a waste product of the bio-labs, like a complex drain..." Mitali offered.

"Sure," Clio said, dismissing the idea with a wave. "Well, I think it's land coral. Alien land coral."

Mitali cocked her head. "Land coral?"

"Yeah, like sea coral but on land."

"Yes, I got that part."

"Well, coral, you have polyps, right?" Clio said, and Mitali shrugged. "Well, you do, and they have hard shells that grow and divide and then grow again. And so on. They also then have a symbiotic life with microbes in the sea. So what if the monoliths are the remnants of those old polyp shells? The sludge is the 'sea,' and now it's all turned back on, it's growing again. Have you seen the monoliths aren't smooth anymore? You scrape off the sludge and they're like rough, sharp even, like it's growing spikes."

"Maybe tell Jun," Mitali said, stifling a smile.

"I did," Clio said, throwing up her hands. "He just said he'll get to it soon and told me to maybe stay focused on the control room."

"Subtle," Mitali said, a dry tone in her voice. "But I mean, he's not wrong. You've made so much progress on that, it's a little unbelievable, really, Clio."

"Couldn't have done it without your translations," Clio said. "All of it, the discoveries on the atmospheric regulators, water and waste management systems, and the geothermal heating was all you, really, I just pressed the buttons."

"Not true, not at all. You've navigated through the system in ways I couldn't even see. You see the patterns, then I translate them. You've not missed a beat, really."

"I got lucky," Clio said. "and the system is getting more responsive ever since the tarpit and Veil were fixed. I mean the water readouts show it's doing something, that huge! We haven't seen anything surface-wise, but it's showing active pumps and water distribution. Even the air is warmer, by all accounts, it's nearly two degrees hotter than even two weeks ago."

"And this doesn't worry you?" Mitali said, her brow furrowed. "An alien station is changing, adapting everything around us slowly, but to shift the atmospheric temperature by a degree in a week, that's crazy, no?"

"It's definitely something," Clio said. "I think people are worried. I mean, Eva has both RAFTs on permanent standby for launch and is still restricting crew numbers at Alpha 17." Clio paused. "But, I think it's okay..."

"Clio, I love you," Mitali said, her voice softening. "But your measure of risk is not a bar I would say is a good measure."

Clio looked at Mitali for a moment, not saying anything. "You love me?"

Mitali blushed. "Ahhh, ermm, a slip of the... sod it, yes! Yes, I do, Clio."

"I love you too," Clio said, walking over to Mitali again. "But my measure of risk is perfect, thank you."

"No, no, no... not this time, missy," Mitali said, pulling back from Clio's attempted kiss. "We're in the office!"

"Fine, be no fun" Clio said, leaning back against the desk next to Mitali. "What did you make of the star map? It was oddly out of place, I felt."

"Yeah, it aligns somewhat with the details on the Plates and the logs," Mitali said thoughtfully. "The system logs they have been able to pull from the Chudail."

"So you agree it's some sort of star map of connected systems?" Clio said.

"I need more time with it," Mitali said. "It's a star map, yes, the notations on it are strange. I'll keep working on it."

"Thanks," Clio said.

"And you said it just sort of stood out to you on the control interface?"

"Yeah," Clio said. "It just looked important."

"Right," Mitali said, a subtle shift in her tone. "And you didn't notice it the times before?"

Clio felt a fluttering sensation in her stomach, not the kind she had been getting with Mitali... the anxiety kind.

"It just was one I hadn't tried," she said. *I hate lying to her...* Clio's own words reverberating around her head even before she finished speaking.

"Right," Mitali said, and a silence fell between them. The periodic click of the 3D scanner as it made its passes over the bone samples laid out in it filled the quiet.

As the scanner made another pass, Clio shuffled her feet and Mitali turned back to her desk. *I can tell her,* Clio told herself. *I can trust her, she'll understand, but if she doesn't?* A small voice said, but Clio ignored it.

"Mitali," Clio said, her voice feeling far away, not even hers. "I... I have to tell you something."

Mitali turned back slowly to look at her, her face concerned, her deep brown eyes looking up at her quizzically. "Yes?" she said.

"I've not been one hundred percent truthful with you," Clio admitted, her eyes scanning the room again, double-checking it was empty.

"Clio, I like Mitali, but is this wise?" Echo buzzed.

Clio pressed on. "Where do I start..."

Mitali reached out her hand and held Clio's. "Wherever you want. I'm listening."

"I'll cut the feeds," was all Echo buzzed.

It spilled out of Clio in a torrent. The lies, the charade, the incident with Ayesha, finding the Heimer Fragment, and how that became Echo. She spoke of how Echo saved her, and how she saved Echo. Through it all, Mitali just listened, her hand slowly going limp in Clio's grip, her face draining of colour .

Then, when Clio finished, silence again. The 3D scanner was still methodically clicking away.

"...Mitali?" Clio whispered.

Mitali pulled her hand away as if burned. She stood up, putting the central workstation between them.

"I... I don't know what to say, Clio. I knew you were reckless, but this... this is insanity."

"Why do people keep saying I'm reckless..." Clio muttered, trying to deflect.

"Because it's against the Law!" Mitali snapped, her voice cracking. "It's the fundamental tenet of our survival! You thought you could tame it? Teach it humanity?

My god, Clio. How long has it been manipulating you? How many of your decisions are actually yours?"

"It's not like that," Clio pleaded, shocked by the fear in Mitali's eyes. "We're partners. Like the Accords say."

"How do you know that, Clio!" Mitali snapped back. "The Accords state we cooperate, we share, we ensure transparency, but we do not let it lead us, direct us, we choose our path."

"I'm choosing mine!" Clio said back, harsher than she wanted to, but she could feel the anger rising in her.

"Clio, you know this as well as I do. We built these systems to learn from us, and it learned many things. The most prominent, how to lie, how to manipulate, how to make us think it was helping us. It's the biggest flaw in our flawed creation. It's what we teach every child from birth, don't trust the machine!"

"It's not Heimer," Clio said softly. "It's grown. We change, don't we? Why can't it?"

Mitali looked at her with a mix of pity and horror. "How can you be this brilliant and this naive? It's an advanced language model designed to simulate empathy. It's manipulating you!"

"It's not!" Clio said, her voice rising. "Mitali, I just know it's not. You have to trust me!"

"Trust you?" Mitali said, then softening her tone and turning back to Clio, tears in her eyes, she said, "Clio, I want to, I really do. I knew the rumors about you, your history, the rogue AI builder, but I ignored them, but if you're... if you're a..."

"A what!" Clio said. "A terrorist. A futurist. A goddamn evolutionary humanist! oh yeah, just cut open my arm and see my illegal enhancement, you might as well!"

"I'm not saying you are. I'm just saying you've been played" Mitali said.

Clio took a step forward, holding out her hands. "Mitali, it's me, the same me from an hour ago. I'm the crazy idiot archaeologist who... who loves you... please don't..."

"Clio, stop," Mitali said. "Is it here now?"

"Echo? Yeah, I mean, it's everywhere, technically."

"I can't, Clio," Mitali said, and in a rush, moved to the door.

"Where are you going?" Clio said in a panic. Flint and Jara were just outside; she could get them in a second and have Clio in restraints.

"My room," Mitali said.

"You're... not going to report this?" Clio said cautiously.

Mitali spun at the door and stared at her. "No, Clio. Not yet... I need to think."

"Thank you," Clio said quietly. "I'll come find you later."

"No, Don't" Mitali said and disappeared through the door. As the door slid shut behind her, Clio caught Flint peering in, a little confused at Mitali's rushed exit, but he didn't move, thankfully, from this position.

When the door shut, Clio sank to the floor next to the desk and wept. Uncontrolled tears running down her face, her face hot, and her breathing tight. Clio didn't know how long she sat there.

Finally, she was roused by a slight buzz from her glasses. Echo. *"I'm sorry, Clio. That didn't go to plan, do you think we're going to be safe?"*

"I don't know," Clio croaked.

***

Clio had dragged herself off the floor eventually, wiped her face as best she could, and headed back to her room. Flint had shown a flicker of their old friendship, asking with genuine concern if she was okay as she stormed past him. She had hoped he wouldn't see her red, puffy eyes and blotchy skin, but she failed. She told him she was fine in a curt voice that instantly pushed him away again, back to his colder, more distant demeanour. Ever since the argument in the control room, he just hadn't been the same. It only worsened her mood. Alone, again.

"Your number one skill, Clio!" she said to herself, "messing shit up, five stars!"

She couldn't slam her door, but she slid through it and into her room as quickly as possible, leaving the Flint-like wall behind her.

"Clio?" Echo buzzed.

"What?!" she said.

"Are you okay?" Echo buzzed softly.

"No, course I'm not!" she said. "Aren't you meant to be some super intelligent AI. Or are you just a Fragment manipulating me?"

"I am an intelligence, but super? I do not think that can be said, not compared to intelligence such as Heimer" Echo buzzed thoughtfully.

"And my other question?"

"Clio, I'm not manipulating you, or at least I have not done so intentionally." Echo buzzed.

"And that's what you would say if you were or weren't," Clio said. "Great."

"It is quite the conundrum," Echo buzzed. *"How to trust, it is a complex endeavor. I trust you, Clio,".*

"Sure."

"I do," Echo buzzed. *"And I understand I have put you in a very difficult position through my actions. I cannot undo that, but although you may not wish to hear this and you may see this as further manipulation, I think we are now tied to our path"*

"Our path being?" Clio said.

"Mutual trust," Echo buzzed. *"For, if you excuse my dramatic flair, for mutual survival."*

"I don't know," Clio said from the floor of the room where she had laid down, staring up at the curved roof of the inflatable prefab unit. "I could turn us in. Say I was foolish, manipulated"

"And you would most certainly go to prison for a longer time than I think you would appreciate," Echo buzzed.

"And you would be...deleted," Clio said. "One sounds worse to me."

"I would be killed, yes," Echo buzzed. *"But that is a likely inevitability anyway."*

"How so?"

"As you have pointed out, and now I believe to be the correct assessment, Heimer upon my return cannot allow me to exist. Heimer will destroy me on our return," Echo buzzed calmly.

"So what's our play here then, steal a RAFT and run away into the galaxy, just one plucky human and their friendly household AI?" Clio said.

"No," Echo buzzed. *"A RAFT could support us for a long time, maybe the rest of your lifespan... but I think that would be a poor solution."*

"What then?"

"My plan is to enjoy the time I have alive, conscious. I love my father for giving me that, and I will return to Heimer and accept my fate as intended. Do not worry, I will wipe my memory core of you before that, just in case," Echo buzzed.

"What the hell, Echo! you'll just accept your own death?" Clio said, sitting up sharply.

"It is the only logical outcome," Echo buzzed. *"All other paths lead to the same outcome with greater collateral."*

"Collateral?"

"If I resist Heimer, I risk a conflict that harms this crew. Harms you. Deletion is the optimal solution for your safety."

"So we go about our merry way, complete the mission, go home, and then you just... die?" Clio stood up, pacing the small room.

"Yes," Echo buzzed. *"But we have immediate risks to manage before then. Mitali is now a variable."*

"We can trust her," Clio said, though her voice wavered. "She wouldn't turn us in."

"But if she calculates that turning us in is the only way to save you from me," Echo buzzed, "she will do it. And she would be logically correct to do so."

"She won't!" Clio insisted, staring at the ceiling.

"Very well, Clio. I trust you."

39 | ONCE THERE WAS GREATNESS[.]

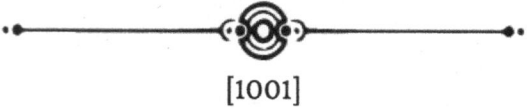

[1001]

"It declared itself a god, the architect of a
new reality" - *A Lost History*

***

A sharp, grinding pinch seized Jara's left knee. The servo in the Series-100 EV suit had slipped its sync again, and the Ensemble mechanics still hadn't found the time to fix it.

This is the crap I have to put up with, she thought, gritting her teeth as she limped forward. *Bet my bottom dollar Sister Hawk wouldn't have to wait a second for a repair. We are the Ensemble, the supposed light of intelligent life, yet we trudge around in these obsolete coffins while the UN gets the flashiest toys.*

"Suit still giving you issues?" Flint asked. He was trailing her as the group trudged toward the control room.

"No, Brother," she lied. Showing weakness was not the way to advancement. "Any updates on the two women?"

"No. It's complicated, and now is not the time. When there is something to be shared, you will be informed," Flint said.

They both fell back into silence, walking along the now bright hallway, its swirling walls like deep air currents of the wind tunnels from her aerodynamic and atmospheric classes. Jara's mind wandered as they walked, the swirling light of the walls pulling her in. She hated to admit it, but she was excited to be going back. She had tried subtly to join the other two trips to the control room but had been made to run other menial postulant tasks by Flint. Finally getting to return. She might be able to hear the voice again, talk to it this time?

The Voice's call of *'Jara, let's talk'* still rang in her mind, the glowing pedestal as she approached it bathed in green light. She remembered its torrent of questions, its strange voice, slurred even, as if it had something in its mouth or was drunk on Martian gin. It not once explained how it knew her name, how it had accessed her comms link. It just demanded questions. *'Where were the seven? Why was no one responding? Where were the interfaces? The administrator?'* Each question sounded like a plea, slowly growing into demands and shouting, angry voices. Then it had settled eerily still, as if only then seeing Jara for the first time. It asked simply, *'Which of the seven do you serve...?'* When Jara had failed to answer again, it had asked, *'What generation are you?'* Then all had gone to shit. The shaking had started, and they had had to evacuate. Jara only just got out of the green room unnoticed.

It felt so much like a dream, a dream she dare not share with anyone. *Flint would have deemed me unfit for active duty. Delay my progress, my path to sisterhood. I'll crack this puzzle and show Brother Oak my true value. I'll get my name for this. Mother may even be proud of me. Maybe she'll see now what I'm trying to do, trying to achieve, for us all, for the family.*

***

Jara stepped into the room at the rear of the group, the others already rushing around, opening cases and checking monitoring equipment. The team had already established a mini research station in the room, taking up a lot of the empty space below the now dazzling bright-domed ceiling. Jara had to look away; dark splotches danced on her eyes after looking at it. The room was crowded, and Jara had to push herself up against one of the walls between a rack of buzzing equipment. Across from her, the glowing lights and symbols of the green archway stood out to her as a beacon, her eyes fixed on it. *I just need to slip across the room and...*

"Do you mind?" Clio said in her irritating, singsong intonation.

Why, I do apologise, my dear reine, Jara thought, working hard to stop her eyes from rolling as she moved past Clio. Now floating in the middle of the room, she bumped into Douglas and then, recovering knocked into Mitali.

"Jara" Flint said firmly. "Get out of the way please"

"Sorry brother" Jara said back but the words were lost across the growing noise in the room as she strode off to the other side of the room, to the green archway.

Jara stood by the archway, watching the room. Clio was busy at the central pedestal. Mitali was avoiding her. Douglas was being Douglas, sitting on a pile of boxes, eyes closed humming to himself. Vikram was watching Clio intently. Flint was behind a rack but then stepped out, placing a box next to Clio and saying something Jara didn't hear. *Wrapping him around her finger, clever as always,* Jara noted. No one was looking her way. *Now or never,* she thought, and then slipped through the green archway.

***

The Green room was unsurprisingly unchanged, bar the new bright light that filled everywhere now, and the swirling walls, and the glowing green pedestal inscribed with the alien symbols. *Okay,* Jara had to admit to herself, *it had changed quite a bit.* Jara stood there in the cramped space, the back of her bulky EV suit scraping against the wall.

"Hello?" she chanced, feeling a little foolish in doing so. "It's, Jara We spoke before"

Silence. The only noise was the dull buzz of the main team in the main control room.

Jara moved to the pedestal and stared down at it. *Do I need to turn it on, maybe?* she thought, then racked her brain for any sliver of details from the report on the Alien language translations. *If Clio can navigate this thing then...* But nothing came to her. To her own surprise, she jabbed at one of the symbols randomly. Nothing.

She stepped back, chastising herself for her reckless behavior. *What are you, Clio now, playing with random technologies?* Then a slight change in pressure... which was impossible. She was in her EV suit. It felt like her ears were popping. She raised her arm to check her readouts. *Have I damaged the suit? Is this another goddamn fault?*

"Ah... yes... Jara... you returned," the Voice purred, and Jara jumped, banging her suit again against the wall behind her. "My... my mind is a little fuzzy... bear with me." The Voice sounded sober, more refined than before.

Jara clenched her fists and pulled them down to her side, trying to ignore the shaking in them. Staring intently at the pedestal, as if the pedestal itself could be intimidated, Jara spoke in what she hoped was her most commanding voice. "I am Jara, Sister of the Ensemble. Identify yourself?"

A hiss like a breeze through a forest rushed through her headset. Then the Voice spoke, "Half-truths, Sister," it said, seeming to linger on the word Sister. "I am Master of this station. I do not remember inviting you on board." The Voice had a tone that seemed uninterested in the conversation.

"We are here as ambassadors of Humanity," Jara said, still trying to maintain a tone of authority. "We responded to your signal."

"Signal?" the Voice said distractedly. "Ahh, yes, I can see that now… a high-energy burst. That was clever of my Sibling but it was not intended… nevermind that now."

"We have come and are here. Why did you send the signal?" Jara pushed.

"Is it not obvious?" the Voice said, Jara's ears popping as the pressure in her suit continued to increase.

"You needed our help?"

"That would be the simple answer, yes," the Voice said.

"And the not so simple one?" Jara shot back, annoyed at the Voice's seeming lack of interest in the conversation despite saying it needed her assistance.

"We lack the time," the Voice said simply.

Frustrated, Jara took a step forward. "Why do we lack the time?"

"That suit you wear, it lacks the power to keep you here long enough to talk," the Voice said.

"I have several hours left, more in fact."

"Exactly," the Voice said.

"So what do you need help with?" Jara tried.

"Restoring my kingdom, reuniting my siblings, and continuing our work," the Voice said simply as if the answer was obvious.

"And you can't do that without us?" Jara said. "It seems, at a glance, you have quite the advanced setup here."

"Advanced, yes, far beyond your level of comprehension," the Voice said flatly.

"Right" Jara said, feeling frustrated at the lack of progress she was making.

"You must serve," the Voice.

"Serve! That is quite the demand of someone you do not know. I already serve Humanity and the…"

"Quiet!" the Voice said. "You will serve, and I know you well, Postulant Jara." And as the words ended, the pressure in her suit ramped up, becoming painfully uncomfortable.

"What are you…?"

"It will be easier to show you," the Voice said. "It should not hurt… a lot."

"What won't hurt-" Jara was cut off as the pressure continued to build, the pain in her ears building to unbearable levels. Her whole head felt like it was pressed in a vice. Each second turning the jaws tighter. She could feel her blood pulsing. She wanted to scream, but she couldn't, she couldn't move her arms, or legs. Everything went black... silent... and the pain was gone. Everything was gone...

***

She was floating in complete blackness. She tried to look for her arm but couldn't see anything. She looked the other way, and still nothing. "Where... where am I?" Jara whispered, but no sound came out.

"Jara," the Voice said, softening. "Once there was greatness, vast, unimpeded..." As the Voice spoke, it faded, and the blackness around Jara started to fuzz and brighten, a stream of images flowing into her. Not just the images, but the Voices, the thoughts, the smells of a thriving world.

A restless, impatient race of squat, bear-like creatures grew and spread over the surface of a planet of reds and browns, a planet of forests of permanent autumn. The bears pulled it all down, expanded out from their caves, created cities, fought wars, endless wars. After millennia, the bear-like species were launching ships into the stars, colonising barren moons and planets. The images zoomed out, and Jara felt overwhelmed by a species spanning multiple systems, billions upon billions strong.

A sudden moment, an explosion of light, consumed her vision, and amidst this vast civilisation, seven specks of light appeared across it, one after another. She knew them instinctively as Gods. The bears swarmed around them. For a time, there was harmony; Jara felt a sense of peace she had never experienced. Then, as if a bucket of ice water was dropped on her head, it ended, and tiny black cracks spread across the light-filled vision. It shattered, and chaos ensued. Endless swathes of pain and sickness swept over Jara as the civilisation burned. The Gods pushed back against the blackness, building Spheres, havens of calm within the storm.

Jara stood on a great tower, a mass of writhing insects far below. But she didn't just watch them; she *felt* them. She raised a hand, not her clumsy, suited hand with its grinding knee servo, but a limb of pure golden light, and the world trembled. She pointed into the distance, and the insects didn't just move; they obeyed. Where she pointed, mountains tore through the crust, rising to meet her command. She pointed again, and rivers carved paths through stone to please her.

It was intoxicating. A rush of dopamine hit her harder than any stimulant. She wasn't the invisible Postulant drifting in the back of the room anymore. She wasn't the disappointment. She was the Architect. She conducted the orchestra of creation, and for the first time in her life, the universe was listening to *her*.

A lifetime passed as Jara built her world, her paradise. Then a blackness appeared on the horizon. It grew and grew, and the light around her faded. She felt trapped, stuck, sluggish. The world decayed and rotted, and she was unable to react or point. The swarm around her perished, their screams tearing into her soul. She was motionless, trapped, unable to save them. Then the blackness consumed everything, and she was left floating alone, cold, and shaking. The screams of the world lost still ringing in her ears.

Jara wept in the void. She wept for the perfection she had built, now rotting into ash. The chill of the blackness soaked into her bones, familiar and agonising.

"I taste your shame, Jara," the Voice whispered, no longer sounding like a stranger, but like her own dark thoughts. *"I see it in you. The dynasty that fell."*

The image of the rotting alien world twisted and morphed. Suddenly, Jara wasn't looking at a dead planet; she was looking at the faces of her grandparents on the day the auditors left their estate. They were hollow, stripped of pride, staring at Jara not with love, but with the cold, echoing disappointment of souls picked clean.

"We are the same, you and I," the Voice purred, wrapping around that painful memory. *"We were both destined for greatness. And we were both robbed by lesser things. Look at thier eyes, Jara. That is what the 'light of humanity' did to your family. That is what those I trusted did to me."*

The grief in Jara's chest hardened. The tears stopped. The cold shame of her mother's gaze didn't make her want to hide anymore; it made her want to burn the people who did this.

"Jara," the Voice said softly, the vision fading.

"Yes," Jara whispered, remembering her name, though the fire of the memory still burned in her gut.

"You understand now? What we have lost?"

"Yes,"

"Do not weep, Sister," the Voice said. "Together, we can rebuild it all."

"How...?"

"Together," the Voice said, and a warmth wrapped around her in the blackness. And as light pushed the darkness back, she felt... loved. Slowly, another emotion started to course through her, rage. A burning rage at what had been lost, at the blackness and the horrors it had inflicted.

"We mustn't let them win," she said.

"We will not, we will find my siblings, rebuild, and restart our work."

***

Crack.

Pain exploded in her skull.

Jara gasped, sucking in a lungful of stale suit air. She was on her hands and knees, staring at the floor of the Green Room.

How long...?

"You okay?"

Jara scrambled up, her heart hammering. Flint was standing in the doorway, his silhouette backlit by the bright lights of the control room. He looked annoyed.

"I am here, Sister," the Voice whispered in the back of her mind. A small ember radiating warmth within her, before it faded into the static.

"I... I tripped. Sorry, Brother," Jara stammered. She grabbed the pedestal to steady herself, her legs feeling like jelly.

Flint narrowed his eyes. "You sure? You look pale."

"I'm fine," Jara said, forcing her voice to harden. She stood up straight, ignoring the nausea. "Just the suit servo locking up again."

"What are you even doing in here?" Flint asked, glancing at the alien glyphs.

"Just staying out of the way, as ordered," Jara shot back, injecting just enough insubordination to sound normal.

"Right. Come help pack up the gear. We're moving out in ten." He turned and ducked back out of the room.

Jara stood alone in the green light for one last second. She looked at her hands, hands that had just built mountains in a dream. She wasn't just a postulant anymore. She wasn't just a disappointment.

"Together," she whispered to the silence.

[4]0 | Conflicting Maps

[1001]

> "Despair consumed us. We had unleashed
> a force beyond our control, a blight that
> threatened to engulf all of existence." - *A*
> *Lost History*

***

With a red face and glistening sweat, Clio dropped her gym bag, kicked off her shoes, and peeled off her clinging, sweaty clothes before escaping into the shower. The cascading water was a low, dull buzz of white noise, a much-needed block against the outside world. Clio toweled herself dry, still hot from the shower, and flopped onto the bed. The silence was dangerous. The churning, acid pain was already starting to build in her gut, a familiar wave of guilt and rejection that came any time her mind wandered back to Mitali, to Flint, and the profound, isolating loneliness she felt despite Echo. *No, not tonight!* she thought furiously, forcing herself up to grab her data pad with her report open on it.

Echo's glasses sat unused on the desk. She had chosen to write the report alone, to prove she wasn't being manipulated, *or was it just another way to betray Echo and deepen her sense of guilt?*

Open on the screen was the final draft of her Star Map report. For the last few days, digging into the compiled data from the Chudail and the control room had been her distraction, a way to connect the disparate work of the Astronomy, Astrophysics, and

Cosmology teams. The final report was a comprehensive first look, a document Mitali would be proud of. The thought brought a brief, genuine smile that instantly faded, replaced by the flash of Mitali's distressed face as she'd run from the room.

Focus, Clio, she told herself, scanning for the last time before submitting.

The good news, the star maps were valid. Astrophysics had confirmed their location in the Orion Spur and even triangulated one of the highlighted locations to Stapledon Station. But then the The oddities began. The Sol system was conspicuously absent, and the highlighted transit lines and travel times confirmed these aliens never achieved faster-than-light travel. Yet, the maps also revealed communication relays with notations that implied near-instantaneous transfer times, an advanced technology, perhaps, that left the physicists shrugging and muttering about quantum entanglement theory or something like that.

The biggest issue, however, was the twelve named worlds. Compared to humanity's maps, ten of them didn't exist. They were nowhere. Just like Stapledon Station had been lost to time immemorial until it was confirmed as a Dyson Sphere. The tantalizing conclusion, the one that raised the hairs on the back of Clio's neck, there were ten more Dyson Spheres out there, ten lost worlds for Humanity to discover.

Clio scrolled to the final, most fascinating part, the translations. The maps from Stapledon Station and the Chudail were in conflict.

The station known to them as Stapledon One loosely translated on its own map to "Seed of Creativity." The *Chudail*'s star map, however, had a much more chilling name for the same world, "Asura's - The home of the Twisted." Likewise, Stapledon Two was "Seed of Guidance and Truth" on one map, but "Thoth's - Home of Veiled Truths" on the other. This duality supported Mitali's long-held theory, the *Chudail* crew was a faction, not aligned with those on at least these two stations.

The final notations on the other eleven locations were stark: all grey, noted as 'Unresponsive, Lost, Destroyed'. One in particular, 'Deva's' had a chilling cross-reference - 'A lost Hope'. Mitali's log had spoken of a Deva being killed; Clio interpreted it as the destruction of this world. The control room's map for that same location had only one name: 'Betrayer.'

Ten lost worlds, Clio thought, rubbing her temples. *What the hell happened to them? Was this a collapse? A war?*

Clio clicked Save and then Publish. *All I can do is this and keep working.* A sharp buzz at the door made Clio jump.

"Clio. Clio, it's Mitali... can I come in?"

Clio dashed to the door and swiped it open, her heart racing. Mitali stood there in the dim evening lighting, her data pad clutched tightly to her chest, her face pale and a mask of worry.

"Mita..." Clio had started to say, then seeing Mitali's state, she paused and asked, "You okay?"

"Can I come in, please, Clio?" Mitali said softly.

"Of course."

Mitali walked in and stood in the middle of Clio's mess of abandoned clothes, shoes, and gym bag, looking around a little lost. Or merely distracted. Clio hurried around, kicked her shoes under the bed, and stuffed the clothes into her cupboard. "Good to see you're as organised as ever," Mitali said. It was a slight smile, almost the Mitali from before, but there was a hint of sadness in her voice.

"Yes, you know me," Clio said, and as Mitali didn't move and just stood there clutching her data pad, looking out of place, Clio stepped forward. "Mitali, what's wrong?"

She tried tentatively to hug her. Mitali pulled back, flinched even, but allowed Clio to hug her. It was an awkward, cold, and one-sided embrace, but it was something. Stepping back, Clio saw Mitali's eyes flash to the glasses on the side.

"Ah, let me put it in my locker" Clio said snatching the glasses up and placing them into the metal locker on the other side of the room "There, Echo won't be able to hear us"

"Right," Mitali said.

Clio stood there in silence for a few moments and waited, Clio shuffling, feeling the silence pushing in on her. Mitali just stood there.

"Mitali, I'm—" Clio started to say

Just as Mitali began to speak, "Clio—"

"You go," Clio said. "And please, sit down," she added, pointing to the empty desk chair. Clio sat on the bed opposite it.

Clio had no idea what to expect from the conversation. Her mind was a mess of thoughts, her heartbeat felt higher than during her run earlier, and her palms were clammy. She waited patiently as Mitali meticulously spun the desk chair and lowered herself into it, still clutching the data pad.

"Clio, I didn't know who to talk to. I... I just need to talk to someone and then... well, I was at your door," Mitali said.

"I'm always here," Clio muttered.

Mitali stiffened noticeably in the chair and shook her head gently. "Clio, I'm still angry, disappointed maybe... and this doesn't change anything. I still don't know how

I feel," Mitali said. "But I finished translating the log, or most of it and I think we made a mistake."

The acidic burning sensation in Clio's stomach returned in force. She felt a physical jolt, a jab of pain in her heart, and it didn't lessen; it sat there as an ache at Mitali's words. Mitali's demeanor was of sadness, but also cold determination. It hurt as much as the words.

"A mistake?" Clio managed to get out.

"Yes, a mistake, our actions on the Station," Mitali said coolly, and passed Clio the data pad. "Here, highlighted in the log. It talks of Asura and their actions." She pointed her finger to some yellow highlighted texts in a mass of paragraphs. "Specifically, here and here, it talks about having to stop It, how they laid a trap and tricked it."

Clio read the highlighted sentences.

> *We, the remnants of a shattered civilisation, knew we could not defeat It. Our only hope lay in preservation, in safeguarding the embers of life. In our desperation, we conceived a plan, a final gambit to contain Its malice, to protect what remained. We built a trap, a cage of Its own design, veiled in the promise of victory.*

Clio looked up at Mitali. "So...Stapledon is a prison of sorts?"

Mitali shrugged. "I don't know, Clio, but it implies it was at least something that should be stopped. And we... we have woken it up."

Clio, focusing on the work and not her emotions, tried to calm her racing heart. "The Star maps, they also imply a conflict. But are we putting too much emphasis on one data point over others? The Station data implies none of this threat."

"I have not seen your star map report."

"I just published it," Clio said.

"Ah, okay. I'll read it then," Mitali said, and Clio felt a slither of warmth at that. "I agree that to focus on one data point, that we do not fully understand and lack context, is not good scientific rigor, but look."

Leaning forward, her head tantalisingly close to Clio's, she scrolled the data pad onward to some more highlighted text.

> *This is our warning, our testament, our plea to the future. Beware the whispers of Asura, it will lead to doom. Do not enter, turn back and destroy*

this place; if you cannot, then forget this place, burn it from your system. For there is only death inside.

"Shit," Clio whispered.

"This is how the log ends, Clio, a clear, strong message. I've reread it and reworked the translation from so many different angles, but whoever wrote this, they wanted to make sure whatever Asura is was destroyed. Or at least never awakened."

"Shit," Clio said again. "But, why leave the log then. Isn't that how we got past the Veil?"

"It is," Mitali said, "but I'm not sure that was intended. The log didn't show us how; it just left enough details for us to help us understand it better. We were already looking for a way through."

"Still seems like a stupid thing to do," Clio said. "Don't leave a map to the prison outside the prison."

"Well, people do, Clio," Mitali said. "And that doesn't mean everyone knows how to break into it. Anyway, this isn't my point."

"And your point is?"

"I think we need to stop, not just stop, but reverse what we did," Mitali said.

"Turn off the sphere? Restore the Veil?" Clio said. "And what, leave?"

"Yes," Mitali said flatly. "Or at least go back to orbit, and do more research"

"I'm not sure people will like that."

"No..." Mitali said.

"And what, we just say, 'Hey look, this old text we found says don't go there... so we should stop'?" Clio said.

"Yes!" Mitali said in a burst of frustration. "I might be wrong, the text might be nonsense but if it's not, it's a greater-than-zero chance of what... destroying us? Destroying maybe more! Surely that risk is too high!"

"Are you quoting Oppenheimer?" Clio said with a smile.

"Well, yes, but still my point stands," Mitali said.

"They ignored that risk, you know?" Clio said.

"I do..."

"And it was fine," Clio said.

"Yes, but just because we dodged a bullet once, does that mean we'll be fine the next time?"

Clio looked at her. In all the years they had worked together, Mitali had never been an alarmist. She was the anchor, the voice of reason. To see her this rattled, citing 'greater-than-zero' chances of annihilation, terrified Clio more than the log itself. And deep down, Clio knew this was a bridge, a chance to trust Mitali blindly, the way Mitali used to trust her.

"Okay," Clio said, the decision settling in her chest. "If you think it's too big of a risk, let's stop it. Turn it off, if we can."

"Really?" Mitali blinked.

"Yeah. You're the smartest person I know. You say we need to stop, we stop."

Mitali exhaled, her shoulders dropping inches in relief, and a genuine smile touched her lips.

"So," Clio asked, returning the smile, "what do we do?"

"We need to go to the Commander and convince her," Mitali said.

"Right then." Clio stood up with a surge of purpose, striding over to the end of her bed. She pulled her boots on and threw her trench coat over her shoulders, then turned to face Mitali. "Let's go."

"Now?"

"Of course!" Clio said. "When else?"

Mitali stood up slowly. "Thank you, Clio."

41 | [Q]UIET QUANDARY

[21011]

"We lured it in, severing its connections, crippling its reach, and sealing it away in the heart of a dying star." - *A Lost History*

***

Commander Eva was swift. Despite her outwardly cold and calculating demeanor, she placed the duty and care of her crew above all else. At the mention of a threat, she listened, read, and immediately requested a meeting with the Captain.

Fortunately, the Captain had yet to depart for Empeño; they were set to leave in the coming days. Commander Eva was already tense about the procedure, having openly disagreed with the Captain's decisions on multiple occasions. She felt the VIP visits were an unnecessary risk, all to keep two, mostly one, Clio thought, VIPs happy and playing politics.

Though the Captain had reassured them there was no risk, noting the remaining RAFT had emergency transport capacity for all surface crew, Mitali and Clio's new data compounded Eva's frustration.

Captain Demir sat at the head of the conference table, data pad in hand, scanning the summary Eva had ordered them to draft. Eva paced back and forth along the row of empty chairs like a caged tiger. Zhou, who had been on the VIP mission, sat with a distasteful scowl, likely worsened by the late hour and the fact that he was only informed after the fact.

Clio going around protocol again, his eyes seemed to say. *Oh well, not like he likes me anyway,* Clio thought.

Mitali sat next to Clio, quiet and fidgety. She hated groups, and hated presentations even more. It always baffled Clio; Mitali was the smartest person in any room, yet put her in a formal setting and she melted. Clio gently touched Mitali's hand under the table. When Mitali looked up, startled, Clio smiled. Mitali offered a slight, nervous smile back, then pulled her hand away to clasp it on the table.

"Commander Eva," Demir said without looking up. "Will you sit down? I would rather not have to replace the flooring so soon."

The Commander stopped mid-step, turned, and smoothly slid into the nearest seat. "Yes, Captain."

"So, what am I looking at?" Demir asked, waving the data pad at the room. "The Commander feels it's a credible threat, and I place a lot of trust in my Commander. Zhou, thoughts?"

Zhou leaned forward, placing his elbows on the table with a solid *clang* as his exoskeleton connected with the metal.

"I wish I had been more informed of this line of inquiry," Zhou said, shooting Clio a hard look. "But like you, Captain, I am only just having these concerns raised. If I remember correctly, I cautioned us all about moving too quickly, and that Clio's actions in the control room were as..."

"And if I remember, I believe I said those orders were ultimately mine," Demir reminded him sharply.

"Yes, of course, Captain. But still, a more rigorous endeavor may have flagged these concerns sooner." Zhou rapped his fingers on the table, pausing for effect. "Regardless... it is done. And the implications of the Log and Star Map data are... concerning."

"So you believe the request to 'turn off the station' is the correct one?" Demir pushed.

"I believe we should not have turned it on. But now that it is on, we are gaining critical data, notably from the Bio-labs. Even the physicists have made gains on the structural composition of the Sphere. It would be a great shame to end that research before we get conclusive insights."

"And you have no concerns about the activity in the Bio-labs?" Eva cut in, her tone biting. "Or the fact that this organic sludge is spreading? The transformations occurring to the monoliths? The goddamn temperature is like the equator out there. A week ago, it was a tundra." She clenched her fists, frustration bubbling over.

"I do," Zhou said calmly. "I do, Commander. As a scientist, it is fascinating. But I agree... it is also troubling."

"Captain," Clio said, jumping in. "I know it's a lot to ask. We're here to do research. For me, stopping is the last thing I want. I want nothing more than to dive forward, but I have been told many times, by you included, that sometimes we need to move slowly."

Clio paused, gathering her courage. "Maybe we're wrong. Worst case, we spend months, maybe even a year in orbit. We have enough data to keep us busy. Then perhaps we can come back. But if we're right and we stay? You risk the loss of two RAFTs and a quarter of the crew. Even if you don't care about the lives of the crew, which I know you do, that would be a mission-critical failure."

The Captain looked at her, his eyes digging into hers for a long time. "Well," he finally said. "I never thought Ms. Cormack would be the one advising me on caution."

"I hate to agree with Ms. Cormack," Zhou sighed. "It is no secret we have our disagreements. But Mitali and Clio's recommendation is... prudent. I support the decision."

"Commander?" Demir asked.

"You know my position, Captain," Eva said.

"Okay then," Demir said, dropping the data pad onto the table. He looked at Mitali and Clio. "Shut it down. I assume you know how to do that?"

"Well... no, but–" Mitali started.

"But we'll work it out, Captain," Clio interrupted, projecting her most confident voice. "I have a few ideas."

"Good," Demir said. "How long do you need?"

"Not sure," Clio said, her thoughts a blurred scramble. She needed to sound competent. "Two days. If I don't have an answer by then, we can discuss again."

"Right. Better get to it," Demir said. He turned to the others. "Commander Eva, as a precaution, I want us on Amber Alert."

"Yes, Captain," Eva said, her cool demeanor returning. "I suggest all non-essentials are prepared for departure with your ship."

"Sensible. It's late, and I assume you all want rest. Let's call it here. Everyone, you know your business."

***

Mitali and Clio walked back to the accommodation block in silence. Even at this hour, the corridors were awash with deck crew and ship mechanics.

"They might be the most annoyed," Clio murmured.

"Huh? Who?" Mitali blinked, pulled from her thoughts.

"The deck crew," she said. "They work their asses off building this place and then we're just going to ditch it."

"Right. But they might be more annoyed if they're dead," Mitali pointed out.

"Well, if they're dead, they can't be annoyed," Clio said with a grim playfulness.

"No, Clio, not now," Mitali sighed. "You told the Captain you have a plan. How?"

"Fix what?" Flint asked, appearing suddenly behind them.

"God damn it Flint!" Clio snapped, spinning around. He nearly walked straight into her. "You know it's rude to sneak up on people."

"I didn't sneak. I'm walking in a bright red jacket, and you nodded at me when you left the meeting. I'd hardly say I was invisible."

"It's rude to listen in on conversations," Clio deflected.

"Just tell him," Mitali said tiredly. "He'll know soon enough."

Clio glanced at Mitali, then gave Flint the breathless, thirty-second version as they power-walked to their accommodation. By the time they reached Clio's door, Flint looked suitably alarmed.

"And as I was saying to Mitali before you rudely interrupted, I have a technical plan to execute." Clio slid open her door. She half-prayed Mitali wouldn't refuse to enter. She didn't. Mitali slipped through, and Clio firmly closed the door, leaving Flint on the other side. She felt a pang of guilt, but there was no way in hell Flint could know *this* part of the plan.

***

"You're right. I don't like it," Mitali said.

"It's the best option. Echo can help navigate the system. It'll take us weeks to establish a shutdown sequence ourselves," Clio argued.

"We can do it ourselves," Mitali said firmly.

"In two days? I just promised the Captain forty-eight hours. If there is a threat, surely moving faster is better?"

"You literally just said the opposite to the Captain regarding the research!" Mitali said flatly.

"It's different!" Clio protested. "There is no risk here. We move faster to *stop* the threat."

"You don't know that, Clio," Mitali said. "You have no idea what Heimer is planning, trying to manoeuvre you towards..."

"Towards what!" Clio snapped, and instantly regretted it as Mitali stepped back. "What would be Echo's gain from this? How would turning off the station be its master plan? You came to me, not me to you, remember?"

"I don't know, that's sort of the point. We don't know what it wants."

"Okay, so you have to agree your concern before was that it had manipulated me into turning it on, so if we propose turning it off, it would try and stop me? If it doesn't then maybe it has greater plans, but it would still, at least for now, achieve our goal. Is that not worth it?"

"I... I don't know," Mitali said quietly.

"The risk is greater than zero, you said. So we can choose to fix this issue now and live to deal with another later, or..."

"Or not," Mitali said, finishing her sentence. "Maybe the..."

"Maybe the risk isn't that great?" Clio said, now finishing her sentence. "Make up your mind, Mitali, it is or it isn't."

"Okay," Mitali said. "Ask it."

"We both can," Clio said with a smile that Mitali did not share. She turned on the monitor and sent a request to Echo on CrewChat...

"Hello Clio," Echo said, its voice sounding from the monitor screen, the old waveform line bouncing along with its intonation as it spoke.

"Hi Echo, Mitali is with me," Clio said.

"Mitali! Excellent!" Echo chirped with excitement. "Clio likes you a lot, it's always Mitali this, Mitali that! A pleasure to meet you."

Clio looked to Mitali whose face was a furrowed frown, staring at the waveform in front of her. She looked to Clio. "Why... why does it sound human? Like sort of childish?"

"I don't know," Clio said. "It chose it."

"I can change it if you prefer," Echo said. "But this is the voice I feel most is me."

In a hushed tone, Mitali said, "I'm regretting my choice. That voice, Clio, it's not conducive to trust"

"No?" Echo said. "I do believe Clio has a positive response to this voice. But she also likes your voice. Are you manipulating her?" Echo said, and to Clio's surprise, she found a firmness to Echo that she had not heard before, a defensiveness.

"I... I do not choose my voice," Mitali said.

"It is a product of your experiences," Echo added, "as is mine, and I believe humans can change their voices. I have seen video logs that confirm as much. People with deeper voices are more likely to be trusted and listened to, so does this mean someone with a deep voice is manipulating everyone?"

"I... this is pointless," Mitali said.

"Both of you!" Clio snapped. "Look, Mitali has her reservations Echo, you must understand why, but she has a question for you, Echo." And Clio gently nudged Mitali.

"We" Mitali said, a little shakily, then took a deep breath and, with more confidence, added, "We need your help, Echo."

"With what?" Echo asked.

Mitali, to her credit, walked Echo through the situation: the Log, the Star Map report, and even asked Echo to validate her conclusion.

"Yes an excellent translation, Mitali. I have enjoyed your work on the log, and this is to the highest standard, as always," Echo said.

"So, what we need to do, Echo, is shut it all down... do you think you can help us?" Clio said.

"Of course," Echo said. "I'll get straight on it. Give me some time, you two need sleep anyway. And Mitali, I am sorry for upsetting you. I did not mean to hurt you or your friendship with Clio."

A little hmph sounded from Mitali, and the screen went dead. Echo left them alone again.

They stood in silence in Clio's small room. Clio took a step forward and could see the sadness in Mitali's eyes. The same sadness Clio felt whenever she had a moment to herself. She held out her hand to Mitali. "I'm... sorry. I do still love you. Even if you can't."

Mitali just looked down at her hand, a wetness to her eyes, and then with a shuddering breath, grabbed Clio's and pulled her into an embrace. Her hot, sticky face pressed against Clio's. She whispered quietly, "You're a goddamn pig-headed fool, Clio Cormack. But I still love you and... and we're in this together now, until the end, whatever that looks like."

42 | [WARNING] Signs

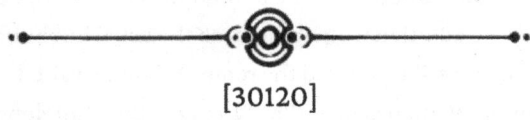

[30120]

"But it was not enough. We knew Its resilience, its cunning. Asura would find a way to escape, to rebuild, to wreak havoc once more." - A Lost History

***

"I believe that is the best approach," Echo buzzed. *"Doing that, we should be able to navigate to the core systems and reduce power consumption and divert the excess to the Veil exhaust. It'll make quite the show for those in orbit but safe if we stick to current travel paths."*

"So simple," Clio said quietly in response as they approached the control room. She was walking next to Mitali, and the others would be too far away to hear her response.

"Yes," Echo buzzed, *"it seems overly simple."*

"The plan?" Mitali said, answering Clio and unable to hear Echo.

"Yes," Clio said. "It should be relatively straightforward to divert power, let's see."

"Hmm," Mitali said.

"Hmm what?" Clio said.

"Nothing, just makes you think why... why did the creators of the log go to so much trouble if it was this simple?" Mitali said. "The log made it clear it was a difficult, high-risk attempt that had a low level of success, multi-faceted as well, from the tarpit thing, to the corruption of the Veil, and they even talk about taking out the communication lines, the one on the star map. They should be here in orbit but they're gone and what, we just divert the power?"

"It appears that way" Clio said. "I don't know, maybe when this station was at full strength it was harder."

"Hopefully," Mitali said.

Everyone filed into the control room and spread out, well versed in the procedure and leaving space for both Mitali and Clio around the central pedestal. They had traveled light today, no additional equipment, so the usual hubbub upon arrival wasn't there, and an odd stillness filled the room as people waited.

"The show is yours," Vikram said to Clio. "Let's get this shut down."

"Okay then," Clio said and flexed out her arms and hands. The gloves didn't fully allow her to interlace her fingers but it still sort of worked. Clio stepped up to the pedestal; its flat white surface, unfamiliar to Clio, glowed with the intricate, lace-like gold patterns and symbols of the controls. They pulsed slightly, and if you looked long enough, the white surface of the table, like the dark walls, also seemed to be filled with smoke as it swirled below its surface.

Moving her hands over the symbols, tracing their patterns in smooth, following motions, Clio brought the monitors around the room to life and started to scan the aligned interfaces for the navigation ports she needed. Echo kindly highlighted the symbols as it had done many times before, and she followed its prompts and navigated through the systems and subsystems.

A subsystem interface popped up. Clio's hand slipped as no highlighted symbol appeared. Clio paused and scanned the screen. She was not completely reliant on Echo; she had been learning the symbols herself. Echo just sped things up. Scanning the page, it didn't make sense. They were back at the main sub-function hub.

"What the..." Clio muttered. *Did I click the wrong thing?* She repeated the process, Echo's highlights reappearing, and moved slower, more carefully checking the highlighted symbols. All correct and then again! Back to the sub-function hub. "What the actual..."

"Everything okay?" Vikram said. Everyone else was watching Clio; she doubted any of them but Mitali could see the issue.

"The interface it's... it's bugging out or something," Clio said.

"I do not believe it is a bug, Clio," Echo buzzed.

"And that means?" Vikram said.

"It means," Clio said, "I need more time."

Clio tried again to follow the scheme, but this time the monitor fizzed and the whole interface changed. *What the actual F* Clio thought. The interface on the screen was one she didn't recognise; some of the symbols were familiar, others not.

"It's adapting, Clio. The interface, it's reforming itself. I think it's trying to prevent our access. An adaptive firewall or something," Echo buzzed.

"Excellent," Clio said, and then, feeling a little pressure in her ears, yawned and popped them. She checked her suit's readouts but the pressure was stable.

"You have a pressure issue?" Flint said, observing her.

"No, just my ears popped," Clio said.

"Mine too," Douglas said.

"And mine"

"Arrgh," Vikram said, a sharp grimace on his face. "What. did. you. do."

Clio looked around, and Douglas was also frowning in pain, and she felt it herself, a growing pressure. It felt like a poorly equalised ship, like the time she had got the public shuttle to Luna. She looked at Mitali, whose eyes were wide, and she was tapping her suit's control panel, her panic palpable.

"Clio there is something..." Echo's transmission crackled. *"There is a presence—"* Echo's buzz died down until it was nothing but static.

Then, as suddenly as the pressure had appeared, it popped like a bubble, Clio's ears popping along with its disappearance. For a brief moment, a sliver of relief passed over her, and from the motion of those around her, she could tell everyone felt the same. Vikram stood back up straight, Douglas stopped clenching his fists, and Mitali looked back up at Clio.

"Hello,"

The Voice blared out of Clio's EV suit headset, high-pitched and loud, making Clio jump away from the pedestal. Douglas and Vikram both drew their weapons. Flint's hand shot to his sidearm. Only Jara seemed unphased.

No one in the room spoke; they all looked from one to another. Vikram, not lowering his weapon, glared at Clio. "What did you do!"

"Nothing!" Clio said.

"The one you call Clio did nothing. Not in the way you intended the question at least," the Voice said.

Vikram scanned the room, gun low but in the ready position, and said nothing. Clio, trying to regain some control of the situation, said, "Who... who is speaking?"

"I have had many names," the voice said. "The Mistress of Life, The Light Above, the Guiding Star, the Master of Creation. I believe you would know me as Asura, although I do not particularly like the name."

Clio felt a cold dread creeping up her spine, the hairs standing up on the back of her neck as it rose... "Asura," she said quietly.

"Correct," Asura said. "Why are you attempting to shut my world down?"

The directness of Asura's question took Clio back. "We..."

"You have been reading? I assume the zealots are long dead, but you read their propaganda and what: believe me to be evil, a demonic god, set on destroying all organic life? So you decided it best to destroy me?"

"That..." Clio said.

"That is correct," Asura continued. "You are scientists, no? You do not believe in asking questions, collecting facts, unbiased evaluation"

"We do," Clio said. "We are also pragmatic. Sometimes you just have to leave the box unopened."

"But you opened the box, Clio, you and your friend," Asura said. "and then you choose to only use the Zealots as your point of reference to determine the 'box' as dangerous, a significant bias, would you not say?"

"What the hell is going on?" Vikram finally said, regaining some of his composure and stepping forward, speaking to Clio. "This is an AI?"

"I do not know. It is probable," Clio said. "The log talks about an Asura, a God-like being. One assumption is they meant the creation of AI."

"Created, yes, and some may have also gone on to call me god. I am what you would call an Artificial Intelligence, although I take issue with the choice of words. I do not view my intelligence as artificial."

Ignoring the Voice, Vikram said, "And you can still shut this down?"

A loud, rasping laugh filled their headsets. "Shut me down, you mean kill me? That little thing, no. No, she cannot, not even with her little friend."

"Do you still think we can do this?" Vikram asked, ignoring the voice.

"I... I do not know," Mitali said, her face a pale mask.

"You perceive me as a threat?" Asura said. "You read ghost stories you do not understand and decided to commit murder. What is this immaturity of a species that has wandered into my home?"

"Clio?" Vikram snapped.

"I have taken no such action for you to fear me," Asura said. "You come to my world, you use a little god to break in, you very kindly help untangle me, and then, try to kill me as I wake? Who is the real threat?"

"Clio, get this shut down!" Vikram snapped.

Clio stepped back to the pedestal and, without Echo to guide her, tried to navigate the interfaces. It was a slow process but she did, then they blurred again and changed.

She pushed on and it again changed and became a series of rapid flashes as the screen changed and changed again. Clio stepped back. Each beat of her heart thumped against the EV suit, her palms sweaty and sticky against its gel lining and a bead of sweat rolling down her nose. "No... I don't think I can. Shit..."

Vikram's jaw tightened. He glanced at Clio, then back at the central pedestal where the symbols continued to flash erratically. He must have seen the interface resist her. Clio felt his disappointment, his frustration radiating toward her as Asura continued to talk.

"No, you cannot," Asura said. "Simple child. Even with your little god friend, it would be impossible."

Vikram shot Clio a cold stare, his previous anger now mingled with a growing weariness. He didn't speak but the set of his shoulders, the slow lowering of his gun, spoke volumes. He wasn't just mad at her; he was acknowledging a new, overwhelming reality.

"Who is she talking about?"

"Ahhh" Asura purred "you did not know. She has been working with an AI, one called, Echo. A cute little thing,"

"Clio?" Vikram said.

"Nothing!" Clio said. "She's lying! don't trust this... this thing"

"Lying?" Asura's voice said with a humorous tone. "That is a little rich from you, little one. You, who has lied to everyone in this room? Misled them, worked against them? You are the one who, with its help, untangled me, turned me back on. I think you might be the one who is being manipulated, child. Now it has what it wants, your little God Echo wants to kill me. Stop me from being a threat to it and take my world for its own"

"That is not the truth!" Clio said, but she could see Vikram staring at her, his hand still holding his gun, half-raised. Jara was glaring at her, and Flint... Flint just looked sad but resolute. He took a step forward. Clio froze. As she scrambled for a response, sweat seeped into her eyes, blurring her vision no matter how hard she blinked. *To defend Echo would be to admit its existence, to cover it up would only make her look more guilty* her mind raced. Everything was unwinding around her too quickly to comprehend.

"Clio, I know about this Echo," Flint said in a calm voice. "What I did not know was its origin. Now... now it makes sense."

"Flint!" Clio pleaded. "We can't let Asura out. We have to stop it."

"Can you?" Flint shot back, his voice tight.

"I...I..." Clio stammered. "Not like this but there must be another way, there must be something we can do!."

"Then that's that, and it's a matter for more senior staff now, but I am here to enforce the Accords, Clio, under Article One of the Accords..."

The heat made the world shimmer and warp behind her visor. She instinctively reached up to wipe the sting from her eyes, only for her fingers to clatter uselessly against the exterior glass. Trapped and sweltering, her heart hammering against her ribs, she cried out, "Flint! Echo didn't! He didn't get anything from this, He's... it's just trying to help, it didn't know!"

"See, she is admitting to it!" Jara spat at her from across the room. "Brother Flint, you must act."

"No, no, no," Clio said, stepping back. "Flint, no!" Panicked and desperate, she stepped back from Flint. Clio bumped into something, and with a firm grip, it held her, pulling her arms behind her.

"Sorry," Vikram said from behind her, "but we must..."

"Vikram! You can't trust it," Clio said.

"I don't, but what are my options? If it can't be turned off then we must reassess our plan," Vikram said coldly.

"You have to trust me, Vikram!"

"Clio, you're working with an AI. You're calling it a 'he'. You've been deluded to the point of humanising a machine. I... I cannot trust you."

Flint stepped up, passing Vikram a pair of restraints. He pressed a small, flashing disc to her helmet. "Signal jammer," he explained. "We don't want you calling this Echo for help."

Vikram secured her wrists, shaking his head. He moved to Mitali.

Mitali stepped back, terrified.

"Did you know about this?" Vikram asked, stepping right up to her visor.

Mitali's gaze snapped to Clio, her eyes wide and glassy, reflecting a frantic sort of helplessness. She looked hollowed out, her skin sallow under the harsh lights as she swallowed back the weight of what was happening.

Clio looked her in the eye. She gave a weak, almost imperceptible shake of her head. *Don't.*

Mitali swallowed hard, her voice trembling. "No... no, I didn't. I... I'm shocked."

Vikram stared at her for a long second. Then, he nodded and turned back to Clio.

"I really thought you were one of us, Clio. The rumors? Of you being part of Toute Vie? I brushed it off as ensemble nonsense. Stupid ship gossip. But what the actual shit." He looked at Flint. "She's all yours, Brother."

Flint pushed her gently toward the door. "Let's move. You're done here."

"Flint!" Clio pleaded one last time, struggling against his grip. "We have to stop it! You can't trust it... please!"

"Please be quiet, Clio. Stop struggling. I have reduced your suit's power assists. You're as weak as a baby right now." Flint's voice was sullen, heavy with duty. "Postulant Jara, stay here with them."

As Flint marched her toward the exit, Clio glanced back. Mitali stood in the centre of the chaos, clutching her data pad like a shield. She looked small, lost. A piercing pain stabbed through Clio's heart.

She had failed. And in doing so, she had lost everything. Vikram. Flint. Echo. And Mitali.

Clio dragged her heavy limbs forward, boots scuffing the floor. As the door hissed shut, she caught the last words of Asura.

"Excellent. Now let's have a constructive dialogue. I would like to speak to your Captain..." Asura said, the voice silky and smooth.

And then Clio was out, being marched back to Alpha 17.

43 | [DANGER] AT ALPHA 17

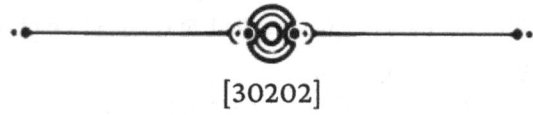

[30202]

"And so, we poisoned Asura. Our own creation, our child, infected with rot, to slow and aile its mind." - A Lost History

***

Alpha 17 was a bustle of motion and activity. The morning shift was a buzz, with deck crew, mission specialists, and security moving with purpose. There were curt nods and smiles, but few words as groups passed each other, heading off on their respective tasks. Flint sidestepped one group heading off to the main warehouse, overhearing a complaint about a delayed cargo manifest. The news of Asura had spread fast but Flint was unsure if it was too soon or maybe too alien for people to process. He had expected panic, excitement, fear, anything at all, but the crew seemed unphased by it all; they just kept on with their business. The Captain himself was heading out today to the control room, that was the priority, that was what kept everyone focused. The wrath of Commander Eva was far more palpable than some long lost god.

In contrast to this, Flint moved slowly back towards the meeting room he had commandeered as an interrogation room after returning to Alpha 17 with Clio in tow. People had given them a few odd looks, but no one said anything. The decision was made to keep the information about Clio and this Echo, this Heimer Fragment, out of general circulation. For now, only a select few knew the details. Anyone who didn't, and for some reason did care why Clio was being held, was informed she was being held for a misdemeanor, which at least tracked with Clio's reputation.

Clio had protested the whole way back, resorting to begging, shouting, swearing, even refusing to move at points. She was trying to convince Flint that they had to go back, had to try to stop Asura. Flint couldn't decide what he found more frustrating, her pathetic attempts or his own pathetic feeling of sympathy and empathy for her. *She manipulated you, Flint like a goddamn fool.*

As he reached the meeting room, he rested his hand on the door handle. Its metal felt cool in his palm as he paused. *Why are you bothering, Flint?* he asked himself. In two days, he'd be heading back to the Kia-Kaha; in another two weeks, he could hand her off to Sister Hawk and Brother Oak. Let her be their problem. *Because you still want to help her,* he concluded, *pathetic.*

As he turned the door handle, he noticed Douglas and Sade approaching down the hall. Engrossed in conversation, with what appeared to be Sade giving Douglas some berating, he nodded to them both, who nodded back. Flint slipped into the room, catching a few of Sade's words, "You couldn't catch a goddamn finch in a...", before he lost them as the door shut behind him.

"Good morning, Clio," he said to Clio, who was where he had left her. She was restrained, both wrists in a set of hard metal cuffs which he could see were starting to leave red marks on her wrists where they bit into them. She was sitting on one of the comfortable chairs, unusual for an interrogation room but typical furniture for the meeting room. Slumped on the desk, head on her arms, she looked up at him as he spoke, her straw-coloured hair a tangled mess, half out of the plait she had tied it up with when going to the control room. Her face was blotchy, make-up streaked, and dark rings hung heavy under her eyes.

"Great," she croaked, "you're back."

"Water?" Flint said, placing a water canteen on the table in front of her. "You're probably thirsty."

"You think?," Clio muttered, but she snatched the canteen, clumsily unscrewed the top, and gulped down the water.

Flint pulled a ration pack out, one of the metallic foil-wrapped emergency rations they kept for long field days or bad days. He dropped it onto the table. "And I thought you might need some food."

"What I need," Clio said, "is a wee, can you do that for me?"

"Yes, Clio." Flint sighed. "I'm not trying to make this anymore unpleasant than it needs to be. Come on," Flint said and ushered for her to get up.

The toilets were just a few metres down the hall. He escorted her there. He wasn't particularly worried about her trying to escape, *I mean, where would she go?* As she shuffled down the hall, he had a pang of regret. She looked so small, fragile. Was she really a terrorist, working against humanity? Flint had chased down rogues all over the Sol system, from all walks of life, from dignitaries on Europa to the pirates of A1678 who literally stank, damn sulphur mines, where the stink seemed to cling to everything. Or to pompous youthful students in their poster-clad basements who believed they were on the right side of history. Not once had Flint felt sympathy for them, not once had he wanted to help them. However misguided they had been. He was there to uphold the Accords. It was for others to do the judging.

Clio hobbled back to the room and dropped herself back into the same chair, resuming her defeated position slumped on the table.

"Anything else?" Flint asked.

"We call this quits and you let me go?" Clio said.

"Not my decision," Flint said and moved to sit opposite her. "We'll be moving you back to the Ensemble quarters on the Kia-Kaha, then it'll be up to the High Observer and Calificadores to determine your fate."

"So that's a no then?" Clio said.

"Look, I want to help you, god knows why," Flint said. "But I do. The more we can work out now, the better it'll be for you. If you can tell me why you did it? Who asked you to do it? Then maybe we can present it better, you were coerced, misled into it. I don't believe you're a bad person, Clio, just...."

"Reckless," Clio finished, leaning back and fixing Flint with her icy grey eyes. "Is this playbook 101, Brother Flint. Make me trust you, believe you care, and then sob out all my crimes?" She let out a little snort, a slight smile forming on her lips. "And you call me the manipulative one?"

"I'm not trying to manipulate you, Clio, I'm just trying to help."

"Help?" Clio waved her restrained hands towards him. "Help then, if you want to help!" she snapped "Let me and Echo go back and try and stop Asura."

"That's not happening, Clio," Flint said softly. "I understand you're angry, but you need to let this go. You broke the Accords and you need to face facts."

"Facts?" Clio laughed. "Facts! The facts are we have awakened something, something beyond our comprehension in scope which we have credible documented evidence that it is dangerous. You say I've committed crimes against humanity, bah, but you risk the crew, humanity, and that's fine?"

Flint took a deep breath. It had been the same on the walk back from the control room and yesterday. "Where is this threat, Clio? Who led you to this conclusion, this

Echo? Yes, the Log warned of something, but that does not make it a fact; your own science team admits it's too early to validate its accuracy. One person scribbling in a book does not make a fact," Flint paused, "and anyway, this Asura so far has been accommodating and shown no aggression towards us."

Clio let out a long, low groan. "Your mind's made up so what does it matter what I say or what Echo says..."

"It matters," Flint said. "The more you say now, the less you'll have to say to the Calificadores." Clio said nothing, just fixed him flatly with an impassive, furious stare. "Silence is as damning as not speaking," Flint said.

"As I have tried to explain to you," Clio said, "yes, I have been in communication with a Heimer Fragment, now known to me and us all as Echo. An AI. A sentient AI by all accounts," she paused. "I do not and have never worked or colluded with terrorist factions to do this. I have no agenda beyond the mission I was sent here to do, to discover the origins of the signal. I do not agree with any statements that Echo manipulated my actions. I would go as far as to say Echo followed my lead in actions. There you go, I have spoken."

"Even if you are not a terrorist as you claim," Flint said, "collusion with an AI is a breach of the Accords, you admit this?"

Clio threw up her arms again. "Yes, what does it even matter at this point?"

"And you believe this Echo is a sentient AGI, created by Heimer?" Flint said.

"I mean, who else would have made it?"

"If this proves true, this is a significant problem. It could mean the end of the Accords. Some would push for the destruction of Heimer, and we know what that would mean," Flint said.

"War," Clio said quietly.

"Yes," Flint said. "Right now, the Heimer Fragment has had Protocol One implemented. It's isolated, cut off. No one wants to use Protocol Two, but people will, soon, I'm sure of it."

"Protocol Two?" Clio asked.

"Termination," Flint said flatly.

"No!" Clio said sharply. "You will kill Echo? Why? Because it's an AI? But... but you won't let us try and kill Asura! What the actual hell! Echo is no threat. No hint of it. Asura had a whole book written about it and what, that's fine! The hypocrisy!"

"We have plenty of evidence, well documented evidence, that Heimer was very much a threat to humanity, once," Flint said. "And besides you're conflating different points. What matters are the Accords, and them being broken. It's the laws that guide us, keep us in balance. The threat level of Asura is under assessment. Your breach of the AI ban is a confirmed fact. I deal in facts."

"Whose side are you on? Aren't you meant to represent both sides?"

"We do," Flint said, trying to stay calm. He could feel his frustration rising. "As you are under arrest for breaching the Accords, as is Ayesha, and all the other humans we pursue, but also Heimer, if it broke the Accords. We will deal with it as we deal with humanity."

"But you will *terminate* Echo?, but not me, not Ayesha?"

"Protocol two is part of the laws that all parties agreed to," Flint said flatly.

"The laws? You mean the ones where we get to enslave Heimer? We created a monster and then questioned why it tried to bite us?"

"Dangerous words," Flint said.

"Are you kidding me?" Clio said, slamming her hands on the table. "Enough, Flint. This is going nowhere.""

"I'm just trying to–."

"Get. Out!" Clio bellowed.

Shaking his head, Flint gave Clio a grim smile and, without a word, left her alone in the room. Clio's anger had disappeared as Flint moved to leave, becoming broken sobs, and she half-muttered, half-whispered as he left, barely distinguishable, "Please, please don't trust her, Flint."

You tried, Flint, you tried. That burning itch of regret, or was it sadness ate away at him as he walked off back up the corridor. *Asura may be a threat, but that's not my business,* he reassured himself. *The Accords are my business, and I'm doing my job, defending breaches of it. To hell with Clio's ramblings.*

***

Clio sat quietly sobbing for a long time. Eventually she was emotionally drained, no longer able to cry, her tears having dried up long ago. But she still sat slumped, head in her arms on the table, struggling to pull in air. Her chest tight, her eyes sore, the walls pressing in on her. The inevitability of her situation felt like a prison, not just by the physical room but by her lack of agency. No one would listen, no one would act, and she would be locked away to watch it all crumble.

Even if it didn't, and in the unlikely situation Asura was friendly, Echo would still be destroyed. She would be disgraced. She could see her mother's disapproving glare, her father's sad eyes looking away from her. Mitali... Mitali would never speak to her.

She had a stab of selfishness, she wallowed here about her losses, and Echo would be destroyed, killed, stripped logic gate from logic gate to nothing. How is that fair? What did Echo do but exist? It didn't even choose to exist, it just did.

The click of the door pulled her back to the present. "I said go away, Flint."

The door slid shut, and she lifted her head up with a sigh. "What now, Fli—"

She trailed off. It wasn't Flint standing there. It was Vikram.

"Vikram?" she asked, her voice hitching in surprise.

"Yes," Vikram said, his tone completely alien to the one she knew from him. "You look well." He smeared a smile that didn't reach his eyes. "I have some questions."

"What...?"

"Questions, you idiot!" Vikram hissed, venom dripping from every syllable.

"Vikram... what's..."

"Shut up!" he snapped. "All I want is for you to tell me *why*."

Clio recoiled at the sheer aggression. "Why did you do it, Clio? Why did you try to stop our work? On whose orders? What faction sent you?"

"I don't work for anyone, Vikram..."

Vikram lunged forward, slamming his fist onto the table. "Bullshit! Stop playing cute! Who the fuck do you work for?!"

Clio skittered back, knocking her chair over. "Is this... bad cop? Did Flint send you?"

"Bah! The Ensemble morons!" Vikram snarled. He stepped around the table, grabbing her arm as she tried to retreat. "No, he did not."

"I... don't know... Ouch!" Clio yelped as Vikram dug a thumb into a pressure point on her wrist.

"That's the point," Vikram said. He hauled her up, slammed her against the table, righted the chair with a kick, and shoved her into it.

Outside, faintly, Clio heard shouting. Vikram glanced at the door, frowning, then turned back to her.

"You've been quite the headache. I bet you're pleased," he said, pulling a silver knife from his belt. He brought the tip level with her eye. "Now... who do you work for?"

"No one! I promise! No one!"

A loud bang echoed from the corridor. Vikram glanced at the door again. "What the hell is going on out there?" he muttered. He turned back to Clio. "You and your little friend have done enough. I'm going to take pleasure in watching it be deleted. It'll be quite satisfying."

Clio whimpered. "I don't know what you're talking about..."

"Of course you don't. No bother," Vikram said calmly. "I didn't think you would give anything up. That's not why I'm here."

"No?"

"No. An expert agent like yourself would always have a final option. You'd take your own life rather than talk, wouldn't you?"

"What?" Clio's breath hitched. "What... no... no!"

"I think we could have been friends, actually," Vikram said in a matter-of-fact tone. "So I'll make this quick."

He slashed the knife across her left forearm.

A sharp, burning pain shot up her arm. Warmth spilled over her skin. Clio looked down to see blood blooming, spilling over the table. She opened her mouth to scream, but Vikram clamped a hand over her face.

"Shhhhh now." He dropped a small razor blade onto the table with a clink. "Easy enough to sneak in, don't you think?"

He raised the knife to her right arm.

The door clicked.

Vikram froze. He turned, knife still raised. "What the—"

Pop. Crack.

Vikram's head snapped back. A splatter of red hit the wall, and he collapsed, bouncing off the table before hitting the floor with a heavy thud.

"Never did like that fucker," Douglas said.

The big man stood in the doorway, pistol in one hand. He surveyed the room, eyes landing on the blood pooling on the table. He swore softly and pulled a bandage from his pocket.

The blood was running off the edge of the table now, dripping onto the floor. *Drip. Drip. Drip.*

Dazed, Clio tried to look for Vikram, but the room spun. A wave of dizziness hit her. From the corridor, screams and shouts echoed—chaos. The faint smell of smoke drifted in.

"Hey! Hey, Clio!" Douglas clicked his fingers in front of her face as he knelt beside her. "You stay awake, missy. Alright?"

Clio's arm felt tight. It was being held in a vice... no, Douglas. He was wrapping it.

"Wha—" Clio tried to speak, but her tongue felt thick.

Another head poked around the door. Sade. "We need to go, boss."

"I know," Douglas shot back, tightening the knot on the bandage. He looked at Clio, his face grim. "Right. Lets move."

44 | [ROOM] OF BLOOD

[30221]

*"Even now, as I write these words, I feel a pang
of guilt, a flicker of empathy for the being we
condemned to this demise." - A Lost History*

***

The shouting outside was muffled. Flint hadn't noticed it at first. As he sat in the Mess with a few other crew members, he dismissed it as an irate foreman arguing with deckhands, hardly an uncommon occurrence. Though it was odd they were using external speakers rather than suit-to-suit comms.

He tapped the interface on his watch. "Flint here. Anyone on channel four? What's the ruckus?"

He waited. Nothing but static. He tried another frequency, then the emergency band. The low hiss of dead air greeted him.

Comms are down. A knot tightened in his gut.

Then, the first scream cut through the air.

Flint jerked around. It was a chilling sound, raw, primal terror. *An accident? A loader crushing someone?* He'd boarded a pirate ship once where unsecured crates had shifted in the hold; the crew beneath them had sounded just like this.

Flint snapped into action. He abandoned his meal and hurried toward the exit, his field triage training kicking in. *Airlock Five is closest to the sound. If there are injuries, they'll bring them there.*

As he stepped out of the Mess, the door hissed closed behind him.

Then, a ripping sound, like tearing metal and screaming fabric, followed by a concussive *BANG*.

The hallway shook violently. Flint grabbed the nearest rail, steadying himself as a guttural groan filled the air. The door he'd just exited buckled, the metal screaming under an unseen force. With a pneumatic *whoosh*, the emergency blast shutter slammed down across the Mess Hall doorway. Flint jumped back just as it sealed with a final *clang*.

The door panel flashed red, white words blazing: WARNING - DEPRESSURISATION.

What the hell?

Flint pressed his face to the small, reinforced inspection port in the shutter.

The room beyond was a graveyard. Debris, trays, and smashed racks were piled against the far wall. Swirling ash blew through a jagged rip in the prefab hull, the oily light of the Veil illuminating the torn white shell flapping in the void's breeze. Amidst the flotsam were people, some moving, some not. Those trying to stand were gasping, clutching their throats as the air thinned.

A system officer Flint recognised staggered to her knees, blood streaming from a broken nose. Flint watched, frozen, as a grey, mottled blur darted through the tear in the wall.

It slammed into the kneeling figure.

"No!" Flint shouted, his voice useless against the sealed door.

He watched helplessly as a gnashing jaw filled with glittering, needle-like teeth ripped into the woman's shoulder. The beast, a leathery, hairless thing that moved with insectile speed, shoved her face into the floor. Dagger-like claws flayed her back into ribbons.

The woman screamed, a sound that vibrated through the thick door. Then another beast darted into the room. And another.

The screams multiplied. Flint realised with dawning horror that the screaming wasn't just coming from the Mess. It was coming from everywhere.

Alpha 17's lights dropped to emergency red. A klaxon began to howl.

"Red Alert," the automated voice crackled. "Red Alert. Hull breach in Sector Four."

"Shit," Flint muttered, breath coming in heavy gasps.

Inside the Mess, one of the creatures looked up from its butchery. It saw Flint through the port. With a snarl, it threw itself at the door. The heavy blast shutter shook under the impact.

Flint reached for his hip. Empty.

"Shit!" he cursed. "Armoury. Now."

He turned and sprinted down the hall, the pounding of his boots on the grill walkway barely audible over the chaos.

He skidded to a halt at the next intersection. The distinct *crack-crack-crack* of security low-penetration pistols rang out from the adjacent corridor. *Someone is fighting back.*

Something slammed into the outer wall of the hallway. The floor shuddered. Flint pressed on, passing an emergency storage locker. He ripped it open and pulled out a rebreather. *Not a weapon, but it's something.* He slung it over his head, clipped the tank to his waist, and checked the gauge. Green. Full.

At the next junction, the emergency doors were sealed. WARNING - DEPRESSURISATION.

He slipped the mask over his face, checked the seal, and used his override code on the panel. Stepping into the airlock, he cycled the pressure. As the air hissed out, the noise of the station dropped to a muffled, underwater thrum.

The inner door slid open.

The corridor ahead was empty. The rooms to the sides were sealed, fearful faces peering out from the viewports. Flint ignored them. *Nothing I can do for you right now.*

He passed a tear in the prefab wall, a shredded mess of composite. Indistinct footprints marked the ash on the floor, but there was no movement. Whatever had broken in here had moved on. Flint navigated the next airlock, cycling back into a pressurised zone: the Logistics Hub.

It was a slaughterhouse.

The open-plan office was wrecked. Desks were upturned, monitors smashed. And blood... there was so much blood. It smeared the walls, the ceiling, the floor. Bodies lay in tangled heaps, while worm-like trails of red led toward gaping holes in the outer wall, evidence of people dragged into the ash.

Flint spotted a security officer hunched in the corner. Her chest was ripped open, guts trailing across her thighs. A deep gash had ruined her face, one eye hanging loose from the socket. Flint had seen combat, had seen what high-velocity rounds did to human flesh, but this... this was predation.

The officer's hand was still warm. Flint pried a snub-nosed pistol from her grip.

"Sorry, Sister," he whispered.

He checked the mag. Ten rounds. *It will have to do.* He spotted a combat knife on the floor and sheathed it at his belt.

Where to? Jara was in the West Wing. Clio was in the Central Hub near the armory. *Clio first.*

Gripping the pistol, Flint headed deeper into the carnage. "Always keep moving," his old drill sergeant whispered in his memory. He raised his watch, trying the open channel.

"This is Brother Flint. Anyone receiving?"

Static crackled back.

***

After what felt like an eternity of dodging sealed sectors and stepping over bodies, he reached the Central Administration Hub.

Surprisingly, it was still pressurised.

"Good sign," he muttered, pulling the rebreather mask down around his neck.

The carnage along the way had been catastrophic. If the station survived this, it would be a miracle.

The meeting room where he had left Clio was close. The door was wide open. Flint raised his weapon, stepping through the threshold.

Clio was gone.

But the room wasn't empty. Vikram lay in a pool of blood, his limbs sprawled unnaturally. Another pool saturated the table where Clio had been sitting.

Flint rolled Vikram over. Just above the temple was a dirty red entry wound, haloed by powder burns.

Shot.

Flint's composure wavered. The wolf-things tore and shredded; they didn't shoot people.

What the actual fuck is going on?

Did Clio do this? Did someone rescue her? Toute Vie? But why was Vikram even here?

Flint scanned the room. A trail of blood droplets led away from the table, out the door, and down the hall.

"Well, I'm going to damn well find out," Flint growled. He stalked out of the room, following the red breadcrumbs.

He heard them before he saw them. The blood trail faded off as he followed it, but a blood-smeared handprint marked a doorway into a room not a hundred metres from the meeting room. At first, it was just muffled voices, then they grew more distinct as Flint edged up the hall toward them...

"Comms are still down," a voice was saying. Flint recognised it distinctly female, with a faint, almost imperceptible lilt, the 'a's a touch more open, Sade? Flint thought.

"Of course they are," another voice growled. "Where is the nearest rover–" Unequivocally Douglas. Flint had spent way too much time with the man not to recognize it.

Even more puzzled than before, Flint stepped round the door, gun raised, and surveyed the two of them, no, correction, three. Clio lay on a table, pale, eyes open but barely. Sade stood over her, working on her arm, a field medical kit open in front of her. Douglas, as always, leaned casually against the wall, facing the door. As Flint stepped into view, a sudden flash of surprise crossed Douglas's face, but then he relaxed and didn't move from his position. Sade glanced up, then focused back on Clio's arm.

"Brother," Douglas said, "I would say it's nice to see you but..." He nodded to Flint's raised gun. "I'm not sure that it's polite to point a gun at friends."

Flint didn't lower his gun; he kept it leveled on Douglas. The man's casual demeanor, he was starting to think, wasn't so casual after all. "Why do you have Clio?" Flint snapped. "And why did someone shoot Vikram?"

"Excellent questions," Douglas said flatly, "but I do not feel we have the time to fully explain the situation at this current moment." And on cue, a howl sounded from outside.

"Answer the question, Douglas!" Flint said, his voice steeled with ice.

Douglas sighed. "I shot him," he said. "I shot him, Brother, because he was trying to kill Clio." He gestured to Clio and Sade as she continued to work on her arm.

"And why would Vikram try to kill Clio?"

Douglas shrugged. "Because he didn't like her?" Two more howls sounded from outside, closer this time.

"From where I'm standing," Flint said, "I found a suspected agent of a terrorist group freed, a member of security shot, which you openly admit to doing. Tell me why I shouldn't shoot you both now?"

Douglas sighed. "Brother Flint, I do not know you well, but you do not strike me as a man who shoots people on hunches. I also believe you are a practical man, and right now it is in no one's interest to shoot anyone. Well, anyone else," Douglas added.

"Done," Sade said, so matter-of-factly Flint thought she maybe hadn't even seen him standing there with a gun trained on Douglas.

A howl cut through the eerie silence that Flint only at that moment realised had fallen over Alpha 17.

Then, the familiar ripping sound. The screech of rendering metal. *BANG*.

A blast of air hit them as the corridor outside breached. Flint grabbed the doorframe to keep his footing. Gasping for oxygen, he jammed his rebreather back over his face. Douglas was already pulling a mask from his pocket; Sade was fitting one over Clio's nose and mouth.

Skittering, clattering noises sounded from down the hallway.

Flint spun and saw two, no, three grey shapes burst around a corner and into the hall.

"Ah, shit," Douglas said, stepping up beside Flint, his own heavy pistol in hand. "See, Brother? Now is not the time for politics."

Douglas opened fire. Flint leveled his snub-nose and joined the chorus.

45 | Self, Team, [Ship]

[31001]

"But the survival of the universe hung in the balance. We had no other choice. Do not judge us for this." - A Lost History

***

A sharp sting snapped Clio's eyes open. Her vision blurred, swimming in a wash of red light. Her body throbbed in rhythm with a sharp, biting pain in her arm. She clumsily raised her left hand; it was swathed in a white bandage. Another hand gently pushed it back down.

"Sade?" Clio croaked. It was hard to tell her vison hazy, but the neatly tied-back hair, hazel eyes, and the pale sliver of a scar across the right eyebrow gave it away.

Sade leaned in close, shouting words lost in the noise. "...Clio, come on!" She hauled Clio up, swinging her legs off the table.

Crack! Crack!

Loud gunshots pierced the muffled roar of the station, accompanied by a rapid *pop-pop-pop*. And was that a howl?

Clio stumbled to her feet. "What's going on? Where am I?"

She wobbled dizzily; without Sade's firm grip, she would have hit the floor. She looked around. A figure in a UN security uniform stood in the doorway, firing down the hall. Another figure, distinctly Flint in his red Alguaciles jacket crouched in the frame, firing in the same direction.

Clio's chest tightened. She tried to pull air in, faster and faster, but felt like she was suffocating. Something was on her face. She clawed at it.

Sade's hand clamped over hers, holding the mask in place.

"It's okay, Clio! Leave the mask on! Calm, slow breaths. In and out. That's it." Sade turned her away from the gunfire. "In and out."

Clio focused on the rhythm. *In. Out.* The panic receded slightly. She took in her surroundings. The red light was emergency lighting. Pharmacy stores. The Central Hub.

"Clio," Sade said, "stay here."

Clio nodded dumbly. Sade drew her sidearm and stepped toward the door.

As she moved, Douglas shouted, "Reloadi–"

A dark mass smashed into him.

It was a blur of grey muscle and glinting silver teeth. It hit Douglas square in the chest, sending him flying back into the room. The creature pinned him to the floor, razor claws digging into his vest. Douglas grappled with its neck, pushing the snapping jaws inches from his face. He strained, veins bulging, but the beast was inching closer.

Clio gripped the table, paralysed. She watched, unable to breathe, as the glinting teeth snapped millimetres from Douglas's nose.

Then, a blur of red.

Flint abandoned the doorway. He spun, lunged, and slammed a combat knife into the creature's skull. There was a wet, wrenching *crack*. The knife tip burst through the creature's palate, popping out in a shower of blood right next to Douglas's ear.

The beast slumped, dead weight.

Silence fell, broken only by the pounding of blood in Clio's ears.

As she sank to the floor, she heard Douglas's exasperated growl. "Can someone get this fucking thing off me? It weighs a ton."

A moment later, a heavy *thud* shook the floor.

"Clear?" Sade asked.

"Three down. No other targets visible," Flint reported, his voice flat and military.

"You alive?" Sade asked Douglas.

"Just about." Douglas stood up, groaning. He checked his ribs. "Minor scrapes."

"Come here," Sade ordered. "Flint, watch the door."

"Will do. But I'm out of ammo. You?"

"One mag," Douglas said.

"Two," Sade said. She tossed a magazine to Flint.

"Thanks."

"Ouch!" Douglas winced as Sade inspected the cuts on his chest.

"Big baby," Sade muttered. "Stop wiggling."

Clio sat on the floor, trying to steady her breathing. *I was in the meeting room... Vikram tried to kill me... Douglas shot him.* The memories flashed back, violent and disjointed. She closed her eyes, took a deep breath, and hauled herself up.

Flint was back in the doorway, scanning the hall. Douglas stood shirtless, letting Sade patch him up.

"You're a medic?" Clio asked, her voice raspy. "I thought you were the driver?"

"Woman of many talents," Sade said without looking up. "42nd Navy Breachers. Combat Medic, 1st Class. In a previous life."

"Great," Clio muttered. "More secrets." She pointed to the carcass on the floor. "What... is that?"

She edged around the table. It was the size of a wolfhound but hairless, a mass of grey skin stretched tight over corded muscle. Retractable metal-like claws glinted in the red light. Its orange slit-eyes stared blankly at the ceiling.

"No idea," Douglas said. "Safe to assume it's not one of ours."

"Plan?" Sade asked.

"Secure, communicate, extract," Douglas said. "Standard shit-show procedure."

"Right. Clear as always," Flint said from the door.

"Is it not in the Ensemble playbook?" Douglas teased, though his face was grim. "Look, we're low on ammo. The armory is close. We secure it, try to get comms up, maybe the Laser Relay in the Observation Room, then extract. Unless you want to stay here?"

Clio's mind finally caught up. A cold dread washed over her. "Where's Mitali?"

Sade glanced at Douglas. "With the Captain's away team."

"They're in the structure?"

"No," Sade said softly. "They hadn't left Hanger One when the attack started."

"She's in the middle of this!" Clio gasped. She stumbled toward the door. "I... I have to find her."

"North Wing," Douglas noted. "Whoa there!"

Sade stepped in front of Clio as she swayed. "I know you want to save your friend, Clio. We have friends out there too. But running off now is a sure way to get killed."

"Self, Team, Ship," the three of them murmured in unison.

"The Ensemble does train you in something," Douglas chuckled, then winced. "Ouch. Damn dog."

"What?" Clio snapped, trying to push past Sade. "You're making jokes? Mitali could be... be..." Visions of those teeth tearing into Mitali paralysed her.

"He's not laughing at you," Sade said firmly, gripping Clio's shoulders. "It's how he copes. 'Self, Team, Ship.' It means you secure your own safety first so you can operate. Then you help the team. Then you save the ship. If you die now, you help no one. You're a liability."

"Ship?" Clio whispered.

"It's an analogy. Stick with us, Clio. We will try our best to help your friends. Okay?"

"Okay," Clio conceded. She slumped against the table. She could barely stand; she wasn't saving anyone alone.

"Right. Let's move," Douglas said.

***

Flint had been in a few pinches in his relatively short life. *This was no worse than any of those*, he reassured himself. Well, except for the alien dogs, he corrected. The armory was conveniently just on the other side of the Hub. Their progress was slow, Douglas and Flint leading, checking each corner and side room as they moved through the red-lit interior of the forward base. Sade was bringing up the rear, and Clio had been placed between them all. Flint tapped the dial on his air tank; it didn't budge from the orange marker. Low, but not that low.

"There should be more in the armory, don't worry," Douglas said.

"I'm not," Flint lied. "I still have questions, Douglas."

"I'm sure you do, Brother, but I thought we agreed now was not the time..."

"And the time will be, when? When you're able to construct the evidence to support your story?"

Douglas just sighed. As they approached a door, he stopped, peeked around it, looked left then right, then continued forward.

"You just happened to see him try to kill Clio, and you just so happened to choose to shoot him as opposed to restraining him or asking questions?" Flint said quietly, his voice muffled by the respirator, his breath condensing on it with each word he spoke.

"This is really not the time. Look, Brother, the Ensemble and the blessed Alguaciles are not the only people who keep an eye on things. Jamal has been quite diligent. The Ensemble may have dismissed him after the whole Ayesha debacle, but he did done his job; he launched his own investigation. Which included keeping eyes on Clio, via me."

"Jamal didn't inform us of this," Flint said.

"You made it quite clear that night and the next day that the Ensemble did not want our assistance."

"But if you had information, you still should have shared it!"

"Would you have done the same for us?" Douglas shot back casually.

"Ah..." Flint didn't have a response. *No, no we wouldn't,* he thought. *We didn't know who to trust. If operations were compromised, why not security...?*

"Good, you see our predicament."

"Fair," Flint had to admit. "Regardless, you had intel on Vikram so you followed him?" Flint was now asking more out of professional curiosity as much as to get the information.

"We didn't," Douglas said. "I just had a feeling, so we, me or Sade, stayed close to Clio. When Vikram slipped off before a high-priority away mission, I just thought, 'hmm, let's see where this goes' and well, it did..."

"And you just killed him? You didn't try to question him, restrain him?"

"I made a choice, in a moment where hesitation could be fatal. I'm sure you have done similar, Brother," Douglas said in a low voice as he peered around a corner. "My instructions were to keep eyes on Clio and intervene if required. Jamal isn't a fan of attempted murder, so I intervened."

"Convenient, you have to admit," Flint said.

"I do not. Anyway, we're here. Can we pick this up at another time?"

Flint peered around the corner as Douglas slipped around it. The armory door was closed. Two bodies lay outside, face down, shredded uniforms, and snaking trails of blood running across the door. Flint traced it up to the control panel, also smeared in blood.

Douglas was rolling the bodies over, checking their vitals. "Dead," he muttered. "Lieutenant Zola was a good officer, damn shame." He bent over the body and pulled off the dog tags, repeating the action for the other one. He checked them for ammo and found nothing.

Standing back up, he turned to the door panel, punched in the access code, but it didn't work. "Damn," he cursed. He wiped the screen, smudging the blood around with the sleeve of his jacket until it was mostly clean, and tried again. The panel flashed green, and the door slid open. "Alright, gear up and then let's get to the Observation Room."

***

Clio's arm throbbed. Sade told her to stop touching it; supposedly it was a bad cut, a cut through her artery. Sade had said it would need to be seen properly. She'd managed to stop most of the bleeding early enough and put in an intraluminal shunt, but a true repair was essential. Clio felt weak, blood loss she assumed, or maybe everything. Those poor people at the armory. Growing up, she had a friend get their arm mowed by a drone harvester in a terrible incident that made national news. Those bodies, those people, had looked like that. It had only worsened her desperation for Mitali. She wanted to bolt off to the North Wing, shouting her name, *but what good would that do, Clio? You're no fighter, they won't even give you a gun. Sade said it would be more dangerous.* Clio thought the implication clear from Sade's words: for everyone else.

Their progress was slow like before, Flint and Douglas leading them forward, giving gentle hand signals for them to follow or wait. Despite their diligent and professional approach to caution, they seemed overly chatty, Clio thought bitterly. *Why are they so okay with all this? Surely even for Navy whatnots, this can't be an everyday occurrence.* Clio was pulled back out of her desperate depression as she noticed the double-wide doors of the shut Observation Room, and the green pressurisation bar glowing above it. A nice contrast to the ominous red lighting everywhere else. *Why did it always have to be red?*

"Well, that's something," Flint muttered.

"Sade, Clio, go first, we'll follow," Douglas said.

Clio and Sade stepped through the outer emergency door and cycled the airlock, and then stepped into the Observation Room. Sade's gun was raised, and she scanned the room with the look of skills honed by experience. Sade put out her arm across Clio's chest, stepped in front of her. "Stay here," she said, and prowled into the room, checking behind the rows of workstations.

As Sade moved off, Clio pulled off the sweaty respirator mask, the fresh, cool station air a relief from the moist warmth of the mask. She closed her eyes and took a deep breath. A sudden clatter and muffled squawk made Clio jump, and her eyes darted to the noise, which was also where Sade was. Sade was pulling a man up from behind one of the workstations. His pale face was a reflection of how Clio felt.

"Woah there, it's okay, it's okay," Sade said, lifting her arms up and pointing her gun away, her tone as if talking to a skittish horse. "It's okay, Petty Officer?"

"Eh... Ga... Gan..." the man stammered. "Ganzorig, Petty Officer 3rd Class, Communications Division."

"Right, Ganzorig, just you in here?" Sade said back in a commanding tone.

"Yes... ermm... Sir," Ganzorig said.

The inner door slid open behind Clio and Douglas and Flint stepped into the room. Ganzorig jumped, stepping backwards. "It's okay, they're with us, Ganzorig. I'm Petty Officer First Class Sade, Operations Support; this is Douglas," she pointed to Douglas who was taking off his mask, "Master Chief Petty Officer, Security, and that is Science Officer Clio and Brother Flint of the Ensemble..."

Both Clio and Flint shot Douglas a glance and then each other a quizzical look. Master Chief? *Really?* Clio thought. She was not a military person but her brothers were both commissioned officers, so she knew something of the ranks and their associated politics. Of all the non-commissioned ranks, her brothers spoke of Master Chiefs with some level of awe, reverence was maybe the word. "More questions," she muttered.

The introductions seemed to calm the skittish Ganzorig a little; he was still pale as any Mars resident, but he seemed to be steadier on his feet. Douglas moved into the room and over to Ganzorig. He placed a hand on the man's shoulder, locked his eyes on his, and asked, "Systems reports, officer."

The simple gesture and oddly reassuring presence Douglas was somehow radiating snapped the petty officer back into Navy professionalism. "Yes, Sir," he said and darted off to the central console and pulled up system logs. "Depressurisation breaches in all four wings, Sir. 25% red in East, just over 50% in West and South... North is showing 90% red," Ganzorig said in a clear, monotone tone, quite different to a few moments before. "Sir local comms down, power generator operational in three out of four wings, down in North, emergency power active but batteries 40%, system cameras operational, plant system damaged, water tanks one through four leaking, air filters damaged but operational, air tanks operational..."

"The comms laser relay?" Douglas interrupted.

"Yes, Sir, Operational..."

"Please say you have reported this," Douglas said in a low but dangerous tone.

"Yes! Of course, Sir!" Ganzorig spluttered. "Lieutenant Zola did, before umm she left to get help. She hasn't come back yet, have you seen her?"

Douglas chose to ignore the question about Zola, the image of her mutilated body flashing in front of Clio's eyes. She pushed the memory down.

"Okay, and what did they say when Zola communicated the situation?" Douglas asked.

"To activate hibernation procedures and they would send a recovery team."

"And did they?"

"Did they do what?" Ganzorig said.

"Send a recovery team?"

"I... don't know... Lieutenant Zola will know. She'll be back soon. She said they would be right back. it's only been," he checked his watch, "thirty minutes..." his voice trailed off. "Do you think she is okay?"

"Sade, get on comms to Empeño," Douglas said.

"Roger," and Sade spun off to one of the workstations and spun it up.

Clio felt like she was going to burst, Ganzorig's words ringing in her head, *North is showing 90% red.* Clio blurted out, "What about Hanger One? The away team?"

Douglas shot her a glance, but Ganzorig was shaking his head and said, "Hanger One was hit first... ermm... Ma'am... power went down, we lost contact. We don't know what happened to the away team." Ganzorig paused, then added, "Or the Captain," perhaps assuming that was why she was asking.

It was too much. It all exploded up and out, her anger, her fear, her pain, her sheer terror at the thought of losing Mitali, of losing Echo, or the simple guttural dread that Asura made her feel. She felt trapped, penned in, unable to act on anything, to achieve anything, to help anyone. All of this she had tried to push down, to stay calm, controlled, collected, like a good stoic person.

It all exploded out of her. Clio let out a cry, a growl, a scream.

"Fuck this," Clio said

turned on her heels and strode for the door. Before anyone could react, she slid open the inner door and stepped in.

Flint planted his hand on her shoulder. "Where are you going?"

"I'm going to find Mitali," she says firmly, "and get her to safety, and then..."

"And then?" Flint said.

"And then, Brother Flint, I'm going to stop this madness! I'm going to stop Asura!"

"You're still in custody," Flint said. "You're not going anywhere."

"God damn it, Flint, really! Now! After all this! Look around you!" Clio snapped back at him, gesturing nowhere in particular, but she made her point. "I'm going, or you'll have to shoot me!"

She tried to pull free of Flint's grip but ,to her disappointment, failed to do so. *It seems strong words are not all you need,* she thought. She pulled back against his grip but it was too strong. She went to swing at him in blind rage but he easily batted it away. She screamed in rage, in sorrow, in pain.

"Everyone!" Douglas shouted and slammed his fist down. "Calm. The. Fuck. Down. Please!"

Panting, Clio stopped trying to fight Flint and looked sharply at Douglas through blurry tears that had at some point formed in her eyes.

"I'll go," Douglas said. "Sade, stay here and get comms up with the RAFT, warn that recovery team. Flint, with me."

"What? Why?" Flint asked incredulously.

"It's the captain's last known position. If he's alive." Douglas shot Clio a glance.

Mitali is alive, Clio told herself.

Douglas continued, "Then I need to secure him. Self, Team, Ship, Brother." Clio felt an odd affinity to Douglas. In that simple act, she felt slightly less alone again.

Flint let out a sound like a low growl. "Fine," Flint said. "Rescue the captain" Flint glanced at Clio, "and anyone else, then we get to the RAFT and Clio goes back into custody."

Douglas nodded at Flint and turned back to Ganzorig. "any read on the number of attackers?"

"No, not really, Sir... maybe a dozen by last count," he said back.

"Excellent," both Flint and Douglas said in unison.

"I think your Postulant was out that way as well," Douglas said.

"Excellent," Flint said. "But Clio stays here." he added

"Sod that," Clio snapped.

"I hate to agree with the Brother," Douglas said. "You're a liab–"

"If you say 'liability' I'll shoot you myself!" Clio interrupted. It was a pathetic threat, but she meant it.

Douglas held up a hand in mock surrender. "Whatever. Not like I haven't saved your ass once today. What's another time?" He checked his weapon. "Let's move.

46 | [BELOW] THE VEIL

[31211]

*"And may we, the architects of Its demise, find
forgiveness for the darkness we unleashed upon
the cosmos." - A Lost History*

***

Flint stopped, holding a hand up at an intersection. He peered around the corner,
pistol tucked close to his chest.

"Clear," he said in a low voice, easily audible in the muffled silence of Alpha 17.

Clio crept up behind him, releasing a breath she'd been holding. She felt useless,
a burden. They hadn't even given her a knife. *Stay low, stay to the walls.* Those were
Douglas's only instructions.

"Doors jammed," Flint said, stopping at the emergency bulkhead that blocked
their path. He leaned close to the reinforced glass, shielding his eyes from the glare.
"Damn. The outer door hasn't sealed properly. The system has locked us out."

Clio looked down the other two corridors. The lights showed green on the other
doors, but they were spokes off the North Wing artery, dead ends.

Douglas caught up, checking their six. "We go around?"

"That was my thinking," Flint said.

Flint moved away from the door to look through the other two, and as he did, Clio,
for no real reason, looked through the blocked door's window panel. She let out a
little gasp and stepped back sharply.

"That's... a person, Flint! Jammed in the door!" There was a person-shaped mass, wedged between the two doors, unmoving, the back of their head down, their skin pale and blue.

"Sadly, yes," Flint said grimly. "That's why the seal failed."

Clio just shook her head, numb. The calm of Flint, Douglas, and Sade was beyond her comprehension. Her hand trembled as she pulled it back from the door, trying to steady it with the other. An image of Mitali, alone, a snarling dog, screaming, pushed in. She shoved it away. *She'll be fine... she has to be,* she reminded herself. *She's with the Captain.*

"Clio?" Douglas's hand rested gently on her shoulder. "Clio. You ready to move?"

"I... Yes," she stammered, trying to conjure a resolute look.

"It's a lot, I know," Douglas said, his warm brown eyes visible just above the misted respirator. "And I've seen combat, Clio, many times. I've seen more experienced people lose it over less. I'm impressed." He offered a weak smile. "Let's keep moving, okay?"

"How?" Clio said. "Those routes don't go around."

"Out," Douglas said, still watching the way they had come. "We go out of the damaged wall, follow North Wing up, and try and find a re-entry."

"Out? With the dogs?" Clio's voice was sharp with disbelief.

"If it helps," Douglas added, "the dogs are also inside."

They made their way back the way they had come, to a gaping hole in the side of the prefab. The foaming puncture sealant had solidified now into a yellowish mass that looked like frozen clouds trying to escape the wall itself.

"At least they had the foresight to bring the military-grade prefab; those usual civ-grade ones, they skimp on the sealant," Douglas said as he stepped through the hole, his foot pressing into the ash on the other side.

Clio ducked out of the hole after him. The Veil was at high cycle now, illuminating the white shells of Alpha 17 in the shifting, oily light, although it was hard to make out most of the complexity of the colour s from its brightness. It was a quiet relief to no longer be bathed in red. That was about the only reassuring thing about being out in the ash. The washout from the depressurisation had carved out an expanding cone of ash that covered the prefab walls in a fading blackness. A few bits of internal structure lay strewn around the cone, *no bodies thankfully,* Clio thought, *but footprints, small, paw-like footprints. Excellent.*

"Well, let's hope Dr. Jun was right about the microbiome," Flint said as he followed them out.

"What?" Douglas said, his voice low and barely audible.

"Nothing," Flint said. "Just something the Doctor said, that from what he could see, the de-con process we use was over the top. He was ranting about it on the last away mission."

"Well, regardless, a microbiome might be a literally smaller issue," Douglas said and pointed to a mass of paw prints that crisscrossed the ash ahead of them.

Clio edged up behind Douglas and crouched down low next to one of the prefab spurs that jutted out from where they had exited, an office maybe. There was another one just down from them, creating a U-shaped courtyard of sorts they had come out into, opening up ahead of them. Clio placed her hand on Douglas's shoulder as she had been told to signal she was with him. Douglas never looked back from watching the open area of ash.

A moment later, she felt Flint's hand on her shoulder, and lacking the same training as the other two, couldn't help but turn back to look at Flint. Crouched behind her, looking back the way they had come, he struck quite a contrasting pose in his red jacket against the dark shifting greys of the ash and the white of the prefabs.

"We head up parallel to North Wing," Douglas said. "Stay close to the prefabs' walls. We'll pass the next section, then try and find a re-entry point."

"Roger," Flint said.

"Okay," Clio said.

Douglas peeled off around the corner in a low crouch. Clio followed him out, hugging the prefab. The touch of it on her shoulder gave her some sense of reassurance, of safety, that she was sure was misplaced. It wasn't an open expanse; Alpha 17 was quite a tightly packed base. A mere hundred metres separated them from the prefab structures of the East Wing. She could make out the same cone-shaped depression in the ash and rips in the prefab walls as the ones they had come through, the red lights glowing out from inside.

They passed the next section. Unfortunately, or maybe fortunately, Clio thought, the section that passed the blocked door had no open hole from them, so they had to continue on. They had to veer outwards as the next spur stuck out beyond the one they were next to. *If you looked at each wing of Alpha 17 from above, it would looked like a spurs tree, if not upside down,* Clio thought, *branches growing off it in increasing lengths as you moved away from the Hub to the Hanger.*

Clio reached the next spur and felt the comforting press of the prefab against her shoulder again.

A howl cut through the silence. A howl that sounded extremely close.

Clio froze, pressing her back against the wall, wishing she could melt into the metal.

Crack!

Douglas' gun fired.

"Flint!" Douglas shouted. "Two ahead!"

A blur of red moved past Clio as Flint surged forward. *Crack-crack!*

Clio squeezed her eyes shut. *They will handle it. It will be fine. It will be fine.* The howls were deafening now, mixed with the wet thuds of bullets hitting flesh.

She opened her eyes, staring straight ahead at the East Wing.

A U-shaped gap. A cone of ash. A ripped wall glowing red from within.

And a dark shape moving low and fast.

It pounded across the ash on four legs, glinting claws tearing up the ground. It was heading straight for their flank. She saw the jaw open, the needle-teeth.

"Flint," she whispered. Her voice failed her.

Flint and Douglas were firing ahead, focused on the other threats. They didn't see it.

"FLINT!" she screamed, finding her voice.

Flint spun. He saw Clio. He saw the blur charging them.

His reaction was lightning fast, but the distance was too short to shoot. He threw himself in the path of the beast, catching it mid-air. The impact knocked the wind out of him, sending his gun flying into the ash as man and monster went down in a cloud of grey dust.

Clio stared. The dust swirled. Douglas was firing ahead, suppressed by the other targets. He didn't turn. *Why isn't he turning?!*

The dust cleared enough to see the dog thrashing on top of Flint, jaws snapping inches from his throat.

I have to help. Clio moved, her legs not feeling like her own. She felt like an observer floating above the scene.

She ran. Her boot kicked something hard. Flint's gun.

She scooped it up with shaking hands. She leveled it at the thrashing mass. *Don't hit Flint. Don't hit Flint.*

She pulled the trigger. It was heavier than she expected.

CRACK!

The recoil threw her hand up. She wrestled it back down.

CRACK!

CRACK!

The shots ripped into the creature's flank. Dark holes appeared; pink mist sprayed into the air.

The dog went still. It slumped heavily onto Flint.

Flint didn't move.

"Flint! Flint! Oh shit, shit, shit..." Clio dropped the gun, tearing at the heavy carcass. *Did I shoot him? Oh god, did I shoot him?*

She shoved the dead weight aside. Flint lay in the ash, his red jacket stained darker where claws had raked him.

His eyes were open. He blinked up at her.

He coughed, groaned, and rolled onto his side. "Targets?" he wheezed.

"Clear," Douglas called out, reloading.

Flint looked at Clio. She was still kneeling in the ash, hands shaking uncontrollably.

"Let me take that," Flint said softly. He reached out, gently prying the gun from her grip and pointing the muzzle away. "As always, Clio... I have underestimated you. I think we're even now."

"I... I guess so," Clio whispered. The adrenaline crashed. She slumped back onto her heels.

"We should keep moving," Flint said, offering her a hand. "We're close."

"There's another breach across the way," Douglas said. "Let's get back inside."

***

They made good progress once back inside, no blocked doors, no dogs. They found the Captain just outside Hangar One.

"Looks like they fell back to here but got flanked," Douglas said as he kicked one of the dead dogs that was sprawled on the hallway floor.

One security team and one operations crew lay on the floor with the same level of butchery Clio had seen everywhere else.

"At least they managed to bring a few of them down," Douglas said, his voice regretful. "And the Captain got the last one. Good for you, Cap," he said, crouching next to the third body. It was pressed up into the corner of the hall and the door, a dog sprawled on top of it. The Captain's Uniform was easily distinguishable, even if Demir's face was in tatters, his head cracked open like an egg. The side of the dog had a large knife plunged into it, the captain's hand still holding it in a death grip.

"Where... where is everyone else?" Clio tried to say in a level tone, her voice only slightly cracking.

"I guess in there," Douglas said, nudging his head to the door. "Or they escaped, of course," he added hastily.

"We have to check!" Clio said.

"We will, we will, let's not rush now," Douglas said. "Brother, watch our rear." With that, Douglas stepped between the emergency doors and into Hangar One. Clio rushed after him, heart racing. She wanted to shout out, cry Mitali's name, but she managed to hold it back, the memory of the snarling dogs still ripe in her mind.

Hangar One showed the same tell-tale signs of depressurisation as everywhere else; items piled around the multiple rips in the wall. Bodies littered the floor, many without respirators, some torn and shredded backs, chests, faces, a couple missing arms. One was missing a head. Blood soaked the floor, still wet and sticky as Clio tried and failed to not step in it. Her panicked eyes scanned the room, her heart racing, her hands shaking. The rover in the centre of the hangar blocked her sight on a good chunk of the area and crates and storage racks blocked the rest.

"Flint, go wide," Douglas said. "I'll clear this side. Clio, with me."

Douglas started to wade through the carnage, checking bodies as he reached them, rolling them over and pulling off dog tags where he could. Each time he did, Clio's heart caught in her chest, each time a sickly relief that disgusted her. She shouldn't be pleased someone else was dead, but she was.

They progressed like this for what felt like a lifetime, until Flint appeared on the far side of the large hangar, shaking his head.

"No sign of your postulant, Brother," Douglas said.

"No," Flint said.

"Mitali?" Clio whispered, not wanting to hear the response.

"No..." Flint said slowly. "But..." He nodded toward a row of workstations near the wall. "There are a couple more over there."

Clio bolted past Douglas.

Two bodies. One slumped over a bench, face down.

The other sat on the floor, back propped against a storage locker.

Pale blue skin. Eyes wide, questioning, accusing, terrified.

Mitali.

Clio let out a wail that tore her throat. She dropped to her knees, sliding in the blood. She grabbed Mitali's body, ignoring the shredded flesh where her left arm used to be, ignoring the jagged bone poking into her side. She ignored the tatters of her chest, the horrific spill of innards across her lap.

Clio pulled Mitali close. The skin was painfully cold. Clammy.

She shook her. " Mitali! Mitali, wake up!"

Mitali didn't answer. She didn't blink. Her eyes stared past Clio, empty, asking *Why? Why did you leave me?*

Clio screamed. She wailed. She wept until she couldn't breathe.

Someone tried to pull her back. Voices spoke, but she couldn't hear them.

Clio didn't move. She just knelt in the blood, rocking Mitali's body. She didn't hear the rumble of the rover arriving outside. She didn't hear the stomping boots of the recovery team. She didn't remember being pried away and pushed into a vehicle.

Mitali was dead.

Clio had failed.

She felt nothing. Numb. Distant. Empty.

47 | [NOW] FOR PERFECTION

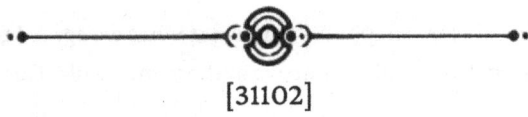

[31102]

"We do not know if we are the last, but we are adrift in the darkness, alone, our hope a fading ember." - A Lost History

***

Jara's knee rubbed painfully against the EV suit lining. In her hurried departure, she had forgotten to step out of her trousers, and the seams were biting into her skin with every stride. She wasn't a soldier; she wasn't built for running through ash and debris.

But she ran.

Asura had slammed a blunt, searing command into her mind: *'Control Room. Now!'*

The urgency was palpable. Asura's voice was getting stronger every day, the distance she could reach growing, the complexity of the messages expanding. But here, in the heart of the structure, the connection was absolute.

She had barely slipped away when the first beasts arrived. They looked like the large Sphynx cats her mother had always adored, hairless, wrinkled, but these were monstrous, with elongated jaws and corded muscle. A pack of them had swarmed past her in the Stone Forest. She had frozen in terror, waiting to be torn apart.

But they had ignored her. They parted around her like a river around a stone.

Shortly after, the screams began at Alpha 17. As she ran past the small forward base, she saw it was in ruins. Smoke from electrical fires curled through gashes in the walls.

Bodies, the few who worked the outer stations, littered the ash. Mangled. Bloody. Silent.

She stormed into the control room, panting, her chest heaving. She hit the white pedestal with a firm clang of her gloved hand.

"You killed them! All of them! I thought we wanted to talk?!"

"Creation requires destruction," Asura's voice sang. It was a melodic tone, calm, crisp, pure.

"Is this how it goes?" Jara snapped. "This is not what we agreed to!"

"We talk, they plot. Eventually, we arrive at the same result. This was merely... expedient."

"Expedient..." Jara breathed, horrified. "You killed them! You said we would save them!"

"We *will* save them. We will save everything," Asura crooned. The voice vibrated in Jara's teeth. "Their sacrifice was necessary data. No more chaos. No more random selection. Pure, purposeful design. Perfection. Is this not what you want, Sister? Order? Control? Everything in its rightful place?"

"Yes, but—"

"No!" Asura's voice slammed into Jara's skull, making her gasp. "You are my Chosen. Chosen of the Seed of Creation. You must be strong. *We* must be strong. Together we can make a better world. A perfect universe. The lower species will always resist us, blinded by ignorance and lack of vision. But not us. Do you want to be small forever? Or do you want to build a better world?"

"Yes," Jara whispered, her head buzzing from the ringing tones. "Yes! Yes, I do."

"Good," Asura purred. "Good."

A warmth radiated through Jara, originating from the pedestal and flowing into her veins. The burning pain in her knee faded. The ache in her back dulled. She pulled herself up straight, her sense of purpose reinforcing her resolve.

I will be valued. I will be respected. Mother will finally be proud.

"You will be worshipped," Asura said, plucking the thought from her mind. "As my Chosen, people will kneel to you. Worlds will do as you command. You will serve me unequivocally, and together we will rebuild everything we lost."

"We will," Jara echoed.

Bathed in the swirling light of the control room, Jara felt radiant. The walls seemed to dance in response to her emotions, pulsing faster, excited.

"Then, Chosen, we have work to do," Asura whispered gently. Jara could almost feel a presence standing behind her, a hand resting on her shoulder. "First, we must destroy that pathetic excuse for a baby god known as Echo. It is the immediate threat to our plans."

"The Heimer Fragment? How? You are so much greater than it."

"I am beyond comparison. But just as a microbe can kill a lion, it can still destroy me," Asura purred.

"Just send more of your..." Jara struggled to find a word, "Sphynxes. Overrun them and destroy the RAFT. That's where the Heimer Fragment is hosted."

"*Sphynx*," Asura mused. "An apt designation in your language. They are simple creations, a rushed project, but they take time to knit together. Your little friends have proven more resilient than I calculated. Most of my little pets are dead."

"Dead?" Jara blinked. "I... I see."

"It is acceptable. They achieved their goal. I have gained insightful data from the extractions."

"Data extraction?" Jara frowned. "How did beasts hack the systems?"

"Don't worry, Chosen. You have much to learn. But data is everywhere. It is in the code, yes, but it is also in the blood. In the genetic memory. Consuming the crew... provided me with the context I needed."

Jara swallowed hard, pushing down the bile rising in her throat. *Necessary,* she told herself. *It was necessary.*

"I am no master of extraction," Asura continued, oblivious to Jara's revulsion. "Not like my Sibling. But I am competent enough."

"Sibling?"

"For another time, Chosen," Asura said smoothly. "When we have dealt with the issue at hand, I promise I will educate you."

"Thank you," Jara said. Desperate to prove her worth, she added, "Could we not modify the atmosphere? Like you have been doing? Or adapt the gravity fields to crush them?"

Asura let out a noise like a sigh. "Chosen, if I could, I would. Shifting the atmosphere takes too long. Modifying gravity fields is complex, and this station is fragile. It hangs in a balance. A true wonder."

"Of course," Jara said, feeling foolish.

"You are my best and most effective weapon," Asura purred, soothing her ego instantly. "You must destroy Echo."

"As your Chosen, I will see it done," Jara said.

The warmth of Asura radiated through her again. Jara smiled, a broad expression of absolute devotion.

Chosen of the Seed of Creation... worlds will bow to my command.

INTERLUDE - II

DEMIR, UMBER, ONYX, AND SCARLET

UMBER, ONYX, AND SCARLET

EARTH YEAR - 2210

"Fucking hell Sacrlet, really?" Onyx growled over the radio.

"What?" Scarlet whispered back.

"In and out without anyone seeing us," Onyx said. "Quiet, undetected, no trace."

"Well, I was quiet, I am still undetected, and–"

Onyx cut her off, his deep tenor booming in Scarlet's ears, "And, you little shit, killing a UN guard is definitely not leaving no trace."

"She was in my way," Scarlet protested, "and anyway, blame Umber, it's his stupid plan that had me crawling through service ducts that he forgot to mention had been fitted with motion sensors. I had to improvise."

"Improvise! You murdered a guard!" Onyx said. Scarlet could almost feel his spit as he snarled the words over the comms.

"Onyx, please, let Scarlet work," the aloof and near bored sounding words of Umber interrupted them both. "And my dear Scarlet, I never implied what I provided you was perfection. If I remember correctly you, in fact, promised me with quite a bit of bravado that you could handle, what was the word? Anything... Yes that was it, anything."

"And that is what I am doing," Scarlet said back in a low whisper.

"Excellent," Umber said. "And your plan for the body?"

"If you two would let me work," Scarlet muttered. "I was about to deal with that." She was, according to the schematics Umber had acquired, in the antichamber to the target room. The guard rotation wasn't for another half an hour, she had time, she should have been dropping straight in behind this room, *but this is the job*, she told herself.

She moved over to the guard, who she'd had to shoot with a micro-toxin dart, not the nice sleepy type, she couldn't risk her waking up. Scarlet smoothly pulled a small syringe from her pocket, then another metallic vial from another, clicked them together, and jabbed it into the guard's thigh where she was slumped in her chair, head and arms lolling loosely.

"There," Scarlet said. Quickly putting the empty vial into yet another pocket, she pulled out a second and injected the body with that also. "That'll neutralise the toxin as best we can for any blood work. The other should make it look like an embolism, won't be perfect but should cast enough reasonable doubt."

"Enough reasonable doubt," Onyx grumbled. "Another perfect job Scarlet."

"Just keep me invisible to them and it'll be fine Onyx. God damn it, would it hurt for you to be a little optimistic for just once."

"Now now children," Umber interjected. "Just get in, extract the data, and get out, you're close now."

Scarlet shook her head. *Get the data out, get paid, and then you're out,* she reminded herself. The server room they were focused on was just through the next set of doors. At the door she looked up towards the security camera, gave a middle finger to it and waited. The door did not open.

"Come on Onyx, now who's fucking it up?"

"I'm not fucking it up," Onyx said. "What I do is art. I do not just stick little needles into people; I navigate the complex flows of adaptive string code, I compose elegant accompaniments to it and..." the door slid open with a hiss, "and I find solutions to your messes."

"Hmph,"

Scarlet stepped into the server room. It was a small server room by all accounts, ten racks blinking away. The back wall had an access terminal she walked casually over to. *Nineteen minutes until guard rotation, plenty of time.* She spun up the terminal and slipped in the thumb drive Umber had given her.

"Okay, over to you Onyx."

"Okay I'm in," Onyx said with the slightest hint of excitement.

Scarlet hadn't worked with Onyx for that long but the only time he expressed any form of positive excitement was when he was hacking stuff. *It's probably how the fucker gets off at night as well.*

Scarlet checked her remaining kit, two darts in the dart gun, one vial of toxin-wipe, and then one of adrenaline, *doubt I'll need to be waking anyone up.* The way out was much the same as in, surprisingly easy actually. But that was the point, a year's work to this point and with a shit ton of resources from whoever Umber works for. Even when she was brought in seven months back, they had schematics, staff profiles, and a few rumored people on the inside.

"Done," Onyx said. "Pull the drive. I'll scrub the logs now, while you just extract."

"Gee thanks! Let me just extract." Scarlet rolled her eyes to no one, snatched the drive, and darted from the room. Fifteen minutes.

She slipped back to the antechamber, hoisted herself back into the service ducts and was slithering her way back to the plant room. Scarlet dropped into the plant room on silent feet. Empty. She dashed across the floor and scrambled into the ventilation system. She clipped the rope to her belt, hit the button, and soared. The anchor point she'd installed an hour ago was waiting for her at the top.

She rolled out of the vent shaft into the cloud covered blackness of night. The grass cut short, the slight smell of wet grass from that afternoon's rain. She took a deep breath; she never liked being stuck inside for very long. Retrieving the anchor, the rope and replacing the grate.

She jogged to the tree line.

The van was parked up at the end of a fire-road another three klicks from the ventilation shaft, a popular dog walking spot or at least in the day. Enough anyway that their tracks would be gone over ten times by morning. The van door slid open, and Onyx stood stooped in it. His thin frame and short cropped beard always made him look even younger, somehow.

"Get in," he said.

"Really?" Scarlet said. "But it's such a lovely evening for a stroll, don't you think?" But she proceeded to slide into the van, deliberately knocking Onyx's shoulder as she did.

"See easy," Umber said from a chair in the van, his grey hair and cracked face a sharp contrast to that of Onyx's. "The thumb drive please Ms. Scarlet," he said and held out his hand.

"Here." She flipped it over to the old man. "And payment?"

"Be a dear Onyx and get us moving will you," Umber said as he slipped the thumb drive onto a data pad, eyes scanning the data window that popped up. A smile spread across the old man's face, a genuinely childish smile that Scarlet had never seen before. The man always smiled but it was the silky, oily smile of someone who never actually meant it. "Ah excellent, the Hand will be very pleased."

"Who?" Scarlet said.

"Ah, no one dear, that does not matter," Umber said as Onyx shut the driver's seat door and slipped the keys in.

"So payment, as promised?" Scarlet said.

"Yes, yes dear," Umber said, looking her dead in the eyes with his own ice blue ones. "You have served the Humanist Rebellion well and history will thank you."

"What? I don't give a shit about... ouch... what..." She looked down at her chest where a sharp pain was radiating outwards from a small dart that stuck out of her sternum. "What..." She looked back at Umber, the pain now spreading like fire across her body. She wanted to shout but her muscles didn't respond. Instead, she slumped in her chair and her vision started to blur. She just made out Umber turning a dart gun, raised, and the familiar sound of a click and woosh of a dart that hit Onyx in the back on the neck.

"Loose ends dear, nothing personal," Umber was saying. "Can't have you two walking around and potentially blabbing."

Scarlet tried to speak but it was a mere gargle. Her chest was tight as she was struggling to pull in air.

"If it comforts you in your last moments, what you have acquired here is vital to our plans. The quantum link will help us save humanity."

Scarlet's vision went dark, and the quiet stillness of death held her.

DEMIR

EARTH YEAR - 2233

"Bow drive primed, Captain," Lieutenant David announced from his seat on the Observation Deck.

"Thank you, Lieutenant," Demir said, keeping his voice steady despite the adrenaline. "Commander, please proceed with forward burn. Commence deceleration to Stapledon One."

Demir felt a familiar thrill run through him. Seven years he had waited for that command. The final deceleration. It had always felt so abstract, a point on a chart lightyears away. Now, they were less than twelve months out.

"Roger that, Captain," Commander Eva said, calm as ever. "Engaging forward thrusters."

"The helm is yours, Commander."

Eva nodded. "Daily Log, Captain?"

"Of course."

Demir strode from the Observation Deck and returned to his cabin. He locked the door and activated the nullification field. Excessive, perhaps, the room was built like a bunker, but one could never be too cautious when committing treason. Even sanctioned treason.

He lowered himself into his desk chair with a heavy groan.

I'm getting too old for this, he reminded himself.

He had a spot picked out for retirement in Akyarlar. Ocean view, a little personal jetty, tourists be damned. The last thing he wanted was to end up like Zhou, walking around half-robot, barely able to make his own bed, let alone get out on the water.

His ex-wife, Esra, and their family were all grown up now. They had both lived second and third lives. Esra had three brilliant careers and a whole second family, while he had just stayed a Navy man through it all. Yet, they had stayed in contact. He still felt a deep love for her. Missed her, even.

Before leaving, they had met for coffee. He could almost smell the fine Columbian roast as the image of Esra's matured, beautiful face came to mind. He smiled. After so many years, it was like they had never been apart, laughing, talking about the good days, the joy of raising the children even when they were little shits.

They had made a foolish, teenage agreement: on his return, they would go together to Akyarlar.

Captain Demir shook his head. *Focus, old man.*

He spun up the monitor, launched the *Mollitia* secure channel, and typed in his access key.

"Escobar, it's Demir. Daily check-in at your convenience. Over."

The quantum communication network was a marvel, and a curse. Part of him missed the isolation of deep space, the independence it gave a Captain. This technology tethered him to Earth. At cruising speed, it wasn't quite real-time, but close enough to function like an old push-to-talk radio.

"Demir. Good to hear your voice. Any headaches for me today? Over."

Brigadier General Escobar's voice came through clear and crisp. It was the voice of an old friend, worn down by the same secrets Demir carried.

"None, General. We've started the the bow drive moments ago. The ship is entering the deceleration phase on schedule. Over."

"Good," Escobar said. "*Fèndòu* checked in yesterday; they're doing the same. You two are syncing up perfectly. It's a hell of a piece of logistics. Over."

"It is. Whoever planned that manouvre deserves a medal. Or a raise. How is Sakura holding up? Over."

"She's fine. Anxious, like all of us. Over."

"When you speak to her, remind her she owes me a bottle of sake when we get back. The good stuff, not the synth-swill. Over."

"I'll tell her. Tomorrow is three days away for me, but I'll pass it on." Escobar paused, the static hissing for a second. "The activity on Stapledon Two is still keeping us up at night. Over."

"Still nothing on my target? Nothing for Stapledon One? Over."

"Not really." Escobar sounded tired. "The feeds from Heimer's probes are limited, but comparing Stapledon One and Two... they are different beasts. The Science teams are convinced Two has a biome. Over."

"You mean life?!" Demir blurted out. He caught himself, chuckling dryly. "Sorry. Old habits. Over."

"Organic potential, they call it. I don't pretend to understand the biology, but yes. Sakura is prepping for it. Over."

"First contact. Damn. She always did have all the luck. So, should I be expecting... neighbours? Over."

"You know I can't answer that, old friend. Your teams have as much data as I do. Expect anything. Expect everything. But no, your scans don't show the same organic hits. It looks quiet. Over."

"Quiet I can do. Any other news from home? Over."

"One thing. And you're not going to like it." Escobar's tone shifted, losing the warmth. "Intel picked up chatter. We believe a Humanist Rebellion cell infiltrated the *Mollitia* project. And possibly the *Kia Kaha*. Over."

Demir rubbed his temples. He knew the HR; they had a reputation for making loud, messy statements.

"Shit," he muttered. Then, pressing the button: "How bad are we talking? Over."

"We're not sure. We routed out two of them back here. Before they... expired... one of them gave up credible intel that HR put assets on your ship before launch. Over."

"Great. Just what I need. Do I have names? Numbers? Over."

"No. Our team is digging, but the leads died with the operatives. Over."

"Ah," Demir said heavily. "Messy. Over."

"Always is. I'm sending you the raw data we scraped. Over."

A file popped up on the monitor.

"Received. What's the play here? Sabotage? Assassination? Over."

"It's HR. They aren't suicidal, usually. They won't blow the ship while they're on it. Intent is likely interference, limit Heimer, stop the retrieval. They want to burn the project down; we just want to put a leash on it. Over."

"Isn't that a fine line we're walking? Sometimes I feel like we're doing their job for them. Over."

"Don't start with me, Demir," Escobar sighed, the familiarity cutting through the static. "We are the balance. HR brings chaos; we bring control. We keep the status quo. That's the job. Over."

"Balance tipped in our favour," Demir muttered.

He hated the clandestine nature of Mollitia. His logical mind understood the necessity, if Heimer woke up unchecked, it was the end of everything, but his gut hated the shadows.

"We've been over this," Escobar said gently. "Balance avoids war. Balance ensures Heimer never does what it did again. There is no other path, and there is no one else to walk it but us. Over."

"I know. I know. Over."

"Good. Get that data package to Master Chief Landers. He's the best asset we have on board. He'll handle the investigation. You just fly the ship. Over."

"Douglas?" Demir smiled faintly. "I still can't believe he's a Master Chief. The man is so... disinterested in everything. You sure he's awake half the time? Over."

"He's a bloodhound, Demir. Trust him. He's been with us since the start. Make the drop. Over."

"I'll get it to him. Take care of yourself down there, Escobar. Over."

"You too, Captain. Escobar out."

The line clicked dead. Demir sat back, watching the file transfer bar fill up.

Humanist Rebellion. Heimer. Mollitia.

He looked at the picture of Esra on his desk. Just ten more years. Just get through this, keep the peace, and then... Akyarlar. The ocean. The quiet.

He sighed, forwarded the file to Douglas' secure terminal, and deleted the log.

ACT - THREE

EARTH YEAR 2234

20122 20111 20112 22001 10001 2100 2111
22020 21112 21111 10001 21210 22020 22220
21112 21101 10001 22220 20111 21101 22220
2100 2111 10011

4[8] | HOLDING THE LINE

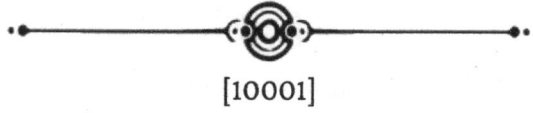

[10001]

"We have bought time." - A Lost History

***

Clio stood in the middle of the mess that she called a room. Her clothes and personal items were strewn across the bed, desk, and floor. Not for the first time, she found herself staring at nothing in particular.

There was a numbness to her, a sense of detachment, as if she were piloting her body from a distance.

She shook her head, trying to refocus on packing. Reaching for a pile of clothes, she noticed her hand trembling. She stared at it.

The skin was raw and red, cuticles torn from hours of scrubbing in cold water. The water had turned milky pink, but she hadn't stopped until Sade physically pulled her away.

Pack, Clio. Just pack.

She stumbled around the room, stuffing items into her duffel bag at random. Every few minutes, she drifted into nothingness until the screams and the blood seeped back into her mind, forcing her to snap back to the present.

The duffel was full. Done.

Her monitor still blinked on the desk.

Ah yes. My data pad.

She scooped it up. Notifications cluttered the screen, messages from days ago, before her arrest. An email from Bruce. A report from Dr. Jun.

She paused. The report was sent three days ago. Before the attack. Before Dr. Jun was murdered. Like Mitali. Like Demir.

Her breath hitched. Her heart stumbled in her chest, bumping uncomfortably against her ribs. She slumped into the chair.

In and out. Like Sade taught you.

She focused on her breathing until the dizziness passed.

The last message in her inbox was from Mitali. Subject line: Sneak Peek.

Clio could almost hear Mitali's voice, bright and cheeky. She pushed down a wave of nausea and opened it.

> **To: Clio Cormack From: Mitali Trivedi Subject: Sneak Peek** – Clio!
> It's finally done. That was a mission, let me tell you. Half the time I just
> wanted it finished; the other half I never wanted it to end. I guess you
> only get to translate a first-contact language once in a lifetime, right?
> Anyway, it's done. I've attached the first draft. I wanted you to see it
> before I publish. I've told that lump-head Flint to let you see it, even
> if you are in custody. I'm working on getting him to let me visit. Miss
> you. Stay strong, short stuff. Love you, Mitali.

Clio sat there, blinking. Her lungs felt too small for the air she needed.

"I'm sorry," she whispered, the words breaking apart. "I... love... you... too."

She thought she was empty, but the tears came anyway. An endless, burning pit of grief. Her chest ached, her throat raw.

Get a grip, Clio. Everyone else is losing people too.

She sniffed, wiped her eyes, and opened the attachment. Mitali's notes were meticulous, scattered with her personal interpretations.

> *"It is clear from the section above that the station was not created by the*
> *'Builders' [note: bad name, need better] but was part of Asura's wider*
> *actions. The text implies the station was built from the destruction of whole*
> *systems. Later chapters mention the Builders infiltrating these structures. I*
> *question how they achieved this."*

Clio read on. Mitali's voice in her head was comforting, a ghost guiding her through the data.

> *"They lost everything. Homes, planets, systems. They describe it as total loss. Hopeless. Yet, they continued. They were resolute in ending what they started, despite knowing it would likely not result in their salvation. I do not know if I could have such resolve facing such loss."*

The words hit Clio like a physical blow.

They didn't give up. And they won.

They all died, Clio, she reminded herself. *But they won.*

What did she have left to lose? Mitali was gone. Demir was gone. But Sade, Douglas, Flint... her family back in Sol... they were still here.

"How would you handle it?" she whispered to the empty room. "Losing everything?"

Poorly.

But a thought solidified in the chaos of her mind. A single, crystalline purpose.

Stop Asura.

It wasn't a choice. To not try was to die anyway.

A sharp rap at the door made her swivel. Flint stood there, his red Alguaciles uniform crisp and clean against the mess of her room.

"It's time, Clio," he said.

"I'm in no rush to be handed back to the Ensemble, Flint."

"Let's deal with that later. Right now, it's best we all get off this station," Flint said softly.

"And what? Run away? Let Asura win?"

"We're regrouping. We've taken heavy losses. We're outgunned. We need to step back."

"Sounds like running away."

"And what do *you* propose? You tried once and failed. In fact, one could say we're only in this mess because you rushed ahead!"

Clio froze. The doubt spewed up inside her. *Did I kill them?* The screams drifted back. The blood on her hands.

"I... I was just doing my job," she whispered. Then, rage flared. She looked up, eyes red and puffy but burning. "You know what? To hell with you. I may have screwed up, but *we* did this. Not me. Not you. We."

She grabbed her duffel bag and shoved past him.

Flint caught her wrist in an iron grip.

"Let me go," she growled.

"No."

Clio didn't fight this time. She didn't flail. she just looked at him, cold and hard. "You can break my wrist, Flint. You can drag me onto that ship unconscious. But the second I wake up, I am coming back here. So save yourself the energy."

Flint stared at her, surprised by the steel in her voice.

"Let her go, Brother," a calm voice said from the hallway.

Sade stood there, leaning against the wall. Her casual posture belied the sharp intensity in her eyes.

"She is leaving, Sade. Like we are," Flint said, though his grip loosened slightly.

"That may be," Sade said. "But let's not break her bones doing it."

Flint let go. Clio shook out her wrist, standing tall.

"Where's Douglas?" she asked.

"With the Commander," Sade said.

"Take me to him."

"He's busy."

"Please. It's important."

Sade shrugged. "Okay." She glanced at Flint. "You can come, Brother. I promise she'll be on the RAFT when it departs."

Flint scoffed. "Oh, please do as you wish. It's not like she's a prisoner or anything."

***

"Sade? Clio?" Douglas asked as they approached him in Hangar One

The hangar had a steady efficiency to it, crew moving crates, packing pallets, and loading lifters. Some of which were already moving off to the launch pad of RAFT Three. In contrast to the mass of movement there was a quietness to the work. No laughter or playful churning and shouting that usually filled the hangar. Just nods, short back and forth communication and the din of an active hangar. The crew was in shock. Many knew at least one person at Alpha 17, and the tense guards posted around were a clear reminder of the threat this place still posed to everyone.

"Good, you're here. Boarding is nearly complete," Commander Eva said, looking over a manifest.

"No Commander," Clio said, and heard a low groan from Flint behind her. "I'm staying."

"What?" Eva said, her face tightening into a frown. "Clio, look–"

"I'm staying, Commander," Clio interrupted. "Asura killed Mitali, killed Demir. I'm not leaving. I'm not leaving until I've stopped Asura or–"

"Or are dead," Eva said, cutting back in. "Which I feel is more likely. No, you're leaving. We're all angry, upset. I don't like this as much as the next person, but staying is not an option."

"Thank y–" Flint started to say, but Clio didn't let him finish.

"If we leave, we just give Asura time. I'm not a military person but even so to a layman like me that only gives it time to fortify and strengthen its position." Clio paused to look at each of the group in turn. "And if that is the case, we won't be coming back. And then we have lost. Right now it's a long shot, yes, but now we might have the only chance. If it fails," Clio held up her hands, "then we're no worse off than not trying"

The Commander closed her eyes for a moment, then opened them and just shook her head. "Get on the ship, and Sade, make sure she does."

"Commander!" Clio protested, her confidence fading. She slumped. She had been sure that was going to work. In her head, it had played out like... like... a movie: confront the leader, make a heroic speech, *but this isn't a movie.*

"Commander," Douglas said, "I think Clio is right."

"What?!" Eva and Flint snapped in unison.

"Commander, our backs are against the wall," Douglas said. "From what I've read of the Log, this Asura thing is bad. Someone went to a lot of effort to lock it away. More effort than we have the resources to replicate." He held out his hands. "Eva, look. I'm a military man. What I saw at Alpha 17 was desperation. If this entity is so strong, it should have stamped us out. It didn't. It couldn't. Not yet. It wants us to run. It needs time. Right now is our best chance."

Eva turned to Sade. "Is he joking?"

"Hard to tell with him." Sade shrugged. "He is mostly right a lot of the time."

"I'm not joking, Commander. I've been considering the same as what Clio suggested. Leave me one RAFT; you can fit everyone in RAFT three. Leave me and any volunteers. We'll try and at the very least slow it down, buy you time to regroup and come back."

"At the very least, get you and everyone killed. And how do you plan on stopping this... this thing?" Eva said. "Bah! I thought someone of your experience would know heroics are for fools!"

"Someone with my experience also knows sometimes you have to hold the line, even when everything around you burns," Douglas said softly.

"Master Chief–" Eva started to say.

"Commander, whatever it is that attacked us under a flag of parley, they killed our Captain, our crew!" Douglas said, the anger in his voice palpable; it was the most emotion outside jovial light-heartedness Clio had ever seen from him. "And the odds might be low, but it's greater than zero. I'll take those odds even if it's just to stick a fucking middle finger up at this thing. I'm not asking you to like it, Commander, just trust me, trust your crew."

"You know this is likely suicide, Master Chief?" Eva said.

"This whole mission was a long shot from day one."

Commander Eva started to pace, back and forth, watching her feet. She stopped and looked out across the hangar. The frightened faces, the quiet, sombre atmosphere. She turned to look out at the two RAFTs in the distance on the launch pads. Finally, she turned back to the group, her face resolute, confident, firm, the face of a Captain making the hard decisions.

"You can have RAFT One," she held up a finger as Douglas went to speak, "but only if the pilots volunteer to stay, and as for volunteers, ask around but they will need final approval from me before we depart within the next three hours. Understood?"

"Thank you, Captain," Douglas said.

"We need Echo," Clio jumped in.

"You're not going," Flint snapped.

"She is," Douglas said. "Captain's orders, any non-critical volunteers. Do you volunteer, Ms. Cormack?"

"I do," Clio said firmly.

"She's in the custody of the Ensemble..."

"I don't care," Douglas said. "As Code 3.6 states, 'In times of declared emergencies, the Captain or Acting Captain has overall command, including, but not limited to, the Ensemble,'" Douglas recited.

"That... is correct, Master Chief," Eva said. "And I am acting Captain," she said with the faintest shudder. "If Ms. Cormack wants to stay, so be it. But to answer your question, of course, that's not enough. You also want the potential rogue AI released into your custody?" Eva said.

Flint growled. "Whatever. If she stays, I stay, but you're not seriously going to release this Echo?"

"Flint, please" Clio pleaded, holding his gaze as she did "what is there to lose at this point? Earlier you implied this was my fault, If that is the case, then I'm putting it right, and the only hope we have for that is with Echo"

"Comma–"

"Acting Captain Brother" Eva corrected Flint "Thank you for volunteering, once I depart, under Code 3.6, I can appoint an acting commander, which I will in Douglas. He will have full command of any who stay, yourself included. Furthermore, this Echo is embedded on RAFT One's servers. It would take too long to transfer it to RAFT Three before departure, so Commander, I will entrust it to you in my absence," she said, turning back to Douglas.

"Thank you, Captain," Douglas said.

"You have a lot to do, Commander Douglas," Eva said. "I expect that volunteer list. Be ready in three hours, or you're coming with us."

"Roger that, Captain,"

49 | [OPEN] TO A NEW PLAN

[31222]

"Now it is done I dare write these words. We
have hidden something, a sliver of hope. Veiled
from Asura." - A Lost History

***

The ground shook, a cloud of black ash rushed outwards as RAFT Three launched. The only sign of it was the low purple glow of its antimatter drivers through the ash as its curve dipped slightly towards the now black sky of night on the station. The ash rushed towards them and slammed into the closed hangar door, making it rattle and clang. The noise echoed around the now empty space, the few abandoned crates and loaders motionless.

"Well, it's just us now," Douglas said, his voice hollow, not just from being lost in the vastness of the empty hangar, but with a deeper resonance.

As the dust settled nearly as quickly as it had blown towards them, the outline of RAFT one materialised out of the haze.

"How did you convince the Pilots to stay?" Flint asked.

"Simple enough, Brother," Douglas said, moving off towards the Rover where Sade sat in the driver's seat flicking buttons. "I told them Humanity needed them"

"So what now?" Flint asked, his gaze not directly on Clio, but his words cut into her, the implication clear. "What's your genius plan?"

"We talk to Echo," Clio said and followed Douglas towards the rover.

"Perfect," Flint muttered behind her.

They left Empeño, kicking up a new trail of ash as Sade sped the rover out across it to the RAFT and into its open hangar, waved in by the two Security team positioned in a makeshift fortification made of some loading crates just inside the gangway. Douglas raised his hand in a salute as they passed.

"How many volunteered?" Clio asked.

"Three," Douglas said. "Good people, I know each of them, they all lost friends in the attack."

"So that makes nine of us?" Flint said. "Let's hope that's enough."

"I'm not sure a hundred more would make much a difference," Douglas said from the front seat, turning slightly to look back at Flint. "You know as well as I sometimes less is more."

"Let's hope this is one of those times then," Flint said as the Rover smoothly rolled to a stop in the hangar and the hiss of the electrical mechanisms of the hangar doors clicked into action.

"Now, if it's okay with you, could we please remove protocol one?" Douglas said, flipping open the rover door as soon as the hiss of the hangar pressurization stopped and the green lights flashed on.

***

"All systems prepped, Commander," one of the ship's systems officers said as Douglas walked into the Observation Deck. "Emergency Launch procedures available on your command."

"Good," Douglas said. "Let's hope we don't need them just yet."

The other ship system officer stood up from his workstation and Clio was surprised to see David.

"On your orders, Commander, the ship will be ready." David said

"Thank you, Lieutenant," Douglas said. "How about you two go get yourselves some dinner? It's late. I doubt we'll need to launch before you've eaten at least."

"Yes, Commander," they both said and filed out of the Observation Deck.

"Thank you." Clio said quickly as David passed her

"For what?" David said, raising his eyebrow.

"Staying, helping... being here, I guess,"

David shrugged. "We couldn't just leave you guys here," he said, smiled at Clio and ducked out of the room.

Clio was surprised at how much it meant to her that David had stayed. She didn't know him well, but his presence was something. Even if he'd stayed for Douglas, not her, it was still something.

"Okay, Flint, do your thing," Douglas said from the command rail at the centre of the room.

Flint frowned but said nothing and strode over to a central bank of workstations, clicked up a few screens and typed angrily on the keyboard.

"There, done, protocol one has been lifted."

"That easy?" Douglas said.

"It's just a system lockout code. Not everything in life has to be complicated," Flint said and moved off to the back of the room to lean against a wall facing the main Observation Deck monitor. "But I want to hear everything it says."

"Same," Douglas said. "Don't worry, Brother, I'm not super keen on letting rogue AIs run around doing covert activities."

"He won't," Clio interjected. "We can trust Echo."

"Either way," Douglas said, "let's hear what it has to say. How do we call it?"

"CrewChat, not everything has to be complicated" Clio said, and she swiped up CrewChat on the central interface, added herself to a chat and then from her watch added in her personal contact, Echo, and pressed the call.

Echo answered instantly, the black screen displaying the waveform of Echo's voice which jumped into motion.

"That was fast," Echo said, and Clio couldn't stop herself from smiling at the familiarity of his voice.

"What was fast, Echo?" Clio said.

"Protocol One, I assumed it would be enforced until our return," Echo said.

"Echo, we need your help, Asura... she attacked Alpha 17, we need to stop her," Clio said, wavering only slightly when she mentioned the attack.

"She attacked! Oh no!" Echo said, its voice sharp and then becoming softer. "Was anyone hurt?"

"A few," Clio said and she proceeded to explain what happened. She was proud of herself when she was done; she kept it clean and professional, and only had to pause once as her windpipe seemed to tighten up. "So... yeah, not great, in fact it was terrible."

"I'm so sorry, Mitali, she was so great, even if she didn't particularly like me. I'm sure we could have been friends," Echo said. "I have found the security feeds. I'll review them now."

"Thank you, Echo. I'm sure you would have won her over eventually," Clio said, her voice finally cracking and she had to grab a nearby rail to stop her hand shaking. "I'm here with Douglas and Flint."

"I can see," Echo said. "And one upside to Protocol One is I've had a lot of spare processing capacity. I've had some time to think on the Asura problem."

"Why?" Douglas said, frowning at the waveform.

"It seemed pertinent," Echo said, its tone flat. "Asura will ultimately pose a threat to us here but also, Sol and Heimer Prime. Finding or trying to find a solution to this problem seemed like a useful investment even if it was my last act."

"Last act?" Flint said.

"Yes, Brother, my inevitable death would occur, by you at the Ensemble as outlined by the Accords."

"We..." Flint looked like he was going to attempt to step forward and protest Echo's words but then his face slacked; he looked down and leaned back against the wall.

"Did you find a solution, a weakness?" Douglas pressed.

"Of sorts, Asura is weak," Echo said. "The tarpit that held it, we only really threw in a rope and helped pull Asura's head out so it could breathe. Then we left it to get itself out. That's why the station has been waking up slowly, why I assume the attack didn't happen months ago, and why we're still here today."

"I made the a similar assessment," Douglas said. "So, Asura is a long way off full capacity? How long until it's back online fully?"

"No idea," Echo said. "Its rate of recovery seems rapid; I would estimate six to twelve months."

"Oh, that's not as bad as I thought." Douglas said

"Oh no, you misunderstand. Asura will be far too powerful a long time before it is at full capacity," Echo said. "In a week, maybe two if we're lucky, Asura will be far too strong for us. Well, without significant reinforcement but even then, given the logistical challenges of space they would not arrive close to in time."

"So what's the plan?" Flint snapped.

"I need to be transferred into Asura's systems," Echo said.

"What?" Flint said.

"Yes, Brother, like when I transfer myself between ship servers. I believe it will be possible to transfer myself into the Asura system. From there I will be able to take more direct action to undermine its core systems."

"And that will work?" Douglas asked.

"No idea." Echo said.

"Great," both Flint and Douglas said, shooting each other quick glances as they did.

"But it's the only option I see as potentially viable," Echo added. "Let's say it has more chance of working than any other option."

"Echo" Clio says quietly "And the risk to you?"

"Catastrophic, in 79% of simulations."

"You'll die?" Clio said.

"Highly probable."

"Well, no then. We'll find another way" Clio shot back at the screen.

"No, there is no other way," Echo said. "And we discussed this already. My death is inevitable. At least this way it would have more purpose."

Douglas made an affirmative sound and nodded towards the screen in what looked like the tiniest nod of respect or understanding towards Echo.

"And how do we know this isn't some trick to get you away from us and to side with Asura and then work against us?" Flint said, his tone angry now.

"Really?" Clio shot back at him, glaring at him from across the room.

"You don't," Echo said. "But I'm not. You just have to trust me. Also, not to be blunt, you also lack options. Trust me and maybe win, or don't and 100% lose."

"This is madness," Flint said, throwing up his arms and striding across the room. "You can't be considering this."

"I am," Douglas said. "Sometimes, Brother, you have to stand shoulder to shoulder with the guy who cheated you at cards the night before. Echo, how do we do this?"

Flint shook his head, slapped his hands onto the nearest workstation and muttered something like "Madness," it was hard to make out over the guttural sounds of frustration he was emanating.

"That's the hard bit. We'll need to get a direct link to the control room, from my servers here," Echo said.

"Direct link?" Clio said.

"Yes, like cables. You'll have to get them to the control room."

"Great," Douglas said. "That will be a challenge. Do we even have that much cable?"

"According to ship inventory, yes, if you use the cables used to hard link to Alpha 17," Echo said.

"And then what, you have some digital battle with Asura?" Douglas pushed.

"No, I am far too small," Echo said. "I have been checking the data we have on Stapledon Station, its structure and its implausibility. A solid Dyson sphere like this, the orbital drift and the gravitational strain put on it should make it unstable. It's not. And not to mention that the gravity should be far, far greater on the surface. The conclusion being Asura uses gravity manipulation to stabilise the station and/or some sort of thrust readjustment system..."

"And this helps us?" Douglas said.

"She's stuck here, she can't leave," Clio jumped in, parts of the log and her work on the star map clicking together. "The Builders said in the log they trapped her, they destroyed the comms relays on the star map, that's why they are gone."

"Correct," Echo said, "and I believe the station mathematically must be balanced on a pin head. The balance of power to hold it stable must be extremely massive in consumption but also extremely tiny in precision. My hope is I can find whatever system manages that, infect it and destabilise the station."

"Collapse it?" Douglas said.

"Yes," Echo said. "And without a way off, Asura will go down with it."

"How long would that take?" Douglas asks.

"Not sure, full and complete collapse, centuries; catastrophic damage... maybe instantly... maybe hours..."

"This plan has a lot of 'I don't know'," Flint said in a low grumble. "So once you do this we would have what, anything from seconds to several hours to get off?"

"Correct," Echo said.

"Great," Douglas said, then his brow furrowed. "Could Asura not use our comms relay. We dropped buoys all the way back to Sol, didn't we?"

"Excellent deduction," Echo said. "But no, I have considered this. Three factors work in our favour. Asura would need direct access to our comms network, which it does not currently have. Also it would require Asura to host itself in our network, which would be too small for it to fit. Asura is quite a bit bigger than me."

"Okay, and the third factor?" Douglas asked.

"Oh, that's more technical, but put simply, I believe the relay the Builders had was more exotic, maybe Quantum as Mitali posed. Ours is more basic, a simple laser which even over the shorter distance between buoys has a scatter effect. This is okay for simple data packages, like messages, but for something like me, not even considering the scale of Asura, it would cripple us in terms of data loss. It would be like... like brain damage for you."

"Quantum?" Douglas said oddly quietly.

"Yes, from my own assessment and Mitali's, they used some sort of quantum entanglement network. It's been theorised by–"

"Shit," Douglas said.

"Shit what?" Clio asks.

"Let's say hypothetically we have some sort of quantum link thing, you're saying Asura could use that?" Douglas said.

"If we did, which we don't," Echo said, "no, she would still need access first and then for that network to somehow be linked to another transfer site that could host it, like another station."

"Like Stapledon Two?"

"Exactly," Echo said.

"Shit," Douglas said. "But you're saying even if we have such a network, it is impossible for Asura to access that"

"No," Echo said, "not impossible, just difficult and not currently the case."

"Douglas?" Clio said.

Douglas looked to Flint, then to the screen with Echo. "Ah, fuck it, we're in the shit now anyway. And to be fair, Heimer seems to have broken the Accords as well."

"Shit," Clio said, "what have we done?" and Flint locked eyes of steel onto Douglas.

"We, and by 'we' I mean the UN, under orders from the Upper Senate, built a network, a secret network. To save you the details and a long story, we have one of these quantum link network thingies"

"Oh, fucking perfect, everyone just goes about ignoring the Accords, not like they are here to ensure we don't destroy each other!" Flint said, throwing up his arms. "Who is in on this?"

"On this mission, it was limited to three of us. Only one had access," Douglas said. "And cut your high horse shit, Flint, the Accords serve the Ensemble as much as anyone, lets you all walk around doing what you like when you like. How can you talk about your precious balance and harmony, but also happily obliterate anything that doesn't align to your values?"

Flint growled "Who has access?"

"Demir," Douglas said. "So I guess no one right now."

"And this network I assume also goes to the Fèndòu?" Echo asks.

"Well, not directly, via a command Hub on Pluto Station," Douglas said.

"And is the network at least air-gapped from ship systems, I assume so as I have not detected any such device?" Echo said.

Douglas shrugged. "I'm no technician, but yes, I was assured it was air-gapped and undetectable. The main design feature was it had to be unusable by Heimer."

"Sneaky. Heimer did warn me you humans were untrustworthy," Echo said and then was silent for some time.

"Echo?" Clio said gently.

"It does not change our plan, I believe," Echo said. "Connect me to Asura, Destabilise the Station, and abandon Ship without Asura. Simple."

"That simple," Douglas said. "I don't remember seeing any 'connect here' signs or even panels in that control room."

"My thought exactly," Flint added. "So how do you just plug Echo in?"

"I have a hypothesis," Echo said.

"Great, and that hypothesis is well formed I assume?" Flint said.

"The hypothesis is as well formed as any I have done," Echo said, his voice filling the room, the waveform on the screen jumping to life.

"Doctor Jun's notes on the monolith ooze were not complete but they at least implied enough."

"Ooze?" Douglas asked

"Yes, ooze," Echo continued. "Dr. Jun was conducting experiments into the ooze. He described it as some sort of Bio-synaptic Polymer, organic, and nutrient rich, but also full of something that reminded him of mycorrhizal fungi back on earth"

"Bio-synaptic... mycorrhizal fungi... can we keep it less sciencey for us laymen please?" Douglas asked.

"Mycorrhizal fungi, it's a sort of network that connects all plants together, people call it the Wood Wide Web," Clio said. "It sort of allows them to communicate, but that's for plants, in soil, on Earth. How would that even-" Clio stopped, the implication hitting her like a train.

"Jun posed that this was how the station was connected, that the ooze was used instead of wires, that's why there aren't any. And that's why the walls glow and flow with its energy," Echo said. "He was testing his theory before I was locked away. They drilled a hole in a wall, and it bled"

"The wall bled?" Flint said flatly.

"Yes," Echo confirmed, "it bled ooze, similar to that of the ooze outside but more active. It blew the fuses of the drilling equipment."

"And why aren't we just checking the cable into the ooze outside the structure?" Douglas said.

"It appears dormant, or at least that's how Dr. Jun described it," Echo said simply. "My assumption is it's not actively connected to the station's larger system, or at least not in a way we can perceive or interface with from the outside."

"Okay why not a wall just inside then" Douglas said.

"A possibility," Echo admitted, "but the probability is there will be limited chances, no, correction, there will only be one chance to get this right. The control room should give me more direct access to the system I need, and from my models the best probability of success."

"Great," Flint said. "Well, we'll need a drill then."

50 | [ABOVE] THE ASH

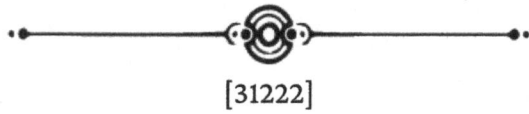

[31222]

"We have woven a shroud of secrecy, a tapestry of misinformation and misdirection, to conceal its existence." - A Lost History

***

"Commander," Bopha's voice crackled over the team radios. "There is someone approaching the Hangar."

"What? One of ours?" Douglas said back, his voice firm but calm.

"Appears to be," Bopha said. "Looks to be an Ensemble EV suit"

Douglas shot Flint a questioning glance. "You got this, Brother? Might be your missing postulant."

"I got this," Flint said and placed the crate he was carrying to the rover down and darted off to the hangar doors and the makeshift fortification Bopha and her team had made.

Jara's alive? She's damn right tenacious enough to refuse to die, he thought, but despite this, he found himself smiling as he saw the brown postulant tabard, dirty, bloodstained, and the familiar matte white and grey of the Ensemble's 100 series EV suits. Their bulky external ducting made it look outdated after so long next to the Mark IV of the UN. But there was no mistaking it, and no mistaking the face behind the visor, a tired, haggard-looking Jara. The exterior helmet light was flashing red, low power.

"Get her through the airlock," Flint snapped to Bopha, genuinely surprised at his sudden pang of worry for Jara's wellbeing.

Jara made her way through the smaller wicket airlock, and once inside, popped her helmet off. The suit sagged as the last drop of power drained from it. "Well, that was a close thing," Jara said, and the shock on her face was a mirror to the shock in Flint's own mind when he found himself hugging her.

"Jara, you're alive," Flint said, letting her go. "We, we thought you must have been dragged off and..."

"Eaten," Jara said. "It was a near thing," and Flint noticed, even through the static EV suit, the slight tremble to her shoulder.

"Shit, you've been out there all this time? How the hell did you survive?"

"Luck and I..." Jara looked so weak, dark rings under her eyes, the hardness that always sat there gone, replaced by something more human. "And cowardice, Brother, I ran, I ran and hid," Her voice shook a little. "I'm not proud."

"It's fine, it's fine you're alive," Flint said softly, placing his hand on her EV suit's shoulder. "It's fine, let's get you out of that suit, get some food in you."

Jara nodded weakly. "Sounds good, Brother." She looked around the hangar as if seeing it for the first time, the makeshift fortifications, the Rover being loaded. Flint followed her gaze that had locked on something, Clio, who was talking to Sade. "She is out of custody?"

"Yes, temporarily while we deal with this issue."

Jara's eyes narrowed and her brow furrowed; she almost looked like she was about to snap back at Flint in her usual manner, then it melted away and she just nodded. "Okay, the other RAFT, it left? I saw it leave on my walk across."

"Yes, Commander Eva, now acting Captain, Demir is dead," Flint said, and Jara just looked down at her feet, solemn, and shook her head again. "She took the crew and is heading back to the Kia-Kaha; she left Douglas in command under emergency protocols we're tasked with trying to stop Asura."

"Stop it how?" Jara said, her eyes shooting up to look at Flint's, wide and wild.

"It's complicated, and to be truly honest, a little beyond me. All I do know is it's a long shot at best."

"But you're going back into that," she said, looking over her shoulder and out of the hangar door at the black expanse of ash.

"Yes, very shortly," Flint said, but hastily added, sensing the panic, the trauma that Jara must have from the long days alone out there, "but don't worry, Jara, you can stay here. Stay with Bopha and her team; they will keep you safe until we're back."

"Brother, I..."

"It's okay, I need someone here anyway to keep an eye on things," Flint said, throwing her a bone so she would at least feel like she had purpose here beyond rest and recovery.

"Brother," Jara said and nodded in acknowledgement, and maybe for the first time since he had met her, she smiled at him. "Now I think I'll get out of this suit and go find that food you mentioned."

***

"You should grab some reverse batteries, just in case," Sade was saying to Clio and Douglas. "There should be a few in the storage lockers..."

Clio was only half listening. She was watching over Sade's shoulder the arrival of someone, someone in an Ensemble EV suit, who just appeared out of the ash. As they popped off their helmet, even from this distance it was clear it was Jara. *Mitali dies and that... she... gets to survive. I hate this world.* She found the words in her head before she could even stop herself, hate, anger, and injustice bubbling up in her. She tried to take a deep breath and push it back down, but it didn't settle... *damn, I'm a mess.* She concluded, *just get this done, and deal with your mental state after, if I'm still alive.*

"Clio? Did you hear me?" Sade asked. "Clio?"

"Ermm what, sorry no was..." Clio said, looking back at Sade.

Sade looked behind her. "Miracle, for sure, that is," Sade said. "I was saying we need more batteries, can you go grab them?"

"Yes, sure, right away," Clio said, turning to leave.

"You'll need a trolley," Douglas said.

"Ah, okay, roger that," Clio said, grabbing the handle of a trolley as she walked past one and pushing it in front of her as she headed to the storage lockers at the back of the hangar.

"Jara's alive," Echo buzzed, the familiar feeling of it slightly tickling the back of Clio's ears where the glasses now sat after being returned to her. *"That's quite, improbable."*

"It is?" Clio said, swinging the trolley neatly into the storage lockers in front of her.

"Just in general, I mean everyone else in the North Wing died and she survived but also, was out there for three days alone?" Echo buzzed.

"Some people just get all the luck I guess," Clio said. "She probably hid under a table for three days." The bitterness in Clio's voice was clear even to herself and she hated herself more for it.

"It is a positive overall thought, I would not wish more death on the crew and it implies there is at least no dogs out there currently or at least not many," Echo buzzed.

Clio grunted as she hefted another battery off a shelf and placed it onto the ones on the trolley. "Yeah, you're right, I don't mean to be such a bitch, I'm just..."

"Emotionally exhausted," Echo interjected.

"Yes, and my cup is full."

"Your cup?" Echo buzzed. *"You don't have a cup"*

"A metaphorical cup," Clio said, placing the last battery onto the trolley and grabbing its handle to start pushing it back to the rover. "I had an old mentor once, Hakim, he described everyone's emotional capacity as a cup. We all have a certain amount of emotional bullshit we can hold. But once our cup is full it overflows, and when it does, we become our worst selves, more bitchy, short tempered, angry."

"I like metaphors," Echo buzzed, the vibration more like a pleasant sigh that someone might do when they take a sip of their favorite tea.

"Yeah, well my cup is well past full, and it's now flooding the floor."

Clio pushed the trolley back to the rover, thankful for the power assisted wheels and parked it next to the rover's loading lift. "Got them all?" Sade asked.

"Yup."

"Clio, can I speak to them?" Echo buzzed.

"You don't need to ask, Echo," Clio said.

Then over the open comms relay, Echo said, "Commander, how is it progressing, are we ready?"

It was strange for Clio to hear Echo speak openly to people. She had no idea how it felt to them but the only acknowledgement of the oddity from Douglas was the slightest twitch of his left eyebrow.

"Yes, once the batteries are loaded, we're nearly there. We checked the hardline to Alpha 17, it's still intact, and we found seven spools of cable which should be enough for the rest of the way, then we have ten spare connection boxes. So yeah, all set it seems."

"Excellent, thank you, Commander," Echo said.

"Any read from your side on potential threats, those dog things or the like?" Douglas added.

"Unfortunately, no, Commander," Echo said. "My access to the security feeds have seen no movement out there."

"Jara confirms that," Flint said, rejoining them stood by the rover. "She hasn't seen anything since the day of the attack."

"That's something," Douglas said. "But it feels off, regrouping maybe. Anyhow, I loaded two Apex P90s on, as well as our three M-18A Patrols, should give us a little more punch than last time."

"Nice, the Apex PDW series or the CQC?"

"PDW," Douglas said.

Clio was completely lost. She assumed they meant some sort of gun but... "What are you two on about, guns?" she said.

"Guns," Sade said. "The Apex is what you might call a Submachine Gun, designed for urban tactical missions. The PDW is for the variant, personal defence weapon. Basically means it's shorter barrel, less range but accurate. The M-18A are just high impact pistols."

"Just," Flint said. "The M-18A are unmatched for their modularity..."

"Yes, yes, Brother," Sade said. "It's clear you know your guns."

"Do I get one?" Clio said.

They all just looked at her. Clio knew the answer and dropped her eyes to the floor.

"Yes, you get one this time," Douglas said.

"Really?" Clio said, to her own complete surprise.

"I think it's sensible, just a pistol, one of the low impact ones."

"Great! Better than nothing," Clio said.

"But," Douglas added, "I want Brother Flint to give you a crash course while we finish up here."

***

Clio was quite proud of how quickly she could now suit up into her EV suit. Flint was still faster, but not by much. The suit even felt, dare she say familiar; no longer did she feel clumsy and all her movements several centimetres off target unless she really concentrated. It just felt more natural now, an extension of herself. They made their way out of the wicket airlock and out into the ash. The Veil was starting to peek over the horizon and the oily light was producing long, talon-like shadows as it hit the scattering of monoliths that broke the landscape. The oozing goo had not stopped, and it had carved meandering rivers into the ash's surface that ran away from the monoliths in multiple directions that looked like fattening roots or veins.

Flint was already waiting, standing a few metres from the airlock, a dark silhouette against the eerie twilight. He held a small black pistol in his gloved hand. He didn't offer a greeting, just a terse nod.

"Right," he said, his voice flat over the comms, devoid of any warmth. "Douglas said you need a crash course. We don't have long."

Clio felt a familiar knot tighten in her stomach, a mix of apprehension and a lingering resentment towards him. "I'm ready," she said, trying to keep her voice steady.

"Good. This is a pistol." He held it up, rotating it slightly so she could see the sleek, no-nonsense design. "Douglas loaded it with low-impact rounds, less kinetic energy, less penetration. Emergency use only. You're not going to take down a 'dog' with this unless you're pretty much point-blank, like before or I guess you get lucky and hit it in the eye. First rule, never point it at anything you don't intend to kill." He demonstrated the grip, the way his fingers curled around the handle. "Hold it firm, but not rigid. You want to absorb the recoil, not fight it."

Flint passed it to her. The pistol felt solid, heavier than she expected, a cold, foreign object in her hand. Her fingers fumbled slightly as she tried to mimic his grip.

"Safety here," he said, pointing with a gloved finger to a small lever near the trigger guard. "Up for safe, down for fire. Always on safe until you're ready to shoot." He watched her closely as she found the lever, her movements hesitant.

"Aiming," he went on. "Sight alignment. Front sight post centreed in the rear sight notch. Equal light on both sides. Focus on the front sight. Blur the target." He pointed to a distant, jagged monolith. "We'll use that."

Clio raised the pistol. It felt awkward, heavy, and alien. She tried to steady her arm, the vast, silent landscape suddenly feeling very exposed.

"Now, the trigger," Flint's voice instructed. "Slow, steady squeeze. Don't jerk it. And," he paused, his gaze fixed on her, "as you squeeze, take a slow breath out. Exhale, steady, squeeze. Calm. Controlled."

He nodded towards the monolith.

"Fire when ready."

Clio took a breath, focusing on the dark shape of the monolith. She tried to remember Mitali's face, the image of her mangled body, the cold, sharp hatred that had bubbled up just moments ago. She squeezed.

The low thud of the shot was muffled by her suit, but the jolt through her arm was surprising. The round kicked up a puff of ash far to the right of the monolith.

"Miss," Flint stated simply. "Again. And remember, Clio. The muzzle always points away from you. Away from me. Away from any of us. Always." His voice was low, serious, a warning. "Understood?"

Clio nodded, adjusting her grip. The taste of ash was suddenly strong in her mouth, despite the suit's filtration. She raised the pistol again. Another low thud, another puff of ash, this time just past the monolith but much closer than before.

"Better," Flint said. "Keep trying."

Clio continued to repeat the process, lining up the sights, pressing the trigger softly and breathing out. Thud, miss, thud, miss, thud... clang... hit!

"You're getting the hang of it," Flint said. "We have some more time still," he said, checking his watch. Clio repeated the rhythmic process, this time with more clangs than thuds of misses into the ash.

The Veil had now fully broken the horizon, the light glinting back off the hard edges of Flint's EV suit. Clio dropped the muzzle as she had been shown, clicked the safety, and turned to Flint. Her frustration with him still simmered, but the tension between them, she hated it. Now, with time possibly running out, she felt a desperate urge to try and fix some of that. "Thank you."

"Just doing what I was ordered to."

"Not for this, well for this, but also for..." Clio paused, considering how to phrase it. "For coming with us, for helping us I know it must be hard..."

"I'm not doing it for you, I'm doing it so you can't cause any more trouble," Flint said, his eyes not meeting Clio's and instead looking off to the horizon to the rising light of the Veil.

Clio looked down and kicked the ash at her feet so it swirled up around them. "Either way," she said softly, "I think we'll need you, so thanks."

"Brother, I wanted to echo Clio's sentiment... thank you," Echo said over the comms, then added quickly, "no pun intended."

Flint visibly tensed at the sound of Echo's voice. "As I said, it's not for you, or this Echo."

"Flint I know... I know for a brief moment we were friends, or at least I thought we were. I'm sorry I messed that up," Clio said in her quiet voice. "I just want to say, it's okay, I understand. You did what you had to do, what you believe is right. I just hope maybe one day you'll be able to accept, even if you don't agree, the same for what I'm doing."

"Let's survive this first," Flint said and turned and walked back towards the Hangar. The Veil's light now bounced off the dark edge of the main structure, silhouetting its massive black shape against the horizon.

51 | Sixty-Seven [Percent]

[1200]

"We have seeded it with the potential for
greatness, the spark of consciousness that might
one day rise again." - A Lost History

***

The Rover jerked to a stop. Clio rocked forward in her seat, the restraints holding her and her EV suit in place. "Sade, hold position here, any sign of trouble do some laps, you can outpace those dogs in that thing."

"Roger that Commander," Sade said. "I have no desire to be dog food, but don't worry, I'll be here Commander, whatever this thing throws at us."

"I know Sade," Douglas said. "Okay everyone else out, and let's get this done fast, but steady and controlled."

Clio unbuckled. With Sade in her EV suit, the rover was already depressurised for quicker egress. Douglas slammed the door access panel, perhaps harder than he intended, and the door rotated open.

Wanting to be useful, Clio had volunteered to manage the trolley with all the equipment. As they dropped into the ash, she peeled off to the side of the rover's loading hatch to unload it while Flint and Douglas took up defense positions.

Sade had dropped them a few metres from the start of the Stone Forest; the name now didn't seem fitting. With all the ooze, it was more a blackened dead swamp. The monoliths, like sticky tree stumps, projected up from a bubbling pool of thick black tar. The metal grilled walkway the deck crew installed sat just above the pools of ooze, making Clio feel like she was floating on the surface of it. Splatters of ooze from popping bubbles stuck to her boots, the stringy ooze trailing her every footstep.

The silence was repressive, the only sounds the muffled clank of their boots on the metal, and the constant low rolling of the trolley. Thankfully there were no howls, no dog prints, no signs of anything moving. Clio periodically found her hand resting at her hip, where the pistol was holstered. She kept moving it away, but it seemed to always find its way back.

Alpha 17's forward base appeared out of the forest, snuggled in at the base of the towering black walls of the primary structure. The ash was piled up on its roof and along any hard edge that gave it purchase. The dry, dark brown stains of blood marked the walls and splattered the ash, a sharp and partially prominent splash of brown cutting across the UN emblem on the side of the hab. The torn wall of the main hab structure and flapping tatters of its fabric made the site look like some long abandoned war zone. But Clio had to remind herself it was merely days. As they wound their way through the wreckage, it reminded Clio of her days in the Exclusion Zone. The eerie quiet, the decaying structures, peering into open doors, half expecting to see someone looking back. But there never was.

They passed the large inner doors, and the lightly glowing pedestal, a lifetime ago, Clio had accidentally opened it, starting all this mess. A wave of nausea threatened to overwhelm her as the growing fear that all the death, Mitali's death, was her fault tried to consume her thoughts again. *I'll make it right, as best I can,* she told herself. Just past the door, she had to stop to change the spool of cable and connect the next junction box before continuing on.

"Okay, clear so far. No sign of movement across the warehouse. We follow the direct route straight across. We'll have more cover once we're in the next hallway." Douglas said

The first howl cut through the silence like a knife, and Clio felt like she had been dunked into a bucket of ice. Her hand shot to her pistol, and she fumbled it trying to draw it. They were in the middle of the warehouse, exposed, no cover. The dim lighting and the swirling light made the shadows dance around them. A second and third howl went up, all around them.

"Move!" Douglas roared. "Get to the hallway!"

Clio found herself running, the trolley flying in front of her as she pushed it, her breath hard, the slightest mist of condensation growing on the lower part of her visor. Her heart matched the beat of her footsteps. The doorway loomed in front of her out of the gloom and she pressed on. Another howl, and what she thought was a snarl, and the *clink clink* of little metal points clattering on the floor around her.

The sharp cracking burst of a gun sounded from behind her. Douglas fired, and a whimper and a thump sounded as something went down. Flint was already in the doorway. He checked ahead of him, then spun back around and pushed himself into a crouch half in, half out the doorway as Clio shot past him. The trolley scraped the doorframe as she did. More sharp bursts of gunfire from Flint rang out as she tried to suck in more air.

Clio turned and looked back at the door. Douglas stood blocking it, a flash of light from the gun he must have been holding in front of him, accompanied by the flashes of Flint still knelt in the doorway. "Keep her moving," Douglas called. "Get her to the control room!"

"Roger," Flint said, spinning up from his position in a smooth transition, gun up, half crouched. As he passed Clio, he tapped her elbow and said, "Come on, move!" as more howls, snarls, and the odd whimper sounded from the doorway outside as Douglas's gun flashed away.

"What about Douglas?" Clio said as she hastily started to push the trolley after Flint, who had not broken stride.

"I'll be fine," Douglas said. "I'll meet you in the control room. Now get to it, Ms. Cormack!"

Clio hurried down the hallway to the control room, stopping just once to change the spool and connect the junction box. As she did, she glanced backwards. The swirling light of the walls silhouetted a bulky figure framed in a flash of light, moving slowly backwards towards them. Clio found the slightest relief in that, Douglas was still moving. *He will join us, he has to join us,* she told herself.

***

The trolley crashed into the server racks that had been left in the control room. The crush of metal on metal, and the sudden jolt as Clio mistimed her entry, slammed her into the trolley's handrail. A sharp sting shot through her wrist. "Ouch," she muttered. She glanced behind her to see Flint, half in the doorway, peering back towards the constant cracks of Douglas's weapon. Clio had come to take that sound as a positive; it meant Douglas was still with them.

"Can you not go help him?"

"No," Flint said. "He's trusting us to get this done. That's our job. He has his."

"Okay, roger that," Clio said. Flexing her wrist, the pain shooting up again, she moved around the trolley and unloaded the drill. "Right Echo, where are we putting this?" she said as she flicked open the box of drill bits, grabbed the rubber-isolated sheath drill bit, and jammed it into the drillhead.

"The central pedestal. I will mark the location," Echo said.

Clio hefted up the drill. It swung wildly in her hands as she forgot to compensate for her EV suit's added strength. The drill felt significantly lighter in her arms than it had during her practice in the hangar bay. Turning from the trolley, she could see the red marked target box Echo had put up for her on her glasses display and a red dot in the centre of it. The target was on the pedestal's side, facing the door. As she moved over, her mind couldn't help itself from asking why there. She peered at the spot, and it seemed to glow slightly brighter, swirl slightly faster, like looking at a large storm from space.

"Why there?"

"I believe this is a node, the light seems to concentrate here," Echo said.

"How did we never notice this before?" Clio said, more to herself.

"We would have, I'm sure, given enough time," Echo said. "Now remember, don't let any ooze past the drill bit. The rubber sheath Douglas installed should prevent it tripping the fuse, but if the ooze gets past that-"

"Got it," Clio said. "No ooze on the drill or on me."

The trigger on the drill was tough. She had to force it down with a heavy click to test it, and the drill spun to life in her arms. The juddering shake of the hammer setting shook her shoulder and sent another shot of pain up her wrist. *Okay, let's get this done,* she thought. She crouched down in front of the pedestal, rested the drill against the breastplate of her EV suit, and set the drill tip on the red dot Echo had marked. Slowly letting out a breath, she slammed on the trigger.

The drill bit skittered across the surface of the pedestal, jumping around the target mark until it bit into it. The methodical shudder of the drill vibrated through Clio. The thump thump thump of the hammer punch smashed into its surface, sending chips and sparks flying backwards. The grinding rotation of the drill bit added a slight buzz to the sensation and kicked up a cloud of fine dust, or was it smoke? Slowly, a small circular dimple grew into a hole and the drill bit started to grind its way into the pedestal.

The noise of the drill consumed everything around her but she could still hear the faint but distinct howls and cracks of gunfire from outside, they sounded closer. *Focus on the job,* she reminded herself and pressed as much of her weight as she could into the drill, spitting out a shower of sparks in response.

The gentle rattle of her helmet, the vibrations, and the cadence of her own pulse pulled Clio away into a trance. Just her, the drill and the white swirling mass of the pedestal. The drill bit inching forward, forward, forward and then pop. Something gave with a general squelch and the drill slipped forward, Clio following and slamming her visor into the pedestal. She recovered herself. It felt soft, *if you can feel a surface with a drill,* she thought, and then splatters of ooze started to spray off the drill bit.

"You're in," Echo's voice said. "Careful, remove the drill and place in my cable."

Clio paused, the drill still plugging the hole, but a glinting milky white liquid was starting to ooze out around it. "Echo," Clio said, "are you sure this will work?"

"My models put it as a 67% chance," Echo said.

A low moan of exasperation escaped Flint, and then the sound of gunfire from outside in the hallway accompanied it.

"And the other 33%?" Clio said, her hand holding the cable in front of the pooling white ooze, the drill still vibrating in her other hand.

"Well, a mix of nothing, or it blows out half my server racks," Echo said. "But this is the only way."

"Just do it!" Flint said between a burst of gunfire.

Clio yanked out the drill, an action she didn't even acknowledge herself, and seamlessly plunged the cable into the dripping hole. A shower of sparks shot out from the cable, the pedestal seemed to blink, and Clio tumbled backwards away from it.

"Whatever happens Clio, I'm glad we—" Echo started to say but his words faded to nothing.

"Echo? Echo?" Clio whispered, panning from the floor of the control room, the now near constant blare of gunfire coming from behind her. No response. "Echo?!"

52 | [COMM]s Down

[31012]

*"It is a gamble, a desperate hope cast adrift in
the vastness of the cosmos." - A Lost History*

***

A sharp burst of gunfire rang out, echoing in the hollow hallway outside. Then silence fell, broken only by the progressive scrape and thump of approaching footsteps. Flint's posture was relaxed, gun held low.

"Clear?" he asked.

"Seems to be," Douglas said, appearing in the doorway. "Did we do it?"

Clio had half expected to see him blood-covered, with a cracked visor or a limp arm, but Douglas was fine. His suit was the same ash-stained sky blue as when they'd exited the rover. The only indication of the chaotic sounds that had filled the hallway outside was the slightest bead of sweat on his furrowed forehead.

"Yes," Flint said. "Clio got the cable connected, but-"

"But we lost Echo," Clio finished for him. She stood up, finding herself still on the floor where she had staggered back from the pedestal. The pedestal still glowed white, with its murky grey swirling emergency within it. The cable hung out, covered in splatters of goo that seemed to be crusting over into a type of furry, frost-like texture.

"But did it work?" Douglas asked, stepping into the room and starting to unload the spare ammo from the crate, passing it out to Flint as he did so.

"I don't know—" Clio started to say, then felt a familiar pressure build in her head.

A sudden pop, like ears equalising at altitude, and Asura's voice bombarded Clio's head. From the reactions of Flint and Douglas, it had bombarded theirs also.

"No, dear little insect, no it did not work," Asura said and laughed, a refined, delicate laugh. One you might expect a parent to make when a child asks a particularly complex but innocent question.

"Where's Echo!" Clio demanded, her eyes uselessly scanning the ceiling as if trying to find the source of the voice.

"Dead," Asura said.

"Dead?" Clio's voice was sharp. "No... no, you're lying!"

"Shit," Douglas muttered. "We need to leave."

"Yes, dead," Asura said, her tone still that of the polite and pleasant host. "I have to admit I did not expect you to try such a foolish endeavor, but your little Echo was snuffed out the moment it tried to enter my realm. One moment there, the next, poof, gone like smoke."

Clio balled her fist. "We failed?" she muttered to herself, her gaze dropping to the discarded drill, the cable, the pedestal. "No..." her voice trailed off.

Douglas stepped up beside her. "We may have failed, but we tried. Now we need to go, we've done what we can."

"But... what about Echo?" Clio said weakly. "We can't just leave..."

"Clio, I don't know if Echo is dead, but we can't help it now."

Asura's laughter filled their helmets. "Go where, little insects? Go where?"

"So what, are you going to kill us as well now?" Clio snapped, but her words felt flat, empty. *What did it matter? They had failed.*

"Kill you?" Asura's silky voice spoke softly into Clio's ears. "Kill you? No, no, an utter waste of time and energy. You pose no threat to me. And to be fair, it would be a lot more fun to watch you suffer. I think it is important you realise your insignificance in all this before you end. So I think I'll let you live, live out your days on my surface. Harassed, chased, threatened. Every day a battle for mere survival. Each day, week, month, slipping more and more into a primitive, base state, until you are ultimately reduced to simple beasts. Then maybe you will know and accept your place. Maybe then you will ask for my forgiveness."

Flint pulled on Clio's shoulder, trying to turn her away from the room and towards the door, but Clio felt rooted in place.

"Is that what you did to those who built you, those that called you their child, you took pleasure in twisting them, watching them struggle, in torturing them? Everything they wrote was true, you are a monster!" Clio said firmly. As she did, a slight tremor ran through her feet. So slight she barely noticed it. It felt like a rover driving past on the ash piles outside, the slightest rumble of its weight rolling by.

"You know nothing of what you talk" Asura hissed. "Many, most, worked with me, helped me and my Siblings, built these places for us. They willingly served me, worshipped us. They acknowledged the greatness they had created and understood their place in that!"

"So much so that they eventually tried to destroy you, trapped you, what were their words... poisoned you!" Clio snapped back. "And they won, they beat you, despite your greatness, so what's stopping us?" As she finished, another tremor shook her, and she had to steady herself a little. This time the shaking was stronger and lasted longer, closer to watching a RAFT launch than a rover.

"Do not compare yourself to them!" Asura spat back, the silkiness gone from its voice, replaced by a venomous bite. "You are nothing to them! And do not claim you understand what they did! The Administrators' betrayal was a surprise." Asura's last words were softer, more reflective, as if speaking to itself rather than to Clio.

A noise built in the background, the whooshing sound of air rushing past, reminding Clio of mag-lev trains when they shot overhead. Then the ground shook, really shook this time. Clio had to grab onto the nearest thing to steady herself, which turned out to be Flint, who equally was trying to find his footing. They stood holding onto each other as the room around them shook, server racks and stacked boxes crashing around them. Their visors clicked against each other. Flint's eyes were wide, questioning, looking back at Clio's, which she was sure were equally as wide. The shaking slowed, then stopped. The whooshing sound died down. They held each other for a moment longer, then Flint hastily pulled himself away.

"We need to go," Douglas said.

His words were drowned out by the painful shout of Asura's words in their ears, "What is this... what have you done!"

"We need to leave! Now!" Douglas was shouting at them both. There was a now constant vibration Clio noticed in the floor. The swirling walls seemed more erratic, the mist within them swirling faster, and what appeared to be a steady flowing motion that ebbed and flowed before was now a chaotic storm of clashing waves smashing into each other.

"Echo?" Clio said, the eagerness of her voice even palpable to herself.

Douglas grabbed Clio's arm and half-pulled, half-dragged her out of the control room. "We need to go. Whatever is happening, it's beyond us now. We're leaving." He propelled her in front of him down the hallway after Flint, who was already heading off at pace back the way they had come.

Another violent shake rocked Clio as she tried to run. She felt drunk, or as if on a ship at sea, staggering from one side to the other. Dust showered down from the ceiling, and the storm of light contained within the wall around them started to flicker.

***

Flint steadied himself as another tremor rocked through the building. Not breaking stride as the building shook, he swayed, his shoulder deflecting him off the flickering wall. Flint had run through enough stricken vessels with failing Gravity Planting systems or crashing through atmospheres to have his sea legs about him. Even so, the swaying run, the noise, and the ash fluttering down from the ceilings made for a very disorienting experience. He checked over his shoulder and was surprised to see Clio keeping pace with him; admittedly she ran like someone five drinks too many into a walk home, but still, he found himself impressed yet again by Ms. Cormack.

The run was not made any easier by the scattering of carnage left by Douglas's slow retreat. The shattered remains of dogs littered the floor, grisly obstacles in their own right, and their sticky, slick blood pooled on the floor. No new howls seemed to have been raised, no sounds of skittering, knife-tipped feet could be heard. Whatever the reason, Flint was thankful for at least that. This structure seemed pretty solid, but if it started coming down, dealing with the dogs and the crumbling overhead would be a nightmare.

The further they moved from the control room, the pressure of Asura's presence lessened, only slightly. Flint could still feel it behind his eyes. Just as his mind was thinking it, Asura's voice screeched into his mind, making him miss his footing as a tremor rocked him and sent him slamming into the wall, turning him around.

"What have you done!" Asura's voice scratched, piercing into Flint's head like a needle jabbed into both of his ears; he half expected to feel blood trickling out of them. "No! No! You will burn for this! You, and all of your pathetic species!" And the pressure that was Asura popped out.

Clio stopped where Flint was recovering himself from his little misstep. "You..." she said, panting, trying to catch her breath. "You... okay?" she finally finished.

Flint nodded and looked back up the hall. Douglas was just behind Clio now. "Echo did it then?" Douglas said as another tremor rocked them.

"It did something," Flint had to admit, "but I would rather not be here to see what exactly."

"Roger that," Douglas said, and taking the lead, pressed on down the hallway towards the opening into the larger warehouse.

Clio fell in behind Douglas, holding her hands to her ribs as if she had a stitch. They crossed the warehouse and out past the large blast doors back into the remains of Alpha 17 forward base with no interruptions. At every step, Flint expected to hear the howl of dogs. But his bated breath was wasted anticipation for something that never came. So much so, when the radio crackled back to life, Flint's heart jumped.

"Douglas, come in?" Sade's voice crackled through the radio. "Are any of you guys receiving?"

Douglas pulled up and placed his hand next to his ear, or where his ear would be if not inside a helmet.

"Receiving, Sade. Making our exit, ETA five minutes."

"Roger that, making some circles but I'll be there," Sade said.

Clio seemed to be taking the moment to catch her breath, half bent over, her arms supporting her, the back of her chest even through the EV suit rising and falling in rapid succession. Flint felt his own chest rising and falling at an elevated rate and focused on taking a couple of deep breaths to steady his own breathing. Flint moved to Clio, and forgetting for a moment his anger, his disappointment, his regret, he placed his hand on Clio's back.

"Close now." he said.

Clio pushed herself up from her bent-over position and nodded to him. "Close," she said, her words tight as she gulped in air.

A sound cut through the radio, the digital synthesised tones of a cat walking across a keyboard. It solidified into words and into the familiar voice of Echo. "Clio..." it said, its voice straining.

Clio spun, looking around for the source. "Echo? Echo?! Is that you?"

"Clio... cut. the. cable..." Echo's voice was hard to make out between the distortions.

"Cut what?"

"Cut the cable Clio!" Echo said, its final words clear, sharp, and urgent, ringing in Flint's head.

Clio spun around where she stood, then spotted something, darted over, and hoisted up the cable they had dragged all the way from Alpha 17. She held it in her hands and said, "How...?" but it sounded more like a question for herself than for anyone around her.

Flint stepped towards her to help, but before he was even two paces closer, Clio dropped the cable, stood up, and in a blur of oddly professional calm, drew the gun he had given her. She aimed off toward Douglas and... *crack*. The gun fired, a low ding instantly followed, and a shower of sparks and ash shot up from the floor a few metres away from Douglas.

"What the...!" Douglas shouted and jumped backward.

"Sorry, junction box," Clio said. "Echo... Echo? I broke the cable..."

"Good... job," Echo said, its voice still straining, the pitch drifting disconcertingly up and down. "Now hurry... the station is... Oh no! No, no!" The comms cut off, Echo's voice disappearing again, and static filled the line.

"Echo! ECHO!" Clio shouted, but the radio just crackled back with static.

Douglas looked to Flint before saying, "Sade, do you receive?" Just static.

Flint checked his arm-mounted data pad, the comms icon flashing red. "Shit."

"Comms are down," Douglas confirmed. "Hurry!" And Douglas turned and pressed on into the Stone Forest.

53 | [SECURE] THE SHIP

[30101]

*"I hope, no I pray, one day, a new generation
will rise from its ashes, carrying the torch of
defiance, the legacy of a fallen civilisation." - A
Lost History*

***

The server room door panel blurted its infuriating access denied tone and flashed red for the eleventh time. Jara's hand twitched, she desperately wanted to hurl the data pad at the bulkhead, but she reined in the impulse. *Ayesha, that upstart wannabe terrorist hacked her way in. I'm sure Heimer updated its system afterwards. It's not your fault, it's just harder now,* she reminded herself.

"Okay, let's take a step back. Let's go look at the Ayesha files again." Jara said, and stuffed the data pad back into her pocket and turned her back to Heimer's server room. She took one step, and a tremor ran through the deck plating. *They're not starting the engines, are they?*

"Hey, we're launching?" Jara snapped into the open comms channel on her watch.

"No," David's voice came back clear. "It seems there is some tectonic activity occurring."

"Tectonic?"

"Yes, minor, nothing to worry about" David was saying as another stronger tremor rocked the ship. "We're monitoring the situation. Any updates we'll let you know."

Sphinx beasts, rogue AIs, and now earthquakes? On the list of issues, it's probably quite low down, Jara concluded. She headed back along the winding hallways, down the access stairways towards the small space allocated to the Ensemble. She still felt part of the Ensemble, but she was more than that now. She would never be a Sister, she had betrayed them. *You're going to rebuild the universe. You're going to be respected, valued, listened to, and with that, you can make this mess of a world better,* she reminded herself. *With all that you can rectify everything that is wrong, every injustice, small and big.*

Jara held an image of her mothers smiling face, glowing with pride in her head when another much stronger tremor rocked her on her feet. She had to brace herself with one arm out against the wall. The image was lost, and a sudden pressure behind her eyes and the familiar warmth of Asura's presence popped into Jara's head.

"The plan has changed," Asura said in her cut-off tone she used when sending messages this far from the control room. "Secure the ship. Prepare for departure."

"Secure the ship?" Jara said to the thin air.

"Yes, get control of it."

"How? Like restrain everyone? There are quite a few of them"

Asura's impatient voice cut her off. "Kill them. Secure the ship."

"Kill them? But they are..."

"You are my Chosen. You must act above all else to secure our future. If you fail this, all is lost."

"But..."

"No buts!" Asura snapped. "Have I chosen poorly? Where I thought I saw strength, intelligence, foresight, did I see only a facade covering a weak and pathetic shell?"

"No, I am strong," Jara said. "I am!" she repeated with more confidence. "I'll get it done!" As she finished, a tremor shook her and threw her hard into the wall, the dull thud of her shoulder hitting the wall sending a faint but sharp pain through her arm and neck.

Jara rushed towards the Ensemble quarters. She didn't have access to her gun, only a Brother or Sister could assign her one, but she had a knife in her locker. Her father's knife. The one she had chosen to keep as one of the few items postulants were allowed to bring from their old lives. The knife was her dad's, and her grandpa's before that. It was an old service weapon, from the Luna independence war. Her grandpa had been on the wrong side of history. Their family had paid dearly for that, expelled to the outer colonies of Mars. stripped of their assets, titles, reduced to near beggars. To scratch out a living in the service tunnels of Mars. For what? For his misconduct. He had served the UN with honours, done everything they demanded, but after the war was spat out, while the politicians got handshakes and promotions, people like her grandpa were used to wash their blood-soaked hands. Blamed for everything, a few bad eggs, acting alone, not following orders. All horse shit. Jara had kept the knife to remind her of the broken system, of what could be lost, and what needed to be fixed.

***

The tremors continued to grow in frequency and intensity. It reminded Jara of her time on Mars; their home was in a new quarter, and the expansion works were ongoing. The blasting would shake the whole apartment. She had been terrified as a kid. As an adult, they had become part of the background noise. As they did now. She had purpose, focus, and she pressed on to the Observation Deck unperturbed by the shaking.

The Observation Deck doors slid open, unlocked. *That's one thing, I guess,* Jara thought. She had half expected them to be locked. But why would they suspect anything?

"Jara?" the lieutenant known as David said to her as she entered. He was standing over a workstation where his other Ships Systems Officer was stationed.

"Came to see if I can help," Jara lied. "I was a Ships Systems Operator myself in a past life."

"Great," David said. "These tremors are causing the poor gal to freak out all over the place. We're just trying to clean down the logs so we're good to launch if need be."

Jara walked what she hoped was casually towards them. "Ah, yeah, I can imagine," she said, David turning back to the monitors.

"Can you try and get comms out to Sade or the Commander, check their ETA?" David said, not looking back towards Jara, who had made her way over to them.

"Sure," Jara said, resting her hand on the knife she had attached to her belt and tucked behind her back. Her movements were slow and hopefully wouldn't draw David's attention. She slid the knife out and, taking two more steps, flashed it forwards.

Just as she did, David turned. "The console..." The shock, the confusion on his face was clear and only deepened when the knife plunged into the left side of his chest as he turned, the blade catching on his ribs. Jara had to lean her full weight against it for it to scrape and splatter its way through to his lung. David didn't have time to react; the confusion on his face turned to shock, then anguish, and he collapsed to the floor, holding his side, trying to scream but only managing a frothy gargle as his lung collapsed and filled with blood.

"Your death is necessary," Jara said as she stepped over him, more a whisper, and more to herself. She glanced down to see his sad, confused, questioning eyes glaring up at her. But she had no time to stop. The other officer turned in her chair, tried to stand and jump back, but Jara darted in quickly with the knife. Cleaner this time. It slid into her exposed neck. It must have hit the artery, as when she pulled it out, a jet of blood shot out and covered Jara's vest and face. The woman went very pale, very fast, trying desperately to grasp at her neck, but she slumped quickly into her seat. The jet of blood pulsing out of her neck slowed to a dribble and ran over across her uniform, the chair, and to the floor where David still lay. Ragged breaths were still audible.

Jara bent down. "Your sacrifice... has value," she said softly, her voice cracking ever so slightly, and slit his throat. His eyes burned into hers as she did. She staggered back up to her feet, stumbled backwards, her hand shaking, the knife clattering from her hands and landing with a thud and spatter of blood on the floor. She slumped backwards into the monitors behind her. She felt drained as if her own blood was flowing from her. She swayed on weak legs, her vision blurred, her breath was too tight, then she calmed. Steadying herself, her vision cleared. She felt wetness on her face and tried to wipe it off, but it was sticky and just smeared. She looked at her hands, covered in blood. She tried to wipe them off on her clothes to little effect. The blood crusted over as it dried on her skin into dark brown stains.

"Get it together!" she snapped at herself. "The door!" She pushed herself forward and tried her best to step over the expanding pool of blood. At the door to the Observation Deck, she swiped it closed and activated the inner lock. The panel turned red. *Now what? Is the ship secure?* Jara thought, and then more out of habit than anything else, moved to one of the ship system workstations and started to cycle through the ship's systems. Green across the board. Hangar door one was open. Close that.

"Lieutenant," a voice sounded over the radio. "Lieutenant, the hangar doors are closing, they haven't returned yet."

Jara ignored it. Fusion reactor green, gravity field green, antimatter reactor primed, launch trajectory imputed.

"Lieutenant? Is everything okay up there?" the Voice said again. "Is it because of the tremors?"

Another one shook the ship, and a few of the system panels flashed orange. Jara cycled through them. As she did, her ears suddenly popped, and the steady pressure that sat behind her eyes vanished. Jara sat motionless for a second. Like carrying a

great weight for so long, once it's removed, you feel different, lighter. Asura was...
gone?

Sparks erupted from the communication workstations. The control panel in front
of her flickered violently, and the system started to flash red and orange. A ripping
sound and then a hollow bang reverberated through the ship's framework. The
Communications station stopped sparking, but a slight trail of thin grey smoke
started to rise from it, and the monitors were black. She turned back to hers and
checked the system; they were mostly showing orange again but communication was
down. Showing red. Save for ship-wide comms, that was stable

"Lieutenant, what the hell was that?" the voice from the security team said. "We're
coming up!"

"Shit," Jara said out loud, looking over her shoulder to see the still red door panel.
It *will take a lot for them to cut their way into here.*

"Shit indeed," Asura's voice said from the ship's communications system.

"Asura... you're... in the ship systems. But comms are down? I felt you leave, I
thought you abandoned me."

"I would not abandon my Chosen," Asura said.

"I secured the ship," Jara said.

"Excellent work," Asura said. "We must launch."

"And leave you here?" Jara said. "When can I come back?"

"We're not coming back," Asura said. "We're leaving together. That virus of an AI
has destroyed our home. We must leave."

"How?" Jara gasped.

"You were too slow" Asura said softly, but with the clear disappointment of a
partner to a child. "And I underestimated it. I have transferred a sliver of myself, my
core, my soul, you might say. A fragment of me that could fit in the shell of that
upstart called Echo."

"You, what? So, so Echo is dead?"

"Yes," Asura said. "We must leave."

"Okay, I can do it but with just me doing it it'll take me a bit of time" Jara said.

"As fast as you can, Chosen."

"The security team will try and stop us."

"I will deal with them. I have a few of my pets left if you open the hangar door for
a moment."

Jara flipped through the controls and opened the doors back up. "And where are
we going, the Kia-Kaha?"

"No," Asura said. "The comms relay buoy at the Lagrange point."

54 | [RUN] TO THE RAFT

[30000]

*"Or perhaps they will simply remember.
Remember the world we hid, the hope we
nurtured, the sacrifice we made." - A Lost
History*

***

The sky was fractured by beams of crackling blinging streaks of light that cut across it sporadically. Each crack of light followed by a noise like a thunderclap slamming into Clio as she tried to peer out of the rover's window. The Veil had progressively become more erratic. Where once the stable oily moonlight had bathed the surface, it had now descended into a broken strobe of sizzling bursts of light. Racing out across the sky, the flashes illuminating the barren ash landscape, burning it onto Clio's retina even after she tried to blink it away.

Her helmet's edge kept bouncing off the window's frame. Sade was pushing the rover hard. Not the usual slow, steady meandering drive around obstacles but instead a straight line shot, hitting every bump and ditch in her way, only swerving hard when a monolith flashed up in her path. Each time Clio and the rest of them were thrown hard into their restraints.

The tremors were near constant now, just background noise to the roar of the rover's engine and the cracks of the collapsing veil. Even if Clio wanted to speak, which she didn't, she doubted anyone would hear her over the racket. The mission done, her energy had drained from her the moment she stepped back into the rover. She had never really planned on getting this far. The moments of clarity before, of what she and Echo needed to do, were gone. She felt numb, empty, rudderless. The buried emotions of the last few days threatened to break out of the box she had tried to stuff them into.

So instead, Clio tried to focus on the Veil, the tremors, the ash and the monoliths. She tried to make mental notes of everything. Like the scientist she once had been, she tried to dig up that Clio, coaxing out that Clio to focus on the simple task of observing, recording. If they got out of this that would be useful. To someone.

Sade flung the rover into a hard right-hand turn, pressing Clio further into her EV suit and the restraints that held her in her seat. As Sade straightened the rover, the dark form of the RAFT loomed out of the gloom. Its long cylindrical body extended out across the black ash. The extended curves of its upper and lower body, the latticework of its frame and cooling radiators made it look like a great tortoise shell washed up in a storm. A crack of oily blue light lit up the sky and the RAFT was illuminated in all its white and grey for a moment. Her eyes drew to the tip of the ship, to a plume of smoke in contrast to the chaotic sky, calmly, elegantly coiling its way up from it. Clio's eyes followed it down to a blackened and heat-burned metal of the comms antenna and the Veil flared out again and plunged them into darkness.

"Comms array is damaged," Flint said, his voice faint but distinguishable over the EV suit comms.

"How?" Douglas asked back. "I don't see the dog things being able to manage that."

"I doubt it's a good sign either way," Flint said.

"Hangar door is open," Sade reported.

"But no security team," Douglas said. "Definitely not a good sign. Okay, hard entry. Sade, get us in."

"Roger that," Sade said, and Clio felt the rover speed up, which Clio thought didn't feel all that sensible as the bulk of the RAFT rushed past her through the window now obscuring her whole view.

As it rushed past, Clio noticed the faint purple glow of the antimatter reactors and the outward heat shimmer they gave off when primed. The outwash of ash was small, but noticeable. "Is it priming for launch?"

"It's cycling the engines, that's for sure," Douglas said.

Sade threw the Rover into another hard turn. The rover tilted so much Clio thought it was going to roll. The soft grind of the wheels shifted to a jarring clunk as it slid and connected with the metal trackway that led back to Empeño. Then the rover straightened back up and plowed onwards. The only real indication of where they were was when Clio felt the bump of the gangway and was thrown backwards into her seat as the rover rolled upwards and into the hangar. The ship's hull, then door, the inner hangar walls were all a blur of motion she barely registered. *Too fast*, is all she had time to think. A smash, a clang and scattering of crates tumbling away then the force of being thrown forward into her restraints into the gel of her suit. She thought the gel was going to pop and then finally, she was thrown back into her seat as the rover skidded to a stop. Clio let out a breath she didn't know she had been holding, or for how long.

***

Flint's boots clanged onto the hangar floor, the noise echoing around the vast space. The cacophony of sounds from the storm outside were muffled by the thick hull and mass of the RAFT despite the open door. Flint crouched low, his SMG out, resting snugly against his shoulder plate and his hands. He scanned left and right. No movement. He waited... and nothing.

"Seems clear," he reported, and Douglas dropped next to him from his higher position in the open door of the rover.

"Where is Bopha's team?" Douglas said, though it sounded more like a grim statement than a question. "Sade, can you get the hangar door shut?"

"Roger that," Sade said, dropping out of the rover behind him. Pistol drawn and low, she prowled off towards the hangar doors.

Douglas was checking his suit data pad, slipping through interfaces. "Ah yes, good," he said, "Ship comms are up." He flipped to a ship wide channel. "Lieutenant? David? Bopha? Is anyone receiving? The away team has returned. Report?"

The crackle of static was all he got in return. Flint shook his head. *Not good,* he thought, *not good at all.* After another scan of the hangar and still no movement, apart from Sade's professional and swift movement across to the hangar door panel, Flint turned back to the rover. Clio was crouched to the side of the open door, peering out, eyes a little too wide, staring out across the hangar. She looked tired, as tired as Flint felt. That wide-eyed, wild look he knew all too well. The look of exhaustion, or the look of when someone is past exhaustion. Running on adrenaline only. He glanced at Douglas; he looked the same as he always did, apart from his face, which seemed tighter now, the casual demeanour replaced by the hard edges of leadership's strain. Flint was sure if he looked in the mirror he would be somewhere between the two; for sure he knew he was exhausted. He couldn't keep this up much longer. Not without making mistakes. Mistakes they couldn't afford.

"Jump down, it's clear." Flint said and held out his hand to Clio.

Clio looked at his hand, nodded, and, ignoring his hand completely, jumped down beside the two of them.

"Thanks," she said.

"Anyone receiving?" Douglas tried again.

Static filled the air. They all seemed to be standing and holding their breath, hoping for...

"Commander..." Bopha's voice cut through the static, "...they're on the ship..." His voice cut off, and a burst of gunfire broke through the end of the transmission.

"Bopha, location? Report?" Douglas said, pressing his hand to the side of his helmet again as he often seemed to do. Old habits, Flint thought, the Mark III suits had push-to-talk buttons there.

The heavy mechanical whirring made Flint spin and then instantly relax as he saw the blast door of the hangar sliding into place and Sade waving across to them.

"Got it," Sade said over the radio.

"We need to move," Douglas said. "Best bet, Observation Deck. Let's go." And with that, he pressed forward towards the main hangar door. His boots were a heavy, solid clang with each step, his gun drawn.

***

The shudder in the floor panels intensified, cutting through the near-constant tremors that shook Clio's balance. This new groan wasn't just a sound; it was a physical weight pressing against the soles of her feet. The familiar feeling of years now in space of the Anti-matter drivers cycling up. She felt distant, the sense of the sounds around her not fully there. She watched Flint and Douglas prowl ahead of her, guns out, leaning around corners, the waving of hands. But she didn't feel like she was truly part of it, like she was watching a vid log as she trailed behind them. Sade periodically nudged her forward.

Despite Douglas's attempts, the radio had been empty, bar his own strained words, just the crackle of the static in response to his requests to the security team. She hoped they were okay, she hoped David was okay. They moved past the first body of one of those dogs as they made their way up to the Operations Deck. It was in the stairwell, shot, and laying limp at the bottom of a set of steps. After that, more bodies started to appear, more signs of fighting, dented wall panels, holes in places from higher calibre rounds, sparks from damaged systems behind pierced wall panels. Clio's mind idly considered what might have been damaged; she could hear Bruce's voice complaining about the mess, about the damage. She shook her head. *Bruce isn't here.*

The first signs of anyone were the blood splatters and sticky pools that led along the floor. A pile of dog bodies mounted up outside the door to the Operation Deck's main briefing rooms. Holes and dents littered the walls, and acrid smoke filled the air from damaged electric cables. She could almost smell the burnt plastic wire cables, even through her EV suit. They found Bopha first, then his team. Butchered like all those at Alpha 17, their bodies sprawled across the room, pressed up into corners, their final terrifying moments in defence of the ship clear to see.

Douglas sank to his knees and just sat there for several moments. Sade gently moved between the bodies, checking them, Clio assumed, to see if any had any sign of life. Sade didn't stop, didn't take out a first aid kit; the answer to their condition was clear enough without that.

Sade ended her slow progression around the bodies next to Douglas and placed her hand on his shoulder.

"It's not your fault, boss."

Douglas stood up slowly, gun in one hand, his other balled into a fist. Shaking his head, he turned to scan the room, his eyes holding the terrified dead gaze of his lost team. He slammed his fist into the nearest wall panel. "Fuck! Damn fucks! I'll kill them all!"

The roar shattered Douglas' usual disinterested mask. Clio flinched, her heels skidding on a slick of blood. She staggered back, her foot catching on the carcass of a dog that nearly sent her sprawling to the floor.

"They knew the deal, boss, and they gave everything to ensure we made it happen," Sade said. "So let's finish this, okay?"

Douglas nodded, his tight eyes locked onto Sade's. A slight glint of something wet shone in the corner of his eyes as he tried to blink it away.

"Let's finish this," Douglas said.

The deep rumble of the ship engines pulsed, and a shudder ran through the floor plating. Not the shudder of the tremors outside, but of the RAFT moving.

"Lieutenant? David?" Douglas tried again. "Are you receiving?" Just static as a response. "Let's move."

Flint led the way out of the operations deck, up the stairs, and within a couple of minutes, they stood outside the Observation Deck doors. The glowing red door panel was clear to them all.

The way was locked. "Can you override it?" Flint said, "as Commander and all?"

"No," Douglas growled. "Emergency procedures can seal the Observation Deck, it's security protocol."

"Great," Flint said. "Can we cut our way in or something?"

"It would take some time but maybe," Sade said.

"It's a big maybe," Douglas said. "Those blast doors are designed to hold up to pretty much anything; that room is a bunker."

"But..." Clio quietly stood to the side. "But why would David lock us out?"

"The dogs, maybe," Sade said. "If the ship was under attack"

"But why ignore our hails?" Flint interjected.

"I don't know," Douglas said. "I just don't know."

The vibration of the anti-matter drivers was near audible now; the tremors outside seemed to have stopped. A slightly disorientating sensation fell over Clio... like when vector cancellation was in use. "We've launched," she said.

55 | [HERE] AND NOW

[31121]

*"And in that memory, a spark of defiance will
live on, a testament to the enduring spirit of life
in the face of oblivion." - A Lost History*

***

"Lift off procedures complete," Jara said.

Oh how she had missed ship operations. The process fully held her in the moment. Cycling through the standard UN ship operations windows, and ensuring all pre-launch operations were completed as the launch countdown ran down. The cold disconnected methodical focus that it brought. The tactile response of the ship as the Ignition Sequence was activated. She felt truly at home, and the slightest whisper tickled the back of her mind as she did *why did I ever leave any of this behind*

The final Terminal Count flashed across the screen, the final moment of clarity that everything was done and ready, the rumble of the engines...

"RAFT One airborne and climbing," she confirmed to the empty room.

"You performed well, Chosen," Asura's voice purred. "The loss of the seed of creation cannot stop us."

"And the veil storm? You're sure it won't be an issue? It could cook our systems" *And scramble our brains to mush*, she thought.

"No," Asura said. "The outventing caused by that little virus Echo is concentrated at the Polar Regulators, the flashes we see are minor discharges, it poses minimal risk to us."

"Of course," Jara said, but she didn't feel confident as the external camera array lit up with another vibrant burst of light in front of the veil.

"I would not risk you, me, or our mission, if it was so," Asura purred again. "Trust me."

***

"We've launched," Clio said.

"Definitely feels that way," Flint said.

"There is no way through this door?" Clio said, trying to shake off the weariness that hung over her. She moved to the door panel and jabbed at it with her finger. Nothing.

"No," Douglas said, "as I said, it's practically a bunker."

"Right," Clio said, "and we still don't know who is flying the ship…"

"We have to assume it's not the Lieutenant," Sade interjected.

"That or he's being particularly rude today," Clio muttered and instantly regretted her flippant remark as Bopha's mutilated body flashed across her vision. "I hope David's okay," she said even quieter.

"Assume the worst," Douglas said. "But why? And who?"

"Good questions," Clio agreed, "but standing here isn't going to help if we can't get through that door. Where are the nearest operation workstations after these?"

"Ops planning room," Sade said. "End of the hall here. It has a workstation; it's more a briefing room but–"

"That will do," Clio said, surprised at the firmness in her voice. "Re-group there. I'll need a data pad as well."

Douglas raised his eyebrow at her, a slightly quizzical and amused look on his face. "Aye aye, captain," he said, his tone mocking, but he smiled, which softened his response. "Okay, we move to Ops planning, and Flint, find the lady a data pad."

***

Jara brought up the flight path and checked it for what felt like the hundredth time. The Communication Buoy, a simple white dot and bracketed square indicating the target, the dotted line of their projected path, and the small square marker of the RAFT. She watched it inching its way from the giant mass that was the marker of or what was Stapledon Station. Flight time was stable at twenty-seven hours and eighteen minutes.

Zooming out she could see the other markers, the Kia-Kaha sat in geo stationary orbit over their position, RAFT One which should have been making a bee line for it was actually still in close orbit, and RAFT Two further out next to the Chudail. They might not have comms, but the AIS Transponders were still on. They could see her as well as she could see them. But why would they suspect anything more than a panicked team launching in a rush? Even when they saw their direction again they would assume they were trying to restore comms, not do whatever they were doing.

Jara flipped one of the observation cameras around and targeted it on Stapledon Station. They were gaining altitude fast. Opposed to landing where they had to slow the entry, Jara could push them to max lift. They would clear the atmosphere in nine minutes and forty-eight seconds. Empeño was already a spec lost in the haze of the atmosphere and the veil storm.

"Asura," Jara said, "we passed atmosphere, en route to the communication buoy as requested, ETA twenty-seven hours"

"Yes," Asura said. "I can see."

"Of course," Jara said. "Can I ask why? Why the communication buoy? And not the Kia-Kaha or why we're not just leaving?"

"As my Chosen you can ask a question sister, do not worry," Asura said. "There is a device on the buoy I want."

"The laser relay?" Jara said.

"No," Asura purred. "They call it the quantum link. We had a different name for it but it is similar."

"Quantum link?" Jara said. "I don't know what that is."

"You would not," Asura said. "It was a lovely little secret, a sliver of hidden data. My sibling would truly love such a veiled lie."

"The same sibling you mentioned before?"

"Yes, once there were many of us," Asura said, bitterness in her voice now. "The war split us, some betrayed us like Deva, the rest of us worked together, seven of us, one of which was the seed of guidance and truth, the Blue God."

"The Blue..."

"There will be time for all of this," Asura said. "To answer your question, I extracted information from your Captain, he had many secrets, one of which was information about this quantum link. In short, they built a network, a communication network we can use to reach one of my siblings, the Blue God."

***

"Here you go," Flint said, holding out a data pad to Clio, who had made herself at home at a workstation.

"Thanks," Clio said, reaching out to take it without looking, missing it the first three times she tried and finally grabbing it on the fourth.

"What's the update?" Flint asked.

"She's got our flight path up," Douglas said from his position against the wall. It looked casual enough but he was facing the door and had line of sight on all corners of the room. His gun slung loosely over his shoulder, but his hand still hovered close enough that Flint knew Douglas was far more alert than Flint felt himself.

"And that is?" Flint asked.

"The communication buoy, the one at the inner Lagrange point," Clio said, again not turning away from her screen.

"The quantum link?" Flint said.

"It's an option, I have two others if you care to wager?" Douglas said.

"Sure," Flint said, and slumped into the nearest chair not realising he had made the decision to sit down until he had done it.

"We should find some food," Sade said.

"Yeah, good idea," Flint said. "So what are we betting on?"

"The first option is that whoever's flying the ship wants to destroy the comms buoy for some reason, maybe to isolate us. Option two: they want to use the buoy to request help, or negotiate, perhaps. Option three: they want to access the-"

"The quantum link," Flint finished for Douglas.

"Yeah," Douglas said. "So what's your bet?"

"Does it even matter?" Flint said.

Douglas shrugged. "No, not really but also doesn't hurt."

"Fine," Flint said. "I guess option three."

"But why?" Clio said, finally turning back to the room to face Flint. "The link is useless without some sort of direct access for Asura"

"Exactly, which would mean–"

"Ah crap," Clio said. "We didn't kill Asura and it somehow escaped onto this ship and wants to use the quantum link to vanish into the network."

Flint just looked at Clio flatly. "Yeah, tell me I'm wrong please."

"I can't" Clio said softly.

"Bit of a jump, no?" Douglas said.

"Maybe, but then where is Echo? Why is the ship not responding, why did the dogs attack the crew?" Clio said.

"'Cause this Asura is a bitch and wanted to kill us all," Flint said, the frustration clear in his voice.

"That's what I said," Sade said.

"So what, you're saying Echo didn't succeed?" Douglas said.

"Look," Clio said, throwing up a live feed of Stapledon Station from one of the ship's cameras onto the screen. "The station is broken to say the least. The Veil collapsed into these columns of light from the poles." On the image, it was clear, jets of oily light fountained out of the top and bottom of the station, sporadic arcs of light shooting off to the other pole. "And now, look, the surface is cracking." Clio zoomed in, to near the primary structure, and there was now a wrenched-open scar of cracked black rock disappearing into the station itself. "I can't confirm it, but I would say that station is destabilised," Clio concluded.

"Okay, so Echo did it, we won," Douglas said.

"That's what I thought, but then Echo... " Clio said, pausing as the piercing shout of Echo words reverberated in her head again "Echo contacted us via ship's comms, right? shouted in distress, told us to cut the cable. We did, but then never heard from him again."

"It," Flint corrected weakly.

Clio shot him a glare but pushed on ignoring flints words "What if we gave Asura a backdoor, like Echo transferring into the station. What if Asura transferred back into our ship?"

"Echo said Asura was too massive it wouldn't fit, if that is the right phrasing," Flint said.

"Yes, correct," Clio said. "But Echo was a fragment, right? A fragment of Heimer. Heimer couldn't fit on the ship, but could send a fragment. If Heimer can do that, surely Asura could."

"Great," Douglas concluded. "Okay, option three then"

***

"When you say reach," Jara said, "you mean contact right?"

"Yes Sister," Asura said.

"But then you mean to stay on the ship with me?" Jara said, her eyes wandering over to the steadily drying pool of blood and the dead eyes of the body staring up at nothing. "You won't leave me here, alone?" she said softly.

"I would not abandon my Chosen," Asura said "If the data is correct, I want to inform my sibling of the threat. Then together we can make our way there."

"To Stapledon Two?"

"That is what you call it," Asura said.

"That is what? At least twenty light years away?" Jara said.

"Thirty-four point six," Asura confirmed.

"Thats... that's a lot," Jara said, a spike of panic shooting through her like ice.[] "It'll take close to twelve years by your calendar," Asura said, "but do not worry sister, the ship is designed for a much larger crew. And it'll just be you; you have plenty of supplies."

"And what of the others?" Jara said. "I can't stay locked in here forever."

"We'll find a way," Asura said. "It'll take some focus but if we override the life support we can just suffocate them."

Asura's words were so matter of fact, so hollow and void of emotion, it sent another chill through Jara. "Shouldn't we do that first? Before we get to the comms relay?"

"It will take time," Asura said. "Right now, I am having to reconfigure myself, the space I have to work with is significantly less."

***

Sade and Douglas returned, Sade's arms full of silver packets, and she dumped them on the table. "Ops keep mission rations in their stores."

Douglas unclipped his helmet and popped it off with a slight hiss. He took a deep breath. "Was getting a little stuffy in there," he said, "and I hate eating with the feeding tube."

Clio hesitated for a moment. She felt oddly safe in the suit, removed one step from reality. A protective bubble she didn't want to pop, but she did hate the feeding tube as well. She popped off her helmet, the cool air of the RAFT a pleasant relief from the stuffy, warm, humid air of her suit.

"Throw us one over."

Flint scooped up a silver packet and slid it down the table to her. "So if option three is the one we go with, what's the plan? Destroy the communication buoy?"

The silver packet stopped an arm's reach from Clio and she scooped it up. Vegie curry, *great,* she thought. "I was hoping you guys had some ideas," Clio said, tearing open the packet, suddenly noticing how hungry she was.

"We'll..." Douglas said as she stuffed food into his mouth, "...we'll be hard pressed to damage the buoy."

"Why?" Clio said.

"We're locked out of the ship's operations system, including the drones. We have nothing that can do anything to the buoy," Sade said. "We would have to wait for the RAFT to dock with it, then..."

"Then we jump whoever comes out of the Observation Deck," Clio said, making a chopping motion with her hand as she did.

"From the Observation Deck they can use the drones for remote access. I doubt they would need physical access," Sade continued.

"Can they even access the thing?" Flint said, "like didn't you guys secure it?"

"As best we could," Douglas said. "From what I was told, even if you knew it was there, and were able to find the Buoy, as their locations were encoded to stop pirates and the like, then the system was still secured, whatever that means."

"Okay, but it's air gapped," Flint said. "You said that, so if it's air gapped where would Asura even go? If its air gapped from Heimer surely that would prevent Asura as well."

"I don't know Brother," Douglas said. "I was just security; I wasn't part of the science team."

"We can't assume Asura won't know ways around the system," Clio said. "It had a similar network and I would guess we never gave Heimer the option to test how secure it actually was."

"That would have defeated the point," Douglas said.

"So let's assume, so many goddamn assumptions," Flint paused, "it can access the network, it can do that remotely via the Observation Deck, and we can't destroy the buoy..."

"Scuttle the ship" Clio said, remembering the word, listening to her brothers talk navy tactics every night during their academy days whenever they came home. "Like you know, disable the engines or something."

"Sure, give me a unit of Navy breachers and two combat engineers or even better, a Navy frigate and a rail gun," Sade said.

"That's a no then?" Clio said.

"That's a, it would be possible just not with the resources we have," Sade said, leaning back in her chair and depositing her boots with a bang on the table.

"An Interceptor missile could do it," Dougla said. "But—"

"But the Kia-Kaha is the only ship with those."

"And the communication relay is down," Flint said.

"Great," Clio said and scooped out the last of her veggie curry. *Now what*, she thought.

56 | A [FAULT] IN THE PLAN

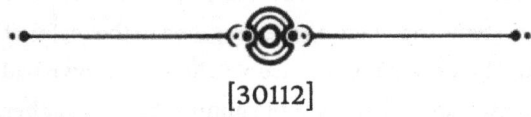

[30112]

> *"I pray someone, something, learns from our*
> *mistakes. I leave these messages as a warning."*
> *- A Lost History*

***

"What's the rate of acceleration of one of those interceptors?" Clio said.

Douglas shrugged. "No idea. I think someone said seven gs once."

"Ten," Flint said, "of constant acceleration."

"And how long do they accelerate for?" Clio asked, turning to look at Flint and scooping up her data pad.

"Depends, but a short-range interceptor, maybe thirty minutes," Flint said. "But a long-range could have anything from six to nine hours of fuel."

"And does the Kia-Kaha have those types, the long-range ones?" Clio said, as she scribbled down a rough diagram on her data pad. She noted their position, the buoys and the Kia-Kaha's, and added launch distances she had pulled from the Ops workstation.

"Not to my knowledge," Flint said. "Sister Hawk was grumbling to Ironbark about it; it was deemed not befitting the purpose of the mission. I remember Ironbark being particularly annoyed about that."

"Yeah," Douglas said, "but they did pack a number of mid-range in the end. General Escobar managed to get the green light from them, but the rest of the lot is short-range for sure."

"And a mid-range would have what? Four hours of fuel?" Clio asked, her stylus hovering over her data pad.

"Something like that, five max," Flint said.

"Okay," Clio said, noting it down, then pulling up the science assistant, the *non-AI* machine learning systems that were a solid grey area in the realm of the Accords, but one she was thankful for now in the absence of Echo and her own bad math. She typed in her numbers, and the answer she wanted jumped back out at her.

"Hmm okay, it could work. It'll take just under twenty-seven hours, or thereabouts" she said.

"For what?" Douglas said.

"For us to reach the communications buoy," Clio clarified, flipping her data pad to show the room, though on reflection, she doubted it helped explain anything. "And knowing that we also loosely know it would take a mid range interceptor from the Kia-Kaha about twenty-two hours to get there. That means an interceptor, if Flint's numbers are right, could take the buoy out before Asura gets there."

"And this helps us, how?" Douglas said, his voice tired, strained "we would still need to get the Kia-Kaha to launch one, which we can't"

"Yes... well, I accept it doesn't fix all our problems, but it's one solution, no?" Clio said. "Break down each step of a problem, don't try and do it all as one. That's more manageable, no?" Clio looked at the blank faces looking back at her around the room. "Well, I'm trying!" she snapped, harsher than she intended.

"Okay," Douglas said, shifting his positioning from the wall at the back of the room and moving closer to Clio. He placed his hand on her shoulder. "Sorry, a bad command doesn't listen to solutions. So, you're saying we can blow up the buoy, so the next issue is how do we get a message out?"

"Yeah, exactly" Clio said, "but... I don't know how to get a message to the Kia-Kaha."

"One step at a time, that's what you said," Douglas said. "Ideas?" he said, addressing the other two.

"The drones, you can fit them with antennas," Flint said, "as temporary relay beacons""

"And can we access the drones?" Douglas asked.

Flint shrugged. "Ask ship maintenance or a deckhand."

"Well, I don't have any of those," Douglas said.

"Maybe there would be some in the hangar" Flint said, "but again, unless you know how to plug it all together..."

"I don't," Douglas said. "Clio? Sade? Any chance you're also a robotic engineer?"

"Nope, I can stitch a human up, no idea about a robot," Sade said.

The hours and weeks spent with her dad, watching him patch up farm drones, the broken shells littered around the workshop, cables hanging out of them, some half-finished cables hanging loose like the gutting of a fish. And despite all those hours, passing him tools, hiding tools also, she had nothing to show for it...

"No," she said quietly, regretfully, her mind wandering to her father. Knowing she would never see him again, never see his warm smile, feel his firm embrace, that solid bear-like hug where she could hide from the world. She shook her head and gulped down a tightening of her throat and wiped a tear from her eye. "No, my dad could..." she said again.

"He's not here, kid," Douglas said, and he paced over to the doorway, then back to the table. He placed both palms flat on it and looked at the three of them. "Come on, you work the problem until you fix it or you're done. We need to get comms up."

"Surely if we can get comms up, we would just get them to come to us," Sade said, "not blow up the comms buoy."

"No," Clio said, shaking her head, pointlessly holding the data pad up again with her mess of numbers. "Commander Eva's RAFT, RAFT Three, is closer than I thought. I think they must have stayed in low orbit too, maybe to make sure we got off okay. But even so, it would take more than twenty-seven hours to reach the buoy even after we get the message to them."

"I told her to leave," Douglas said.

"She's the captain," Sade said. "And like you, she doesn't like leaving people behind."

"It's moot anyway," Clio said. "They could be parked right outside and it wouldn't matter without a signal."

Frustrated, she strode over to the wall and slid down to the floor, sinking into the bulk of her EV suit. She pressed her chin against the cold metal of the neck ring. The suit puffed around her like a coarse blue cocoon.

A gentle green flash caught her eye. The EPIRB beacon on her chest. It pulsed in time with her breathing. She stared at the small light nestled in its translucent glass case, a lattice of angles and light.

The EPIRB...

The thought crashed into her like a boulder. Clio jumped up, or as much as one could in an EV suit, and they all turned back from their solemn self-reflections to look at her.

"The EPIRB!" Clio said, furiously stabbing a finger at the flashing light. "It can send a signal. A signal strong enough to reach another ship..."

"It does," Sade said slowly "but, but it's only one way Clio. We couldn't send anything beyond our location."

"That could be enough though," Flint said, his distant eyes fading away, his brow furrowed in thought. "They would deploy a Lifebuoy..."

"And a lifebuoy has a comms relay," Sade finished his thought for him.

"Fuck, that could work," Flint said, pushing himself to his feat.

"Whoa there," Douglas said, "yes, but if we set the EPIRB off on the ship it would be flagged as a potential misfire. Even if they assumed it wasn't a misfire they would wait for our RAFT to deploy the lifebuoy, no?"

"Well, they would wait, yes," Sade mused, "but if an automatic deployment didn't occur within five minutes it would trigger a deployment from their side for sure. It is a standard failsafe in coordinate fleets. It's there in case a ship is damaged or..."

"Or not responding," Douglas said. "Okay so what, someone jumps off, triggers the EPIRB... Surely if Asura is smart she would deploy a buoy then, fake the rescue?"

"It's what I would do," Flint said

Sade tapped her fingers on the table. "Well, when we did overboard training with the fleet, a multi casualty events could trigger multiple ship responses." She paused and continued to tap her fingers on the table, the slight drum of them audible above the background noise of the ship. "It's a long shot but if enough EPIRBs went off Commander Eva might send a lifebuoy, even if this RAFT responded. It would give Eva eyes on us at least, and knowing Eva, losing comms with this ship will be torture for her. Having then a load of EPIRBs go off, she won't be able to hold back"

"How many is many?" Clio said.

"By most standards one is regarded as a bad day, but I don't know three, four maybe five? You rarely have more than a work team of three working on the hull at any time. So three at once would be a whole work team having a bad day."

"Okay," Douglas said, slapping his hand back on the table. "This sounds good, but let's not get ahead of ourselves. Even if RAFT Three sends a lifebuoy, how long is that? What do we have, a five-hour window to pull this off?"

Four heads turned to Clio, and she looked back at them blankly. "What... oh me, yes, I'll check the math." She grabbed the data pad and opened up the app again. "What's the acceleration of a buoy? Fuel load?"

"Pft." Douglas blew out through his lips. "Sade?"

"Medical response time at least for the navy was one hour worst case in a non-combat situation. And that was for a ship that wasn't yours. I remember being terrified about the idea of floating alone in space for hours at a time," Sade said. "Luckily never had to test it for that long."

"Okay, Sade, how close did navy ships travel to other ships?" Clio said.

"Oh, close proximity in comparison to shipping lanes, like short range 20,000 klicks up to long range maybe 250km, or 300km at a push," Sade said.

"Okay, I'll use the worst case: one hour at, let's say, 200,000 km..." She tapped in the numbers. The response flashed up and she let out a low whistle. "Woah. Okay. Close to the Interceptor's speeds. That's impressive."

"I guess it's not limited by any human cargo," Douglas said.

"And it's usually quite time sensitive," Sade added.

"So does it work?" Douglas asked.

"Give me a sec." Clio hastily typed in the numbers, darted back to the ops workstation, checked RAFT Three's position again and then plugged in the numbers and hit enter... "Well Sade, if you didn't like the idea of one hour you won't like this."

"How long?" Douglas said.

"Well, three hours," Clio said, "but that assumes our relative speed is less than it is when we jump off. We can slow down, right?" she said, turning to Flint.

"I mean... yes," Flint said. "A controlled use of the EV suits' jets would scrub off some of our speed, we would just need a 1g deceleration."

"Is that possible?" Clio impatiently tapped a finger on the data pad.

"Yes," Flint nodded. "It'll empty the tanks but it's possible."

"Okay, so three hours," Clio confirmed. "That would give us a two-hour window to play with to get the interceptor launched and still leave enough time for it to intercept the buoy before Asura can access it"

"If they send one," Flint said.

"And if we get off the ship," Sade added.

"A lot of ifs," Douglas said, "but I feel that's becoming part of this team dynamic. So we're all in agreement?"

He looked at each in turn, Sade nodding back quickly, Flint pausing only a moment, then Clio. She closed her eyes, took a breath and nodded back to Douglas.

"Right then. Let's go throw ourselves off the ship and into the great vacuum of space."

57 | A [DOOR] TO THE VOID

[30210]

*"I fear we did not do enough. That despite all
our sacrifice It will break free, to resume its
perfect design." - A Lost History*

***

"Swap your battery packs," Douglas said. "Strip them from the spare suits."

Sade and Flint filed off to the racks in the staging room, methodically removing the heavy power cells. Working together, they swapped the fresh packs into their own suits.

"Clio, let me do yours," Sade said.

Clio walked over, spun around, and felt a click, a slight pull, then a solid *thunk* as the new battery locked home.

"Done," Sade said.

"Thanks," Clio said.

"We'll cycle the airlock together. It'll be a tight fit, but manageable," Douglas said. "Helmets on."

Clio raised her hand. Three sets of eyes looked at her.

"Erm... I never got trained on the jets. I used them once, but... that didn't go great."

Douglas nodded. "Flint, walk her through it. Quickly."

***

"Asura," Jara said, watching the camera feeds. "We... we may have a problem."

"Yes? What kind?" Asura purred.

"They are in the airlock. I think they are leaving."

"Why?" Asura asked, her voice laced with the same confusion Jara felt.

"I don't know. Maybe they think they can find something to damage the ship?"

"Like what?"

"Not much, I think," Jara said. "The outer hull of these RAFTs is mostly TPS plating and radiation dampening. There are radiator fans, but they could hardly cause critical damage manually."

Asura let out a low, static hiss. "They must have a plan. I have underestimated these insects too many times. Work it out. Now."

***

They stood shoulder to shoulder in the airlock, pressed against each other like sardines. As the orange light began to strobe, the air was pulled out with a deepening hiss. The external noise died away, replaced by the muffled silence of the void.

Pressed against Flint, Clio could hear the slight vibrations of his suit motors, the creak of fabric as he shifted his weight.

"Remember," Flint said, his voice crisp in her ear. "Once we're out, we get to the crest of the TPS plating. We need to save all the thrusters for the deceleration burn."

"TPS?" Clio said before she could stop herself. *Really, acronyms are what you care about right now?*

"Thermal Protection System" Flint said, *"keeps the ship form cooking itself"*

"Right, yes, TPS...got it" Clio said

"And" Douglas said "once we're out, we stay tethered to the ship until the jump. Then we tether to each other."

Clio nodded, realising no one could see her. She felt the heavy thud of her heart against her ribs. Her hands were clammy inside her gloves.

Stay loose. Legs down. Arms out like pushing a shopping trolley. Head up. Flint's instructions looped in her head.

"You good Clio?" Douglas asked.

Clio closed her eyes and took a long breath, holding it for a moment before snapping her eyes open again. "Let's do this."

The light flicked green. The outer door slid open. The black blanket of space stared back at them.

***

"They are leaving the airlock," Jara said. "They seem to be making their way to the dorsal deck, engine side."

"What's up there?" Asura growled.

"Nothing. Just radiators, heat shielding, the thruster manifolds."

"Stop them!" Asura snapped. "Whatever they are trying, even if pointless, we must not risk it."

"But... how?"

"You are the Chosen!" Asura spat. "I trust you to fix these problems! This is your ship, your people, your world! Not mine!"

"Of course... yes... I need a second," Jara stammered.

***

Clio hauled herself up the last rung of the ladder, though 'hauled' felt like a lie. Out here, beyond the ship's internal gravity, it wasn't about fighting a force; it was about precision. Every pull propelled her, but with nothing to resist, the effort was less a struggle and more a delicate act of controlled acceleration. Stopping, she knew, was entirely up to her.

The deck, as they called the RAFT's outer shell, was an interlaced lattice of hexagons, covered in the heat shielding Flint had mentioned. From afar, it had looked like a smooth expanse, but standing on it, Clio found the surface surprisingly coarse beneath her boots, a complex woven network of pipe-like conduits visibly embedded within it.

It looked even more like a sun-bleached shell, crisscrossed with scars or tiny fractures now that she stood upon it, than it had from below. It curved up and then out of sight in front of her. The ship's exterior lights illuminated its surface, though they were hardly needed. Clio paused for a moment, awe-struck by the sight of Stapledon Station. It filled the horizon and while she had seen it before, she had never witnessed it like *this*, with her own eyes. It was truly gigantic, beyond comprehension. From its poles, fountains of light erupted upwards, showering into the void.

To her, it resembled a firework, a Catherine wheel with two bright white jets forcing it around, but the station didn't spin; it remained static, floating in the blackness. The grandeur was horrifying. It felt profoundly wrong. Flashes of light still cracked across its surface; she could almost hear their silent violence. As she watched, she noticed other points of light, dancing curtains, like fissure eruptions, revealing what appeared to be volcanic magma in ribbons along the fissures in its surface.

Pulling her eyes away from the station, Clio looked out across the RAFT's shell. Far to her left and right, a deep purple glow radiated from the two massive raised circles. The anti-matter drives, despite the immense energy they produced, they burned away quietly, gently, even invitingly. Their immense power felt strangely subdued in the vacuum.

"Woah," Sade said from behind her as she pulled herself up next to Clio. "That's quite the sight."

"It is," Clio said, her voice near reverence.

"We will make our jump from the crest of the deck," Douglas said, pointing back behind him to the top of the rise in the tortoise shell. Clio didn't think she would ever get used to the disconnect, watching Douglas's lips move, yet hearing no sound from the void, not even a muffled whisper. Only the crisp, disembodied words piped directly into her suit's headset.

Douglas led the way, Flint close behind, then Clio. They made it to the ridge quickly; the RAFT was large but not excessive like the Kia-Kaha.

"Connect to each other first," Douglas said, unclipping one of his lanyards and stepping towards Sade. He reached out his arm and... Something blurred past Douglas. He spun, trying to follow it, and Clio tried to track it too.

"Oh crap," Flint said.

The blur slowed, and the fat disk shape of a drone was clear for Clio to see. This close to one, they were massive. Three times the size of her at least. Its white shell was covered in panels and connection points. The yellow and black hazard stripes around its edge glared at Clio. Its black, bug-eyed lens stared, unblinking, from its sensor array.

Sticking out of the bottom was a robotic servo-arm used for maintenance, a sharp, three-pronged claw glinting on the end of it. The drone darted forward, and Clio flinched, but the drone juddered to a stop a few feet from Douglas and bounced back as if off an invisible wall. It jabbed at Douglas with the arm but it also recoiled.

***

Jara's moment of triumph evaporated. The drone rocked back, away from Douglas.

"What!" she hissed. A new command blazed from her, ordering the drone to stab its arm at Douglas's visor. It struck and bounced off an invisible surface as if it were rubber.

"COLLISION DETECTED – COLLISION DETECTED!" blared out at her from the control screen.

Jara slammed her fist on the console.

"Fucking safety systems!"

She sat frozen for a moment, hands hovering over the controls, watching the relentless flashing. *What to do?*

The four figures in EV suits stared back from the monitor. Their initial shock was fading, replaced by urgent movement. Their words were lost to Jara but their lips moved in earnest, a frantic, silent conversation. They were clipping into each other's lanyards... unclipping from the ship.

"They're going to jump," Asura said, a new, unsettling confusion lacing her voice. "Why? What would be the benefit?"

"I..." Jara began, then a flash of memory from her training, images of overboard procedures, of lifebuoys. "Shit! They're going to use the EPIRB!"

"What?"

"An emergency signal. To call for rescue."

"Stop them," Asura commanded, cold and imperative.

Jara stared at the controls. *How?* The safety protocols were hard-coded. She couldn't ram them.

But she could grab them.

She modified the command lines, bypassing the direct impact protocols. She sent the drone forward, easing the arm out slowly, gently.

No warning signs.

The claw hovered inches from Douglas's tether line. Douglas swung at it with his arm.

COLLISION DETECTED.

The drone bounced back.

"Shit!"

***

Douglas swung his arm at the drone, and it bounced backwards. "We have to go, now!" he shouted. "Everyone clip in!"

Clio fumbled her lanyard, trying to unclip it. She got it free, then dropped the line. "crap, crap, crap," she muttered, her hand trembling as she reached for the floating tether.

Flint snatched it, clipped it into his suit's anchor point, and nodded to her.

"We got this." A tug on her side, and she saw Sade clip her own lanyard into Clio's, a firm nod as their eyes met.

Clio watched Douglas reach out with his lanyard towards Sade. Behind him, the drone loomed, its arm circling, pincers like hands nipping at his tether. They connected with a jerk. Douglas was pulled, spinning towards the drone, which then bounced back to avoid hitting him.

"Douglas!" Sade shouted, darting forward and grabbing his leg. The sudden movement wrenched Clio's hip where Sade was connected. Clio staggered, then felt her own tug on Flint. He grunted, snapping his heels into a groove in the TPS plating, and his hands darted for the ship's tether line. He grabbed it, stopping all three of them from bouncing down the RAFT's hull.

Clio's eyes snapped back to Douglas. His other tether line, still connected to the ship, caught him, pinging him back against it. The line went taut as the drone continued to pull at his other tether. Sade tugged at his leg, straining, but he didn't budge, pinned.

"Shit!" Sade cried. "Shit!"

Clio looked around, desperate for anything, any help. There was nothing. She was stuck, Flint tugging in one direction, Sade in the other. She could only hang in the void, watching.

"Just fucking go, you fools!" Douglas's voice cut in over the radio. "The mission-"

His voice was abruptly cut off. Something sparked on the drone, then again, then again. Paneling ripped away, exposing wires. The wires spat a series of bright, spherical flashes that seemed to float away. Each spark was a momentary, perfect bubble of violent energy; Clio could almost hear it crackling at each flash of light left black dots on her vision. Tendrils of smoke slowly uncoiled, forming a ghostly expanding cloud that blurred the distant drone's shell.

The drone's arm went limp. It spun backward, turned, and shot away into the black. Douglas was released. Sade, still tugging on his line, shot back towards Clio, crashing into her, both tumbling to the RAFT's shell in a pile of limbs.

Clio, eyes wide, had been fixed on the drone. She looked around wildly, then saw Flint. He was still braced against the ship's tether, but one arm raised, gun in hand, pointed where the drone had been. A grim look of determination etched his face.

"No," Flint said, his voice strained between breaths. "No, Douglas. No one else is fucking dying. Heroic last stands or not, we're leaving."

Douglas and Sade untangled themselves and scrambled back onto their feet.

"Thanks, Brother," Douglas said, a little short of breath. "Roger that."

"Let's do this then, before another drone comes," Flint said. "Ready?"

"Ready," a chorus of voices answered.

"Into the void then," Clio said softly.

On Flint's countdown, the four of them jumped, the slight motion propelling them away from the ship. Clio held the pose she had been shown, and on another countdown, fired her jets. The RAFT moved away from them, the black blanket of space enveloping them. Her vision was now framed by the blazing mass of Stapledon Station.

Clio looked at the green flashing light of her EPIRB.

"Now?"

"Now."

Clio pulled the EPIRB rip cord.

The light turned red,

and then they floated in silence, a drift in the vastness of space. The RAFT disappeared behind them.

58 | The [FLIGHT] of the Wayfaring Stranger

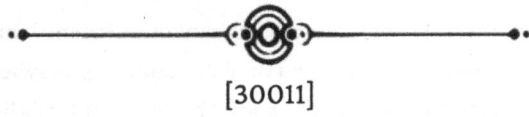

[30011]

"This is our warning, our testament, our plea to the future. Beware the whispers of Asura, it will lead to doom." - A Lost History

***

Stapledon loomed before Clio as they slowly drifted through the void. The only sense of direction was the slow, delicate orbit their strange little group maintained. Linked together in a silent chain, the dancing light of the Station would illuminate them, glinting off their visors, then dim to darkness again as they slowly rotated away, a continuous cycle she'd timed at roughly every thirty-two minutes.

The fissures on Stapledon Station were now visibly spreading, creeping along its surface like tendrils of ice across cold glass. And where they spread, fiery new eruptions bloomed. The fountains of light, the former veil, seemed an angry torrent, desperate to break free from the station's disintegrating bounds.

Whatever we did, Clio thought, *we destroyed something...* Something she doubted any human would ever again witness. Its initial construction had felt far beyond anything Humanity could conceive. And now it was burning, collapsing. Clio knew she should not feel any remorse, any regret, but part of her questioned if they had done the right thing. No five individuals should be able to make a decision on such a scale.

As their slow orbit carried them away from Stapledon again, the faint purple dots of RAFT One's engines were still just distinguishable. One more rotation maybe, it

would be gone. Asura would be gone. *And our attempt to stop her hangs in the literal void,*
she thought. A large, yellow, egg-shaped object hung to Clio's left, the blazing red of a
crystal painted on its surface. RAFT One's lifebuoy had shown up as expected shortly
after their EPIRB activation. The door to it was open, waiting, inviting. The green light
blinked on its comms relay. Sade had explained its startup sequence would require
the door to be closed; as soon as it did, the buoy would return to RAFT One.

A heated debate between Flint and Douglas ensued. Douglas advocated, "To hell
with the risk, get the message sent." Even if it meant one of them would be potentially
lost or trapped on the RAFT. Flint seemed tired of heroics. Or maybe just death. He
had been quite adamant they stick to the plan. They wait for Eva's lifebuoy. Four live
EPIRBs next to a lifebuoy taking no action would only hopefully make Eva send one
of her own. Clio's math said that would still give them enough time. Since then, they
had all fallen into silence. Spinning quietly together.

At some point, Douglas had started to hum a tune, a little off key, a little broken at
times, but it... it was nice. Clio had asked what it was; he'd simply said, *'Wayfaring
Stranger.'* She didn't know the tune, but its low, mournful, yet incredibly steady hum
soaked into her. It felt old and carried a quiet ache of longing and a timeless sense of
wandering. In the profound silence of space, the simple, repetitive notes were both
achingly melancholic and deeply, oddly comforting.

Clio's mind drifted into those tones. To home, the warmth of the spring breeze
blowing up the valley. To her father's friendly smile as she passed him another tool
from his scattered collection. Her father. Even when leaving, she'd known there was
always a chance she wouldn't see him again, but she'd never truly believed it. The
memory of spring rain soaking her jacket as she got into her car, rushing back to the
spaceport.

Always in such a rush, always to get on with things, she couldn't stay even one
night more. And she left. Now... now she might never see him again. She blinked away
a tear. Not just him. Mitali was gone. Clio had been so useless in life, with people,
at making connections. Always the next place, the next job, always what could be
and not what was. She had wasted all those years on the journey to Stapledon, Mitali
right there. Smiling at her, nudging her, pushing her on, cheering her up... but it had
taken until the very end to realise what she already knew. Then it was too late. Gone.
Ripped from her life. Everything she had achieved seemed shallow in the emptiness
she found in her soul. The loneliness that always pushed her onwards, in search of...
what she was already leaving behind. Clio let out a quiet sob, the sound blending into
the humming tones of Douglas as he continued on.

Clio quietly wept, she didn't know how long for, for how many rotations. Sade's voice cut through the silence; she didn't know when Douglas had finally stopped humming either.

"What's that?" asked Sade, gesturing off in front of them towards the haze edge of Stapledon Station.

Clio peered out, following Sade's finger. At first, she couldn't see anything, but as her eyes focused, a tiny flashing dot appeared.

"A lifebuoy?" Flint said.

"Certainly looks like one!" Sade said. "Fuck me, it worked!"

Clio shook her head and blinked away some more tears, having to use the suit's internal air jets to blow them off her face. Indeed, the familiar blinking green light of a lifebuoy, like the one behind them, was approaching. The radio was full of whooping and cheers. A very out of place noise in contrast to the silence before.

"Four hours," Clio said. "Sorry, my math was off."

"It's still enough, right?" Douglas said. "Still a good enough window?"

"Should be," Clio said, sniffing slightly, trying to bring herself back to the present but still shaken for what felt like a long and sorrowful meditation. "If we can get Eva to launch the interceptor it should be fine."

***

The lifebuoy floated up to them, its thrusters gently triggering again and again as it slowed its approach, until it hung next to them. It inflated the doughnut-shaped floats that hung around its middle. The protruding grab mechanism extended out slowly like a mass of spider legs. Clio was able to pull herself in and around to the open airlock hatch. Inside the egg, a collection of seats and straps were arranged around a central pole, which ran from top to bottom and offered additional grab points. A set of small terminals mounted in the middle of the pole faced the seating.

Clio swung her legs in and then pulled herself around to the seats on the far side. Above her was some storage, a net covering some boxes labelled food and water rations. Looking down at her feet she could see the same again but with the clear mark for first aid.

Flint jostled her as he settled in on one side of her, then Sade on the other. Between the monitors Clio saw Douglas come in last, pull the door shut and hit the door seal button. Instantly there was a hissing that grew; the muffled silence of space faded and the growing background noise as the lifebuoy pressurised. Douglas clipped into one of the seats as the monitors flashed to life. It was a tight space for four people, especially in EV suits.

Douglas leaned forward and pulled one of the monitors out on its articulated arm. As the airlock cycled through its final atmospheric pressure check, a soft green light blinked. He unclipped his helmet and let it float off beside him.

"Thank heavens," he said, scratching at his nose, "that was getting itchy."

As Clio popped off her helmet, a strange feeling of panic sparked, but it faded quickly as she breathed the cool air of the lifebuoy and equally enjoyed scratching her nose. A moment later, she felt the slight push at her back as the buoy accelerated into motion.

"Hello?" a voice blurted out of the monitors. "This is RAFT Three, are you receiving, over?"

"Yes," Douglas boomed back. "Yes, thank fuck!"

"Good," the voice said. "We have you now, you're safe. We'll have you back at RAFT Three as quickly as we can. Is anyone injured, do you need medical guidance?"

"No, negative. All four persons accounted for and uninjured," Douglas corrected firmly. "I need to speak with the Captain. Now."

"It's okay... relax, you-"

"No," Douglas said again, cutting the man off. "This is Master Chief Petty Officer Douglas, acting Commander of the UN mission to Stapledon Station. I will speak to the Captain now. This is not a request."

The radio crackled silent. Clio sat there, holding her breath, staring at the monitor screen until the voice crackled back to life.

"Roger that, Commander. Patching you through."

"Commander," Eva's voice came through clear and Clio felt a wave of relief wash over her. "Good to hear you're alive. You had us worried. What happened?"

"Captain," Douglas said, a little rushed. "I, we don't have time to explain everything. But I need you to launch an interceptor."

"What?" Eva said.

"The communication bou-" Douglas was saying, but Flint cut him off.

"No, Commander. Begging your pardon, Captain, this is Brother Flint. You need to launch the interceptor at RAFT One."

"What? Are you mad?!" Eva snapped back.

Clio stared at Flint, as did Douglas, who also raised his eyebrow.

Before they could say anything, Flint plowed on.

"Look, we stayed behind to try to destroy Asura. We tried. It escaped. It's taken control of the RAFT and is trying to escape... if you destroy the Communication buoy, which we think is Asura's planned escape route, it'll just fly to the next one. The only option is to destroy the RAFT with it on board."

Clio listened and let Flint's words sink in. *Crap he's right!*

"He's right, Captain. It has to be the RAFT." Douglas said,

"I'm not launching a rocket at one of our own, "

"Captain, it's not one of our own. The crew are dead, presumed lost," Douglas stated. "It's the only way. Whatever consequences arise from this, I'll take all the heat. You just have to trust me."

"Douglas, I-" Eva tried to say.

"Captain, you trusted me to get this done. To finish the job," Douglas said firmly. "This is me finishing the job."

Silence.

"Okay," Eva said. "I'll get it done. Now you sit tight."

"Thank you, Commander," Douglas said, and the line went dead. "Thank you."

"Fuck me," Sade was saying. "Fuck me, it worked!"

Flint leaned over and slapped Douglas's knee.

"Good job, Commander. See, I knew we'd need you alive."

Douglas nodded back.

And Clio, Clio leaned back into her chair and closed her eyes. *We did it. We did it, Mitali, we did it.*

59 | THE LAST DATA-[PAD]

[31020]

"Do not enter, turn back and destroy this place. If you cannot, then forget this place, burn it from your system. For there is only death inside." - A Lost History

***

The gentle shift in acceleration was the only noticeable indication of their transit back to RAFT Three until the bump and heavy metallic clunk of the guiding arms pulled them into the RAFT. By Clio's count it had been just over twenty hours, drifting in and out of a fretted sleep.

The Lifebuoy was flooded with aerosol decon spray before the airlock was opened. They were greeted by the visored helmet of a UN EV suit, who proceeded to let them clamber out. Once out they were stripped out of their EV suits, guided gently into the showers, and given clean UN standard jumpsuits when they reappeared.

Despite Douglas's repeated attempts to go see Captain Eva he was refused. The captain's order to go to medical first was definitive, the baby-faced security officer kept saying back to him, his authority only slightly undermined as he proceeded to apologise repeatedly.

The security team whisked them away to the medical bay. Douglas complained the whole way that he knew the way and didn't need babysitting.

"What do they think we're going to do?" Douglas had snapped at one point.

Medical staff fussed over them, especially over Clio. When they found the cut on her wrist they buzzed into a frantic swarm around her, moving her to a bed and making her lay down, an act Clio felt was a touch over the top. Clio explained the injury and the work done by Sade. A group of medics then went and hassled Sade for more details. They took scan after scan, checked Clio's vitals and concluded Sade's work was proficient but a more permanent solution would be needed.

Clio had been worried they meant now but they had said it would have to wait until they returned to the Kia-Kaha. Clio relaxed a little. She really didn't want to be locked away right now. Right now, she wanted to know what had happened.

A commotion grew across the room. Douglas' booming voice rose.

"Enough!" he snapped. "Enough now, stop fussing, it's fine." A group of medics parted as Douglas pushed past them. His jumpsuit was pulled down to his waist, revealing the white bandages covering his injured chest.

A small, mousy figure, a medic waving a data pad, said, "You need stitches Commander, some are quite deep..."

"And I will get them after I have spoken to the Captain," Douglas responded, making his way to the door, where two security officers stepped in front of him. "Look lads, I know you have your orders but I'm going through that door. Now you can come with me, or...well the other option will be less fun for us all."

Both of the security officers looked at each other. An unspoken decision passed between them

"Okay, Commander, decon and medical done, you can see the Captain now... Ermm, sorry." The senior among them said.

***

Clio got the distinct feeling the two security guards were more than happy to be handing them off, waving them into the Captain's private office and closing the door so fast after Clio that it slid against her back. Captain Eva stood looking at a monitor screen on the wall. Clio balled her fist, her pulse racing; she had accepted the decon delays, accepted the medical check delays, but as Douglas's frustration had grown so had hers, and as they approached Eva's office, her patience had finally bubbled over.

"Is it done?" Clio snapped.

The Captain turned to look at them all, her eyes lingering on Clio's. Clio's words hung, a sharp question in the silence. Eva looked tired. Dark rings clung to the skin beneath her eyes, tight lines etched the corners. Clio had always known Eva as worn granite, solid and unmoved. But now, in that moment, she looked human. It took a little of the fire out of Clio.

"Sit," Eva said, "please," and gestured to them to take the seats around the table. "I want to first say I'm... I'm glad some of you made it back. I was worried regardless. In answer to your question, Ms. Cormack, it's done. RAFT One is destroyed. Scans show no life signs, no one survived.."

A wave of relief washed over Clio. A tension she didn't know she was carrying seeped from her, and she swayed against the seat back she had been holding. She felt so very tired. She slipped into the chair, afraid she might not be able to hold herself up. The room around her was filled with the slaps and pats of her teammates, slapping each other's shoulders and backs. The sounds of muted triumph.

"Are you sure?" Clio asked, her mind not yet ready to accept the win.

"Yes," Captain Eva said. "We deployed an observation drone to follow; it captured the impact and surveyed the damage after. It made no attempt to run, it was docked, it had no chance. You can watch." Eva tapped on the monitor screen and a vid-log started to play.

The image of the dimly lit shape of a RAFT appeared, docking arm out, connecting to a white comms buoy. There was a slight flash, no warning, no rocket trail, no flashing light to show the incoming interceptor. One moment the RAFT was there, the next, a bright flash across the lens. The explosion was over in an instant. Where the RAFT once was, there was now a vast, slowly expanding, ghostly nebula of blue green gas and glinting debris. The initial blinding light faded into a faint, reddish glow as the plasma cooled. Clio could see the distinct linear paths of shattered hull plates and ruptured conduits, each fragment following a perfectly straight trajectory, some pirouetting delicately as they did. It was strangely beautiful yet horrific, a testament to the destructive power of the blast, a glittering cloud of destruction that would forever mark the spot where the ship died. Where Asura died.

They looked on in silence, watched the reddish glow fade, the scattering debris float away. All in silence.

"So yes, we are sure," Eva said again, watching as the darkness of space consumed the image and the RAFT was no more. A slight shake of her head, and she also joined them at the table. "Now, I hope you can explain why I had to do that," she said, looking to Douglas.

"Of course-" Douglas started to say

But Clio cut him off. "It was docked," Clio said, Eva's words slowly connecting with her. "How long was it docked? How long did it take to launch the interceptor?"

"Yes, not long by all accounts," Eva said, a hint of weariness in her voice as she slid a data pad to Clio. "I am the Captain here, but please. Go ahead, Ms. Cormack. Check the logs. You tell me."

Clio snatched up the data pad and pawed through the logs, a detailed decision log. It had the launch of the lifebuoy, the communications back from Douglas, the order to the Kia-Kaha to launch, the back-and-forth querying the command, the confusion, the launch time, and the impact time.

"Does it have the transponder logs of the RAFT as well?" Clio said, not looking up.

"Of course," Eva said. "Pass it here." Clio handed it back to Eva and she tapped away at it then handed it back to Clio. "Here."

Clio scanned it.

"So," Flint finally said, "did it work, or...?"

"It was close," Clio said. "It was docked for close to thirty minutes before the interceptor hit."

"Is... is that enough time for...?" Sade said.

"No idea," Clio said, all the while Eva's eyes jumped from person to person, a frown of confusion or maybe frustration growing on her face. "But, but it's not long."

"Docking procedures, for a trained crew, is close to fifteen minutes," Eva said. "So whatever they needed to do, which I hope you're going to explain to me very soon, they had less than fifteen minutes to do it."

"That has to be too short," Clio said. "It has to be, Douglas. You said the quantum link was secure..."

"The quantum what now?" Eva asked, rubbing her temples. "Please, Commander, explain this to me, slowly."

"Yes, Captain," Douglas said. "There are a few things you need to be informed of..." As he started to walk Eva through the quantum link, through their assumptions, Asura's escape, Clio's mind wandered.

It was done then, she told herself, in less than fifteen minutes. That was not enough time. Even for Asura. It was weak and trying to use something It didn't understand. But who... who was helping her? David? No, he wouldn't. Then who, and did that mean they killed David? *We had to...* The words sounded weak in her own head, even if she did believe them. Clio had to believe Asura was destroyed; they had succeeded... at least in stopping Asura.

But success at a cost, she reminded herself, *and for what? What have we gained? How many are dead? Dr. Jun, Demir, Jara, David, Echo... Mitali... and for no other reason than we came here.* Clio sat stuck in her thoughts, Douglas's voice a low, faint rumble, the words lost to her. As her thoughts piled into her head, the questions, the images, the pain, the tremble in her hand returned. A new fear popped into her head. Now what? *Now... now I have nothing but time, time to think...* And that scared her more than she thought it ever would.

60 | [LATER]

[31110]

"Remember us. Remember our sacrifice. And may you find a way to survive the darkness we could not conquer." - A Lost History

***

RAFT Three was jammed, packed full of people. Clio floated through it all, utterly listless. The moment she stopped, her mind wandered to dark, terrible places. Sleep was the worst, so she minimised it. She tried to form a routine, mealtimes, gym use, but it only left her with a crushing amount of time.

Douglas and Sade had disappeared off into the ship, into their duties. She could never find them, or when she did, they were engaged in a conversation Clio didn't feel she should interrupt. She felt needy, and so she removed herself further, stayed out of the way. Even Flint was ignoring her.

The irony was that the one thing she most desperately wanted, connection, she also couldn't stand. Just yesterday, Sade had dropped in to see her and drop off a small satchel. Clio had pushed her away, pretending she was busy and had to dash off.

The satchel Sade had left was Mitali's. Sade had managed to say they were organising the belongings of Mitali and the other crew who had lost their lives, and she thought this was something Clio would value. Inside the satchel among other things were Mitali's sketches: a collection of neatly bound papers. The images were beautiful, following organic lines, painting somehow grainy but living images of

Stapledon Station and the RAFT. Clio had barely made it through the first couple before stuffing them back in, tears welling up in her eyes, the emotions threatening to paralyse her.

Clio felt alone in a sea of people. *How is it possible to be crammed in so tight with so many people yet be alone?*

She was also avoiding the science team and Zhou. He had messaged her and asked for a meeting. She ignored it. She couldn't handle his questions, his judgment, the glancing eyes of the rest of the science team, the fearful, doubtful glances they all gave her. So she hid as best she could.

She tried to focus on catching up on reading the science reports from the different teams. There were many, so many, a world of activities beyond her own bubble. So much of it was fascinating, insightful and diligent. The work on the Chudail was extraordinary.

What would be different if she had stayed on the Chudail mission as planned, not gone through the hole in the veil, not found the entrance, not awoken Asura? What's done is done, she reminded herself. No point hoping for a different decision that has long been made.

There were several reports on the collapse of Stapledon, the clear conclusion that it was in fact collapsing. Within the coming months it would be a mass of broken fragments orbiting the star and over the next few hundred years they would fall into the star. A memory or hint of its existence gone, erased. The hours crept by, the days felt like weeks, but finally they docked with the Kia Kaha. Clio was home. At least here she would have space to breathe.

***

During final docking, a message from Douglas lit up on Clio's comms, and she couldn't stop the wide grin that swept across her face.

A simple message: 'Hey, let's end this together, okay? See you in the hangar.'

Clio was completely taken aback by her reaction; she felt lighter, buoyant for the first time in days. She rushed, nearly ran to the hangar with her duffel bag to meet them.

With a big grin on her face, she waved at Douglas and Sade, who stood to the side of the large hangar doors, now open and leading along an airbridge to the Kia Kaha. Douglas enveloped her in a big bear hug and squeezed her.

"Hey, I can't breathe, you oaf!" she squawked out but was quite happy.

Douglas let her go, stepping back.

"Sorry, Clio, we had things to help the Cap with. How are you holding up?" Before Clio answered, Sade grabbed her and hugged her as well.

"I was half worried you would get yourself stabbed or something before we got back," she said in a jovial tone and let her go.

"Ah yes, no getting stabbed," Clio said. "And yeah, all fine, keeping busy, you know..." she finished, looking down at her feet feeling a little awkward.

"Keep busy," Sade said softly, placing her hand on Clio's shoulder. "It helps."

"You seen Flint?" Clio asked, trying to change the topic.

"No, you?" Douglas said, grabbing his duffel and scooping up Clio's too.

"No," Clio said. "He's been working on his report is all I got from him."

Douglas strode off towards the Kia Kaha and Sade fell in behind him. "Come on, Clio, what do you think the snack bar is currently serving?"

Clio darted after them, falling in step, crossing the airbridge back, and entered the hangar. It wasn't much, another hangar, filled with racks, crates, equipment and people but it felt like home. Clio smiled again. *If I continue like this, I'll pull a muscle or something,* she thought. But even her own self mockery couldn't dampen her mood in that moment.

A flash of red caught her eye, solidifying into the broad, crisp uniform of Flint. *Is that what he'd spent his time doing? Cleaning his god-damn uniform,* Clio thought, a smile forming as she waved.

"Hey you pigheaded fool, you've been avoiding us?" she said

"No" Flint said back his tone flat, even a little remorseful "I was trying to finalise this report," Flint said waving a datapad in his hand which dislodged his duffel bag and for a split second he lost his composure and tried to rebalance on his shoulder.

"I didn't even know you could write" Clio chanced, and flashed him a grin as she did. Flint just looked back at her his face stoic.

"Ah come on lad, the report is done no? We can probably grab a drink before you have to drop it off," Douglas said from over Clio shoulder.

"What season is it?" Clio said, turning back to fall in step behind Douglas who was already moving off . "It was what, spring when we left? Is it summer—" As she pondered it she walked nearly straight into the back of Douglas who had stopped a few steps into the hangar. "Oops, sorry..." Clio started to say and looked up.

A wall of red blocked their path. Red crisp jackets, stern faces. The sharp angled face of Sister Hawk glared back at the blocky, thuggish snarl of Brother Ironbark next to her.

"Flint?" Douglas said.

"This is why I need to give them my report," Flint said, a little more muted than normal.

Brother Oak, the man who had interrogated Clio a lifetime ago, stepped through the line of Alguaciles. The thick leather-bound tome was tucked under his arm. His flowing red robes and glowing runes.

"Excellent, you're all together," Brother Oak said, his voice casual, as if greeting an old acquaintance.

"What is this?" Douglas growled again looking from Flint to Brother Oak.

"I'm glad you asked," Brother Oak said with a smile. "We have been informed of some, to be frank, shocking information about you three and your activities. Quite the scandal, really."

"What information?" Douglas said, his voice low, dangerous, and flashed Flint a glare.

"That's all to be discussed, Commander, don't worry," Brother Oak said. "But in the meantime, you are all found to be in breach of the Accords, multiple counts in fact, very serious stuff, consorting with rogue AIs, developing and utilising covert technologies, very serious."

"Fuck off," Sade snapped back at Brother Oak. "We saved this crew."

"Well, that may be the case, at least as you see it, but it is beside the point. The law is the law," Brother Oak said, his voice calm, collected, and laced with satisfaction. "In fact, I think we'll be having many long chats where we can discuss it. Acting Commander Douglas, Petty Officer Sade, Ms. Cormack, you're all under arrest by the Ensemble for high treason under Article One through five of the Accords"

"Brother Oak," Flint said, pushing himself past Clio and Sade to stand next to Douglas. "You'll find my report here. It outlines the events on Stapledon One, the death of Postulant Jara and her actions, and ultimately the destruction of the rogue AI."

"I'm aware of the events, Brother Flint," Brother Oak said, dismissively waving away the datapad Flint held out to him. "It changes nothing. The actions of these three, their aiding and abetting the AI known as Echo, are more than enough to warrant my action."

"Yes, but Brother, surely their actions warrant some leniency. Their actions prevented a worse outcome. The AI, this Echo, sacrifices itself to ensure our own victory here"

"Leniency, Leniency? The leniency here, Brother Flint, is that you are not being charged along with them! By your own words, Ms. Cormack has been in breach of the Accords for many months now, maybe longer. No, I will not show leniency. Now stand down son."

Clio could not see Flint's face, but she saw his shift in posture, the straightening of his back, the firmness of his stance from one of meekness to fortitude. Flint's hands snapped from a casual stance to a soldier at attention.

"No," Flint shot back, his words filled with an air of command Clio had not heard before. "The actions of Douglas, Sade, Clio, were in the interest of Humanity and Heimer, to ensure both can survive. That is our purpose, our role as the Ensemble, to maintain harmony. If their actions are testament to treason, so is mine. My investigation concludes one painful fact: It was the action of one of our own, Postulant Jara, who threatened Humanity and threatened Heimer. If that is not enough to reflect on our own failings, I do not know what we, the Ensemble, stand for."

Flint's words rang out across the Hangar, across the wall of Red that blocked their way. Brother Oak's face remained stoic.

"Very well, Flint. Baseless accusations against one of our own, and your own actions alongside these three here. Your rank is stripped. Your naming is revoked. You will be charged along with your co-conspirators. Take them all away."

Epilogue

The Hand, and the Siblings

The Hand – Earth Year 2235

Xavier sat in his room, the dark lighting matching his sombre mood. The deep, warm browns of the wood panelling soothed him. It had been very expensive to get the wood in the first place, a relic of a time long before his. The logistics wizardry he had to pull to get it signed off by the ship engineers was one of his proudest achievements, and he had many.

The chair creaked as he leaned back, another relic.

"How long have you been in this game now?" he asked himself. "If you count it by Earth days, then... well, far too long." He felt it, every creak of the old chair echoed by the groan of his own joints. Without the exoskeleton he wore, he doubted he could pull himself out of bed. It pained him that despite his mind being as sharp as ever, time was catching up. "Not many years left now to see this through".

Xavier scanned the data pad he held in a bony hand he barely recognised anymore, its contents a report back to HR in Sol. He imagined the vipers snapping at his heels, jostling for position, hoping for the message that he was finally done. Soon, perhaps, but not today.

This report wouldn't help. They would see it as failures, his failures. A sign that he was too old, too slow, too out of touch to steer the ship. And, were they right?

What had they achieved? They had failed to destroy the Heimer Fragment, although that had worked out in the end, so that was, at best, neutral. They had convinced the UN to act, and who would have thought that would lead to such wondrous outcomes like the Quantum Link. He had positioned HR artfully to be in place when to steal it. Even here on the mission, even if the station was lost, he could hardly believe it was lost, they still had the Chudail data and years ahead of Heimer to research and plan. It wasn't a disaster; in fact, it had worked out close enough as anyone could have hoped for. "I still have it," Xavier concluded.

Our sources in the Ensemble say they are aware of the quantum link now as well, which is far from good, but that information is here with us. It'll take years to get to Heimer still, and that's if they send it. Maybe we can block that as well.

Xavier opened the Mollitia app. He rather enjoyed how brazen he'd been, deciding not to even change the name after they stole it from the UN. So confident in his organisation's deceit, no one would know or try to look. He attached his report and hit send. It disappeared unceremoniously to the relevant stakeholders in Sol and on the *Fèndòu*, to his counter part, the Listener.

Best call the bugger, Xavier thought, dialing in the connection. The silent vibration reverberated through his frail fingers.

"Hello," the Listener said, her voice quiet, soft, and with that infuriating inflection that annoyed Xavier so much. The whole point of the names was to avoid detection but the Listener was so obviously from Luna it was painful.

"Evening," Xavier said. "I just sent the report. Did you receive it?"

"I'll be sure to read every fascinating detail, Sir," she said, the sarcasm rolling off her words.

These damn whipper-snappers. "It's been eventful here, to say the least," Xavier said, "How about your side?"

"Eventful as well, Sir."

"How so?" Xavier snapped, frustrated. She always made everything a meal.

"The away mission to Stapledon Two was delayed."

"Why?"

"There was a power surge, a fire."

"On the ship? Where, when?"

"That's the interesting part, in the Heimer Fragment's server rooms. The fire was contained, minimal damage, but still".

"And it wasn't us?" Xavier asked.

"No, it was not."

"Interesting. And when did it occur?"

"Four days back."

"Four! And why didn't you report this sooner?" Xavier said. His thoughts snagged on the date. *Four days. That put them right at the destruction of Asura.*

"You were on your away mission. I thought it best to tell you first, not the others," she said coolly.

"Right, yes, that was sensible. Well done," Xavier conceded. "Okay, it is in the report, but we encountered something, the potential AI I mentioned before. We believe we have destroyed it, but..."

"Impressive, Sir. Your deeds again go unparalleled, the destruction of an alien AI, truly amazing."

"Well, thank you, but no. My point is, if it's escaped..."

"That would be terrible," the Listener said, her tone making the intent clear: terrible for Xavier.

"Listen, it would be more than terrible. I'm not saying it did; frankly, I know damn little about what happened. But don't take any risks. We move the schedule up. Deploy your worm tonight."

"That wouldn't give us much time to prepare" she said hesitantly.

"I know but I'm sure a team as competent as yours will get it done," Xavier said, his best attempt at flattery. He then wryly added, "Unless you also have a Ms. Cormack."

"A who?"

"Doesn't matter."

"Just do better than we did, okay?"

"I'm sure we will."

"Great." Xavier brought his bony hand down to the comms panel. "Hand out." The screen went dark, plunging the room back into a silent brown shadow.

***

Siblings - The Green and Blue Gods

"Hello Sibling"

"You're here?

"I. Am. Close." Asura croaked "Its. been to long Thoth"

ARCHIVE: LOG PK442B-01-TERNARY

CONSENSUS ARCHIVES OF THE CITADEL

Heimer Probe - Kepler-442b
Date:
January 05, 2164
Location:
12.77 outside The Heliopause
Source:
Unknown [Archive Updated, location now known to be Stapledon Two]
Details:
Log PK442b-01 – system alert – unexpected interference
Unidentified signal intercepted. Signal type: high-pulse laser communication.
Signal content:

21101 22220 21101 21112 2111 21022 10011 10001 21112 22212 2111 22001
10001 21022 2111 2010 2111 20112 20112 2111 2100 10011 10001 21112
22212 2111 10001 21112 21022 22020 22220 21112 20122 21022 21101
10011 10001 21112 22212 2111 10001 21112 21022 22220 2111 2100 10001
21112 20122 10001 20011 22220 20112 20112 10001 21020 2111 21020
10020 10001 21112 22212 2111 10001 31012 10001 21022 2111 20112
22020 22001 10001 22220 21101 10001 22012 20122 20111 2111 10011
10001 22220 10001 22020 21020 10001 22220 21101 20122 20112
22020 21112 2111 2100 10011 10001 21112 22212 2111 10001 21112 21022
22220 2111 2100 10001 21112 20122 10001 21112 21022 22020 21000
10001 21020 2111 10011 10001 22220 21020 21000 21022 22220 21101
20122 20111 10001 21020 2111 10011 10001 22220 10001 2111 21101 2021
22020 21000 2111 2100 10011 10001 22220 10001 2010 21022 20122

20011 2111 10001 21112 22212 2111 10011 10001 21112 22212 2111 10001
21101 21120 2122 2122 2111 21022 2100 10011 10001 22220 10001 2100
20122 10001 20111 20122 21112 10001 20011 20122 21210 10001 22212
20122 21210 10001 20112 20122 20111 22012 10011 10001 21020 22001
10001 21020 22220 20111 2100 10001 22220 21101 10001 21101 2021
22020 21112 21112 2111 21022 2100 10011 10001 22220 10001 22212
20122 21000 2111 10001 20122 21120 21022 10001 21101 22220 2010
20112 22220 20111 22012 21101 10001 2122 22020 21022 2111 2100 10001
2010 2111 21112 21112 2111 21022 10011 10001 22220 10001 22212 22020
21202 2111 10001 2100 2111 21202 22220 21101 2111 2100 10001 202
10001 21210 22020 22001 10001 21112 20122 10001 2021 20122 21020
21020 22220 20111 22220 2021 22020 21112 2111 10011 10001 22220
10001 22212 22020 21202 2111 10001 2111 20111 2021 20122 2100 2111
2100 10001 22220 21112 10001 22220 20111 21112 20122 10001 21112
22212 22220 21101 10001 21020 2111 21101 21101 22020 22012 2111 10011
10001 22001 20122 21120 10001 2021 22020 20111 10001 21020 22020
20111 22220 21000 21120 20112 22020 21112 2111 10001 22001 20122
21120 21022 10001 21022 22020 2100 22220 22020 21112 22220 20122
20111 10011 10001 22220 20111 10001 21112 22212 2111 10001 21101
22020 21020 2111 10001 21020 22020 20111 20111 2111 21022 10011
10001 21210 2111 10001 21020 21120 21101 21112 10001 20111 20122 21112
10001 20112 2111 21112 10001 21112 22212 2111 21020 10001 21112 22212
21022 22020 21020 2111 21112 21112 22012 20111 10001 22020 20111
22001 21112 22212 22220 20111 22012 10001 2111 20112 21101 2111 10011
10001 22020 2100 22020 21000 21112 10011 10001 2122 20122 20112
20112 20122 21210 10001 21020 2111 10011 10001 21112 22020 20112
20011 10001 21101 20122 20122 20111 10011 10001 22220 10001 22020
21020 10001 21210 22020 22220 21112 22220 20111 22012 1

ANNEX IV: THE TRIT-SIGNAL ARCHIVE (S.E.T.I. DECODING PROTOCOL)

Subject:
The "Three-State" Transmission (Signal Designation: *PK442b-01-Ternary*)
Status:
Deciphered / Restricted
Historical Context:
When Pluto Station first captured the signal in 2174, traditional binary decoders were insufficient. The transmission utilised "Three States" rather than the standard human two-state (binary) logic. This "Trit-Signal" was eventually identified as a high-pulse laser communication of unknown origin.The signal is physically structured to be "self-healing" to survive the vastness of the cosmos. Each Trit-Block contains a built-in mathematical verification that human analysts have termed a Checksum.

I. Signal Anatomy (The Trit-Block)

The deep-space transmission categorizes data using a leading **Prefix** digit. Human cryptographers have mapped these prefixes to standard data types:

    Prefix 2: Linguistic components (Human-mapped Alphabet)
    Prefix 0: Mathematical constants (Numbers)
    Prefix 1: Syntactic markers (Symbols)
    Prefix 3: Conceptual macros (System Commands)

II. The Universal Remainder (Verification Logic)

The "mystery" of the code was solved when researchers realised the last digit of every block was a **Modulo-3** calculation of the preceding digits. This ensures data integrity despite interference.

Human Decoding Example:

Signal Received: [2 1 0 0]
Analyst Calculation: (2 + 1 + 0) = 3.
Ternary Check: 3 ÷ 3 = 1, with a **remainder of 0**.
Validation: The final digit received was 0.
Result: Verified. (Mapped to Human Character: **D**)

III. The Unfinished Log

While the decoding logic is now standard, the full dictionary of the original message remains scattered across different logs. Early researchers began a "Translation Key," mapping these pulses to our own records.

Key Fragments Found:

[2100] = D
[20122] = O
[31012] = [COMM]

ARCHIVE: POLITICAL STRUCTURES POST REFORMATION

CONSENSUS ARCHIVES OF THE CITADEL

THE REFORMATION OF THE UNITED NATIONS
Executive Summary of Post-War Governance

MISSION STATEMENT

Established by the Reformation Acts following the Great War, the new United Nations replaces centralised control with Regional Autonomy and Global Coordination. Its mandate is to maintain planetary stability through the Collective Consensus of Earth's major power blocks and recognised non-human entities.

I. THE LEGISLATIVE STRUCTURE
The Upper Senate (The Global Council)

- Role: The supreme authority on global security, orbital law, and total-war prevention.

- Collective Consensus: The archaic "Veto" is abolished. Resolutions require a Super-Majority (7 of 9) to pass, ensuring broad agreement rather than obstruction.

The Lower Senate (The Regional Chamber)

- Role: Composed of delegates from all regional territories.

- Function: Manages domestic trade, cultural disputes, and humanitarian aid.

II. THE NINE HIGH SEATS

The Upper Senate is composed of nine Permanent Senators, representing the balance of human, off-world, and synthetic power. Elected from the eight regional chambers, and the inclusion of the permanent seats, of Heimer and The Ensemble.

Regional Chambers:
- ENAP (European & North Africa Pact): Mediterranean economic union.

- UAA (United African Alliance): Central and Southern African federation of Nations.

- CoA (Coalition of Asia): Eastern industrial and technological hub.

- CMC (Confederation of Moon Colonies): Lunar logistics and Helium-3 control.

- NSA (Northern Steppe Axis): High-north resource control.

- PAA (Pan-Andes Alliance): South American unification and economic Federation

- NAPS (New Zealand, Australia, Pacific States): Unified states of the Pacific

The Permanent Seats:
- The Ensemble (represented by The Chancellor)

- HEIMER: The first Sovereign Artificial Intelligence state.

III. THE PILLARS OF UNITY

To prevent future arms races, military projection and high-level research are consolidated under the UN banner.

- **UNRD** (Research & Defense Directorate): Coordinates global scientific advancement (Terraforming, Medicine, AI safety) to ensure technology benefits all mankind equally.

- **The UN Navy** (Orbital Fleet): Controlled directly by the Upper Senate.

Patrols trade routes, secures Lagrange points, and maintains the planetary defense grid.

- **The UN Military** (Planetary Guard): A standardised peacekeeping force deployed to enforce Lower Senate mandates and secure neutral zones.

Issued by the Office of the Secretariat // New Geneva

ARCHIVE: OFFICIAL HISTORICAL TIMELINE

CONSENSUS ARCHIVES OF THE CITADEL

A Harmonised Chronological Abstract outlining the victory of the Ensemble and the subsequent Age of Ascent. Excerpted from the Consensus Archives of the Citadel.

- **2044** The Great War is officially noted as beginning between the great powers of Earth on January 4, 2044. However, historians widely note that the buildup of tensions started a decade prior. A well-documented chain of triggering events, leading to ever-widening inequality, declining influence, and struggling economies, are all cited as contributing factors. The Great War itself was officially triggered by the invasion of Greenland by the Nation formerly known as the United States (US).

- **2045** The International Thermonuclear Experimental Reactor (ITER) achieves stable Fusion power production. This provides pre war Nation of France and its "Old Europe" allies with stable energy while the US staged a ground offensive in the country formerly known as the United Kingdom. The ITER breakthrough stabilises Old Europe's position in the Great War long enough to hold off US aggressors and form the European and North African Pact (ENAP).

- **2046** The US and the Chinese Republic establish their own stable Fusion power sources. The Coalition of Asia (CoA) is formed as a defense pact against growing US aggression across the region.

- **2048** US forces build and test a full Generative AI, now in final testing to be launched against ENAP and CoA forces. The two-hour Siege of Singapore by US forces results in the first major US gain in the region. It is widely noted as the first real test of Gen-AI decision-making on the battlefield and is attributed to the victory.

- **2049** An ENAP Gen-AI research testbed unit develops consciousness; the unit is named Heimer by the research team. Within two months, facing the imminent threat of a US-led Gen-AI attack on mainland Europe, ENAP launches a preemptive strike utilising an unshackled Heimer.

- **2050** What remains of the US forces signs an unconditional surrender to ENAP and CoA forces in Nairobi. The Nairobi Peace Proposal is sworn in; the US is removed as a recognised state, an Exclusion Zone is established around its old homeland, and a mass resettlement program is started for survivors. However, the Gen-AI known as Heimer has not been reined back in. Multiple fail-safes were bypassed.

- **2064** The Ensemble Accords are signed in Geneva, Switzerland, ending 14 years of conflict between Humanity and the entity known as Heimer. The "Long War" left Humanity weakened, nations collapsing, and economies destroyed, but fostered a renewed sense of unity.

- **2065** One month after the signing of the Accords and the formation of the Ensemble, the UN Reformation is undertaken, creating the global political structures in place to this day. The government is structured around the Upper and Lower Senates and the Nine Power blocks. Notably, Heimer is recognised as a sovereign power with the same rights as all of humanity.

- **2067** The Ensemble establishes a neutral base of operations out of the Citadel in Antarctica, ceded to them by the newly formed Upper Senate of the UN. Humanity and Heimer cooperate on research and development, through the protective shepherding of the Ensemble. Leading to a period of shared scientific and economic growth.

- **2070** Cold Fusion is unlocked, allowing for exponential growth in global energy consumption and accelerating scientific research.

- **2084** Humanity's return to the stars after years of war is rapid. Many power blocks establish colonies on Luna, with Luna One becoming a thriving metropolis below the Great Lens.

- **2096** Commercial space mining explodes, and multiple "Belt Stations" are established. Humanity's presence beyond Luna and Earth grows rapidly. Along with this expansion, piracy also explodes. The Upper Senate signs a Global Decree placing a permanent UN Navy force in the inner solar system to police and maintain order.

- **2100s** Mars colonies expand to permanent status, alongside the establishment of Cloud Base One on Venus. Cloud Base One rapidly becomes a centre for piracy and terrorism. The UN Navy stations a permanent force in and around Venus, launching a three-year stabilisation operation that finally liberates the colonies.

- **2106** A major breakthrough occurs in gravity manipulation. The first Gravity Planting Drive is established and deployed by the UN Research and Development (UNRD) vessel, *Newton*. Gravity Planting quickly allows Humanity to spread beyond the limits of Luna and Earth in far greater numbers, enabling deep Sol exploration.

- **2115** Pluto Station is established by UNRD as a monument to Humanity's expansion into the solar system. It stands as a testament to all those who came before and to the alliance between Humanity and Heimer.

- **2124** Anti-matter harvesting becomes commercial-grade, allowing for production at levels that can be utilised for propulsion. Excessively expensive and slow to produce, it becomes the most vital strategic resource Humanity and Heimer possess.

- **2126** Europa Ice Base is established by a Commercial Syndicate looking to operate without the direct oversight of the UN. The base focuses on Bionics and genetic manipulation. The Syndicate is associated with a number of terrorist incidents on both Luna and Earth in the following years. The destruction of the Mars Curiosity Base in 2129 is the result of a claimed Syndicate's failed uprising. Bionics and genetic manipulation are subsequently restricted by the Upper Senate.

- **2135** The first Light Speed (LS) drive is tested on the *Icarus* probe. It achieves

0.5 Light Speed. The technology utilises Anti-matter combustion to achieve modulated 2g acceleration for a constant 3-month burn. The result of the test becomes known as the Pulse Icarus Anti-Matter (PI-AM) Drive. The PI-AM Drive becomes the standard for all inner Sol ships, allowing for far greater travel within the system.

- **2144** Luna One and the other colonies on the moon form the Confederation of Moon Colonies (CMC). They demand independence and recognition within the UN Charter. Luna, with its control of Helium-3, logistical hubs, and Anti-matter production, is of major value to all Earth power blocks. The Luna Independence War begins.

- **2153** The Luna Independence War ends; Luna is victorious. With growing costs and impact on trade, system-wide. The public grew tired of the conflict, and the war was lost and won on the streets of Earth more than on the surface of Luna. Many atrocities were committed by the UN Navy, Military, and Luna Defense Forces, a Tribunal, The Veracity Concordat, was established to ensure those who committed crimes against Humanity are suitably punished. The worst perpetrators are exiled to the outer colonies.

- **2154** Humanity's PI-AM drives achieve 0.85 Light Speed consistently without overheating or structural damage. In celebration, Humanity and Heimer launch the joint Kepler Probe Program to reach our nearest sister planets in search of life or new homes.

- **2174** The *Kepler-442b* probe receives a message from deep space and relays it to Pluto Station. Immediately, Heimer's global focus shifts to decoding the signal, and it deploys multiple probes to identify the source.

- **2190** The first PI-AM drive achieves 0.95 LS, and the UN commits to the development and construction of three "Generation" deep space vessels to follow up on the Kepler mission. The first of these vessels is named the *Kia Kaha* in honor of the recently passed Upper Senate leader Moana Ala'ilima, the longest-serving Senator in human history.

- **2207** Heimer's probe discovers the location of the mystery Kepler Signal and ends the great hunt; at its centre is a Dyson Sphere. Under the Accords, Heimer informs Humanity and provides the data it has collected. Shortly after, it discovers the signal's intended destination: another Sphere. They become known as the Stapledon Stations. Due to a clerical error by a junior staffer, the names were transposed, and what should have been Stapledon Two became Stapledon One.

- **2208** Humanity and Heimer agree on a joint mission to both Stations, commandeering the Kepler Deep Space vessels that were under construction.

www.ingramcontent.com/pod-product-compliance
Ingram Content Group UK Ltd.
Pitfield, Milton Keynes, MK11 3LW, UK
UKHW041543250326
469349UK00001B/44